"The Night I
In this Mike Ha   r
the first time, the celebrated private eye stalks
an old flame . . . in the dark . . . in the rain.
It's a perfect night for a love gone bad.

"Home Is the Place Where" by Bill Pronzini
A ramshackle tourist trap at the crossroads of
nowhere is the stopover for a desperate bounty
hunter at the end of his rope—and the end of
the line.

"Family Values" by Matthew Clemens
Opening old family wounds may be good for
the conscience, but they bleed like the devil.
Ask the P.I. who unearths a nasty little secret
at the base of a client's family tree.

**"The Girl, the Body and the Kitchen Sink"
by Martin Meyers**
Tailing a suspicious husband sounds simple.
But when the husband is a film director and
your client is an icy dame right out of Central
Casting, chances are you might get shot on
location.

**. . . and a line-up of 12 more top-drawer talents
who deliver the goods with the hard,
swift kick of a .45.**

MYSTERY ANTHOLOGIES

PRIVATE EYES

EDITED BY

Mickey Spillane

AND

Max Allan Collins

A SIGNET BOOK

SIGNET
Published by the Penguin Group
Penguin Putnam Inc., 375 Hudson Street,
New York, New York 10014, U.S.A.
Penguin Books Ltd, 27 Wrights Lane,
London W8 5TZ, England
Penguin Books Australia Ltd, Ringwood,
Victoria, Australia
Penguin Books Canada Ltd, 10 Alcorn Avenue,
Toronto, Ontario, Canada M4V 3B2
Penguin Books (N.Z.) Ltd, 182–190 Wairau Road,
Auckland 10, New Zealand

Penguin Books Ltd, Registered Offices:
Harmondsworth, Middlesex, England

First published by Signet, an imprint of Dutton Signet,
a member of Penguin Putnam Inc.

First Printing, February, 1998
10 9 8 7 6 5 4 3 2 1

REGISTERED TRADEMARK—MARCA REGISTRADA

Printed in the United States of America

PUBLISHER'S NOTE
These are works of fiction. Names, characters, places, and incidents either are the
product of the authors' imagination or are used fictitiously, and any resemblance
to actual persons, living or dead, events, or locales is entirely coincidental.

CONTENTS

INTRODUCTION
BY MAX ALLAN COLLINS

When Marty Greenberg and I teamed with Mickey Spillane to produce a series of new anthologies in the tradition of the great detective pulps *Black Mask* and *Manhunt,* we decided to make each volume thematic; and an obvious—an inevitable—theme for a Spillane anthology was private eyes.

After all, Mickey's Mike Hammer is one of the "big three" private eyes the genre has produced: Dashiell Hammett's Sam Spade and Raymond Chandler's Philip Marlowe, of course, being the other two.

This is not to say other fictional private eyes haven't made their mark—Ross MacDonald's Lew Archer and Robert B. Parker's Spenser are but two examples; Sara Paretsky's V. I. Warshawski and Sue Grafton's Kinsey Millhone are stellar examples of the recent commercial success of fictional female detectives.

But Hammett set the standard with shifty hard-bitten Spade, and Chandler embellished the model with an evocative, poetic first-person voice and the notion of a modern-day knight via his Marlowe. Spillane's po-etry—and his knight—may have been rough-hewn, but his hard-hitting, postwar sex-and-violence approach revitalized the form, and set sales records that remain unbroken, worldwide.

We decided to invite some of today's top crime writ-ers—as well as some talented new blood—to create not just private-eye stories, but—in the Chandler/Spillane tradition—*first-person* private-eye stories.

The voice of the private eye has been a key element since the late twenties and that era's two seminal fictional P.I.s: Hammett's nameless Continental Op and Carroll John Daly's Race Williams.

Daly—the inventor of the modern-day cowboy that is the private eye—isn't read much today, though periodically some industrious publisher puts out an edition of his work. Spillane was a huge Daly fan, and Daly's private eye Race Williams is rightly viewed as Mike Hammer's daddy.

Mickey says he never cared much for *The Maltese Falcon,* the novel that introduced Sam Spade; he much preferred Hammett's Continental Op tale *Red Harvest,* a blood-fest in which bodies pile up and a two-fisted P.I. carves out rough justice with his two fists, one of which often brandishes a blazing rod.

Both Hammett and Daly made their mark as short-story writers in *Black Mask* and other crime pulps, the likes of which just aren't around anymore. Probably the major reason Daly has not endured—where Hammett and Chandler have—is that Race Williams's creator just wasn't much of a novelist; his books are uneven, episodic affairs. It was in short stories—colorful, emotional melodramas with vivid titles like "Hell With the Lid Lifted!"—that he shone, providing inspiration for the future creator of Mike Hammer.

In the 1950s *Manhunt* picked up the *Black Mask* short-fiction torch, and, not surprisingly, Mickey Spillane was a regular contributor. But since then, venues for short, tough fiction have been few and far between.

This series of anthologies is, we think, a step in the right direction.

Mickey Spillane has written numerous short stories

and novellas during his long career—in the 1940s at Timely Comics, he turned out scores of short-short fillers sandwiched between four-color comics (many of which he also scripted). Throughout the 1950s, when he and Mike Hammer had made each other household words, Mickey regularly appeared with short fiction in *Manhunt* as well as such men's magazines as *Cavalier* and *Saga*. Amazingly, however, Mickey never published a short story about his most famous creation. . . .

That's right—with the exception of a Shamus Award-winning *Playboy* condensation of the 1989 novel *The Killing Man,* there has never been a Mike Hammer short story. Any number of anthologies of "best" or "famous" detective stories have had to explain the absence of a Hammer tale: Mickey never wrote one!

Or did he?

Brace yourself for italics—the manner in which a certain writer places emphasis on the truly important passages in his work. . . .

Our lead story marks the first publication, anywhere, of a 1953 Mike Hammer short story—"The Night I Died."

Originally designed as a radio script, "The Night I Died" has all the classic Hammer elements: a noir mood, hard fast action, revenge, loyalty, betrayal, sudden love, sudden death. It's a vintage Hammer novel in microcosm.

Several years ago I ran across the unproduced Hammer radio script—which, with its consistent Hammer narration, was essentially a short story—in Mickey's files. The author—that is, *"writer"* (Mickey doesn't see himself as an "author")—has allowed it to be set up in short-story form, and given permission for its publication here.

Mike Hammer is joined, in this anthology, by some of the most popular private eyes of our day.

Bill Pronzini's "nameless" detective appears in "Home Is the Place Where," a quietly poetic yet powerful tale; Jeremiah Healy's Boston P.I., John Francis Cuddy, makes a grim but humane excursion into the dark recesses of drugs and parental concern in the mini-novel "Lessons"; Robert J. Randisi's Nick Delvecchio explores a crime as sad as it is modern in the deftly written "A Favor for Sam"; and Michael Collins's one-armed investigator Dan Fortune takes on man's inhumanity to man, among other animals, in the tense, terrific "Can Shoot."

Other notable fictional detectives make appearances in this volume: the current lively crop of female P.I.s is well represented by Barb D'Amato's Cat Marsala in "See No Evil," a crackling private-eye procedural worthy of Ed McBain; multiple Edgar-winner William L. DeAndrea, one of the best latter-day proponents of the Ellery Queen school, serves up his TV troubleshooter Matt Cobb in a hard-hitting novella, "Killed in Good Company"; Ed Hoch's aging P.I., Al Darlan, appears in "An Eye for Scandal," a clever, surprising tale about politics and tabloid scandal; and Martin Meyers revives his 1970s series character Patrick Hardy in "The Girl, the Body, and the Kitchen Sink," a loving, wryly politically incorrect valentine to the classic paperback private eye.

As in *Murder Is My Business* and *Vengeance Is Hers,* the previous anthologies in this series, we have invited some newer writers to contribute, and the results make for gratifying reading: in "Diver," James Traylor (my co-author on the critical study *One Lonely Knight: Mickey Spillane's Mike Hammer*) explores the death of a youth through the eyes of a melancholy, middle-aged detective, Bob Crawford;

Ted Fitzgerald, a respected reviewer of mystery fiction whose short fiction is also attracting attention, tackles sensitive subject matter in his disturbingly topical "Nicole"; Matthew Clemens, whose award-winning fiction at the Mississippi Valley Writers Conference has consistently caught my eye, combines humor and compassion in the shocking "Family Values"; and Arthur Winfield Knight, in "Easy as Pie," presents a quietly evocative tale of a P.I. on an errand of mercy.

Two of suspense fiction's best, most popular writers present stories featuring first appearances of private eyes: horror star Rex Miller gives us "Sideways," a haunting slice of smaller-town P.I. life; and Stuart M. Kaminsky sets forties Hollywood dick Toby Peters aside, temporarily, for the sad, funny "Snow Birds."

Finally, my own private op, Nate Heller, tangles with scam artists and his own semblance of a conscience in "Kaddish for the Kid," a true-crime tale of Chicago in the thirties.

Any notion that private-eye stories have a "sameness" is disproved by this collection. What these stories have in common is also what separates them: each has its own distinct voice. Many less-than-astute critics "explained" the Spillane phenomenon by talking only about sex and violence; what they missed (and they missed so much!) is the hypnotic quality, the sound, of an unforgettable voice echoing through urban canyons.

Mike Hammer is about to walk down the street on a rainy New York night.

Who can resist joining him?

THE NIGHT I DIED
A Mike Hammer Story
BY MICKEY SPILLANE

You walk down the street at night. It's raining out. The only sound is that of your own feet. Then you hear another sound and you look across the street and see the blonde.

The blonde.

The girl you've been looking for for two whole years. She's blonder now. A little bit heavier but on her it's okay. And more beautiful than ever. She had to be more beautiful than ever. The girl you've been looking for for two years but never wanted to see again in your life.

So you follow her for a little while, then out of force of habit that's two years old, you cross the street and stay behind her. Yeah, even from there she hadn't changed. All the grace of a cat was in her walk and maybe some of their animal instincts, too.

Maybe she heard me.

Maybe she just felt me.

That's the way it always had been. Her steps got slower and shorter, then she stopped altogether and there was Helen.

Lovely, lovely Helen who I loved so much—but was going to kill in just another minute.

The gun in my pocket that had gotten warm from my hand felt cold all of a sudden. Cold and almost too heavy to lift, but I got it out of my pocket and had it in front of me when I reached her. She still had those deep green-tinted eyes that could laugh at you . . . even when you were dying . . . and now it was Helen who was dying and she could still laugh.

"Hello, Helen."

A long pause. "Hello, Mike. Do I get it here?"

"That's right. Here, Helen. Just like I said it would be. The next time I ever saw you, wherever it was . . . and now it's here."

"All right, Mike."

"It won't hurt much, but I'm not worried about that kind of pain. What I want you to feel will be right inside your mind. A slow, agonizing pain that wants to scream but can't make a sound because it's all inside you. It's life screaming because death is catching up with it . . . and all you'll be able to do is lie there listening to that silent screaming and the last thing you'll hear will be my feet walking away."

"Not even a kiss good-bye, Mike?"

"Not even a kiss good-bye. The last one was two years ago. That one will hold me. . . . That was a real kiss . . . a real kiss of death. *Remember it, Helen?*"

Sure she remembered it. How could she ever forget it? The kiss of death. Hers. Two years ago was the night I died. But there was a time before that . . . many nights before. The time we met.

There was a party going on. You know the kind . . . all the Broadway wheels spilling champagne and someplace in the background a soft piano setting the mood. I said my hellos . . . but I didn't like the people I was forced to associate with and was ready to leave when I saw her. . . .

There was loneliness in her . . . loneliness and something else that didn't belong there. Fear. The kind of fear that didn't belong at a party like this one, with a crowd like this one.

Then our eyes met over the heads of everybody and suddenly the room seemed to empty slowly until there was nobody there or even in the whole world except the two of us.

And fear.

I walked over to her . . . looked at her and could feel my spine get crawly.

"I came alone," I said.

"So did I."

"Then you're with me."

I didn't expect the mist that flowed into her eyes. A wisecrack maybe, but anything except the mist.

"For how long?" she asked.

"Forever?"

She paused. "I think . . . I wish it could be . . . forever."

"Let's get out of here."

Her scared cry overlapped my words: *"No!"*

"What's scaring you?"

That surprised her.

"Yeah—it shows, kid." I paused. "Let's get out, girl. Nobody'll ever bother you while I'm there. I'm funny that way."

"Forever?"

"Maybe forever. We have to start sometime."

So we went, the two of us . . . and fear. Fear that was there when she told me her name was Helen Venn, fear that was with us in a cab and stayed like an invisible shroud when we walked through the park.

"It's . . . a pretty night, Mike."

"Maybe."

She turned her head and looked at me, the swirl of her hair a golden waterfall in the moonlight.

"There's something wrong with your eyes, Mike."

"Yeah, I know. They don't look at you . . . they watch you. That what you mean?"

"That's right. What are they watching?"

"A kid in trouble. It's all over you. Why, Helen?"

"It's quite a story." She hesitated. "I think . . . Mike!"

Footsteps ran toward us, jostled into us, but the dark shape veered off, into the mess of shrubs. I ran after him, but he was gone.

"He got away," I said, breathing hard.

"Please don't go after him!"

"Don't worry. I couldn't find him in there anyway. Look . . . remember I said this could be . . . forever?"

"I remember."

"Then we go someplace and sit down. We'll hear some music and you can talk to me. Whatever it is, I want to hear it all."

So we went someplace and talked, a little place with soft lights—softer music. Then she told me.

"There isn't too much, Mike, but what there is . . . well, it's deadly. Look at me. Big, beautiful . . . even educated. Some might say I'm lucky. But I'm not. I'm just one of thousands more like me who are caught in this . . . rat trap of New York. Then I met a man. He was quite a guy. I went head over heels for the dirty . . . him. Then he was killed. Shot. It was only then that I found out who he was. Marty Wellman."

"Marty. *He* was your guy. . . . That slob was the biggest hood the Syndicate ever turned out."

"I know that now. Do you know why he was killed?"

"Sure. Someplace he had a couple of tax-free millions stashed away. It's a good reason for murder."

"Now do you know why I'm scared?"

"Tell it to me."

"They . . . or whoever the killer is . . . thinks I know where it is." She paused. "Mike . . . I'm tired of being afraid. I'm tired of walking the street afraid to look back and more afraid to look ahead. I'm tired of looking at my front door night after night, waiting for it to open slowly until I see a killer standing there with a gun in his hand. Mike . . . I'm tired, do you understand? Tired of living . . . afraid of living anymore. Mike . . . I want to die. I want to so bad I'm going to do it myself. I'm . . ."

"Shaddup!"

"No! I . . ."

"Shaddup, I said."

She did.

"I'll get him for you, girl. He'll never bother you again. He'll never bother anybody again."

"The police . . . they never . . ."

"I'm not the police."

"Then . . . it still might be . . . forever, Mike?"

"We can make it go however we want it to go. But I'll need some help from you."

"You can have . . . anything you want from me, Mike."

And forever started that night.

It started when Helen took me to the place Marty Wellman used to run, a smooth bistro catering to the uptown trade that ran as far as up to Ossining on the Hudson. Those who were popular that far up made the back room a gambler's paradise and a sucker's grave.

No, she wouldn't come in. She stayed in the cab and that's the way I wanted it. There was muted music and indirect lighting. The coatroom was jam-packed but there wasn't a dozen people at the bar. The rest were digging their graves behind the curtain alongside the bandstand.

I walked up to the bar and sat down.

"Yessir," the bartender said.

"Gimme a beer."

"Yessir!"

He brought the beer and moved away.

"Hey, feller. Come here a minute."

"Yeah?"

"How long have you been here?"

"About two years."

"You knew Marty Wellman, then, didn't you?"

"Yeah, I knew Marty."

"*What* did you know about him?"

"Nothing."

"Don't walk away, friend."

He paused. "Friend . . . look. If you're just a wise guy . . . get out by yourself. If you're a tough guy I'll toss you out. You know?"

"Friend . . . *look.*"

I held my coat open just enough so he could see the leather of the sling that ran across my chest. I didn't have to show him the .45 that was under it.

"I'm a tough guy, friend. Real tough. Different from the other kind. I'll tell you my name. Just once. Then you talk . . . understand. It's Mike . . . Mike Hammer."

"Yeah. . . ."

"Who owns the place now, friend?"

"Me . . . I do. There's my license on the wall."

"Swell. Who runs it?"

"Me . . . I—"

"Friend . . . from where you stand maybe I don't look mad enough to do it, but you're going to be hurting awful bad with a slug in your leg."

"Ease off, will you, I'm trying to tell you. . . ."

"Never mind, Joe," another voice said. "We'll tell him."

Whatever the guy behind me had in his pocket pressed hard against my back. The bartender tried to grin but it looked a little sick.

"Much trouble, Joe?" the guy asked.

"Not too much, Dave. He's got a gun."

"He won't have it long. Get up slow, bud. You know where to go or should I steer you a little?"

That was a laugh. Go? I could find it with my eyes closed. Sure, I went . . . nice and orderly, too . . . through the crowd at the wheels, around the dice tables, then up to the door marked private and I didn't even have to knock.

There were four of them in there . . . plus a languid redhead. But only one of them counted.

His name? Sure, you remember him . . . Carmen Rich. The boy with all the muscles. The rising star in the world that lived at night. You heard of Buddy Whiteman, too, the slick gunslinger from Miami who was always at Carmen's arm. And now there they were.

"This the guy?" Carmen asked.

"Troublemaker at the bar," Dave said.

"They never learn, do they?"

"Not until we teach them, Carmen."

"Maybe you got a good idea of what's going to happen to you, feller. You want to speak, say it now."

"You slimy thick-necked jerk," I said. "You scrimey punk . . ."

"Take him, Buddy. Take him good."

"Yeah, take me," I said. "But before you start, remember something. There's a gun at my back but there's one under my arm and I can get it out a second before I die and in that one second I can plant a slug between your eyes and maybe the Miami boy too and if living is that cheap to you, go ahead and take me."

Nobody moved.

They sat there watching me . . . and they knew. That kind could always tell.

Carmen said, "Hold it, Buddy. . . . What's the angle?"

I laughed. "Me . . . and a dead man. Marty Wellman. Why did he die? Who killed him? There's your angle."

"I'll pay for that information," Carmen said.

"So will a killer."

"I don't get you, guy."

"Nobody ever does."

"Have a cigarette?"

"No thanks. I'll stick to my Camels."

Carmen clicked his lighter, puffed his cigarette. "Why'd you come here?"

"Let's say to see you. The guy at the bar owns the joint and you run it. So Marty left a will."

"That's right. Marty left a will."

"You don't leave a gambling concession in a will, Carmen."

"You know me?"

"Yeah. And you know me, too. Mike Hammer. Maybe you heard."

Carmen paused. "I heard."

Whiteman said, "I hate these bigmouthed characters. Let me take him, Carmen."

"I'd like to see you try it, Buddy," Carmen said. "It'd be real funny. He'd actually die just to pump one into both of us."

"Nuts," Buddy said.

"Buddy . . ." Carmen said. "If you try it . . . I'll kill you myself. I know this guy."

"He's pulling a bluff and . . ."

"*I'm* not, Buddy," Carmen said. "I've seen some of the dead men he left behind him."

"So you know why I'm here," I said. "You have any answers?"

"You should know the story," Carmen said. "Someplace Marty had money stashed away. Two million is a good haul."

"Where, Carmen?"

"Would I run this joint if I knew?"

"Okay," I said. "I was just asking. Now I'll ask around other places. You better be on the square, feller. Otherwise I'll be back."

I pulled away from the guy behind me. "Hey . . . what is this?" he said.

"Let him go, Dave," Carmen said.

I laughed and shut the door on them.

A croupier was calling out as I slid my bar stool into place. "Hey, friend . . . gimme a beer."

"Yessir, what can I . . ."

The bartender's eyes were wide.

I said, "They didn't do it to me, feller."

"I don't get it," the bartender said softly.

"You will, feller . . . if you work that buzzer behind the bar on me again. I said I was different from the other kind of tough guy. You know?"

"Yeah," the bartender said, dragging it out.

"I'm getting out now. . . . Just remember me if I ever come back."

Sometimes it's good to be a guy who doesn't have to worry about the rules. You can learn things that are clubs to hold over somebody's head and you can prowl the night until you find the ferrets . . . human animals who live by invading the dens of the rats.

But first I went to a rat.

He was dressed in gray from his head to his shoes. His hair was mousy color and his eyes were the kind you see peering out of holes in the wall.

Sid Pollack was a rat. On his paper they called him a columnist, but a lot more on the outside called him a rat. He was living by night in a gin mill on Third

Avenue that had taken on the taint of respectability
lately.

"Hi, Sid."

"What do *you* want, Hammer?"

"You."

"Scram."

"There was a court case. There was a witness. There
was a big lie told and a stinking murderer got off
free." I paused. "There was a night a week later when
the killer called on the witness and passed over an
envelope with ten grand in it."

His voice was hushed. "You dirty . . ."

"Shut up or I'll break your back right over the
bar stool."

"What do you want?"

"News. Who runs the Syndicate since Marty Wellman got hit?"

"You ought to know."

I just looked at him.

"Okay . . . lay off," he said hurriedly. "So it's Carmen Rich."

"How?"

"He moved in. There's another way?"

"Not without an army, there isn't."

Sid smirked. "He's got an army."

"Yeah?"

The reporter spoke slowly, with contempt. "You
crazy fool. He's got Buddy Whiteman. He's got a kill-
batty jerk who'll knock off the whole town if he says
so. The Miami Kid is the fastest thing you ever saw
with a rod. You stick your head out. I'll be giving you
a two-line obituary in my column and glad to do it."

"Why haven't the cops tagged Buddy Whiteman?"

He laughed. "The cops. The only thing they haven't
got to hit him with is evidence, you jerk you. Maybe
after you . . ."

I slapped him.

He dropped his glass and stopped laughing.

"Don't ever laugh at me, Sid."

The cops? No, don't fool yourself. They don't make any mistakes. They're good boys to keep on the right side of. One in particular. Meet him yourself. His name is Pat Chambers . . . Captain of Homicide. We were buddies, so I could speak to him. We were buddies, so he could speak to me.

"You know, Mike," Pat said, "if anybody but you asked me for information on Wellman, Rich, or Whiteman, I'd hold them for questioning. What are you up to?"

"That isn't an answer."

"First *you* tell *me* things."

"A woman is slowly dying because a killer is loose. I like that woman."

Pat paused. "Helen Venn?"

"You're a brain, Pat. It's her."

"Be careful, friend. She's marked."

"I know."

"We kept a tail on her after Marty's death. She's marked. . . . We know that . . . but we don't know how, why, or by whom."

"The paper never said much about Marty catching it."

He threw the sheaf of papers on his desk; they scattered. "There's the file on him. A few pictures, too. That one there is the last he ever had taken."

It was a police photo, a garish head-on shot of Marty Wellman, the muscle kid. Too handsome for his own good. Too big and broad for anybody else's good either.

He looked pretty sharp sitting there at his desk in a dressing gown that was open to let his chest hair show through. His head was turned to one side and a cigar was tight in his pretty teeth.

Yeah, pretty sharp. The only trouble was that he was pretty dead, too. The bullet hole showed right over his ear.

".38 slug did it," Pat said.

"He got it cold?"

"No . . . warm, sort of. The desk drawer was open and a snub-nosed .38 was right where he could get it. Notice his hand. It's still lying almost on the rod. He must have sat there with the thing in his hand."

"It was a hard two million he had, Pat."

"I'll tell you something, kid. We found out about that. The two million was a bluff. He never had it. He called that bluff his insurance dough for retirement and used it to bank himself into control of the Syndicate's gambling setup in town here."

"Some use money . . . some use a bluff . . . and some use an army."

"What?"

"Nothing. . . . Helen Venn. What about her?"

"Beautiful . . . and lonely. Marty cultivated her. That was another bluff, only she didn't know it."

"I'm glad he's dead."

"Oh, it wasn't all his fault. You know dames. If she hadn't been looking for a push ahead, she wouldn't have hung out with the money boys. First it was Earnie Haver. Then Salvy Slocum. Big Ed Smith got in line and finally it was Marty. She was quite a girl to get a yen for."

"Yeah."

"You say it funny, Mike."

"Yeah. Was she really a pusher, Pat?"

"Oh . . . I wouldn't say so. A kid blinded by the bright lights, let's say. She checked clean."

"Do we talk about the Syndicate?"

"Do you mean Carmen Rich?"

"That's right."

"No, we don't talk."

"Carmen too big to talk about?"

"Let's stay friends, kid."

"Sorry," I said.

"We don't talk because it's a sealed case. It's being worked on."

"Okay, Pat, thanks." I stood. "I'll dig around. Anything turns up . . . I'll buzz you."

"Swell," he said. "Do that."

I had asked rats first. They didn't know. Then the cops. They wouldn't talk. There were still the ferrets . . . sharp-eyed little people who walked in the shadow of the rats and knew everything they did. All you had to do was get them to open their mouths.

On the Bowery I found my ferret.

He was sleeping in a doorway dreaming big dreams and living under a blue sky someplace that was warm and comfortable. . . . He didn't like it too much when I woke him up.

"Hello, Jake."

"Hey . . . hey . . . cut it."

"It's me, kid—Mike Hammer."

He scrambled to his feet, scared.

"Come here, come here . . . what's the matter with you?"

"Look, lemme alone, Mike. Just lemme alone."

I held his arm and hauled him in close until the sour whiskey smell of him was right under my nose.

"What's the matter with you? You want a fin or a train ticket? I'm not too good to speak to, am I?"

He groaned loudly. "Mike . . . look, lemme say it fast. . . . The word's out. They're gunning for you. You ain't healthy no more."

"Who?"

"Who knows? The word's out. Mike . . . lemme go."

"Sure, Jake. Just answer me something. Why did Marty Wellman die?"

A long hiss escaped his lips. He was scared. "Mike!"

"Why, Jake . . . *why*?"

"There's talk . . . it isn't loud talk because if it gets heard somebody gets killed. Marty . . . he had to die. You know, the king is dead. Long live the king. He got pushed because somebody else wanted in."

"Carmen?"

"Honest, Mike, I . . ."

"Okay, I won't push you. But the talk I heard had two million bucks in it."

"Marty was flat. He borrowed fifty grand from a Chicago outfit. That sound like two million?"

"No." I gave him a fin. "Here—buy yourself a steak."

"Thanks."

And that was all the ferret had to say. No . . . he wouldn't have said another word. He was one more guy the fear had gotten to.

So now the word was out.

Somebody wanted . . . me.

"Don't move, mister," a voice said.

My boy Dave from the bar. The second time he held a gun on me.

"Sucker," he said. "Sucker. You would've had it easy if you didn't nose around. Come on."

"Where?"

"There's a car over there."

"Suppose I don't?"

"Try it."

"Yeah . . . yeah."

He wasn't fast enough.

Somebody should've told him. This is New York.

You let them find out for themselves here. I stepped past him, .45 in hand, hearing the last little sounds he was making, aware of the complete silence that hung over the Bowery while a hundred eyes saw a kill that a hundred mouths would never speak about except among themselves.

But the dead man proved a point. I was important. Then I knew just how important. . . .

Important enough for two more of Carmen's boys to be on top of me, and I never saw the other one. I heard the swish and thud of the sap. . . .

"We can't go out to the island," a voice was saying.

"Then use the park," another voice said. "We can pull over, dump him, and blow."

"Suppose somebody hears the shot?"

"For the kind of dough we're making, you want Social Security?"

"Aw, shut up."

"Here's the place. Pull over."

They carried me out. They dragged me through the bushes and around a jutting tooth of rock like you find in Central Park, then they dumped me. The fat boy pulled the gun from his pocket, checked the shells, then flipped the cylinder back. . . .

I played it just a little too slow. Too slow. The louse got me with the gun butt and I had it good . . . just long enough to hear them get away.

But I wasn't too bad off. One dead man earlier still told the story. I started to get up . . . then my hand closed around a flat little pad and I thought how I had missed it earlier when I had chased somebody else into these same bushes . . . somebody who had been waiting for Helen and me ripped it out of his coat pocket when he tried to get me off his back.

I wrapped my handkerchief around it, stuck it in

my pocket, and got up. It wouldn't take long to reach the street . . . or get a boy to run my package up to Pat's office.

It was enough for the night. Enough. I called a cab over and gave the driver Helen's address. . . .

"Hello, Mike," she said. "It's so good to see you."

"Helen. . . . You look different, kid."

"I . . . *feel different*, Mike. I'm . . . not afraid anymore."

"You'll never have to be afraid again."

"But . . . you look different, too, Mike."

"Somebody else told me that once, too. They said they could always tell when I killed somebody."

"Mike! You killed . . ."

"What difference does it make. The pressure's off you now. They turned the heat my way." I hesitated. "You're beautiful, kid. Why? Why?"

"Why what, Mike?"

"Why do I love you so fast? What happens to a guy to make it so quick? Why, Helen? Why did a guy have to die tonight? Why is it I love you so much?"

"Maybe it's because I can love, too. I thought I loved before . . . but it wasn't like this. Nothing like this at all. I don't have to . . . work to love you, Mike. It's just there. It's something that makes you and me the only two people in the world. Something that is life and living . . . and love. Love . . . it makes fear seem so small and pitiful. When you love like this there isn't any room left for fear at all. Mike . . . remember you said forever?"

"Uh-huh."

"And I said I'd do anything in the world for you?"

"Yeah. . . ."

"And you said forever had to start sometime?"

"And forever starts . . ."

"Tonight, Mike."

Then you come into the mist once more because there's a killer loose and you're ready to start again. It's a day and a night later, and another day and a night and all along the way voices whisper to you while you wait.

They're after you, Mike.

Hey, Mike . . . watch it.

Pal . . . pal . . . a guy with a rod . . . he was here before . . .

And you listen without answering . . . but you listen. You see them. You know their faces . . . faces that are all alike . . . faces of hunters . . . but you move too fast . . . then you're ready to move and you watch and wait for a long time before you have him right.

He comes out of a building finally . . . and for the first time he's alone. You say . . .

"Carmen . . ."

Then he spins around and while the crazy fear is still on his face and the scream in his throat, there's a crashing thunder of a shot. . . .

And Carmen Rich fell with the blood, a wild angry stream spurting from his throat, and you know the party isn't over yet. . . .

So you run and run until you're in the clear and stand there panting your lungs out . . . then another long day and then you begin to wonder and at last you get an idea . . . and see Pat again.

He spoke slowly, softly: "Mike . . . all I know is what they let me know. Sure Carmen is dead. They all die sooner or later, but someone's ready to fill in. No matter what the papers or the politicians say, we can't stop the Syndicate from operating."

"Who filled in, Pat?"

"I wish I knew. I wish I knew."

"Guess."

"Somebody who's here now. A million-dollar enterprise doesn't go without a president for long. But who? I don't know yet. By the way . . . the prints we lifted from that pad of yours. They belong to a guy named Ben Liter. Small-time hood. Mostly petty raps. What's the pitch?"

I snorted.

"Something?" he asked.

"No . . ." I said. "No . . . nothing, Pat."

Nothing. Always nothing. Even the voices that whispered told me nothing. In a way it was funny, all of it . . . from a bartender who owned a bar worth a fortune . . . but didn't run the business . . . to dead me . . . to guys in the bushes . . . to a new president. Toast. The king is dead. Long live the king. Ahhhh.

The queen.

Helen.

Tonight was rain and Helen and tomorrow the king could live and die but tonight was the queen . . . and live.

So I went back to the apartment. I got out of the cab. It was quiet . . . dark . . . and late, so that's why I heard him . . . and maybe why I followed him. Then there he was, going into the same building as I was. . . .

"Buddy!" I said.

He took two shots at me and I clawed my .45 out from under my arm and took pursuit.

And there we were, alone in the darkness, the back fences of the alleys crowding us, the rain a muffler that blanked out sound but we each knew the other was there and someplace where I could hear him breathing was the new king who was ready to kill my

queen and for the first time I was the white knight
and I laughed. . . .

"Buddy . . . you won't get out alive."

"You're kidding, feller. You're just kidding. You
know who did it to Carmen? You know *why*?"

"Yeah," I said.

"Carmen was too big too long. I been small long
enough. It's my turn now. I'm going up. Then you
know what? I got everything I ever wanted. *Everything*. Nobody . . . understand . . . nobody . . . gets in
my way. Nobody stops me or gets in my way even. Not
you, nobody." He laughed. "Not even Mata Hari."

"They were big dreams, Buddy," I said. "You've
had it."

"No," he said. "*You* get it. You and anybody in
my way."

There was just that one exploding pain in my belly
that smashed me into the ground . . . hard, wet, and
the breath was gone for long seconds. There was that
fuzzy feeling that I had known once, a long time ago
in the stinking jungles of a Pacific island . . . but even
then it hadn't been this bad . . . and then the king
stood over me to put the final one in my head.

He shouldn't have been so gracious. . . .

His laugh was a whisper as he came over and he
was still laughing when I shot him.

You could hear sirens someplace . . . they faded as
I stood up, stopped altogether as I walked and all the
sound I could hear was the rushing waterfall in my
ears . . . but somehow I got up to her apartment . . .
opened it with the key she had given me and staggered in.

My queen was beautiful . . . beautiful . . . standing
there in that single light. Beautiful and mine.

And I was dying. . . .

"Mike?" Her voice was querulous.

"They're dead, Helen. It's one way of stopping the fear."

"Dead?"

"Carmen Rich . . . he didn't matter. Buddy Whiteman." I paused. "He mattered. He's dead, Helen, but I'm the only one who knows. You'll never have to be afraid of anything again. I'm the only one who knows."

"Mike . . . ?"

"The death photo of Marty Wellman. He had his hand on a gun, so he was afraid of a killer. But his head was turned to look at something else. Even with a killer in front of him, you'd be the only one he'd look at. The only thing he'd take his eyes off a killer for. And one other thing. It was small and wouldn't mean much except to me. The guy who watched us in the park . . . he was a small-timer. A guy with services for rent . . . but not to a big organization like the Syndicate, Helen. To you, maybe, but not the Syndicate."

"Yes . . . it was me, Mike. Me and Marty at first, but he wouldn't give me what I had earned. He had to die. You know that, don't you? Carmen?" She shook her head. "He wasn't the strong one I needed. I wanted someone who could act . . . quickly, decisively. Someone who could respond to my . . . love . . . without anyone knowing it. Someone ready to do whatever I asked him to . . . no questioning . . . nothing." She shrugged. "That was Buddy Whiteman. The Miami Kid, they called him."

"Forget them, honey," I said. "It's over now. There's only you and me . . . for a few minutes at least."

"Mike . . . there's not even a few minutes. I'm scared again. I wanted so much. I almost had it . . .

then I did have it . . . for a little bit. Mike . . . I'm going to have it for all time. I'm going to have the world at the snap of my fingers. Not a little bit . . . everything! Buddy killed Carmen for me." She laughed shortly. "He was going to kill you, too. Mike . . . you see, here's how it is. Buddy got ambitious, too. That was the sad part of it. He and I planned the kill of Marty and did it. But he had ambitions and as long as I knew his part of the murder, I was in his way. Juries seldom convict a woman, you know. So it had to be either Buddy or me. One of us had to die and I didn't like to kill anyone myself . . . so I chose *you*, Mike. . . ."

"But . . . I . . . loved you, Helen."

"And now you have to die, Mike. I can't even let you have that few minutes to speak to the police when they come . . . and they will come, you know."

"I know."

The knife was in her hand . . . a long slim little thing that came close slowly. It came up closer . . . and I couldn't move out of the way at all.

"Mike . . . believe something. I really love you, Mike."

"I know, Helen. So now I die. But don't count on living too long, Helen. Someplace we might meet again . . . no matter where it is, you'll die, too, Helen."

"It will never happen that way, Mike." She sighed. "Mike . . . I'm sorry."

She thrust the blade.

Die? Yeah, that was the night I died. It wasn't my skin and bones. No, my flesh had to live even though I didn't want it to.

But something else had died that night. Something more important than what you see when you look in the mirror.

My thumb found the hammer and pulled it back.

"Really here . . . Mike?"

"Really here, Helen."

"Not even a kiss good-bye, Mike?"

"Not even a kiss good-bye. The last one was two years ago. That one will hold me. That was a real kiss. A kiss of death. Remember it, Helen?"

Sure, she remembered it, all right. She came closer, with her arms reaching out for me and I wasn't supposed to see that same sliver of steel that she had used before.

"I really love you, Mike."

"And I really love you, Helen."

And then the only sound you hear is the gunshot, and her cry. And the sound of your own feet, walking down the street at night.

HOME IS THE PLACE WHERE
A "Nameless Detective" Story
BY BILL PRONZINI

It was one of those little crossroads places you still find occasionally in the California backcountry. Relics of another era; old dying things, with precious little time left before they crumble into dust. Weathered wooden store building, gas pumps, a detached service garage that also housed restrooms, some warped little tourist cabins clustered close behind; a couple of junk-car husks and a stand of dusty shade trees. This one was down in the central part of the state, southeast of San Juan Bautista, on the way to the Pinnacles National Monument. The name on the pocked metal sign on the store roof was BENSON'S OASIS. There were four cabins and the shade trees were cottonwoods.

No other cars sat on the apron in front when I pulled in at a few minutes past two. Nor were there any vehicles back by the cabins. The only spot to hide one on the property was in the detached garage—and it was shut up tight. Maybe something in that, maybe not.

Heat hammered at me when I got out, thick and deep-summer dry. In the distance, heat haze blurred the shapes of the brown hills of the Diablo Range. It was flat here, and dust-blown, and quiet. The feeling you had was of isolation, emptiness, and displacement in time. For me, it was a pleasant feeling, not at all unsettling. I like the past; I like it a hell of a lot better than I like the present or the prospects for the future.

It was even hotter inside the store. No air-conditioning, just an old-fashioned ceiling fan that stirred the air in a way that made me think of a ladle stirring bouillon. Under the fan flies floated in random lethargic circles, as if they'd been drugged. The old man behind the counter at the rear had the same drugged, listless aspect. He was perched on a stool, looking at a book of some kind that was open on the countertop. A bell had tinkled to announce my arrival but at first he didn't look up. He turned a page as I crossed the room; it made a dry rustling sound. The page was black, with what looked to be photographs and paper items affixed to it. A scrapbook.

When I reached him he shut the book. It had a brown simulated leather cover, the word *Memories* embossed on it in gilt. The gilt had flaked and faded and the ersatz leather was cracked: the book was almost as old as he was. Over seventy, I judged. Thin, stoop-shouldered, white hair as fine as rabbit fur. Heavily seamed face. Bent left arm that was also knobbed and crooked at the wrist, as if it had been badly broken once and hadn't healed well.

"What can I do for you?" he asked.

"You're the owner? Everett Benson?"

"I am."

"I'm looking for your son, Mr. Benson."

No reaction.

"Have you seen him, heard from him, in the past two days?"

Still nothing for several seconds. Then, "I have no son."

"Stephen," I said. "Stephen Arthur Benson."

"No."

"He's in trouble. Serious trouble."

Face like a chunk of eroded limestone, eyes like

cloudy agates embedded in it. "I have no son," he said again.

I took out one of my business cards, tried to give it to him. He wouldn't take it. Finally I laid it on the counter in front of him. "Stephen was in jail in San Francisco," I said, "on a charge of selling amphetamines and crack cocaine. Did you know that?"

Silence.

"He talked the woman he was living with into going to a bondsman and bailing him out. The bail was low and she had just enough collateral to swing it. His trial date was yesterday. Two nights ago he stole a hundred dollars from the woman, and her car, and jumped bail."

More silence.

"The bondsman hired me to find him and bring him back," I said. "I think he came here. You're his only living relative, and he needs more money than he's got to keep on running. He could steal it but it would be easier and safer to get it from you."

Benson pushed off his stool, picked up the scrapbook, laid it on a shelf behind him. Several regular hardback books lined the rest of the shelf, all of them old and well read; in the weak light I couldn't make out any of the titles.

"Aiding and abetting a fugitive is a felony," I said to his back, "even if the fugitive is your own son. You don't want to get yourself in trouble with the law, do you?"

He said again, without turning, "I have no son."

For the moment I'd taken the argument as far as it would go. I left him and went out into the midday glare. And straight over to the closed-up service garage.

There were two windows along the near side, both dusty and speckled with ground-in dirt, but I could see reasonably well through the first. Enough daylight penetrated the gloom so I could identify the two vehicles parked in there. One was a dented, rusted, thirty-year-old Ford pickup that no doubt belonged to the old man. The other was a newish red Mitsubishi. I didn't have to see the license plate to know that the Mitsubishi belonged to Stephen Arthur Benson's girlfriend.

Cars drifted past on the highway; they made the only sound in the stillness. Behind the store, where the cabins were, nothing moved except for shimmers of heat. I went to my car, sleeving away sweat, and unclipped the .38 Smith & Wesson Bodyguard from under the dash and slid it into the pocket of my suit jacket. Maybe I'd need the gun and maybe I wouldn't, but I felt better armed. Stephen Benson was a convicted felon and something of a hard-ass, and for all I knew he was armed himself. He hadn't had a weapon two nights ago, according to the girlfriend, but he might have picked one up somewhere in the interim. From his father, for instance.

The stand of cottonwoods grew along the far side of the parking area. I moved over into them, made my way behind the two cabins on the south side. Both had blank rear walls and uncurtained side windows; I took my time approaching each. Their interiors were sparsely furnished, and empty of people and personal belongings.

The direct route to the other two cabins was across open ground. I didn't like the idea of that, so I went the long way—back through the trees, across in front of the store, around on the far side of the garage. It was an unnecessary precaution, as it turned out. The farthest of the northside cabins was also empty; the near one showed plenty of signs of occupancy—clothing, books, photographs, a hot plate, a small refrigerator—but there wasn't anybody in it. This was where the old man lived, I thought. The clothing was the type he would wear and the books were similar to the ones in the store.

Nothing to do now but to go back inside and brace him again. When I entered the store he was on his stool, eating a Milky Way in little nibbling bites. He had loose false teeth and on each bite they clicked like beads on a string.

"Where is he, Mr. Benson?"

No response. The cloudy agate eyes regarded me with the same lack of expression as before.

"I saw the car in the garage," I said. "It's the one Stephen stole from the woman in San Francisco, no mistake. Either he's still in this area or you gave him money and another car and he's on the road again. Which is it?"

He clicked and chewed; he didn't speak.

"All right then. You don't want to do this the easy way, we'll have to do it the hard way. I'll call the county police and have them come out here and look at the stolen car; then they'll charge you with aiding and abetting and with harboring stolen property. And your son will still get picked up and sent back to San Francisco to stand trial. It's only a matter of time."

Benson finished the candy bar; I couldn't tell if he was thinking over what I'd said, but I thought I'd give him a few more minutes in case he was. In the stillness, a refrigeration unit made a broken chattery hum. The heat-drugged flies droned and circled. A car drew up out front and a grumpy-looking citizen came in and bought two cans of soda pop and a bag of potato chips. "Hot as a bitch out there," he said. Neither Benson nor I answered him.

When he was gone I said to the old man, "Last chance. Where's Stephen?" He didn't respond, so I said, "I've got a car phone. I'll use that to call the sheriff," and turned and started out.

He let me get halfway to the door before he said, "You win, mister," in a dull, empty voice. "Not much point in keeping quiet about it. Like you said, it's only a matter of time."

I came back to the counter. "Now you're being smart. Where is he?"

"I'll take you to him."

"Just tell me where I can find him."

"No. I'll take you there."

Might be better at that, I thought, if Stephen's close by. Easier, less chance for trouble, with the old man along. I nodded, and Benson came out from behind the counter and crossed to where a sign hung in the window; he reversed the sign so the side that said CLOSED faced outward. Then we went out and he locked up.

I asked him, "How far do we have to go?"

"Not far."

"I'll drive, you tell me where."

We got into the car. He directed me east on the county road that intersected the main highway. We rode in silence for about a mile. Benson sat stiff-backed, his hands gripping his knees, eyes straight ahead. In the hard daylight the knobbed bone on his left wrist looked as big as a plum.

Abruptly he said, "'Home is the place where.'"

"How's that again."

"'Home is the place where, when you have to go there, they have to take you in.'"

I shrugged because the words didn't mean anything to me.

"Lines from a poem by Robert Frost," he said. "'The Death of the Hired Man,' I think. You read Frost?"

"No."

"I like him. Makes sense to me, more than a lot of them."

I remembered the well-read books on the store shelf and in the cabin. A rural storekeeper who read poetry and admired Robert Frost. Well, why not? People don't fit into easy little stereotypes. In my profession, you learn not to lose sight of that fact.

Home is the place where, when you have to go there, they have to take you in. The words ran around inside my head like song lyrics. No, like a chant or an invocation—all subtle rhythm and gathering power. They made sense to me, too, on more than one level. Now I knew something more about Everett Benson, and something more about the nature of his relationship with his son.

Another couple of silent miles through sun-struck farmland. Alfalfa and wine grapes, mostly. A private farm road came up on the right; Benson told me to turn there. It had once been a good road, unpaved but well graded, but that had been a long time ago. Now there were deep grooves in it, and weeds and tall brown grass between the ruts. Not used much these days. It led along the shoulder of a sere hill, then up to the crest; from there I could see where it ended.

Benson's Oasis was a dying place, with not much time left. The farm down below was already dead—years dead. It had been built alongside a shallow creek where willows and cottonwoods grew, in the tuck where two hillocks came together: farmhouse, barn, two chicken coops, a shedlike outbuilding. Skeletons now, all of them, broken and half-hidden by high grass and shrubs and tangles of wild berry vines. Climbing primroses covered part of the house from foundation to roof, bright pink in the sunlight, like a gaudy fungus.

"Your property?" I asked him.

"Built it all with my own hands," he said. "After the war—Second World War—when land was cheap hereabouts. Raised chickens, alfalfa, apples. You can see there's still part of the orchard left."

There were a dozen or so apple trees, stretching away behind the barn. Gnarled, bent, twisted, but still producing fruit. Rotting fruit now.

"Moved out eight years ago, when my wife died," Benson said. "Couldn't bear to live here anymore without Betty. Couldn't bear to sell the place, either." He paused, drew a heavy breath, let it out slowly. "Don't come out here much anymore. Just a couple of times a year to visit her grave."

There were no other cars in sight, but I could make out where one had angled off the roadway and mashed down an irregular swath of the summer-dead grass, not long ago. I followed the same route when we reached the farmyard. The swath stopped ten yards from what was left of the farmhouse's front porch. So did I.

I had my window rolled down but there was nothing to hear except birds and insects. The air was swollen with the smells of heat and dry grass and decaying apples.

I said, "Is he inside the house?"

"Around back."

"Where around back?"

"There's a beat-down path. Just follow that."

"You don't want to come along?"

"No need. I'll stay here."

I gave him a long look. There was no tension in him, no guile; not much emotion of any kind, it seemed. He just sat there, hands on knees, eyes front—the same posture he'd held throughout the short trip from the crossroads.

I thought about insisting he come with me, but something kept me from doing it. I got out, taking the keys from the ignition. Before I shut the door I drew the .38; then I leaned back in to look at Benson, holding the gun down low so he couldn't see it.

"You won't blow the horn or anything like that, will you?"

"No," he said, "I won't."

"Just wait quiet."

"Yes."

The beaten-down path was off to the right. I walked it slowly through the tangled vegetation, listening, watching my back trail. Nothing made noise and nothing happened. The fermenting apples' smell grew stronger as I came around the house to the rear; bees swarmed back there, making a muted sawmill sound. Near where the orchard began, the path veered off toward the creek, toward a big weeping willow that grew on the bank.

And under the willow was where it ended: at the grave of Benson's wife, marked by a marble headstone etched with the words *Beloved Elizabeth—Rest in Eternal Peace.*

But hers was not the only grave there. Next to it was a second one, a new one, the earth so freshly turned some of the clods on top were still moist. That one bore no marker of any kind.

I went back to the car, not quite running. Benson was out of it now, standing a few feet away looking at the house and the climbing primroses. He turned when he heard me coming, faced me squarely as I neared him.

"Now you know," he said without emotion and

without irony. "I didn't lie to you, mister. I have no son."

"Why didn't you tell me he was dead?"

"Wanted you to see it for yourself. His grave."

"How did he die?"

"I shot him," the old man said. "Last night, about ten o'clock."

"Shot him?"

"With my old Iver Johnson. Two rounds through the heart."

"Why? What happened?"

"He brought me trouble, just like before."

"You can state it plainer than that."

A little silence. Then, "He was bad, Stephen was. Mean and bad clear through. Always was, even as a boy. Stealing things, breaking up property, hurting other boys. Hurting his mother." Benson held up his crooked left arm. "Hurting me, too."

"Stephen did that to you?"

"When he was eighteen. Broke my arm in three places. Two operations and it still wouldn't heal right."

"What made him do it?"

"I wouldn't give him the money he wanted. So he beat up on me to get it. I told him before he ran off, don't ever come back, you're not welcome in my house anymore. And he didn't come back, not in more than a dozen years. Not until last night, at the Oasis."

"He wanted money again, is that it? Tried to hurt you again when you wouldn't give it to him?"

"Punched me in the belly," Benson said. "Still hurts when I move sudden. So I went and got the Iver Johnson. He laughed when I pointed it at him and told him to get out. 'Won't shoot me, old man,' he said. 'Your own son. You won't shoot me.'"

"What did he do? Try to take the gun away from you?"

Benson nodded. "Didn't leave me any choice but to shoot him. Twice through the heart. Then I brought him out here and buried him next to his mother."

"Why did you do that?"

"I told you before. 'Home is the place where.' I had to take him in, didn't I? For the last time?"

The stink of the rotting apples seemed stronger now, nauseating. And the heat was intense and the skeletal buildings and fungoid primroses were ugly. I didn't want to be here any longer—not another minute in this place.

"Get back in the car, Mr. Benson."

"Where we going?"

"Just get back in the car. Please."

He did what I told him. I backed the car around and drove up the hill and over it without glancing in the rearview mirror. Neither of us said anything until I swung off the county road, onto the apron in front of Benson's Oasis, and braked to a stop.

Then he asked, "You going to call the sheriff now?" Matter-of-factly; not as if he cared.

"No," I said.

"How come?"

"Stephen's dead and buried. I don't see any reason not to leave him right where he is."

"But I killed him. Shot him down like a dog."

Old and dying like his crossroads store, with precious little time left. Where was the sense—or the justice—in forcing him to die somewhere else? But all I said was, "You did what you had to do. I'll be going now. I've got another long drive ahead of me."

He put his hand on the door latch, paused with it there. "What'll you say to the man who hired you, the bail bondsman?"

What would I say to Abe Melikian? The truth—some of it, at least. Stephen Arthur Benson is dead and in the ground and what's left of his family is poor; the bail money's gone, Abe, and there's no way you can get any of it back; write it off your taxes and forget about it. He wouldn't press for details, particularly not when I waived the remainder of my fee.

"You let me worry about that," I said, and Benson shrugged and lifted himself out of the car. He seemed to want to say something else; instead he turned, walked to the store. There was nothing more to say. Neither thank-yous nor good-byes were appropriate and we both knew it.

I watched him unlock the door, switch the window sign from CLOSED to OPEN before he disappeared into the dimness within. Then I drove out onto the highway and headed north. To San Francisco. To my office and my flat and Kerry, the woman I loved.

Home is the place where.

SNOW BIRDS
BY STUART M. KAMINSKY

The answering machine made a screeching sound like a cat sliding down a tile roof. When it finished rewinding, I examined the silent rusty air conditioner in my office window and hit the PLAYBACK button.

If we don't count the three people who didn't leave messages, the two calls from the collection agency in Tampa that wanted me to pay the $4.50 I owed as copayment on a visit to the Doctors' Hospital Emergency Room, and the incoherent call three days earlier from Lorraine Stitch, this was the first message I'd had in two weeks.

"You there, Mr. Fonesca?" came one of those tough old men's voices. "You are, pick up the phone. You're not, it's a little before nine in the a.m. on Tuesday. Names Ames, Ames Delaware. I'm hard to reach, but I got work for you maybe. Easiest way to get me is be there when I call later, about five, or come over to the Round-Up Restaurant a little after noon. I'm there most days for the special."

There was a little click and three beeps. My watch said it was ten to noon. I turned off the machine and decided to try to coax the window air conditioner into a hum of cool air. I promised it eventual repair. I promised it appreciation. I promised, but I lied. I hated the son of a bitch. I hated it almost as much as I hated my '86 Toyota and with as little reason. The air conditioner had come with the toolbox-size office.

It hadn't worked with enthusiasm in the three years I'd been in the nameless two-story office building behind the Dairy Queen off of Highway 301 that runs along the east end of downtown going north and south to nowhere.

The Toyota had even less to feel guilty about than the air conditioner. I'd bought the car new and ran ninety thousand miles on it, most of them in Chicago, but a lot of them since I set up shop in Sarasota.

I gently pushed the gray ON button and the air conditioner heaved into sluggish wakefulness. I didn't breathe. Which was probably the healthiest thing to do in the coffin since there was no air worth the intake. The air conditioner shuddered and began to hiss out air and drip brown water. I diagnosed it as electrical emphysema.

Sarasota in the summer runs in the mid-nineties every day, humid every day, rainy every afternoon. Maybe I was fooling myself but it didn't seem any worse than Chicago in the summers and it was sure a hell of a lot better than St. Louis in the summer. I grew up in St. Louis. The winters weren't bad. The summers almost killed me.

"Fonesca," I said aloud, a malady of those who live alone for long periods of time, "I think you've got a . . ."

And then the air conditioner died. I pulled the plug. The living will she may have left in the form of a warranty would have expired when I was still with the State's Attorney's office in Chicago. I thought of burying her and decided instead to let her remain in the window, maybe forever or until I moved. I opened the window and looked through the holes in the screen at a sweating fat woman in white shorts mopping her brow, tugging at her kid, and ordering something at the D.Q. window.

I liked Dairy Queen when I moved to Sarasota. I'd grown to hate it after only two or three thousand shakes, dipped cones, and buster bars.

I looked at my desk, a turn-of-the-century teacher's desk complete with the empty hole where an ink well had once sat, at my wooden garage sale chair that I thought would match the desk when I bought it. I had one other wooden chair, a steel filing cabinet, a typewriter, a small bookcase with two or three law books and a few dozen horror novels, and a movie poster on the wall, an original of *Mildred Pierce,* my most valuable possession. I'm a sucker for melodrama.

I opened the door to a wash of wet August heat, went out, kicked the door shut, and heard it click. My office is on the second floor in a cracking pink concrete office building. The offices all open right out on an outdoor landing. There's an overlap on the roof, but it leaks. It wasn't raining yet, but it didn't matter. I was already damp with sweat and in no mood to go to my apartment and change into a clean shirt. Besides, Ames Delaware did not sound like the kind of client who would be offended. I've been wrong before, but I have the uncanny ability not to learn from my mistakes. It keeps me young and bewildered.

I had my own parking space. I got it free from Sonny the manager of the D.Q. In exchange, I promised to keep an eye on his place when he was closed. About a year ago I'd actually caught a couple of kids trying to break in. They were local pink-neck teenagers who were divided about whether they were looking for money or for frozen burgers. That had been my biggest case since moving south.

Sonny was handing the fat woman in the white shorts a giant chocolate dip. Her blond kid reached for it. She wacked him with the back of her hand. He didn't cry. I waved at Sonny and he waved back as I pulled out.

My Toyota has no air-conditioning. I didn't need it back in Chicago. Couldn't afford it in Sarasota. I have not been a success on the Gulf Coast, but I hadn't been unhappy either.

I pulled out onto Washington, which is 301, turned past the remnants of the old White Sox Spring Training Stadium across the street, and headed for the Round-Up. The Round-Up is one of the many oddball restaurants in Sarasota, a town known more for its well-heeled tourists and wealthy retirees who lived on the offshore Keys than its cuisine. There are some good restaurants and there is a hell of a lot of variety including the Round-Up that boasts on a red-on-white sign in the window, THE BEST CHINESE TEX-MEX IN FLORIDA. Few challenged this claim, especially not the homeless who wandered past every day. The Round-Up is on Second Street, not in the best neighborhood in town.

Sarasota is rich, but even the rich need maids, supermarkets, police, firemen, tailor shops, and shoe stores. There is a middle class and a lower class in Sarasota and everyone, even the snow birds, the well-to-do who come down only in the winter from as far north as Canada and as far east as Germany, knows it.

Parking was not rough in front of the Round-Up, not in the summer. Parking isn't rough anywhere in Sarasota in the summer. There's plenty of parking and no lines at the restaurants or movies.

The Round-Up wasn't packed but it wasn't empty and there was good reason. The food is cheap and spicy, the service fast, and no one hurries you out. You can nurse a beer or even an iced tea with a pitcher in front of you while you watched the Atlanta Braves on Cable. Round Harry, the owner, was a

Braves fan, a transplant from Atlanta more than a dozen years earlier. He was round when he came to Sarasota. He had gotten more round. The Round-Up was not a quiet place. Harry wheezed when he walked, the Braves game bellowed, drunks poured drinks for each other with shaking hands, and a pride of lawyers, sales managers, real estate dealers, and knowing locals talked deals and the hometown loud enough to be heard.

I spotted Ames Delaware in ten seconds, the time it took my eyes to adjust from the sun to the near darkness. The place wasn't big but the tables weren't jammed together. There was leg and elbow room and the smell of beer and something frying. The Round-Up was supposed to look Western. It didn't, but it did look like a run-down bar and grill. The grizzled old man sat at a two-chair table in the corner, his back to the wall, Wild Bill covering himself from a sneak attack after drawing Aces and Eights.

He looked up at me from what looked like a plate of chop suey over nachos. I pegged his age at about ten degrees below the temperature outside. His hair was white and cut short. His eyes were light, probably blue-gray and as I walked toward him I saw none of the telltale red or yellow in the whites that gave away the lifetime drinker.

"Fonesca," I said, stopping in front of him.

He pushed his chair back and got up holding out his hand. His shirt was a red flannel with the sleeves rolled up and his jeans were faded but clean. I couldn't see his feet but I was sure he was wearing boots.

"Ames Delaware," he said, sounding more like George C. Scott than he had on the phone. "Anyone ever tell you you look like that guy in the movies?"

"Charles Bronson," I tried.

"Other guy," he said. "Ned Beatty. Have a seat."

I sat.

"Order something," he said. "On me, no strings, no obligations. Food's kinda nuts but it's not bad."

I nodded at Round Harry who was sweating in spite of the almost cool air. He wiped his hands on his apron and shouted, "What'll it be?"

"I'll have what he's having," I shouted, pointing at Ames Delaware.

"Suit yourself," Harry shouted and went about his business.

Ames Delaware wiped his mouth with a paper napkin and looked at me.

"I know people," he said. "Mostly. Get it wrong sometimes."

"Who doesn't?"

"Got your name out of the book," he said, ignoring me. "Not much choice. Small town. Could have had more choice in Bradenton, but I'm on one of those mopeds so I decided to stay cheap and local. Your listing was the smallest."

"I appreciate your confidence," I said.

"Don't joke on me, Mr. Fonesca," he said gently. "I'm country, but I'm no dolt. We can laugh together but not at each other. You can't stop yourself, then we can just have us a lunch, talk about the gators and the blue water and white sand and say good-bye."

"I'm sorry," I said. "I'm big city. Sometimes I don't know when I'm doing it."

"Apology accepted," said Delaware, taking a bit of whatever it was Harry now placed in front of me in a steaming blue metal bowl along with a glass of dark beer.

"Special," said Harry. "Mandarin Nacho Supreme."

He departed and I looked at Delaware.

"You in a hurry?" he asked.

"No," I said.

"You gonna talk to me straight?"

"I'll try," I said, drinking some beer and looking down at the brown stuff in the bowl.

"How's business?"

The Braves must have done something interesting. Harry and some of the customers groaned, and one shouted, "You see that?"

"Business is bad," I said.

Delaware nodded. "Then you got time to concentrate on what I'm gonna give you."

"Depends on what it is," I said.

"How old are you, Mr. Fonesca?"

"Call me Cal," I said. "I'm forty-one."

"Your people?"

"My pe . . . My mother was Hungarian. My father was Mexican."

"Was?"

"Both dead."

He nodded and ate some more. "You a good man?"

I shrugged. "No, but I'm an honest one. I can prove it. You can see my office."

"Lots of crooks are broke," he said. "They just don't know how to do thievin' right. But I believe you. Background."

"Life story?"

"Make it short," he said.

I drank half a glass of beer and said, "Short version. Went to college. University of Illinois. Social work. Guy I knew in school offered me a research job for a law office. It paid better than social work. I took it. Guy I worked for ran for office and won. State's Attorney. I went with him."

"Where?" asked Delaware, his eyes watching me carefully.

"Cook County, Chicago. I became an investigator.

Got pretty good at it. Chief Investigator for the office. Married a secretary. She died in a car accident on Lake Shore Drive."

"When?"

"Three years ago."

"That when you came down here?"

"That's when I came down here," I said. "Packed the Toyota. Headed for Key West. Never got there. Stopped in Sarasota and got hypnotized by the white sand on the beach. Put out a shingle, sweated out a license, and lived on what little I brought in and what I had saved."

"Family?" he asked.

"Nope."

"Sad story," he said, wiping the bottom of his plate with a wad of sourdough bread.

"Nope," I said.

"Good, I don't think so either. Like a man who doesn't feel sorry for himself." He let out a very small burp. "Sorry."

"Excused," I said. "My turn."

"Ask," he said, sitting up and pushing his plate away gently.

"What do you want?"

"Amos Sprague," he said.

"Amos Sprague," I repeated.

"You might want to take notes," he said. "You ain't got a book I've got one."

"I've got one," I said, pulling out my small imitation leather notepad.

"Sprague left Jackson Hole a little more than a year back," he said. "I tracked him slow through a sister of his in Yuma, a dentist he went to in Truckee, a car dealer he bought a Dodge pickup from in Texarkana. Got him down to here. Lost him. Need some help."

"Can I ask why you've spent a year looking for Amos Sprague?"

Some business guys at the table behind me let out a whoop of laughter. One of them started to choke.

"We were partners," said Delaware. "He took the money out of our joint account on a Saturday afternoon and took off in the company truck."

"Your business?"

"Cattle feed, a little land," he said.

"How much did he take off with?"

"Two hundred thousand dollars even. He left eighteen hundred."

"And you want your money back?" I asked.

"Or Amos Sprague dead," he said. "I can't live dignified or die justified with this unfinished between us."

"So I find Amos Sprague and tell him to give you your money back or . . ."

"Tell me where he is and I shoot him between the eyes."

"Seems simple enough," I said. "My fee is . . ."

"Contingency and some cash out flat," said Delaware.

"I don't . . ."

"I've got a little over four hundred to my name. I'll give you half and a week. You can't find him in a week I get me a job and raise enough to find someone who can. You find him and get the money back and I give you twenty thousand. Simple as that."

"Fair enough," I said, toasting him with what remained of my beer. "What can you give me on Sprague?"

He reached down under his chair and came up with a stained brown envelope with the aluminum clasp long gone. He placed the envelope in front of me. His knuckles were arthritic, not really bad but getting there fast.

"Got a picture, copy of his birth certificate, list of things I remember about him. That's it. I spent close to a month wandering this town looking but I ain't seen him. He could broil his hair and get a new nose and I'd know him, but I ain't seen him."

"Maybe he's not here anymore," I tried as I finished the special. It wasn't half-bad.

"I figure he is," Delaware said, standing up and pulling his worn brown wallet from his back pocket. "I feel it. Could be wrong, but . . ."

He counted out ten twenty-dollar bills and laid them in front of me.

"I'm trusting you, Calvin," he said. "Only made one mistake about character in my life. That was Amos and I've paid dearly for it. I'll pay the man on the way out and you can find me in here every lunch till the money runs out. Then it depends on whatever hours I work if I got to work."

I stood up and took the hand he held out.

"I'm on the job," I said.

He nodded and walked to the bar. He was wearing boots.

When Ames Delaware left, I pushed my plate and beer out of the way and opened the envelope. Most of the business crowd was gone. It was after one. I ordered a pitcher of iced tea with my newfound wealth and asked Harry if he had ever seen the guy in the photograph that had been in the envelope.

"Old guy asked me the same," he said, breathing garlic over my shoulder. "Doesn't look like anyone I know. Or maybe it does. People come, go. You know."

I thanked him and looked at the photograph as I sipped my iced tea. Amos Sprague smiled up at me showing no teeth. He looked familiar, but I didn't trust the feeling. Sarasota itself is spread out and has only about fifty thousand permanent residents, but the rest of the county and Manatee County to the north brought the numbers up over two hundred thousand.

I tried not to think of what I'd do or say when and if I found Sprague. I'd probably try to talk or scare him into giving Delaware back whatever remained of the stolen money, if anything remained. If there was nothing left, I'd probably tell him to get his ass out of Sarasota before Delaware put holes in him. It depended on how Sprague behaved when I found him, if I found him. I didn't like the idea of Ames Delaware wandering around for what remained of his life in the hope of killing his ex-partner. I liked Ames Delaware. I even liked the idea of twenty thousand dollars. I could live for two years on twenty thousand, maybe more. I thought I was reasonably content, but the vague hope of money had shaken my peace of mind and given me dreams of a new air conditioner and a new low-cost used car from Rent-A-Dent.

Ten minutes after leaving the Round-Up, two of my wishes were answered and life got more complicated than I wanted it.

I knew someone had been in my office as soon as I opened the door. I could tell you that I sensed it, that I immediately noticed that my chair had been turned just two degrees or that I had some clever simple device attached to my door. I knew because the office was cool.

"Hi," the man in the loose-fitting white linen shirt said, looking over his shoulder at me.

"Hi," I said back.

The front of the air conditioner was off and he was tinkering away at the insides with a pocket screwdriver.

"I've got it going but I don't have the right tools," he said. "Needs a new coil. The filter needs cleaning.

Wiring goes back to when I was being shot at by the Chinese in Korea, but it'll run awhile."

He put the front back on the air conditioner, snapped it in place, and turned to me.

"Thanks," I said, moving behind my desk. "Who told you it was broke?"

He was one of those little wiry guys, full of energy, almost bouncing on his toes. I figured him for around sixty. Graying hair cut short, big clean teeth, a smile that said he had other things to do.

"No one," he said. "Got something I could wipe my hands with?"

He held out his hands to show me the grease from the air conditioner and I reached into my desk drawer for D.Q. napkins. I held some out to him and he took them.

"I'll wash when I get home," he said, wiping away some of the grime. "Trash?"

I held up my battered trash can with the National Basketball Association pennants on it. He wadded the napkins and threw in a three-pointer.

"I didn't want to sit in here waiting for you without the cool air," he explained. "Besides, I had nothing to do and a Sprague abhors idleness and broken things. They call out to be repaired, tended to."

"You have a feeling for inanimate objects," I tried, feeling the first effects of Harry's Round-up Special in the pit of my stomach.

Sprague rubbed his well-shaven chin with the back of his hand to keep it from getting grease dirty.

"No, but it drives me a little crazy to see things not working that should work. If they can't be fixed, junk them. That's what I say."

"That go for people, too?" I asked.

Sprague smiled and shook his head.

"Never thought about it that way, but maybe so.

You know you look a little like that actor on television. Little round guy with curly hair."

"Ned Beatty," I said.

"No, not him. I'll think of it later."

The air conditioner made a sound like the one my father made when he passed a kidney stone. Sprague and I both waited. The air conditioner survived the crisis and hummed on.

"Well," said Sprague, straightening his well-pressed tan slacks and crossing his legs. "I'm going to satisfy your curiosity and then I'm going to make you an offer. This could turn out to be one hell of a good day for you, Calvin."

"Please," I said. "Just call me Mr. Fonesca."

Sprague tilted his head to one side like a goofy parrot and nodded.

"I've been waiting for Ames to find me for a year," he said. "I could have just shot him back in Jackson Hole and dumped his body in the wilderness. It would have welcomed him. But I'm not a killer and besides, I wanted him to suffer."

"Two questions," I said. "How did you find me and why do you want Ames Delaware to suffer?"

Somewhere beyond the D.Q. and the old White Sox stadium, a car screeched and hit something that may have been another car. Neither of us paid much attention. The number of drivers over the age of eighty in the county probably equals the population of Jackson Hole.

"I've been waiting for Ames. I told you. He's been in town more than two weeks showing my picture, asking for me. Word got back to me through some people I'd told to be on the lookout for him. They got a couple of hundred-dollar bills each and I got the information."

"You're very generous with Ames Delaware's

money," I said, leaning forward to give him the un-blinking stare of the impassive prosecutor.

"Oh," he said with a chuckle. "I plan to get a lot more generous. I've had someone following Ames for the last four days. They saw you with him at the Round-Up, asked the bartender who you were, and . . ."

"Here you are," I said.

"Here I am," he agreed, sitting back and folding his hands in his lap.

"Answer to question number two," he said. "Ames Delaware's father swindled my father out of his five-state livestock feed monopoly back in 1927. I grew up listening to my father tell the tale. He figured Tris Delaware owed us at least three hundred thousand dollars. Ames knew it. Knew how his father had made the money Ames put into our business in the winter of 1959."

"And you waited thirty-two years to get the money back?"

"Thirty-two years," Amos Sprague concurred.

"There are those who would say that whatever Ames Delaware's father did to your father, it has nothing to do with what you did."

"I am aware of that," said Sprague. "And I am aware that among those who would say this are many who uphold the law. I choose to think of this as a blood feud, a matter of family honor, of justice through the generations."

"Bottom line here, Colonel," I said.

"Bottom line is, how much did he offer you? I know Ames. He offered you a percentage if you found me and got my father's money back. He couldn't do much else. He can't have more than a few hundred dollars left."

"Twenty thousand," I said.

My stomach was doing more than complain now. It was sending out warnings of doom, but I kept a straight interested face.

"Room's cool and you're sweating," said Sprague.

"Indigestion."

"I'll give you twenty-one thousand cash. No income tax to declare. You buy yourself a generous supply of Pepto-Bismol, get a new air conditioner and plenty to spare. I gather you are not an ambitious man."

"You gather right."

"I am an ambitious man," he said. "You know the office supply building going up over on Clark near Swift?"

I nodded.

"Mine," he said. "Got my money tied up in it. You find Ames. Tell him I'm dead. I've got a new name now. A new life."

He reached into a pocket in his white shirt and pulled out a folded piece of paper he handed across the desk. I took it, opened it, and flattened it out. It was a death certificate for Amos Sprague dated six months ago in Manatee County.

"It's a fake," he said. "Doctored. A good one though. I haven't used it for anything. I've been holding it for Ames Delaware. Now you can deliver it and take home twenty-one thousand dollars. I'll put it in a brand-new wallet which I will throw in free of charge."

I folded the death certificate and handed it back to Sprague.

"You're saying 'No,' " he said, placing the certificate back on my desk.

"I'm saying 'No,' " I agreed. "I don't have much, Mr. Sprague, but I do hold on to the belief, maybe the illusion, that I have integrity."

"And an empty refrigerator, and a bad stomach, and . . ."

I held up my hands, but he didn't stop. He just changed direction.

"Then so be it," he said with a great sigh as he stood up. "I am not giving Ames Delaware one nickel unless he wants to polish my shoes. He will have one devil of a time proving I am Amos Sprague. He will have another devil of a time getting me extradited for a civil crime in Wyoming. He will run out of money and go madder than he is, which is fine with me, though I know he will be a considerable nuisance."

"He says he'll shoot you between the eyes if you don't pay him," I volunteered.

"Recourse to violence has always been the way of the Delawares," said Sprague, walking to the door of my office.

"It's how the West was won," I said, trying out a smile.

"Tom Bosley," said Sprague. "That's who you look like. The father on *Happy Days*."

"I'm glad you remembered."

"All right, Mr. Fonesca," Sprague said, one hand on the door handle. "I will meet Ames Delaware. You know the park at the end of Lido Key?"

"I know it."

"Past the parking lot, on the east side, the beach on the inlet, not on the Gulf side."

"I know it."

"Eleven in the night tomorrow, after the park closes. You come alone, you get a wallet full of money. You bring Ames and he is unreasonable, you get a dead old man and a lot of explaining to do."

"A dead old man?"

"I do not consider myself an old man, Mr. Fonesca. I am sixty-six and more than vigorous. I married a woman of forty-one in this very town six months ago and she is now with child. Think about it."

He left and I sat going through my drawers in the hope of finding something that would stop the alien inside my stomach from bursting through. I found a half bottle of black shoe polish, three used and useless disposable Bic razors, a receipt for a rebuilt alternator for the Toyota, and something that looked like a pre-scription bottle without a label. The bottle had some liquid in it. I threw it in the wastebasket. My shot was shorter than Sprague's. I gave myself two points.

An hour later after spending part of Delaware's money on my digestive system, I sat in the Selby Library finding out about Amos Sprague. It wasn't hard. I'd stopped first at the County Records Office on Ringling Boulevard, a gallstone's throw away from the Round-Up. The new office supply building was owned by Malcom Amos. I checked the papers for the six months, which took about two hours, and found that Malcom Amos had come to town from California to spend the rest of his life in retirement enjoying the Gulf waters and the good life. He was already on the board of directors of the Sarasota Opera Company, the Asolo Theater Company, the Sarasota Ballet Company, and various charities. He had married the once married and once divorced Marcia Charvet of Venice and they had a home on Longboat Key.

I doubted if Marcia and Malcom had met through the *Herald-Tribune*'s matchmaker column. She was, if her pictures did her justice, a class act.

My stomach was better. Not perfect but better. I drove to my apartment on Bee Ridge Road, a one-room in a concrete courtyard across from a mall that supplied all my needs: Big Macs, video rentals, pizzas, pharmaceuticals, and used paperbacks. My apartment building, the Crescent Palms, looks suspiciously like the grandfather of my office building. My apartment is a studio only a little larger than my office. But it's cheap and the air-conditioning is central. I keep it clean. It's easy and dirty depresses me, almost as much as I was depressed when my Toyota groaned to a stop in front of my apartment door and kept running after I turned it off.

I wished I had never seen Ames Delaware or taken his money. I wished I had sloshed myself with Bull Frog 36, put on my Chicago Bulls cap, and gone down to Siesta Beach with a Dean Koontz novel. I wished, but wishing didn't make it so.

I spent the rest of the day watching videotapes and trying not to think. I watched *Dr. Cyclops*, *Battleground*, and *Mildred Pierce*. I took a bath and put nothing in my stomach but warm milk and Tums. When I went to bed, I still didn't know what I was going to do.

I didn't decide that till I walked into the Round-Up a few minutes after noon the next day. Ames Delaware was sitting in the same chair at the same table eating what looked like a green omelette. One of the CNN women with dark hair monotoned on from above the bar on the latest series of slaughters in a breakaway country in Europe.

The place wasn't nearly as crowded as the day before. Probably because half the customers had died after eating yesterday's special.

"Hungry?" asked Delaware.

"No," I said, sitting across from him.

He worked at his teeth with his tongue and stared at me. I looked over at Harry behind the counter and indicated that I wasn't ordering.

"You found him."

"He found me," I said. "I'm giving your money

back, Ames. Minus gas money and the cost of a pack of Tums. I'm out."

He looked down at his food, took a bite, and shook his head.

"Don't work that way," he said. "We have a deal. We shook on it. Man's word is his word or what's he got."

"That's pretty much what I told Sprague," I said.

"There, you see," said Ames Delaware. "I figure since you want out Amos said he wouldn't give me my money."

Harry was hovering over our table now with not much to do besides take care of his customers since the Braves game hadn't started.

"You look a little pale, Calvin," he said, breathing into my eyes.

"Special yesterday didn't agree with me," I said.

"No," he replied, standing up and wiping his hands on his apron, which I was beginning to see as fetishistic behavior to clean his hands of the indigestion he caused.

"Sat fine with me," said Delaware.

"You got to get in shape, Calvin," said fat Harry, moving away. "Get a checkup, too."

"Well?" asked Delaware when Harry was safely serving a couple at a nearby table.

"He says your father stole the money from his father," I said.

"Not so," replied Ames Delaware. "That's old business. Between his dad and mine. My business was with Amos. I ain't responsible for poverty, wars, all this race stuff, or bad blood between our fathers. Damnation, might as well tell George Moon-Toes he's got the right to put a tomahawk in my head because my granddad maybe shot a member of his tribe."

"I see your point," I said.

"You got no choice if you got any sense."

"He won't pay you," I said.

"Then I'll shoot him dead. Either way it ends it."

"And you go to jail for the rest of your life."

"Maybe yes, maybe no. I can be long gone on my moped and a few gallons of gas in less than a day and I don't leave much of a trail."

"He's married," I said. "His wife's going to have a baby."

"Then she'll have to bear it, wean it, and bring it up without its father," he said. "Knowing Amos, he's got a horse of a life insurance policy. I figure she'll be better off without him."

"You're being hard, Ames."

"I'm being straight, Calvin."

"He fixed my air conditioner," I said.

"I was always good with animals. He was always good with machines. That ain't no reason to let him live."

There wasn't much point in going on with this. If I didn't get the two of them together, Ames would find his old partner eventually. Either Amos would hire someone to get rid of Ames or Ames would shoot Amos Sprague. Either way the police would want to know what the hell had been going through my mind to let it happen. I knew what the police would say if I called them. Two old men are always threatening each other in Sarasota. What could they do about it? When there was a crime, they'd be there. And when it did happen, I'd have some tough explaining to do. I could pack up and leave town, but I liked it here.

I arranged to meet Ames Delaware at my office at ten-thirty that night. He knew where the D.Q. was. He promised he wouldn't bring his gun. Not this time.

"Maybe we can work something out," I said, getting up.

"He sees reason, we can work it out. Way I see it, I've got nothing to lose. He's got everything to lose."

He had a point. I didn't want to see it, but he had a point.

I spent the rest of the afternoon in my office reading *Midnight,* doing crossword puzzles, and looking at a dying palm tree through the window.

The moped putted up just before ten-thirty. I stood up and listened to the clop of Ames Delaware's boots on the concrete steps. He knocked at the door and I told him to come in.

"Mind if I leave my helmet here?" he asked.

"No safer in here than on your bike, but sure."

He placed the red helmet on one of my chairs.

It took us twenty minutes to drive to the park. We could have made it faster but the bridge to Bird Key was up. Lights glittered along the bay on our right and left in the condos, hotels, and homes along the shore. Across the bridge and beyond Bird Key we drove around St. Armand's Circle where the Snow Birds and well-to-do congregated in fashionable shops and ate at some of the town's better restaurants.

We went left along Lido Beach to the end of the Key and I parked in the lot of a nearby beach motel. The chain was up across the parking lot at the park. Ames Delaware started to get out while the Toyota was still sputtering.

"Remember," I said. "I get a chance. If that doesn't work, you leave with me and I'm out of it."

"You get your chance," he said and got out of the car.

We crossed the road and walked around the parking-lot chain. I didn't know how often the police patrolled the park after closing, but it was hard to keep people out since the beach ran into the park on the Gulf side.

We listened to the surf, the gulls, and the crunch of

parking-lot stones under our feet as I led the way past picnic tables and through a thin line of trees onto the narrow beach. Across the inlet, the lights from the houses looked friendly but far away.

We were early. Amos Sprague wasn't there.

I moved to the shore with Delaware and looked into the clear moonlight water. A ray about the size of a large kite glided just below the surface of the water no more than a dozen feet out.

"Ames," I said. "It's beautiful here."

"That's a fact."

"Being alive is not bad."

"Depends. You're talking to the wrong man, Calvin."

At that point, the right man came walking through the trees about thirty yards up the beach. A small white heron skittered away from him. Amos Sprague walked erect, surefooted in our direction, a little man with a mission. Ames Delaware took four or five steps in his direction.

I stepped between them when they were about a dozen paces apart.

"Hold it," I said. "I talk. You listen. You both agreed."

They said nothing.

"Compromise," I said.

"There's no compromise about this," said Ames Delaware. "Told you that. He gives me my money back and I let him live."

"Money is mine, my father's," said Amos Sprague. "I told you that. He gets out of town and I let him live."

"A new partnership in the office supply business," I tried.

"No," said Sprague.

"Cash money," said Ames Delaware, standing tall, a rush of warm wind bristling his hair.

The white heron had wandered back and stood a few paces behind Amos Sprague in the moonlight.

"That's it," I said, clapping my hands. "That's it. We're leaving now. I'm preparing a report and turning it over to the police in the morning. I'm also giving a copy to my lawyer."

That part was a lie. I had no lawyer.

"Can't work like that," said Amos Sprague.

"Can't," agreed Ames.

"I'm not a violent man," said Amos. "I told you, but I see no options here. I've got a business, a wife, a child on the way, and family honor. I'll live with a necessary sin."

My stomach warned me even before Amos Sprague turned his head toward the dark shadows of the trees along the beach. A man stepped out toward us, the moon spotlighting him. He was lean, somewhere in his thirties, and wearing a T-shirt that said "Tone Def" on it in red letters. He also carried what looked like a shotgun.

There was nowhere to run and no one to call. I had a vision of the ray in the water going for my dead eyes.

"This is crazy," I said.

"No argument from me," agreed Amos Sprague as the man with the shotgun moved toward us.

When the man was about a dozen paces from us, he started to raise the weapon. It was about halfway up when Ames Delaware pulled what looked like a Buntline special from under his shirt behind his back and fired twice. I don't know where the bullets hit but the man with the Tone Def T-shirt went down on his back and flung his shotgun toward the bay. Birds and squirrels went chattering mad in the brush and trees.

Ames turned the pistol toward his old partner.

"Money's all in my wife's name," said Amos evenly. "You can shoot me dead but you'll never get a dime of the money your father stole from us."

"Then you're a dead man, Amos Sprague."

"Hold it," I said. "Someone must have heard the shots. The police . . ."

Ames Delaware wasn't listening. I pushed his gun hand and he fired. The white heron squealed, shed tail feathers, and dropped. Amos Sprague didn't move. He could have made it to the trees when Delaware fired but he chose to stand his ground.

"Stand aside, Calvin," said Delaware evenly.

"You've got my curse, Ames Delaware, and a wish you had children so they could carry it, too," shouted Amos Sprague.

"I can live my last years with your curse, Amos, but not your memory."

The shot cut through the night. One shot. No more. Amos Sprague went down.

Ames Delaware returned the long-barreled gun to his belt and turned to me.

"It's done," he said.

"You lied to me," I said. "You said no gun."

"So did Amos. If I didn't lie, you'd be a dead man."

He was right and I suddenly needed a toilet. A car, maybe two, was racing across the gravel in the parking lot beyond the trees and picnic tables. A pair of headlights cut through, bouncing toward us.

"I regret the bird," said Delaware.

"It was my fault," I said. "I hit your arm."

"Gun was my father's. It ends fitting."

Footsteps came crashing through the brush branches and a pair of flashlights found us.

"Put your hands up," came a less-than-steady voice behind the light.

I put my hands up and so did Ames. The two police-
men moved toward us past the dead men.

"On the sand," said one of them. "Arms behind
your back."

I moved as fast as I could. Ames didn't budge.

"Can't do that," he said.

"Old-timer," came the voice drawing nearer. "I'm
in no mood."

"Don't go on my knees," said Ames. "For man nor
God. I'll take the consequences."

And he did. When they took us into the station
back on Ringling Boulevard right next to the county
jail, Ames took full responsibility, told the police that
I had come to patch up an old quarrel and that Amos
had set us up. He told them I'd tried to stop the killing
and that I had no idea that he had a gun or might
use it.

It was not with charity and goodwill, but on the
advice of the public defender that they simply let me
go home with a red mark on my file.

They kept Ames and I testified at the inquest. The
guy with the T-shirt was a drifter named Burt Hemp-
hill. No indictment on that one. But Ames was turned
over for shooting Amos Sprague.

The story stayed on the local front pages and the
television news for five or six days. Ames Delaware is
awaiting trial. I invested what remained of the two
hundred Ames had given me in food and a tune-up for
the Toyota. Ames's moped is sitting in the corner of
my office.

I visited Ames at the lockup this morning.

His chances of getting off, according to the public
defender, look pretty good. I told him if he gets off we
might consider becoming partners. He didn't say no.

DIVER

BY JAMES L. TRAYLOR

1

I had never been to the club, but I'd heard the name—Metroplex.

I'd always thought it sounded like a fight in which someone landed a low blow.

A teenage boy was dead there.

I was in the dark blue BMW I had rented recently for another job. It had been part of the cover then, but I found that I liked the damned thing. But I hardly qualified for vilification as a yuppie. At forty-two, I was just a businessman, except my business was pain—human anguish.

Dale Maleske had been a seventeen-year-old senior at Wheeler High School, Marietta, Georgia. For most of the 1980s Wheeler was locally famous for being one of the top five football teams in the state. It was also known as the teen suicide capital of Cobb County. Dale was the sixth so far this year and it was only just past New Year's.

January is one of the few unpleasant times in Atlanta. For the past three years running, January 6 and 7 had been local holidays because of snow and ice storms. Hell, one year in the 1970s the town was closed down for a week. The Northern immigrants snickered and told stories about how "Southerners couldn't drive." In East Cobb anyone born south of Philadelphia took a lot of jabs.

There wasn't anything unusual about Dale's death except that he just happened to decide to end it all by jumping off the overhead railing of the Metroplex's sunken bandstand and dance floor. The crowd had told the police that he was a jumper, just another body slammer who, instead of jumping onto the top of the crowd from the front of the stage, had opted to leap from the overhead to the cavernous expanse of bodies below. Usually, these jumpers were caught by the crowd, got a little contact high from the thrill, and went home safe and happy. This time the crowd parted and the boy's body hit the floor like a javelin.

The mother, Neely Maleske, a thirty-eight-year-old divorcee with three kids (Dale was the oldest), a slightly underpaid job, and an attitude about men in general, had been referred to me by a neighbor, Basia Hiatt. I'd done a slight favor for Basia some years before that obviously had meant more to her than to me.

By the time I talked to Mrs. Maleske, the funeral was over, the police had come and gone many times, and I, Bob Crawford, was her last hope of knowing the truth about her son.

"I refuse to believe that Dale was a jumper, a suicide," she told me.

We were sitting in her great room in a subdivision off Sewell Mill and Murdock, right in the heartbeat of fashionable East Cobb. Neely Maleske looked poised and confident sitting there, a likely guardian of a five-bedroom, three-and-a-half-bath traditional home, paid for and kept up by her hard work and the support checks.

"I'm sure that it's hard to accept, Mrs. Maleske, but the police are almost always correct in these cases. If they believe Dale jumped, he probably did."

"Damn, Mr. Crawford, if he'd been depressed, I'd have known it. I'm his mother!"

I ignored the shrillness, the sharp rise in her voice. I didn't want to encourage her. "Tell me about Dale's behavior the week before the fall. Anything peculiar? Out of the ordinary?"

I was fishing. You did a lot of it in this business.

"Well, the only thing peculiar was Dale's wanting to go downtown to that punk club, that Metroplex."

I knew the place; in a real run-down section the city fathers want to condemn only to erect their Fabulous Falcons' new stadium. I was for the dome on it; it would protect unsuspecting small plane pilots from seeing the worst team in professional football merely by accident.

She was wandering all around the subject, not quite coherent. "Had he ever mentioned the Metroplex before?"

"No, not really. I knew he liked 'new music' as he called it. He'd listen to people like Rotten Gimick and Camper van Beethoven, but I thought he preferred something more sedate for concerts."

She paused, walked over to a coffee table, came back with a copy of *Creative Loafing,* a local tabloid.

"I used to read this for the investigative stories, but Dale read the entertainment ads. One of his friends told him there was an all-ages show for some band I'd never heard of. Said it was 'speed metal' or some such. I finally agreed to let him go with two of his friends—Brian Hammond and Robin Zimla. They both live in this neighborhood."

"You trust these boys?" I asked.

"I suppose. I'd talked with them many times. They never said anything that sounded weird or anything."

"Did you talk with them after your son's death?"

"Yes. They came and told me they were sorry. They never thought anything like that would happen. That

it just didn't seem like Dale. That he'd been wired
that night—much more than normal."

" 'Wired,' they said. Does that mean anything special to the peer group?" I asked.

"I assume they just meant more excited than usual,"
she replied. "They didn't make a big deal of it."

I noted the addresses of the two friends. I'd need
to speak with them and eventually, inevitably, of
course, the police—but not just yet.

"Did Dale have a girlfriend?"

"No one steady, but he dated several. Lately it
seemed to be mostly Katrina and Ashlee. I think he
liked Ashlee the most."

Her eyes turned away from mine and gazed out the
bay window. "She was the last person to leave his . . .
grave. She said she missed him terribly, that she didn't
know he was that upset."

"Was she at the club? Does she know anything?" I
felt like I was floundering. It all looked like a typical
package: divorced working mother loses touch with
teenage son, a mother who doesn't recognize when
the boy is in trouble.

She gave me a snapshot of Dale and Ashlee. So far
I didn't know anything about either of them.

I got some more names and addresses of Dale's
friends. I already felt they were the key.

Dale had died Saturday night. Last Saturday night,
I kept telling myself. It was now only Thursday. He'd
been examined and probed, eulogized and prayed over,
dead and buried, and only five days had passed.

2

The Plex—that's how the crowd knew it—is right
smack in the middle of downtown Atlanta. But not
the part with the Hyatt Regency, the Ritz Carlton
(downtown version), and the Peachtree Plaza. It's only

a block north of the Omni Hotel and office complex (where the Democrats held their National Convention in 1988) and more appropriately the Club Rio that will always be associated with underage girls, porno videos, and Rob Lowe.

The hotel and office area is staunchly Republican— or would be if the Southern Democrats would admit it. The Metroplex sits resolutely worlds apart from that affluence. The club caters to disenchanted youth. The kind with spiked hair (even if moussed), leather jackets, lewd T-shirts, and hollow animas.

It also appealed to the curious. Today I was one of them.

I was surprised to see the place had its own attended parking lot. Somehow that seemed incongruent for a counterculture club.

I gave the attendant three bills (little ones) and self-parked my car; it was the only BMW. I resisted a temptation to look over my shoulder as I walked away.

The Club's name was painted in huge black stencil letters on the side of the rough brick wall— M E T R O P L E X. There were perhaps twenty people loitering in the general vicinity of the entrance. None seemed to be particularly hostile, but then my outfit wasn't business suit and tie either. I was only about twenty-five years older than most of them.

I walked up to the ticket booth. "I'd like to see the manager."

"Six dollars." The scraggly girl did not look up.

"I just need to talk to the manager."

This time she looked up. "Six dollars."

It was hopeless. I slid over the two bills. By this time, the head was back down but an angular hand pointed over her shoulder to a very dark hall. I walked the way she pointed, following crowd noise and what turned out to be taped music. It was loud enough for me, live or not.

I knocked on a door that read: M A N G E R.

"Yeah," was the only response I got.

I pushed the door open. "I'm Bob Crawford. I'm looking for the manager."

"Yeah, what for?"

There was a nameplate on his desk.

CARL TROWER
THE BUCKS STOP HERE

"Mr. Trower." I extended my hand.

He took it and said, "Crawford, you said. What do you want?"

"Dale Maleske."

His eyes narrowed, got a little darker.

"His mother asked me to see if I could find out any more about his death. I operate a little security company in Buckhead." I was sure he knew Buckhead; I didn't think private detective would impress him.

"I've told that story already. To the police and to the papers. You want to see the spot? We taped it off and painted it; the crowd dances on it every night. They push to get there. Call it Big Slam."

My eyes showed I didn't know what he was talking about.

"Ever been to a club like this?"

"No," I told him.

"I didn't think so. Come with me; you need to see this once for yourself."

By now the tape was over. The first band came on. A poster whizzed by—CREAMOZOIDS. Silently, I wondered.

The music was loud, rhythmic, but not melodic. Occasionally I picked up a lyric—usually a four-letter word—followed immediately by rapid guitar bursts.

"That's speed metal. This band's really hot in LA, lucky to get 'em here, even on a Thursday."

By now I'd figured out speed metal meant loud and real fast, but it didn't make me like it.

He led me past a long bar, the overhead decorated with photos and T-shirts of groups that had played the club—The Dead Zone, Dead Elvis, The Dead, The Damned. The decor seemed alphabetized.

More images came quickly. The bar was separated from the dance floor by chicken wire. That ploy allowed people over twenty-one to get a drink while the all-ages bunch got to see the group, buy T-shirts and Coke (the bottled variety).

From the edge of the steps leading to the dance floor, Trower pointed. "There. Right in front of the singer." I could see part of a painted outline. They'd probably have to paint again soon.

He gestured, pointed above his head. "He jumped from there."

I had to take three steps out onto the dance floor to see where he pointed. I saw another strip of tape from the overhang. I guessed it might be twenty feet. Plenty high enough if you landed wrong. Or wanted to.

In front of the singer, I saw several guys—and one girl—launch themselves up over the heads of the crowd and get passed along for a while until they got dropped to the floor. Several were bumping into others—slamming. A perfectly descriptive word.

"Can I go up there?" I pointed up as he had. He nodded, indicated a stairway.

"We tell 'em not to jump, but usually a few do. We know it's dangerous, but most like to get a little scared."

No one was near the rail. From that point, it felt as if I was directly over the singer. The words were more understandable. I didn't like them any better but now I knew why. Leaning over the edge toward the microphone, all I could see below was cleavage. Before, I had only been vaguely aware that the lead singer was female. The clothes of the group and the audience were pretty much unisex. As I pulled back over the rail, I snagged my jacket. Near the tape was a splinter.

Trower was already headed down the stairs. Back in the office he seemed reluctant to give any real answers.

"I don't know why he did it. No one's ever done it before and killed himself. I certainly didn't want him to."

"Did the police close you down?" I asked.

"Yeah, dammit. On a Saturday night of all nights. I make half my living Saturday nights."

"The crowd here looks pretty rough."

"Nah. It's all show. Usually the bands are rougher than the crowd. You should have been here the night the guy jumped. The Butthole Surfers were here. Ninety percent of the acts we get in here, we can't even put their name in the Atlanta papers." He paused for a moment. "But that night was a tough crowd. Strange, too."

"In what way?"

"Oh, I don't exactly know. Well, I do, too, but it's not something you want to tell the cops. I can't stop these people from doing something in the parking lot and coming in here. The whole crowd that night was wired or something special. Much flashier than usual."

"Did you know this Maleske kid?" I asked.

"Nah. Musta been his first time." He paused and looked at me directly for the first time since my visit. "But I'll never forget him."

3

I didn't want to talk to Dale Maleske's friends, particularly the girlfriends. My neighbor's daughter, my mentally adopted daughter, was too recently dead for me to want to do that.

The only reason I could make myself go was the point of pain in Neely Maleske's eyes. She was hurting as I had hurt.

I turned the BMW off Johnson Ferry onto Chadd's Ford. I had decided I'd only talk with the special girlfriend, Ashlee Duke, she of the Southern name but as it turned out Northern descent.

I'd called ahead to arrange the interview. The neighborhood didn't like little surprises such as P.I.s wandering around asking questions, legitimate or otherwise. I took a deep breath, rang the bell.

"Mr. Crawford?" she asked. "I'm Brandy Duke, Ashlee's mother. Come in." Her voice did not have the low, sweet sound of a woman from the South.

We walked into a fashionable great room. Lots of windows, big fabric chairs, projection TV screen. In the shadow, I saw blond movement.

"This is my daughter. I'll just stay here with you, of course."

"Yes," I said. "No problem."

Ashlee had on pedal pants, an exercise top, and little tiny imitation track shoes with L.A. Gear in the pastels on the side. She looked as fast as I felt slow. She had the taut breasts, big nipples, and tight ass that only seem to last about thirty seconds when girls are very young.

"Ashlee."

"Yes." No sir, no nothing, no Southerner.

"Tell me about Dale. Why did he do it?"

"I don't believe he did! He loved me!"

Her mother broke in. "Ashlee, don't be absurd. You'd only gone out with him for six months."

"Well, you're sleeping with that guy Tom and you've only known him two months," the daughter retorted.

Brandy was also a blonde, but the breasts were larger, the ass not quite so tight, and she wore no ring.

"Ashlee," I interjected, before an argument could start. "Did Dale say he was depressed, or felt bad or anything?"

"No, he wasn't depressed. He wanted to go to the club with Brian and Robin. That's all he talked about for a week. How cardinal it'd be!"

"So you don't think he even had it on his mind?"

"No; and I told the police that, too. They didn't even listen."

"Sometimes, they're like that." I paused, looked around the room. "Was he happy?"

"Yes, I've told you. He was even happy about the . . ." She stopped suddenly, her pale cheeks blanching whiter, then turning red.

She jumped up, ran from the room. Her mother looked at me, said coldly: "You'll have to leave now, Mr. Crawford. My daughter and I have much to discuss."

As I drove away from that no longer cloistered existence at Chadd's Ford, I headed toward the house of the other girlfriend, Katrina Waverly. Neely Maleske had told me that they called her "star" but it was all beyond me. She'd told me she had "no idea" either.

Katrina was a cold call. All I had was an address and the fact that Dale had dumped her for Ashlee.

The girl answered the doorbell herself.

"Katrina? I'm Bob Crawford. Dale Maleske's mother wants me to talk with you a little about what might have made him kill himself."

She was the brunette version of Ashlee, except that she was more physical. She was darker, almost olive, with long brown hair, long legs, and heavy doe-deep eyes. If you judged solely on beauty, Ashlee would lose.

She stood impassively, her eyes narrowing, me the enemy.

"I just came from Ashlee's. She seems quite upset. More than just about Dale. I got the impression you might know why."

"That bitch! She stole him from me. Made him sleep with her. I'm a good girl. He just walked away." She stopped her tirade, then turned to me again: "Bitch!"

"Would you mind talking to me about Dale?" I wanted to get back to business. She was drowning in teenage angst. My chest felt stuffed, overburdened.

"I guess it's okay. Let me call Dale's mom to check on you." She closed the door quickly. I didn't want to point out to her that if I had not been legit she would have been assaulted long before now.

The door opened quickly. "Come in. She says I should motor it for you."

"Thanks. Do you know why he would want to commit suicide?" Even I was getting tired of the question.

"No. Not really. I suspected that Ashlee might be pregnant, but I don't think he'd kill himself over that."

"You sure she's pregnant?

"Pretty. I heard she was late. Very late."

"Did Dale know?"

"I guess. They were together everywhere. Her mom was gone a lot. They had the house to themselves."

"He never said anything to you, one way or another?"

"No. He . . . I guess he was ashamed of it. I'd put him off about sex. I guess she didn't."

I looked at her hard. "But he didn't seem worried about the baby, Ashlee, or anything?"

"No . . . He was the same ole Dale—good-looking and carefree. He'd have probably loved the kid. He was that way."

There was nothing more she could say. She didn't know anything that could help me understand his death.

I drove away to a Dunkin' Donuts, downed a fresh coffee, and scribbled on a yellow pad. I made a stupid chart: Dale—Dead; Ashlee—Pregnant; Katrina—Virginal; Neely—Distraught; Brandy—Entertained; and Bob—Stymied.

I needed to talk to Dale's two buddies on that trip to the Metroplex—Brian and Robin.

I caught up with Brian Hammond while he was on break from running Billy Bob, the singing mechanical bear at Show Biz Pizza. He smelled cheesy, but he had that muscular jock look—big shoulders and tiny hips—that goes over well with the under twenty set.

He eyed me suspiciously as I walked up, but didn't move from leaning against the wall at the rear of the restaurant.

"Whatcha want?"

I sat down next to him, pulled my arms around my knees. "My name's Bob Crawford. I'm working for Dale's mom. She doesn't want to believe that he committed suicide. Did he?"

"No fucking way, man. He was having too much fun splitting Ashlee."

It was impeccable teenage logic, but I believed it. "What about that night? Do you know how it happened?"

"Sure. That was gorillaed from the start. Dale really wanted to see the Surfers. I wasn't that much into it but I'd never been to the Plex, so I said, what the hell."

My mind was drifting as he ran on with the story.

"Dale went down to get a Coke or something, came back looking all sweaty. Said he'd heard something that scared him, he wasn't sure what."

"Did you tell the police?" I asked.

"Yeah. But they didn't pay much attention because they didn't like me calling them the 'fuckin' blues.' They just ignored me. But he was scared, wanted to leave fast."

"His mother doesn't know this, Brian."

"I never told her. After the police wouldn't listen to me, I just didn't care anymore."

"What did he hear? Did he say anything specific?"

"Well, I couldn't make much out of it," Brian continued.

Brian was beginning to look restless. Already he'd talked more by himself than any teenager I'd met in months. His eyes were starting to turn away. If I didn't move in, he'd be gone.

"Surely, he said something more than that," I suggested.

"He said something about false men and no men and true men. It didn't make shit for sense."

I knew that if I didn't ask the right questions, he'd be gone and all my hopes of finding Dale's killer. This was the key. Why did he do it? What had he heard? Why didn't he just tell Brian what scared him?

"It was a deal, I guess." Brian broke into my thoughts. "At least I think he meant it was a deal."

"A drug deal? Why would that have scared him so much?" It didn't make any sense to me either.

"He wasn't scared about no deal. He was scared about the money. That he wouldn't get it."

Brian was confusing the hell out of me. "The money. What money?"

"The money from the deal. He needed it because of Ashlee. Because she was pregnant." Brian stopped talking for a second. "He thought that he'd be able to get her out of trouble. And himself."

I stopped him. "But he didn't know where any money was."

Brian laughed. "That's just the point. He did know. That's what he heard. And he needed it bad."

Brian paused for a moment. "Dale said if I'd read about World War II in history class and actually watched those dumb black and white newsreels they used to show us I wouldn't be such a dumbass."

"What'd he mean?" I asked.

"I couldn't figure it out. Said he'd seen a slogan on President Truman's desk. I didn't know what he was talking about."

"He didn't say anything else?"

"Yeah. One thing. I'd forgot. Something about a 'block of ice.' Shit, they didn't use block ice at that place."

My stomach muscles drew in. I hoped my face didn't change. I wanted him to keep talking.

"Dale wouldn't tell me anything else. Except he never thought he'd have to turn someone in."

"Turn someone in?" I asked.

"Yeah. To the police. He was excited. Said he had to get something before we left. That the police would need it."

"What was he after?" I was eager—this would answer the entire Dale Maleske question.

"He didn't say. He just went off."

"You follow him?"

"No. I tried to, but he waved me off. I said okay. By then, I was more interested in the band."

"And you never saw him alive again?"

"No. I heard the shouts and looked up and saw him coming down. He fell headfirst right into the crowd."

I was trying to close the time gap in my mind. It really wasn't coming together. Brian had turned the story around for me.

I left him there nibbling his pizza.

4

I was drawn to the club, that noisy place where the boy had lost his life. I'd spent days thinking about him, his face, his friends, his death—I hadn't known him before I'd made that first trip to the club, but I felt like I knew him now.

Dale was smart. He'd told Brian just what was going on at the club but Brian's world was too small. Mine was an old world, and for one instant Dale had been there with me.

He'd died in a second-story slam dance. The crowd had just parted and his head—instead of being cushioned by the dancing bodies below—had gone straight into the concrete floor. But I knew it wasn't suicide. Brian Hammond had convinced me it was murder. I just couldn't put the picture together. I felt the answer there, just waiting for me.

I walked up the stairs to look once again at the railing. I knew there was something I'd missed, something the police had missed. I knelt there, carefully examining one of the precious few clues I had, that jagged place in the wood where the fabric from his shirt had caught.

The police thought suicide. I knew they were wrong. I'd been to the spot. I'd felt the push; his mother felt the pain.

It was right then as I looked over the railing that I knew for certain that Dale Maleske had been murdered.

It was the tiny bit of fuzz stuck in the wrong side of the rail. But that's not what made it murder.

There at the club, men knew no truth. This was a false house. A plan for rebellion where the misfit was champion, where only money counted. And to the crowd, bucks was all.

Leaning over the rail, I knew Dale's line to Brian pointed to his killer. Then I remembered Carl Trower's motto—"The Bucks Stop Here." True men and blocks of ice merged the old with the new. You didn't have to be a whiz to know about ice, but I'd bet the mortgage that Brian had no clue about Harry Truman.

Dale thought it was funny, told Brian to beware the true man. Brian didn't know what he was talking about.

But I did. Now it was not just a killing joke, it was murder.

I could see a tiny fragment of fabric in the railing on the far side when the lights swung round, reflecting. I leaned over to get a better view.

My head spun. The dance floor stood suspended but enlarged below me. It started to move slowly. I turned my head, like the feeling you get when you're falling off a bicycle or about to be in a car wreck.

Time froze. I didn't even feel the push.

I thought I'd leaned too far. I couldn't regain my balance. I was slipping away, thinking about how to get my feet in front of my head when I hit . . .

My legs hooked on part of the railing, one foot caught in a slat. Pain shot down my body. I reached out by instinct, grabbing at air, grabbing at anything.

My fingers found fabric, then a belt. Other fingers pushed, tried to loosen them.

The closeness of the other body pressed in on me. I held on but my sense of balance was lost. The sickness of vertigo overcame me. I held on to the belt as we tipped over. My brain screamed—TWIST, dammit!

Our bodies fell to the same floor that killed Dale Maleske. My elbows hurt, my knees hurt. I didn't remember the landing.

I looked down at the body beneath me. The face looked funny. The eyes had no glow, a coldness was all that came from the face.

Carl Trower was dead.

I struggled to my feet. As I looked down I could see Trower's head in the center of the little square he'd painted onto the dance floor, his head pointed directly to the ceiling.

My gut ached. Dale was dead. Even now I didn't know everything. Maybe I could find out before I called his mother. She'd want to know why. And I had to have a reason, even if I made it up. People demand reasons; they must have explanations; they must know.

I struggled to my feet. The crowd around me parted. I heard a voice. "Somebody call an ambulance."

"Yeah. And the uniforms. Get 'em here, too."

I stumbled over to an empty table, sat down. Someone stuck a drink in front of me. I didn't look up.

Dale was in my mind. And Neely. And myself.

My thoughts were crowded with darkness. I could feel the staleness of the club and the stagnation of a dream. Another promise unfulfilled, another future voided, another youth dead. It wasn't supposed to happen that way in the calm affluence of Chadd's Ford, a Yankee bastion nestled in the new monied South. Carl Trower had killed Dale Maleske, but the murder would not so much be his fault as it would be the area's, my birthplace, saddled once again with second-class dismissal. Cursed and vilified by the transient looters, those corporate minions, transferred from their cold homes to our sun, feeling only the physical warmth, never the warmth of the people.

I looked at the empty glass in front of me. I could hear the sirens outside. I only had to imagine the blue lights.

I just sat, waited for the police. I'd known from the start their turn would come.

AN EYE FOR SCANDAL
BY EDWARD D. HOCH

I suppose the trouble at Darlan & Trapper Investigations really started when my young partner Mike Trapper found the girl of his dreams and married her last Christmas Eve. That was seven months ago, and though I had to admit the sight of Marla Downs Trapper entering a room could still pump the blood through an old man's veins, she'd been making my life hell from the first day after the honeymoon.

Mike was a rich man's son who'd walked into my one-man agency a few years back with money to invest when I needed it worst. He became my partner instead of the hereditary lawyer his father had expected. He was tall and blond, young enough to be my son, and I think at first I loved him like one. But Marla Downs had expected a bit more when she married him, and I think the shock of helping him with his income taxes was more than she could stomach.

"Marla thinks we should take a wider range of cases," he told me one day in April. "We want to buy a house and—"

"She told me," I muttered, flipping through the morning mail. "She told me the day you got back from Bermuda."

"Well, I think she's right. There are people around with big money to pay for information. People like Tommy Deckler."

"The tabloids? You want me to go to work for the *Midnight Sun*?"

"Marla says—"

"I know." I was the first to admit that business hadn't been good. In the first few years after Mike and I became partners things had picked up, but it proved to be only temporary. Now his original investment was long gone, and I wouldn't have blamed Mike for walking out on me.

"—that you've got to stop doing free jobs for old friends and buckle down to making a profit for this agency."

"I guess when you reach my age there are a lot of old friends with problems."

"If you won't go after the profitable end of the business, at least let me do it, Al."

"Did she suggest that, too?"

"I'm suggesting it."

So I'd let him do it. I tried not to think of the sort of agency Darlan & Trapper was becoming, even while we started to show a profit for the first time in years. Though he'd always talked about his cases and often asked my advice, Mike decided it was best not to mention these special clients until the final bill went out. To me, shadowing a rock singer to catch him in bed with a fifteen-year-old girl was no better than the messy divorce cases I used to shun in the old days.

So in late July, on a Monday afternoon when we happened to close the office and head for home at the same time, I wasn't really surprised when I asked him what he was working on and he replied, "You don't want to know, Al. It's one of those messy jobs you hate so much."

He was right. I didn't want to know.

* * *

It must have been four in the morning when the ringing telephone awakened me. I had a cordless one that I kept by my bedside and I rolled over to pick it up. I don't know who I expected, but it certainly wasn't Marla Trapper.

"Al, this is Marla," she began, talking fast. "Mike woke up with terrible pains in his side and I've got him over at Northpark emergency."

I shook the clouds from my head. "What is it?"

"They think maybe his appendix. They're going to operate."

"I'll be right over," I promised.

I threw on my clothes and drove across town to Northpark Hospital, only half-awake. The streets were virtually empty at this time of morning and I was there within fifteen minutes. Still, it was too late to see Mike before they wheeled him off to surgery.

"The doctor is reassuring," Marla told me, ceasing her pacing long enough to give me a quick kiss on the cheek. "Thanks for coming."

"I guess there's nothing to do but wait."

"I told him he's been working too hard. This case has him running around like crazy."

"Which one is that?" I asked.

She glanced around the waiting room nervously. "You know!" she answered quietly.

I merely grunted, not wanting to admit that Mike had told me very little of late.

During the slow hours that followed, I had an opportunity to observe Marla at length for the first time since their marriage. She was a bit thin for my taste, but certainly sexy. Her smile was the sort that seemed directed at you alone, and even her casual sports clothes were colorfully eye-catching. Sometimes I wondered why she'd married Mike Trapper, unless it was for his share of the family money. I was cynical when it came to love, having gotten my own divorce long before such things were fashionable.

"How old are you, Al?" she asked suddenly as our wait passed the two-hour mark.

"Pushing sixty. Old enough to retire if I could afford it."

"You look younger," she told me, and I wondered what had brought forth this improbable compliment.

Our conversation was cut short by the arrival of the doctor, a hospital staffer named Ericson. "Mrs. Trapper? Your husband is fine. It was a ruptured appendix, just as we thought. He's resting nicely and he should be able to go home by the end of the week."

"Can I see him?"

"He's in the recovery room. He won't be fully conscious yet, but you can slip in for five minutes."

I insisted she go in alone, and went back to my chair in the emergency waiting room. Already I was thinking about phoning his clients and explaining that he'd be out of action for a couple of weeks. Marla was back in five minutes, looking relieved. "He knew me," she said. "He's still pretty much out of it, but he mumbled something about seeing you first thing in the morning."

I glanced at my watch. It was nearly seven o'clock. "I'll come back in a few hours, after he's rested."

"Thank you, Al."

We still hadn't hired a regular secretary for the office, but I phoned the service and hired a temp for the week. It had worked out in the past when we were both busy on cases, and this promised to be a busy week. Then I set the alarm for ten o'clock and tried to catch a couple hours of my lost sleep.

By the time I returned to the hospital, Mike was fully conscious, conversing with Marla in his room. "How you feeling, boy?" I asked him.

He managed a wan smile. "I'll live. Of all the crazy things to happen to me!"

"Better men than you have lost their appendix."

"They caught it just after it ruptured," Marla said, "before it could do real harm."

"How are things at the office?" Trapper asked.

"Fine. I hired a temp for the rest of the week to answer the phone."

"You've got to take my cases, Al."

"They can wait."

"This is Tuesday and I won't be out till Sunday or Monday! Then I'll be home resting for another week or two. I'm talking big bucks!"

"What is it?"

"The file's in the top drawer of my desk. It's just legwork, but it needs to be done this week."

"Since when do we get big bucks if it's just legwork?"

Mike Trapper winced a bit as he tried to shift position in the bed. "It's politics. The party conventions are coming up and Tommy Deckler—"

"Deckler again!" He was the publisher of the *Midnight Sun*.

"He's got money, Al, and it's nothing illegal."

"Go on," I managed, just barely.

"A lawyer named Hugh Barnstable wants his party's nomination for Congress, but Deckler says there are rumors about him cheating on his wife. He had me checking various hotels in the district where Barnstable stayed during the past year."

"So he can run a front-page story and ruin the man's career?"

"It's a character flaw, Al. The voters have a right to know."

I turned away for a moment, feeling sick and depressed. I remembered Mike Trapper the day he'd first walked through the door of my office. He'd had principles then, or at least I thought he did.

"How much money?" I heard myself ask, and the question alone made me no better than he was.

"Our regular rates plus expenses during the investigation, with a bonus of ten thousand if we find something."

It was a measure of our financial desperation that an extra ten thousand could seem like big bucks, especially to Mike. But he was building up business for the agency, from whatever quarter, and if he could bring in a job like this every week or two it added up. Distasteful as the job might be, I knew that I'd follow through for him. That's what partners did.

"All right," I agreed. "I'll look over the file. When you're back on your feet, we need to have a long talk about the direction the agency is taking lately."

"Thanks, Al."

I left the hospital feeling slightly unclean.

The service had sent over a temporary secretary-receptionist named Elizabeth Farr. She had brown hair and a good figure, with a pleasant, intelligent face hidden behind large round glasses. "Mr. Darlan?" she greeted me. "You had two calls, one from Maxim Realty and the other from a Mr. Tommy Deckler."

"Thanks." I took the slips. Maxim Realty was the landlord, asking about the overdue rent. "Do I call you Betty, Betsy, Liz, or what?"

"Elizabeth will be fine," she answered with a smile.

I grunted and sat down at my desk, in no hurry to return Tommy Deckler's call but knowing it had to be done. After spreading out the file on the desk before me, I dialed his number. It was his personal line and he answered immediately. "Deckler here."

"This is Al Darlan returning your call."

"Darlan, I heard Mike Trapper's in the hospital."

"Word travels fast."

"I get a list of all newly admitted patients. What's wrong with him?"

"Had his appendix out. He's coming along fine."

"Be laid up for long? He's working on a rush job for me."

"We talked about it. I'll take over till he's back on his feet."

"Well—" He hesitated. "Maybe we'd better get together. You free for lunch?"

I hadn't thought about eating. It was ten after one. "I guess so."

"One-thirty at the Colony Club. All right?"

"I'll be there."

As I was going out the door Elizabeth asked, "Do you have any typing for me?"

"You could make some new labels for these file folders," I suggested. "Use Mike's electric typewriter. Mine's an old manual with dirty keys."

Tommy Deckler was at his table when I arrived, seated with a slightly younger man. Tommy was in his late forties, with conservatively short hair and a pencil-thin mustache. His seersucker suit was rumpled. He introduced the other man as Simon Lang, his editor on the *Midnight Sun*. "A drink first?" he suggested after we all shook hands.

"Not while I'm working."

"I thought all private eyes—"

"I don't like that expression, Mr. Deckler. In fact, I don't much like you. My partner's sick so I'm filling in for him."

"You come right to the point."

The waiter brought menus and I ordered a club sandwich with a fancy name. Lang wasn't eating and I decided he'd stopped by just to meet me. "Simon's a great editor," Deckler said as Lang departed. "He uses his girlfriend to bring in some of our best stories. Cheaper than hiring your partner to check on Barnstable."

"I don't want any part in sleezy journalism," I told him. "Hugh Barnstable doesn't mean a thing to me, but I don't care for assault by tabloid."

"I only hired Mike to learn the truth about the rumors we've been hearing about Barnstable and some woman."

"With a nice bonus for verifying them."

"Naturally positive information is more valuable to a newsman than no information."

"What's the name of this woman? I didn't find it in Mike's file."

"The name I was given was Connie Strand. I know nothing more about her. The word I have is that they shared a hotel or motel room one night in the spring when he was drumming up support in the district. He wasn't yet an officially declared candidate so he might have felt it was safe."

"The congressional district includes half the city plus two adjoining counties. That's a lot of territory to cover. Why can't you assign a couple of reporters to it?"

"The word would get out too fast that I was snooping around. This way if there's nothing to be found nobody gets hurt."

It made sense, but it didn't make me like the assignment any better. "How many of these jobs has Mike done for you?"

"This'll be number five, I think. Don't you have records?"

"I didn't bother to check. How soon do you need the information?"

"This week. The state convention opens Monday.

The story would have its biggest impact in next week's issue."

"I'll do the best I can."

We parted with a handshake and I went back to the office to study Mike's list of hotels in the area.

After checking in at the hospital on Wednesday morning and finding Mike in good spirits, I drove out to the next hotel on his list. It was a newly restored place with a golf course and tennis courts, more of a summer resort than an overnight stop for salesmen. This was the sort of place where checking the records was easy. It took me only ten minutes to convince the reservations clerk that she should check the computer for a list of five names. Three of them I'd made up on the spot. The other two were Connie Strand and Hugh Barnstable.

"Sorry," the young woman told me. "Nothing on any of them."

"Thanks anyway."

I'd hardly expected to find anything on my first stop, but I quickly learned it was to be a frustrating day. Roadside motels passed by quickly, and in most cases I knew before checking that Barnstable would have used an alias if he'd booked a room in any of them for a tryst. I spent the day standing at registration desks while reluctant clerks thumbed through stacks of cards—or even, in one case, flipped the pages of a big black ledger that I thought had gone out with nickel candy bars. The few places with computerized reservations were a treat, but they helped me no more than the others. I decided I was going about this in the wrong way.

That evening I phoned Deckler at his home. "Find anything?" he asked.

"Not a thing. Frankly, I think this is a waste of time."

"What do you suggest?"

"Who gave you the tip in the first place? That's the person who has the information we need."

"I can't reveal my source. That was part of the agreement."

"Then get back to your source and tell him I need more information. If I can't have the hotel and the date, I need to know where I can find Connie Strand."

Tommy Deckler sighed. "I'll see what I can do. If I don't call you right back, it might take a day or two."

"Call me anyway. I'll wait by the phone."

I was at my apartment, and while I waited I flipped through the evening paper. There was a picture of Hugh Barnstable on the first page of the local news, with a story about the nominating convention and his official declaration, due the following morning.

Deckler called back in ten minutes. "We're in luck. My source is willing to meet with you, but on explicit terms. It must be tonight. Drive to the parking lot at Sailor Field—"

"The baseball stadium?"

"That's correct. You should arrive there thirty-five minutes from now, exactly at eight forty-five. The game will have already started, but there'll be plenty of spaces. Park your car and place your identification inside the front window where it can be seen from outside. Leave your doors unlocked and wait."

"All right."

"One other thing."

"What's that?"

"You must make no attempt to learn the informant's identity or even to see her face, which will be covered. Understand?"

"It's a woman?"

"That's right."

I felt a growing unease. "Do you know her identity?"

"Of course, but there's no need for you to. Think of her as Ms. Deep Throat."

"Sure." I hung up and headed for the ballpark.

I pulled into the parking lot at Sailor Field exactly at eight forty-five, paid my fee, and drove down the line looking for an empty space. When I found one I pulled in and slipped the ID from my pocket, laying it flat on top of the dashboard. Then I waited.

There was a roar from inside the stadium, signifying something good for the home team. A few late arrivals scurried from their cars to the gate, but no one approached me. It was getting dark fast. Maybe that's what she was waiting for.

Exactly at nine o'clock the door on the passenger side opened and a figure slipped in. She was wearing black slacks and a dark bulky sweater that seemed too warm for the mild night air. A dark silk scarf was wrapped around her head and lower face, leaving only her eyes visible.

"Good evening," I said.

"You're Al Darlan, the private detective?"

"None other. That's my ID by the windshield. Why all the secrecy?"

"This wasn't part of the deal when I talked to Deckler. I was to be kept out of it. But he said you needed more information and he didn't want to tell you the wrong thing."

"That was wise. I work a lot better with information I get firsthand. Now let's get down to business."

She glanced toward the backseat, though by now it was too dark for her to see anything. "No tape recorder?"

"I'm too old for these modern gadgets. Let's just talk."

"What do you need to know?" Her voice was firm and she sounded educated. An Eastern college, probably. Not Boston, not New York, not the South. Maybe not Eastern. Maybe middle American. Ohio or Indiana.

"Hugh Barnstable is supposed to have spent a night—one or more nights—with a woman named Connie Strand. Correct?"

"It's a suspicion, based upon certain evidence."

"Checking the area hotels isn't working. They would have used other names. I need to know the nature of this evidence."

She was silent for a moment and another cheer went up from the stadium. Finally she answered, "I can't tell you about any evidence. I can give you the name of the place they stayed, if you need it."

"I need it," I assured her.

"The Daisy Inn, just outside Limeport on Route Five."

I jotted it down on my pad, certain that it hadn't been on Mike Trapper's list. "Can you give me a date?"

"Somewhere around late April. I'm not certain."

"All right. I'll do the best I can."

"I'm leaving now." As she spoke the words the car door opened and she slipped out into the darkness.

I waited in the car for about thirty seconds, remembering I'd been warned not to try learning her identity or seeing her face. Then I figured, the hell with it. I left the car and headed toward the stadium gate, the direction she seemed to have taken. Lighting in the parking lot was far from adequate, and I couldn't spot her among the occasional figures still walking through the shadows toward the gate. I came to the chain-link fence, and through it I could see people running down to the refreshment stand or restrooms between innings.

That was when I tripped and almost fell. A man was lying on the ground, huddled against the fence in the shadows. "Are you all right?" I asked, starting to lift him. Then I saw the blood on the asphalt and jerked my hands away.

He was dead, and even in the dim light I recognized him as Tommy Deckler's editor, Simon Lang.

When you're in my business you learn early when to report bodies to the police and when to walk away fast. This was definitely walking-away time, and that's what I did. Trying to explain to the police what I was doing there in the first place would have been next to impossible.

So I waited till the next morning and read about it in the paper: "Midnight Sun Editor Slain in Stadium Parking Lot." Simon Lang had been stabbed twice in the chest and the police were calling it an attempted robbery, even though his wallet was still in his pocket. They figured the robber had been scared away after he stabbed his intended victim. Tommy Deckler called it a horrible crime and stated that he'd take over editorship of the *Midnight Sun* himself pending appointment of a new editor.

I stopped by the hospital and found Mike walking in the hallway with his wife. "How are you, Marla? How's our patient today?"

"A lot better before he read the morning paper," she complained.

"What happened, Al?" he asked at once. "Is it connected with the case?"

"I was there but I don't know what happened."

"You were there?"

"Meeting a source that Deckler put me on to.

Maybe Simon Lang was part of the meeting, but if he was I didn't know it."

"I've got to get out of here!" Mike said.

Marla put a firm hand on his arm. "You're not going anywhere but back to bed! Al can take care of the office."

"I wanted to ask you one thing," I said as he started back reluctantly. "Did you check a place called the Daisy Inn?"

"I don't think so. Is it on the list?"

"No. It's down near Limeport."

"Some of those little inns are nothing more than bed-and-breakfast places. I never thought to check on them."

"I'll do it. I might find something."

"Be careful," Marla cautioned. "If this killing was connected to the case—"

"Probably just a coincidence," I tried to reassure her.

I got to the office around eleven and found the temp, Elizabeth Farr, slitting open the junk-mail envelopes. "Do you want a book on home alarm systems?" she asked.

"No time to read it. Any calls?"

"The landlord again."

"Thanks." I noticed a little black-and-white TV on the corner of her desk.

"Hope you don't mind. I brought it from home. There's not much doing around here."

"Story of my life. What's on?"

"That politician, Hugh Barnstable. He's announcing his run for Congress."

I glanced at the fuzzy screen. He was blond, in his late thirties, and the handsome sort that attracted women. Apparently he'd attracted Connie Strand. I went over to my desk and started sorting through the first-class mail Elizabeth hadn't opened. Nothing seemed urgent.

"—going to be with him every step of the way," someone on the television was saying.

It was the voice that got to me. I'd listened to it in a darkened car for only five minutes, but I'd have known it anywhere. "Who's that?"

"His wife, Gretchen."

I walked back to her desk and stared at the television. There was no doubt about it. Gretchen Barnstable was Ms. Deep Throat.

I told Tommy Deckler I had to see him, and an hour later we met again at the Colony Club where we'd lunched on Tuesday. "This is getting to be a habit," he told me with a smile. "I should start deducting these lunches from your bill."

"Tuesday's lunch was different," I pointed out. "Simon Lang was here, too."

"God, it's terrible about poor Simon! I can't imagine what happened."

"Do you think she stabbed him?"

"Who?" He looked blank.

"Ms. Deep Throat. Maybe he was trying to learn her identity."

"Simon wouldn't do that," he said, but there was a hint of uncertainty in his voice.

"Did you tell him about last night's meeting at the stadium?"

Now he was really edgy. "I may have called him. Yes, I guess I did, after I talked to you."

"Then Ms. Deep Throat could have killed him to keep from being identified."

"Why would she do that when I already know her identity?"

"She gave me the name of the place," I said, changing the subject.

"What was it?"

"I'd better check it first. Could be a false lead. I'll drive out there this afternoon."

As we parted, Deckler asked, "Do you really think she might have stabbed him?"

"Somebody did. What about his wife and family?"

A shrug. "Divorced years ago. He had girlfriends off and on, but he kept his personal life pretty much to himself."

"Do you think it was attempted robbery?"

He looked away. "Simon wasn't a baseball fan. I never knew him to go to a game. He was there for some other reason."

Route 5 ran south of the city, through a rolling countryside dotted with farmhouses and occasional crossroads stores. It didn't take me long to find the Daisy Inn, a moderately large Victorian house set back from the road at the end of a curving driveway. The entrance hall was impressive, and I was immediately greeted by a robust man in paint-spotted overalls.

"Welcome to the Daisy Inn. You looking for food or lodging?"

"Information."

He seemed perplexed at this. "What sort? We don't have any tourist maps—"

I showed him my ID. "Al Darlan. I'm trying to trace the movements of some people back in April. I think they may have stayed here."

"I'm Jack Rosserman. I own the place."

"Then you're just the man I need. I understand you have a little bed-and-breakfast operation here."

"That's right. We also serve dinner on weekends."

"Would you have records for the last week in April?"

"Oh, sure. What's the name?"

"Hugh Barnstable."

"Barnstable. Seems to me I heard that name just recently. Was he in the news?"

"I couldn't say."

"Well, I can tell you he stayed here. I got a reason for remembering it. There was a long-distance call from his room, and I had to write him for payment."

"Now when was this?" I asked.

He dug around in a desk set against one wall and came up with a copy of a letter. "Barnstable stayed here the night of April twenty-ninth. When my phone bill came in the middle of May I found a charge for a person-to-person call from Connie Strand to Felix Strand in San Diego. It came to nearly ten dollars and I wasn't about to pay it."

I was beginning to understand how Gretchen Barnstable had learned of her husband's infidelity. "You wrote and told him this in the letter asking for payment?"

"Sure did."

"You sent it to his home?"

"That was the only address I had. A check came back a week later."

"From him?"

"Sure! Who else?"

"Connie Strand shared the room with him that night?"

"Yeah."

"But Barnstable registered for both of them?"

"That's right."

"You have no address for Strand?"

"Didn't even know the name till I got the phone bill."

I thought about that. "If it was a person-to-person

call, it must have shown Felix Strand's telephone number in San Diego."

"I guess it did," he agreed.

"It would be a great help to me if you could dig that out."

"Maybe tomorrow when I get time. I'm pretty busy today."

I took a twenty-dollar bill from my wallet. "It would help me a lot to have it now."

"Well, maybe I could look."

He went back to the desk and found the phone bill almost immediately. "Another twenty if I can use your phone to call this number."

Rosserman pocketed the money. "Go ahead."

I dialed the number in San Diego and waited while it rang. Finally an elderly voice answered and confirmed that he was Felix Strand. I cleared my throat and said, "I'm with the telephone company, sir. We're trying to confirm a long-distance call made to your number by a Connie Strand on April twenty-ninth."

"Yes," the old man answered. "It was my birthday and Connie phoned me. I'm seventy-nine years old."

"That's very good. I was wondering if you could give me your daughter's address and phone number. I need to check some other billing with her."

"Daughter? I have no daughter." The voice sounded momentarily confused.

"I thought—"

"Connie is my son. Conrad Strand."

"I see."

"He's a window dresser at Peachum's big department store back there. I'll give you his number."

When I hung up, Jack Rosserman was looking out the window. He turned to me and asked, "Satisfied?"

"You didn't tell me Connie Strand was a man."

"You didn't ask."

I went back to my car feeling baffled and just a bit foolish.

It was almost closing time when I reached Peachum's Emporium back in the city. I caught up with Connie Strand just as he was leaving the display department on the third floor. "A private dick?" he asked, studying my ID.

"That's right. Where can we talk?"

He was a slender man of about forty, with a brown mustache and pale blue eyes. "What's this about?" he asked.

"Hugh Barnstable."

I thought he winced slightly at the name. Glancing at his watch he said, "There's still time for a cup of coffee at the Snack Shack. It's on this floor."

I followed his lead to a little roped-off area of tables and chairs, with some planters and a straw roof furnishing the decor. He got us two cups of coffee and we chose a table in the corner.

I came right to the point. "You spent the night of April twenty-ninth with Hugh Barnstable at the Daisy Inn on Route Five. There's no point in denying it. I spoke with the owner and also with your dad in San Diego."

"Why'd you drag him into this?"

"Only to locate you. I gave him no details."

He studied me over the rim of his cup. "Are you the one blackmailing Hugh?"

"What's that?"

"Did you send him the note demanding fifty thousand dollars?"

"I know nothing about that. When did he get the note?"

"Yesterday." He sighed and closed his eyes for a few seconds. "I make no secret of my sexual preference, but in politics it's entirely different. Hugh's got a wife and he wants to run for Congress. I respect that. I'm just sorry someone found out about us and is trying to use it against him."

"Why did he tell you about the note?"

"Why? Because he thought I'd written it!" There was a touch of bitterness in his voice now. "We broke up in May. I haven't seen him since then, except on television."

"If you didn't send the note, who did? Who else knew about the two of you?"

"Well, you found out fairly easily. I guess other people could, too."

I thought of Barnstable's wife. "I guess they could. Did you know a man named Simon Lang?"

"The one who got killed? Never met him." He smiled for the first time. "I've never had any dealings with the *Midnight Sun* people."

I downed the rest of my coffee. "Thanks for your help," I told him.

It was a crazy case and I still couldn't see my way clear to the end of it, but I knew I had to speak with Hugh Barnstable and get a look at that blackmail note. I decided the best way to do that was through his wife. I didn't need to get the number from Tommy Deckler. I looked it up in the phone book.

"Barnstable residence," she answered, perhaps ready to pass herself off as the maid, but I recognized the voice at once.

"Mrs. Barnstable, please don't hang up. This is very important. We had a chat in my car last night, at the ballpark."

"I think you have the wrong person."

"Your husband is being blackmailed."

"By you?"

"No. I think it ties in with the killing in that parking lot last night."

She gave a slight gasp. "Simon Lang."

"That's right. It's more than a coincidence that Deckler arranged our meeting and his editor turned up dead at the same spot."

"Do you think he's involved?"

"I don't know. I need to see a letter your husband received yesterday."

She was silent for a moment. "There was a letter—"

I decided to take a chance. "And you opened it."

"I never open his mail!"

"You opened the letter from Jack Rosserman at the Daisy Inn. Otherwise you wouldn't have known about Connie Strand."

"Have you found her yet?"

"I think your husband should tell you about Connie Strand. Do you have the letter?"

"Of course not! I resealed the envelope and left it for Hugh."

"What did it say?"

"The sender wanted fifty thousand dollars to keep quiet about the night at the Daisy Inn. It said instructions would follow."

"Then there'll be another letter."

"I—I think it came today," she replied quietly. "But I was afraid to open it."

"Can I come over?"

"I don't think that would be wise."

"I have to see that letter, Mrs. Barnstable. It could tell me who killed that man Lang."

"Does it matter?"

"It could matter very much. If he was the blackmailer, your husband might have killed him. Or you yourself."

"No!" She made it a whisper more than a gasp.

"I'm coming over," I said, and hung up.

*   *   *

The law business was profitable and Hugh Barnstable had never been a poor man. Their brick house in a fancy suburb seemed almost too large for just the two of them. Gretchen Barnstable answered my ring with a nervous look on her face, as if she'd been expecting some avenging angel. Maybe that's what I was.

"He'll be home for dinner any minute," she told me. "You shouldn't have come here."

"And you shouldn't have been running around parking lots in the dead of night. Why are you so anxious to ruin your husband's political career?"

Without the scarf over her face she was attractive if not beautiful. Younger than her husband, I guessed— maybe thirty-five at most. "We've been growing apart for years, though that letter from the Daisy Inn was my first evidence of actual infidelity. I did nothing about it for weeks, but when he told me he was running for Congress all I could see was more of the same. I tried to stop him through Deckler's rag."

"Show me the letter before he comes."

She handed it to me, still sealed, just as we heard a car pull into the driveway. There was no time for steaming flaps now. I ripped open the envelope with my finger. The typed letter on plain paper was brief and to the point: "Bring fifty thousand in hundred-dollar bills in an envelope noon Friday, addressed to B. Franklin. Leave at desk in Ritz Hotel."

Gretchen Barnstable read it over my shoulder. "That's the same typewriter as yesterday's note. I recognize the filled-in letters. Needs cleaning."

There was no time to say more. Hugh Barnstable entered the room and asked, "Who are you? Gretchen, who is this man?"

"He's a private detective, Hugh."

"A private— What in hell is going on here?" He

spotted the note I still held. "Have you been opening my mail?"

"I'm investigating a murder—"

He swung a fist at me, his face distorted in anger. "Get out of my house or I'll have the police on you!"

I dropped the letter and blocked his fist with ease, then retreated. I wasn't looking for a fight, and he was twenty years younger than me. "You'd better tell your wife everything," I advised as I went out the door.

On Thursday morning I phoned Gretchen's number and she answered. "Can you talk?" I asked. "This is Al Darlan."

"Yes. He's gone."

"Did he tell you about the Daisy Inn?"

"My God, I never dreamed—"

"What's he going to do?"

"Withdraw from the race. I told him you were working for Deckler, and he doesn't want it spread all over the *Midnight Sun*."

"I'm not going to tell Deckler what I found. I'm not in the scandal business. If that makes a difference—"

"Thank you. I'll tell him."

"And don't worry about the blackmail letters. I'll handle that."

Elizabeth was busy typing when I reached the Darlan & Trapper office. "I thought I'd get some of your files in shape while I'm sitting here." The TV was turned on but the sound was inaudible.

"Good idea. You're efficient enough to work here full-time, if we could afford you."

"I've been thinking of settling into a permanent job."

"We'll see what Mike thinks when he's out of the hospital."

"That reminds me—his wife called. They're anxious to hear about the case."

"I should have stopped by this morning but I was anxious to get in here."

"Busy day?"

"Wrap-up day. I'm doing a final report for Tommy Deckler." I took the plastic cover off my battered typewriter. "Maybe you could type it up for me after I rough it out."

"Be glad to."

I stuck a blank sheet in the machine and started pecking. After a few minutes Elizabeth took her newly labeled file folders and walked over to the drawers. Her skirt was straight, ending above her knees. I walked up behind her and slipped a hand over one breast.

"What is this, Mr. Darlan?"

"I'll tell you." With my other hand I started to raise her skirt.

"What—?"

I grabbed the knife and yanked it from the sheath on her thigh. "Is this what you used to kill Simon Lang?" I demanded, spinning her around and into a chair.

"What are you talking about?"

"When I was in high school I dated a girl once who carried a knife in her stocking top. She scared the hell out of me, but it taught me to spot the bulge of a knife under a clinging skirt. Now are you going to talk before I call the police or after?"

"I've done nothing wrong!" she insisted.

"Except murder your boyfriend and try to blackmail Hugh Barnstable. His wife pointed out to me the filled-in letters on the typed notes. They came from a dirty typewriter just like my old machine here. The first note arrived on Wednesday, the day after you started work. I recognized my typewriter right away but it made no sense until I remembered that Simon Lang had a girlfriend that Deckler credited with bringing in some of their best stories. It occurred to me that someone working as an office temporary would be in a perfect position to pick up news and gossip, either from talkative employees or from business files. When Lang got word of a possible story he'd have you watch for an opportunity, perhaps paying bribe money to the agency, and get yourself assigned where he wanted you."

"If that's all true, why would I kill him?"

"Because this time was different. He got you the job here to find out what I uncovered before I reported to Deckler. But you saw it as a perfect chance to blackmail a congressional candidate. My old typewriter with its easily matched letters was perfect for your scheme. If necessary I could be framed for the crime and you'd simply disappear. I think you told Lang at the ballpark Wednesday night and he flew into a rage. He wanted no part of blackmail. So you stabbed him and decided to follow through on your own. The fifty thousand, if you got it, would have been the first of many demands."

"None of this proves I killed him."

"Only Gretchen, Deckler, and Lang knew about the ballpark meeting. Deckler had nothing to gain by killing his editor, and I couldn't believe that Gretchen had done it. After all, Lang's boss already knew of her involvement. Why kill Lang to keep it secret? But I realized that Lang might have told his girlfriend and even brought her along. If you'd written those notes on my typewriter, you were that person. You even brought a TV to work yesterday, to follow news reports of the murder investigation. As for proof to satisfy a jury, it looks like there are traces of dried blood still on the guard of this knife. And I'll bet that they match Simon Lang's blood."

Later, when the police allowed her one phone call, she didn't call a lawyer. She phoned Tommy Deckler instead and offered to sell him her story for a quarter-million dollars.

SEE NO EVIL
BY BARB D'AMATO

"I hate mysteries. This kind anyway," Harold McCoo said. He pushed his swivel chair around to hand me my cup of coffee.

"Mysterious coffee?"

"Oh, hell, no. It's Sulawesi Kalosi. Aromatic with a gently woody undertone. Javanese type."

"What, then?"

McCoo is Chief of Detectives, Department of Police, City of Chicago. He didn't get to that position by wasting a lot of time. He shoved a large pile of paper toward me. "I want a favor, Cat."

"Anything for you."

"An investigation. And we're going to cut you loose some money for it, too."

"You don't have to—"

"Yeah, I do. I want you official. You're gonna need to see confidential documents. So confidential that even the subject, Officer Bennis, isn't allowed to see them."

"Documents about what?"

He sipped his coffee. McCoo makes very good coffee. "You know, Cat, people don't change. We've got lemons in the department, Piltdown men, but they show up pretty soon. You take an officer like Bennis, eleven years on the job, not one problem. He was in Six for eight years. His commander there has nothing but praise for him. He's been in One for three years

116

now, and even though Commander Coumadin's an idiot, he admits Bennis has been professional, no whiff of brutality. He's been a street officer all that time, not a desk man. He's not going to suddenly up and *execute* somebody."

"I suppose not. I take it somebody thinks he did. Was there some sort of danger—?"

"He thought the guy had killed his partner."

"That's a reason."

"Not much of one. Somebody who's been on the street eleven years—he's been in tight places before, and he's had threats against his partner before, and a zillion times he's been scared. It's that kind of job."

"Okay. That makes sense."

"But they're going to destroy him. The Office of Professional Standards is gonna make an example of him. When the complaint is sustained, they'll suspend him. And there's a rumor they're thinking criminal prosecution."

There had been a lot of talk in the Chicago media that OPS didn't often sustain brutality complaints. The process for investigating complaints, they said, was a washing machine: stuff went in dirty and came out clean. There was some truth to that, too, but much more in the past than now.

"And this Bennis—"

"Isn't the kind to do something like this. But it looks like he did. And the OPS investigator, Hulce, is out to get him. The hell of it is, his story has holes."

"Bennis is a patrol officer? You're Chief of Detectives. Why is it your problem?"

"The detectives do the initial investigation."

"And?"

"Ah, I know the kid slightly."

"Oh, really?"

"I knew his mother, once upon a time. What we need, Cat, is a fresh eye on it."

"I don't do whitewashes."

"Hey, I'm not asking for a spin doctor. I need a private eye. There's something wrong someplace and a good guy is gonna suffer. I don't have the time to deal with it, and everybody here is either strongly pro or strongly con, both of which I don't want. I want you to look at the papers without me giving you any predigested ideas. Here." He patted the stack of paper. "You figure it out."

"Oh, well. If you've got the money, honey, I've got the time."

The Furlough bar was never going to be a photo opportunity for *Architectural Digest*. There were no ferns, no hanging plants, nothing green and growing in the whole place, unless there was something alive under the slatted floor at the beer taps that nobody knew about. The front window hadn't been washed since Eisenhower was president and was now a uniform, suede-finish gray, about the texture of peach skin. Thirty years earlier Royal Crown cola had given out signs for doors with little slots where the proprietor could insert the times the place was open. The Furlough's hadn't been replaced since it was first attached; several numbers had fallen sideways and some had fallen off, so the sign now read that the bar was open Thursdays from   :00 to   .

The Furlough was owned by two retired cops and was diagonally across the street from the Chicago Police Department's central headquarters at Eleventh and State. I was supposed to meet my people at the bar at three-thirty p.m. They would have just got off an eight-hour tour.

When I walked in, I could feel emotion in the air.

It wasn't me, wasn't because a female had walked in. There were a couple of women cops in the bar already. The tension was there before I arrived. I could see it in the spacing of the people around the bar. My two cops, whose pictures I had seen in the Chief of Detectives' office, were sitting alone at the far end of the zinc bar. One was Officer Susanna Maria Figueroa, a short, young white woman. Sitting next to her was her partner Norm Bennis, a stocky black man of about thirty-five, ten years older than Figueroa. His head was down between his shoulders. Then there was a gap of four stools, followed by two white men, one tall and one pudgy with a shiny pink face, a black woman whose elbow leaned on the bar and whose hand cupped her chin, and another, older white man next to her.

The bunch of four were carefully not looking at Figueroa and her partner.

I walked over to her. In these situations, I make as much effort as possible to look like a fellow cop. I'm not; ordinarily I make my living as a reporter. Generally speaking, cops don't love reporters.

I said, "Hi, I'm Cat Marsala."

They looked at me with a total lack of enthusiasm, the way you might look at a parking ticket on your windshield.

But they had orders from the Chief of Detectives. Figueroa said, "I'm Suze Figueroa. This is my partner, Norm Bennis."

He extended his hand. If Figueroa looked glum, Bennis was sunk in an abyss of gloom. But his face had laugh lines. Which currently were not being used.

I shook his hand.

"Let's go over there," Figueroa said. There were three tables in the place. Their tops were about as big as lids from Crisco cans. If all three of us wanted to put our elbows on the table, there wouldn't be room.

"What's the matter with these other guys?" I mumbled to Figueroa, cutting my eyes toward the four at the bar. "They mad at you for something?"

"Trying to cheer us up," Figueroa said.

"So I yelled at 'em," Bennis said.

"Oh." I waited, but neither spoke. "All right, you two. You know why I'm here."

"Because I killed a guy," Bennis said.

He took a break then, bringing back three beers. I wanted to hear the story from them before I read the documents, but I didn't want to be jacked around all afternoon, either. I said, "Talk!"

Bennis shrugged. "I don't see what you can do about it."

"Humor me."

He said, "Okay, okay. We're on second watch. It's about two in the afternoon, Saturday, we're in the car we usually get and we're maybe an hour, hour and a half, to the end of the tour. There's an in-progress call. Citizen calls 911, describes it as a rape and he's right. One thirty-one responds. The woman is cut and she's yelling to the car that the asshole has a knife. A second unit, one thirty-six, responds and when they get in sight of the woman, the jerk was taking off. One thirty-one follows him to an apartment building. We hear the radio traffic and get over to the building. Mileski and Quail in one thirty-one have separated. Quail to the back door and Mileski to the front. They've got the place buttoned up, so Suze and I run into the hall. Far as we know the asshole's raping somebody else. There's an apartment door open, and a woman yelling."

"She was saying 'You idiot!' in Spanish," Figueroa said.

"So we go in. Long, dark hall. In the apartment, the shades are pulled most of the way down, because the woman who lives there is watching soap operas.

"We run in, and the guy's standing in the living room—name's Zeets—and the TV light is glinting off the knife and he says he's gonna kill us. Figueroa draws on him and screams 'Drop the knife!' about yea zillion times. So do I. Finally the asshole throws the knife on a chair. I've got my service revolver out by now and I hold it on him while Figueroa starts to cuff him, except I can't see hardly at all because the light from the windows, what there is of it, is behind them.

"Then, like in a split second, he whips around with one cuff on and grabs Figueroa's gun and they lurch back away from me. They're wrestling for the gun. I know it, but I'm supposed to stay back and take aim, which I do, but I can't see much. It's too dark. They're wrestling back and forth and then there's a shot. I figure Figueroa's been shot.

"I can't see who's got the gun, and they're still struggling, but I can see the guy's outline and I fire at him." He stopped a second and looked at me doubtfully. "You know that if we fire at all, we're supposed to try to kill him? I mean no winging him in the hand, that cowboy kind of stuff."

"I know."

"I fire six times. He drops." Bennis ducked his head. "Basically, he's dead."

"So. I don't see what's wrong."

"His mother and two sisters were in the apartment. They're saying I didn't need to shoot him. They're saying it was obvious that Figueroa had the gun. All three of 'em."

"Oh."

"I'm gonna be suspended or fired. Probably fired.

And they're talking about prosecution for man-slaughter."

"I understand. That's scary."

"No you don't."

I never like it when people say I don't understand something. Personally, I think I'm pretty sympathetic. But Bennis was so upset, I forgave him. "So tell me."

"It's not the manslaughter thing. I love this job."

His voice was filled with frustration and anger. Bennis and Figueroa seemed to have relaxed their initial distrust of me somewhat. I asked Figueroa, "Is that what happened? What Bennis says?"

"Yeah. Zeets and I both had hold of the gun when it went off. Thank God it was pointed up. Went into the ceiling."

"So you back up Bennis?"

"Totally." She punched Bennis's shoulder lightly. "This is a good man." For just a second real affection came over her face. "All he wanted to do was save my life."

The mutual trust in their relationship was obvious. Out in the street, alone, in danger, in the dark—sure, two cops had to trust each other. It was horrible when an officer was paired with somebody he couldn't rely on. In this case, clearly, they leaned on each other every time they hit the streets and neither had let the other down.

Rising, I said, "All right. I'll be getting back to you."

As we moved to the door, the pink-faced officer at the bar said, "Hey! You gonna help Bennis?"

"I hope I—"

The woman officer said, "They're gonna railroad our buddy."

Another cop said, "OPS ain't any better than civilians."

"Yeah, your basic citizen'll turn on you in two seconds flat!"

"They see a mugger you're their best friend."

"Hear a noise in the night—"

"Teenagers *congregatin'*—"

"Guys passin' around little bags of white stuff—"

"But you grab the mugger and next thing they're screamin' police brutality."

"I ever tell you about the time I chased these two guys down the alley off Van Buren near Plymouth Court?"

Suze said, "Yeah, Mileski, you did."

"*She* didn't hear it," he said, pointing to me.

"She doesn't want to, either."

"Three a.m. and not one breathing soul around. Responded to an alarm at a jewelry store. Two guys they're sharing about one neuron in their heads between the two of 'em, but one of 'em had a sawed-off shotgun."

"Very illegal!" the woman cop said.

"Guy takes a shot at me, misses, and they both run. I'm in pursuit. My hat flies off, I'm outta breath, but I manage to hang on ta my radio. Run 'em down after six blocks. The jerk with the gun falls over a gas can somebody threw out, loses the gun, I cuff him, pick up the shotgun in one hand, got my service revolver in the other—we're talking two-gun Pete here—aim 'em both at the other guy, who's too fat to climb over the fence and escape, and the guy gets so scared he starts to cry."

He stopped and looked at me. "Well, great!" I said, wondering what he was getting at.

"Brought 'em both in. Single-handed. Know what happened to me? No department commendation. No nothing!"

"That's too bad."

"But!" He said it again, "But! *But!* They gammee a fine for losing my cap!"

"Oh."

"That's nice, Mileski," Bennis said. "But we're trying to have a private conversation here now."

"Oh, well, excuuuuse me."

However, there really wasn't much else to say. I nodded to them and said, "I've got the papers. I'll be in touch."

I thought I'd been encouraging, but apparently the sight of me had not made Bennis think he was saved. As I went out past the ancient bar sign, he said softly to Figueroa, "It's hopeless."

Armed with nine pounds of CPD paperwork, twelve ounces of coffee, and a half-pound bar of chocolate, I settled in at home for a good read.

There were sixty pages of photocopied photos alone: crime scene photos, autopsy photos, and spent pellet photos. Typed statements from the mother and both sisters, headed OFFICE OF PROFESSIONAL STANDARDS, the interviewer being the OPS investigator C. Hulce. A transcript of the radio activity that afternoon. Typed statements from Figueroa and Bennis, also interviewed by C. Hulce. Interviews with Mileski and Quail. An interview with the rape victim whose case had started all this off. A plat of the apartment, with the position of the body. Another plat of the apartment with the position of the officers at the time of the shooting. Copies of the hospital reports, labeled "Emergency Room Outpatient Report"—Figueroa had been cut on the jaw during the scuffle by the barrel of her own gun. Releases allowing the hospital to give the reports to the OPS. Consent forms. A dozen Shooting Investigation Reports. Disciplinary Action forms. A fifty-page document called "Summary

to the Commanding Officer." Something called a
Weapon Discharge Report. Evidence lists. Diagrams
showing the position of the wounds on the body. Autopsy protocol from the pathologist, addressed "Cook
County Institute of Forensic Medicine." Inventory of
the officers' weapons. Ballistics tests. One sheet from
ballistics stated that the bullet reclaimed from the ceiling matched Figueroa's gun. A Waiver of Counsel/
Request to Secure Counsel. Both Bennis and Figueroa, who was not charged but was questioned, re-
quested counsel. And about a hundred one-page
things headed "Supplementary Report."

An army may travel on its stomach, but a police
department travels on its paperwork.

One printed sheet advised the officer of his or her
rights. While they could have counsel, as far as the
department was concerned, that was about all they
got. They had no right to remain silent. If they remained silent, they would be "ordered by a superior
officer to answer the question." If they persisted in
refusing to answer, they were advised that "such re-
fusal constitutes a violation of the Rules and Regula-
tions of the Chicago Police Department and will serve
as a basis for which your discharge will be sought."

I suppose it is a privilege, not a right, to remain a
police officer. And I suppose they need to be able to
get rid of the crazies, but it certainly had Bennis
pinned down so that he had to answer them. And he
seemed to have made some mistakes.

There was a sheet of charges. Boiled down, he was
accused of (1) discharging a firearm without justification, and (2) failing to give a true and accurate account
of the incident relative to the shooting of Jorge
Sanabria.

His primary accuser was the dead man's mother.

OFFICE OF PROFESSIONAL STANDARDS
26 Mar 93
CR #9956291

Statement of witness, Benicia Sanabria, relative to the
incident that led to the death of Jorge (Zeets) Sanabria on 12 Mar 93 at 1400 hours.

Statement taken at 1121 S. State, Chicago IL 60607

Questioned by: Inv. C. Hulce, Star 337,
                            Unit 243
Date & Time: 26 Mar 1993 at 1320 hours.
Witnessed by: Inv. Clarence Summerset,
                            Star 633, Unit 243

Hulce: What is your full name, address, and telephone number?
Sanabria: Benicia Sanabria, 731 W. Sangin, 312/555–
   8997.
Hulce: What is your marital status?
Sanabria: I am a widow.
Hulce: Are you giving this statement of your own free
   will, without the promise of exoneration or reward
   of any nature being given to you?
Sanabria: Yes.
Hulce: Do you work? If so, give the name of the company, address, telephone number, and length of
   employment.

My eye skimmed down the page to:

Hulce: What is the relationship of Jorge Sanabria to
   you?
Sanabria: He is my only son.
Hulce: What occurred on 12 March 1993 about 1400
   hours at your home that resulted in the death of
   Jorge "Zeets" Sanabria?
Sanabria: I was home. I work Sunday through Thurs-
   day. Suddenly Jorge came running in.
Hulce: Was he carrying anything?
Sanabria: He was. Well, yes, he was. It was a knife.
Hulce: What happened then?
Sanabria: Then, well, then he said, "They're after me,"

and my daughter said—um, she called him a name and she said, "What did you do?" and he started swearing. And my daughter said something about Jorge disgracing her and then a police officer came into the front of the hall. The door, our door to the hall, was still open, and the man said, "Police officer, come out!" or something like that. But he stayed in the hall and then two other police officers came in. And Jorge backed into the living room.

Hulce: Describe them, please.

Sanabria: One was a woman. She was short and dark-haired and I think she was possibly Chicana. The other was a black man. Taller but not tall.

Hulce: What happened then?

Sanabria: Then they all yelled, "Put the knife down!" But Jorge didn't.

Hulce: Did he say anything to the officers?

Sanabria: He said words I will not repeat. But that's no reason to shoot him dead.

Hulce: Then what happened?

Sanabria: They said to get back, so I am standing in the doorway to the living room. I can see in at an angle, so I do not see the man well, but the woman and Jorge. Jorge threw the knife on the chair. The woman put one handcuff on Jorge. Then he threw her back and grabbed her gun. And they struggled for the gun. He should not have done this, but that's no reason to shoot him dead.

Hulce: Then what happened?

Sanabria: The gun went off. The woman had pointed it at the ceiling, and then Jorge lost hold of it. Then the man shot him dead.

Hulce: After the woman officer had regained possession of the gun?

Sanabria: Yes, after. Two, three seconds after. And I shouted, "Stop, you are killing him." But he did not stop.

Hulce: Was it bright enough to see?

Sanabria: Oh, yes. Very bright enough. The shades were pulled down, but not all the way. And, the television was on. It gives light. Off and on. Depending on—how do I say this?—whether the behind part of the picture—I know, the background—whether it is bright. You could see just fine.

Hulce: After reading this statement and finding it to be what you said, will you sign it?

Sanabria: Yes.

Both Sanabria sisters confirmed what their mother said. The younger girl, however, had been in the kitchen throughout the event, and could only report what she heard. Both girls were well spoken and specific, although the older one had some angry comments about the police.

Then there was Bennis's side:

OFFICE OF PROFESSIONAL STANDARDS
26 Mar. 1993

Statement of accused, Officer Norman Bennis, star 31992, Unit 001, relative to allegations that on 12 March 1993 at approximately 1400 hours, inside a first-floor apartment at 731 W. Sangin he discharged his firearm without justification, resulting in the death of Jorge Sanabria. It is further alleged that he failed to give a true and accurate account of the incident relative to the shooting of Jorge Sanabria.

Statement being taken at the Office of Professional Standards, 1024 S. Wabash, Chicago IL 60605.

Questioned and typed by: Inv. C. Hulce, Star 337, Unit 243
Date & Time: 24 Mar. 1993 at 1335 hours.
Witnessed by: Attorney Frederick Melman FOP
1300 E. Chicago Ave.
Chicago IL 60611
Inv. Clarence Summerset, Star 633, Unit 243

Bennis prefaced his remarks with the formula the

FOP counsel would have given him. And both he and C. Hulce seemed to have fallen victim to creeping officialese.

> *Bennis:* I want to say that I am not giving this statement voluntarily, but under duress. I am giving this statement because I have been advised by the Police Department regulations that if I do not I will be fired from my job.
>
> *Hulce:* Relate what happened on 12 March 93 at 1400 hours in the apartment at 731 W. Sangin that resulted in the death of Jorge "Zeets" Sanabria.
>
> *Bennis:* I ran in past Officer Mileski, who was guarding the front door so as Zeets wouldn't escape. My partner, Officer Figueroa, was ahead of me. A woman was in the doorway of the apartment screaming at Zeets. He was brandishing a weapon, a knife with a six-inch blade. I said drop the knife. He backed into a dark room and Figueroa and I followed. We had our guns drawn. Figueroa said drop the knife. The room was very dark. After being cautioned many times, he threw the knife onto a yellow and pink flowered chair. Figueroa began to cuff him. Then he suddenly threw her off and he jumped her and they were struggling. Her gun went off. I could not see well because of the lack of light, but when I saw a silhouette which I knew to be Zeets and not my partner, even though they were close together, I fired. Fearing for my life and for the life of my partner, I discharged my weapon six times.
>
> *Hulce:* Then what happened?
>
> *Bennis:* Then the woman I now know to be Mrs. Sanabria ran in and she said you've killed my son, and the woman I now know to be Anne Sanabria started to hit me . . .

That was about it. I flipped pages until I found Suze Figueroa's statement. It was almost exactly like Bennis's. Not so much alike that I thought they had rehearsed all their answers with each other, but they certainly had talked it over. Still—that was natural, under the circumstances. Figueroa's statement added one detail. She said that at the instant when her gun went off, she and Zeets each had one hand on it, because Zeets had pulled her other hand away, and it was Zeets pulling the trigger that actually caused the discharge. Then his hand came off the gun. But because of the darkness she was certain Bennis couldn't see Zeets's hand had left the gun.

A sheet headed FINAL INCIDENT REPORT/RECOMMEN-DATION OF INVESTIGATOR, written by C. Hulce, OPS investigator, concluded that Bennis did not have to shoot, that the incident was over and Figueroa had regained control of her gun before Bennis started firing, that he could see well enough to know that the danger was past, since he had been able to describe the pink and yellow flowered chair. The light level had been confirmed by the Sanabrias, Hulce added, and Bennis, therefore, had not only fired without justification, but had lied in telling the investigators that he could not see. "Since Officer Bennis was able to describe the chair both in pattern and color, it is unreasonable to claim that he could not see the victim and the other officer."

Hulce believed that Figueroa had also lied in saying Bennis couldn't see Zeets's hand was off the gun, but they apparently weren't pushing a charge against her.

Unspoken was Bennis's motive. That he had been enraged at the attack on Figueroa—which certainly was life-threatening for a few seconds—and had killed Zeets intentionally.

An idea of what had really happened was taking shape in my head. Looking through the hefty pile of documents, I finally found the transcript of the radio traffic. I read it three times. It confirmed my theory. What I needed now was to hear the actual radio transmission, live, as it happened that day. No problem. McCoo could set that up. If I called him first thing in the morning, we'd probably be able to hear it in the afternoon.

I met Figueroa and Bennis in the anteroom on the fifth floor. The windows looked over Chicago to the west. Somewhere out there a dusky feather of smoke rose from a fire. Bennis's arms hung drearily at his sides and his eyes were half-closed. He flopped into a plastic chair.

"What do you know about the Sanabrias?" I asked them. "Can you claim they aren't reliable witnesses? They certainly have reason to be biased."

Suze looked at Norm. "They—yes, I suppose. Zeets, you know, had been dealing drugs for years."

I said, "I hear some hesitation in your voice."

"Well, it's the old story. The wild son, two hard-working daughters. Zeets has a long sheet for attacking women. The mother is a good person. Very nice. She works washing and packaging vegetables in a supermarket. The older daughter is a stockbroker. The younger daughter's still in high school. She's an honor student—"

"And?"

"I don't feel very comfortable characterizing them as petty crooks who'd swear to anything."

I watched Norm as he rose suddenly and went to stand next to the window. The shade fabric was yellow and cast a mustard glow on his face. I said to her again, "And?"

"And these are—jeez, these are my people. In some sense. I'm not very comfortable with the, you know, putting the image on them. The image of the sleazy Hispanic."

Norm said, "Shit!"

Then we got word to go into the hearing room.

Investigator C. Hulce, Office of Professional Standards, turned out to be Corinne Hulce. She was a short woman with strong shoulders and a hungry mouth—a jackal of a woman. McCoo sat next to her, wearing his indulgent face. Also in McCoo's office were Commander Coumadin, Bennis's commander in the First District, and Melman, the attorney retained for Bennis by the Fraternal Order of Police.

We went through the introductions in a spirit of great caution on everybody's part.

Then Coumadin said, "Play the tape. That's what we're here for."

I had read the transcription, but hearing it was very different. Even though it was only voices, all the urgency was there. I could imagine the tension in the Communications Room, as well as on the street, as the incident developed.

The dispatcher said, "One thirty-one," which meant beat car thirty-one in the First District.

Officer Quail said, "Thirty-one."

"I have a woman screaming for help at 110 West Adams."

"Ten-four," he said, acknowledging the call and also by code that he was in a two-man car.

"Thirty-three," said the voice of a woman officer.

"Go ahead, one thirty-three."

"That alarm you gave me? The manager says it's gone off four times this week. Plus, there was a runner there. The call you had said no runner."

"Thanks, thirty-three. We'll get onto it." It was important for alarm companies to tell the police when they were sending runners. Otherwise, a cop coming on the call could think the runner was the burglar. "While you're there, thirty-three, we have three teenagers beating up a man at State and Jackson. Citizen called it in."

"Ten-ninety-nine, squad."

"I didn't know you were a ninety-nine unit," the dispatcher said. Ninety-nine meant a one-man car. "Let me know if you need backup."

"Will do."

Quail's voice said, "Thirty-one."

"Go ahead, thirty-one."

"We have an attempted rape here! We need a unit to take the woman for medical attention. Subject took off westbound."

"Okay. Uh—one thirty-six?"

"Thirty-six."

"See the woman at 110 West Adams."

"Ninety-nine."

"Do you have a description, thirty-one?"

"Yeah, uh, male white Hispanic, twenty years old, black hair, light complexion, wearing black Reeboks, black shirt, Levi's." This was a description that would distinguish him from at best half the young adult males on the street.

Quail's voice said, "Squad, thirty-six is here. We're in pursuit."

"Other units, the suspect is . . ."

The dispatcher repeated the description. Half a minute passed. Some officer said, "Hezz foggl ztt!" the transmission garbled. There was a series of gasps, as if somebody was running and trying to talk at the same time, then, "—any other units he's dangerous!" Then, "We got him! He's going into a building at 731 West Sangin."

The dispatcher said calmly, "Twenty-seven? You in the area? Can you back up thirty-one?"

Norm Bennis's voice said, "Ten-four. We're three blocks away, westbound on Jackson."

There was another half minute or so without any transmissions. This was the period, I knew, when Suze and Norm pulled up in front of the building on Sangin. They found that the two officers in thirty-one had split up, one to guard the back door and one in the front hall.

Bennis's voice again: "One twenty-seven."

"Go ahead, twenty-seven."

"Thirty-one has the suspect isolated in a first-floor apartment. He's supposed to have a knife."

At the same time, the dispatcher was saying, "Anybody in the vicinity?"

"Twenty-nine. I'm at Monroe and Michigan. I'll roll on over."

There was a short period of silence. Then Bennis said, "Twenty-seven."

"Twenty-seven, go."

"We probably got enough units. They have him bottled up at 731 West Sangin, and we're going in, squad. One of the neighbors says he ran in carrying a knife and screaming."

"Twenty-seven's giving a slowdown," the dispatcher said, conscious that every unit in the area would be wanting to give chase.

A few seconds of buzzing, somebody with an open key on his radio, then Suze's voice: "We have the suspect in an apartment at—hey!"

A new voice screamed, "Always after me!!!"

Suze yelled, "Drop the knife! Drop the knife!"

"Put down the knife!" It was Norm's voice.

Suze: "Put down the knife!"

"Drop it!"

"Drop it! Drop it!! Right now!"

"Yeee—"

"Down!"

"Cuff him!"

"Hands behind your back!"

"Bastards!" This was the unknown voice.

"Ten-one! Ten-one!" somebody said. It sounded like Bennis, but high-pitched. Ten-one means officer in trouble.

The dispatcher started to say, "Units in one, we need backup at 731 West Sangin," but the other noises overrode. We all knew that every unit in the area would be screaming to a halt and turning toward the incident.

"Shit! Goddamn!"

Dispatcher: "All units stay off the air. One twenty-seven has an emergency."

"Hey! Back off!"

A shot. That would have been Suze's gun.

"Shit! Ahhh! Shit!"

There were two shots. Then one shot. Then two or three more, fast. Then there was a sound like metal scraping on a sidewalk, but so unnerving that I thought it was actually a human voice, screaming.

"He's hit!" somebody said.

Immediately Bennis's voice said, "Twenty-seven. We need an ambulance here." His voice wasn't panicky, but it was tight as a guitar string.

The dispatcher said, "Fire's rolling, twenty-seven."

"Right," I said to Commander Coumadin. "That makes everything clear."

"What?" He realized this was not a commanderlike answer, so he said, "In what way, Ms. Marsala?"

"Norm was right. He was telling the truth. And so was the family. They were both telling the truth. The family and your officers."

"But they disagree."

"They disagree and they're both right. They were both telling the truth."

Investigator Hulce snapped, "That's not possible."

"Suppose I show you that it is. What happens?"

"We—well, of course we'd drop the charges."

"And clean up Bennis's record?"

"Certainly," she said huffily, not believing me.

"Play the tape again."

Hulce rewound the tape after a nod from the commander. I said, "You have a synchronous tape that tells the time this was recorded, right?"

Hulce said, "Right."

"Stop and mark when I tell you." Hulce glanced at the brass, hoping they'd slap me down for giving her orders, but they didn't. The tape began to play.

The dispatcher said, "We have a woman screaming for help at—"

We listened as three minutes passed. Then, Norm Bennis's voice said, "They have him bottled up at 731 West Sangin, and we're going in, squad."

I said, "Mark tape." Hulce punched a button and a different voice said, "Fourteen oh-three hours, fifteen seconds."

The drama unfolded again, unseen, with the strange, occasional sounds from radios where the key was briefly opened, like flashes of light in darkness. We heard the commands to drop the knife. We heard the shots. I said, "Now!"

"Fourteen oh-three hours, fifty-seven seconds."

"Only forty-two seconds!" Suze said.

I said, "Right. Forty-two seconds from the moment Bennis entered the house to the moment he fired."

Bennis said, "It seemed like five minutes."

"To you. But not in terms of the actions you described. Everything happened very, very fast."

"He's not going to get off because of *that*," Hulce

barked. She added sententiously, "An officer has to be able to make split-second decisions."

"That's not what I'm talking about."

Norm Bennis was studying me and finally spoke. "Tell me." And the seriousness of Bennis's situation must have made even Hulce sympathetic for a couple of seconds, because she shut up.

"Bennis really couldn't see. It was too dark. He did the best he could. He and Figueroa had been driving around for more than six hours. They came in from outdoors. His eyes hadn't adjusted to the dimness in the apartment. Mrs. Sanabria and the daughters had been inside all day. To them it was bright enough. Have you ever walked into a dark restaurant from outdoors? You can't see, and you bump into things, but everybody inside is zipping around carrying trays and pouring drinks and doing fine."

"But he told us the exact color of the chair!" Coumadin said.

I made my voice as patient as I could. It wouldn't do Bennis and Figueroa any good to tell their commander he was an idiot. "By the time they were calling for ambulances, Commander, his eyes had adjusted to the dark."

Hulce was fuming. And why not? She wouldn't look good as a result of this; she should have figured it out herself. I fixed her with my sternest look. She should have thought it out thoroughly before putting Norm through hell. Then I turned to the FOP counsel, Melman.

"Ask an eye doctor. You'll get some figures about just how long it takes a thirty-five-year-old human eye to adapt under those circumstances."

He nodded, then smiled and nodded again more briskly.

In the stretching silence, Bennis jumped up, came

over with all the laugh lines on his face laughing, pulled me up out of the chair, and kissed me on the forehead.

"Unprofessional behavior!" Suze Figueroa said. "Give that man thirty days!"

KILLED IN GOOD COMPANY
BY WILLIAM L. DEANDREA

My eyes burned from something worse than tear gas. I squinted as tightly as I could, but I had to keep my eyes open a crack, to follow the yellow cone the flashlight made in the smoky interior of the cabin. To try to find Doug Empsey and drag him the hell out of there, even though I could tell from what was happening to me, it was surely too late.

Outside, I could hear Ethel Eden's hoarse voice telling me to hurry. It was nice to have encouragement, but it was superfluous. If I didn't find Empsey *that second* I'd have to—but there he was. He was between the small frame bed and the rough wall of the cabin, on the floor. There was a window there—maybe he'd been trying with his crippled hands to get it open. To get some air.

Air. That was the idea. I'd been holding my breath as much as possible behind a wet, thick scarf that I'd wrapped across my face, but I'd risked a few inhalations, every one of which had been a mistake. I burned inside now, and I had to get out.

There was no time to be gentle, now. I dropped the flashlight, put one knee on the rumpled cot, braced myself with one gloved hand, and with the other, I grabbed him by the collar of his T-shirt and pulled.

I cursed as the fabric started to tear, but the rip hit a seam and stopped, and Doug Empsey came flying over the cot like a marlin being hauled into a boat.

I didn't stop to admire him. Instead, I got to my feet and started dragging him. My eyes felt like chunks of meat grilled on a skewer by now, and I couldn't see much, but I could make out the rectangle of light that was the open doorway. I made for it.

Empsey had seemed to weigh practically nothing when I pulled him over the bed, but he got heavier with every step as my air and energy gave out.

Finally, with a scream, I got him out the door and dragged him about seven feet away from the cabin. I took a bleary-eyed look at him for a second, but I couldn't make out any features, just a mass of red, blistered flesh. He might still be alive, but I couldn't do anything more for him. I staggered on a few more steps, then collapsed on the cool grass, still crisp with the early autumn morning frost. Each breath was a new river of fire, and my eyes were melting and dribbling out of my head.

From behind me, I heard small footsteps and a slamming door. Ethel had shut whatever was in the cabin back inside. I wanted to applaud her, but I couldn't think of anything but the pain.

"Don't rub your eyes!" she commanded, and my hands stopped halfway there.

"I hear sirens," she said. "Help is coming."

"Uh-awww, uh-auggh," I said. That was supposed to be "What about Doug?"

Either she understood me, or she filled me in figuring I'd want to know, which seems more likely. "Doug's dead," she said. "It's . . . horrible."

It flashed through my mind that this woman had covered countless wars, famines, and disasters around the world over the last thirty years, a period in history particularly rich in them. If *she* thought something was horrible. It probably was.

I wanted to ask her how I looked, but it was too

much trouble. I passed out before she could have answered me, anyway.

It was the sort of letter it would take a whole new
mind-set to respond to. I wasn't especially interested
in resetting my mind, but that's why God gives us
girlfriends.

"You've got to do this," Roxanne said. She pulled
her knees up under one of the extra-large T-shirts she
liked to sleep in. It was Saturday morning, and we
were at my borrowed apartment on Central Park
West. The mail had arrived. There was nothing worth
noting except a cream-colored envelope with GO Productions and a Manhattan address printed in the corner. It was addressed to "Mr. Matthew Cobb" which
usually meant junk mail. Anybody who knows me at
all usually skips the "mister" and keeps it to "Matt."

Still, since it purported to be from a production
company, I figured I might as well have a look. It
presented a little mystery.

It's not unusual for a TV executive to get mail from
production companies, and I do work for the network
as Vice President in Charge of Special Projects. And
it's not unusual for people to get the wrong idea about
just what Special Projects is, since the name was deliberately chosen to be obscure. What we do is try to
keep the network's nose—or as much of it as the public and regulators can see—well wiped. We do everything too nasty for Public Relations, and too sensitive
for Security.

It _is_ unusual, however, for this sort of mail to reach
me at home, since I am the beneficiary of what seems
to have turned out to be the longest and most luxuri-
ous sublet in the history of New York City. The original deal was that I would watch the apartment on
Central Park West for Rick and Jane Sloan, college

friends of mine who would rather live in a tent studying endo-cannibals in the Mato Grosso than have bar-
becued chicken brought to their door by the local deli,
mere fools they.

In any case, I watch the apartment and their dog.
Spot is an attack-trained Samoyed with black nose,
black eyes, and perpetually smiling black lips the only
contrast to his cloud of pure white fur. I'd been sitting
him so long, I'm sure he had completely forgotten I
wasn't his master.

Anyway, we were lazing around the apartment. Spot
was allowing himself to be petted alternately by Roxanne and me. And I opened the letter and read it.

"Oh, for God's sake," I said.

"What is it, Matt?" Roxanne wanted to know.

I chuckled. "Maybe I shouldn't tell you. It says here
it was specifically sent to me at home so the network
wouldn't have to know about it."

She brushed some black hair from her eyes and said,
"I am not the network."

I forbore to point out that she was the granddaugh-
ter of the network's founder, and still the largest single stockholder.

"Come on," she insisted. "What does it say?"

"Oh, all right. It's from somebody named Gary
Oshen, head of GO Productions. Dear Mr. Cobb, bla
bla bla, in case you prefer not to receive this kind of
communication at work, bla bla bla, this letter.

" 'I have received a grant from the Max N. Serra
Foundation to produce a film I plan to call *No Secrets*.
In it, I plan to gather some top investigators from all
fields, and have them talk about various aspects of
their craft, both in individual interviews and in a
roundtable format—' "

I interrupted myself. "Why is he telling me all this?"

Rox told me to read on. I did so. " 'Such famous

names as Sheriff Lamar Briggs of Georgia, private eye Doug Empsey, and Pulitzer Prize-winning investigative reporter Ethel Eden have already agreed to attend. Your participation would make the film complete, assembling an official policeman, a reporter, an individual private investigator, and (yourself) an investigator whose skills are at the disposal of a large corporation. The core of the film would be a roundtable discussion,' bla, bla—"

I looked up from the page. "Is he out of his mind? I'm a TV guy. The investigations are an unfortunate by-product of the job I happen to have."

Roxanne's dark eyes were big with mock innocence. "So?" she said. "Sheriff Briggs probably thinks of himself as a speeding ticket guy who gets stuck with investigations, too."

"Come on, Rox. He fights crime for a living."

Roxanne laughed. "Matt," she said, "I love you, but you're awfully dense sometimes. What the hell do you do? The only difference is that Lamar Briggs does it for the people of his county, and you do it for my grandfather's grasping corporate octopus."

I was a little defensive. "Well, trouble turns up."

She nodded sympathetically. "Funny how that happens in a glamorous multibillion-dollar corporation in the public eye."

"Yeah." I started sticking the letter back in the envelope. "No sense rehashing those old scandals for a panting public. I'll send regrets."

Rox shook her head. "You've got to do this," she said, pulling her legs into her T-shirt.

"Why?"

"Because you want to. You know you do."

"It's embarrassing."

"Hey, this is me, Cobb, remember? Your lover? The woman who knows you better than anybody on earth? You do a good job of hiding it, but you've got an ego the size of the Empire State Building. You love the idea of being included in company like that."

"They're world famous! I'd make an ass out of myself."

"You ought to be used to that by now."

"Oh, thank you, darling."

She smiled sweetly. "It's quite all right, love. Now, you go ahead and do this. I'll never forgive you if you don't."

That wasn't the end of it, of course. We argued about it the rest of the weekend. But the outcome was never in doubt. By the end, I knew that deep down I *did* really want to go and confer, converse and otherwise hobnob with the Master Snoopers. Giving us an excuse to do what we really want to do anyway is another reason God gives us girlfriends. Monday morning, I told Gary Oshen I'd be glad to be there.

The get-together was set for Columbus Day weekend in Maine, at Empsey's Nest, a hunting and fishing resort run by Doug Empsey and his daughter since his retirement from the private-eye business.

I got off the plane in Orinoo alone. After nudging me into the trip, you would have thought Roxanne would have come along, but she had a big exam on Tuesday (the woman's hobby is academics—she has more degrees than a Celsius thermometer by now) and she wanted the long weekend to study.

A square, solid woman about my age dressed in plaid corduroy and L.L. Bean duck boots said, "Cobb?"

I admitted it.

She put out her hand. "Hi. I'm Sharon Empsey. Since I was in town anyway, I thought I'd meet you and take you to the lodge."

I told her thanks, and climbed into the passenger seat of an Isuzu Trooper, the back of which was filled with groceries. It was a tight squeeze to get my little suitcase in.

"Doesn't look like you brought a gun or any tackle with you," she said.

"Nope. I had my fill of guns in the army."

"Nam?"

"Fringes. I was an MP."

"Important job," she offered. Her utterances were clipped, but her voice was lovely, low and smooth. She had dark hair drawn back in a no-nonsense ponytail, and her cool blue eyes were glued to the road.

I shrugged. "It got to be a drag," I said. "Two million Americans sent over there to fight Communists, and they send me over to fight Americans."

"So you don't shoot. Don't fish, either?"

"I'm a city boy. Never got the urge."

"We don't have a lot to offer at the lodge outside of hunting and fishing," she said. "Hope you don't get bored."

"I've brought a few books to read. And the company should be interesting. If all else fails, I can catch up on my sleep."

"You don't look that tired. As for the company being interesting, don't count on my old man. He doesn't talk much, and when he does, he's usually asking questions. Private-eye habit, I guess."

That made sense. Since I, too, was supposed to be one of the ace investigators, I figured I'd uphold my image and ask a few questions myself.

"Am I the first one here?"

"Nope. Lamar Briggs got in yesterday. Gary Oshen has been around for days, making a nuisance of himself. Right now he's painting the lobby."

"Don't tell me. He has a color he thinks will look better on film."

"Yeah." Sharon Empsey smiled a little. "How'd you know that? Most people I tell about it think I put him to work."

"I work in television," I said. "He's doing the painting himself?"

"He's doing everything himself. Far as I can tell, he's a one-man show."

"I guess the Max N. Serra Foundation didn't overload him with money."

"Nah. He's not even paying for the lodge. I agreed to let him use it—figured it would be good publicity. And it will be nice to see Dad back in the public eye again. Not that you could get him to admit it."

"Your father's being difficult?"

"When is he not? But this time he's been impossible. According to him, I shouldn't have let anybody use the lodge without his permission—hell, I've been running this place single-handed since I was twenty. He never pays attention to what I do, and I've kept the place profitable every year, which is more than he ever did. Now he just stays in his cabin halfway up the mountain and comes down a couple of times a week to complain about something."

"Shame."

Sharon smiled again. "Yeah, well, I think he misses the chase. Now, with his arthritis, he can't even hunt and fish as much as he used to. Anyway, he came around. You're here, the movie is going to be made, Dad is going to participate."

Her face was suddenly serious. "Though that was a near thing, too."

"How's that?"

"When he found out Ethel Eden was going to be here."

"I thought they were great friends."

"Once they were. At one point, I thought Dad was going to marry her. Then the Skeggens case got between them."

"I remember hearing about that one, but I didn't catch up on all the details."

This time, the smile was a little twisted. "I'm sure you will before the weekend is out. Suffice to say, my dad and Ethel wound up on opposite sides. There may be some fireworks when the two of them set eyes on each other again, though I wouldn't bet what kind."

"You're eager to see it happen, though, aren't you?" I asked.

"What are you talking about?"

"You want to see them back together. That's why you let Oshen use the lodge and talked your dad into going through with it. You're playing matchmaker."

"Oh, I am, huh? In the marriage sense or in the boxing sense?"

I sized her up. I had hit a nerve, no doubt about that, but she wasn't giving anything away. "I don't know," I said at last. "Could be either. You tell me."

"I've told you too much already. It's a gift with you detective types, isn't it? People just shoot off their mouths to you. Well, forget it. If I were making matches, I'd make one for myself. As much as I love the wilderness, it's no place to meet guys. Are you taken, cutie?"

That called for a double take, and I did one. I saw she was smiling, which made me feel better.

"As a matter of fact I am," I said.

"Figures. Here's the lodge."

She checked me in, then showed me to a room that was clean, comfortable, and rustic. No phone, no TV, no radio. It was, as she said, a place for people who wanted to get away from it all. She told me there'd be a get-together in the lobby at six o'clock, and left me to my book.

I read for a while—*Justice at Nuremberg*, by Robert E. Conot. Now *there* was a criminal case. Of course, there wasn't a whole lot to do in the way of investigation, since the Nazis were so proud of themselves they kept detailed notes on every depraved thing they did.

When it was time, I headed for the lobby. On the way downstairs, I tried to remind myself that these people, as much as I might admire them, as much as they had accomplished, were still just people, and I shouldn't embarrass myself or them by gushing on them. It was the sort of thing I used to have to tell myself a lot in my early days with the network, when I kept meeting the Greats of Show Biz. Since then, I've become pretty blasé about show biz. But finding killers and exposing corruption are slightly more important than pretending to be a frontier doctor, and the people I was about to meet had been doing it for years.

Actually, the first person I met was Gary Oshen. If you move in certain circles anywhere in the United States or Canada, you've met dozens of him—he was a Filmmaker. One word. Capitalized. Two m's. They run around, documenting the things in life that the networks never get around to covering, living on grants and small film festival prizes, and occasionally doing a commissioned film for a charity or government project or something. I probably sound as if I'm putting them down, but I don't mean to. Part of what's wrong with the media in this country is that too few people produce it. These men and women redress the balance a little.

Gary Oshen was a recognizable subspecies—somebody with ambitions beyond cheap documentaries. He might make it, too. He was pushy enough.

"Matt," he said. A hand stuck out from the forest of photographic gear that hung about his torso. "I'm so glad you could come. I hope you had a pleasant trip."

"Not bad at all. Nice color you picked for the lobby."

"Good, good. The airport's pretty busy for a town this size, because the University's nearby, of course. Listen, would you mind going up to the top of the stairs again and coming down? I want to get the entrance of all the participants—you know, 'Cobb takes the case!' "

I looked at him. He was smallish, with coarse black hair, wire-framed glasses, and the youthful smile of a Jewish Howdy Doody.

"I thought we were going to talk, and you were going to film what happened."

"Oh, well, you work for the network. You know we've got to open up the film a little. Let in a little air."

I decided to give him a chance. I went back up the stairs and descended again. He passed. He didn't try to ask me to do it again. Then he gave me a release to sign.

"Okay, after this, forget I'm here, okay? Just mingle. The rest of them are in there." He pointed to a room off the lobby I hadn't been to before. "Have fun!"

I heard the camera whirring behind me as I went. I was glad he was using high-speed film. I didn't need some hot spotlights cooking my eyeballs while I was trying to be natural.

"You're wrong," I said to Oshen as I went in. "They're not all here."

"You're not supposed to talk to me now."

"Where's Empsey?"

"He'll be here. Talk to the other guests."

So I did. A tiny woman with short, soft brown hair and a tall, white-haired man were sharing a drink with Sharon Empsey, who in a long skirt and a silk blouse looked rounder and softer than she had in flannel and corduroy that afternoon.

They were talking about the weather—Oshen was going to love that for cinematic potential. I waited for a lull, then I said, "Hi."

Sharon introduced me to Ethel Eden and Lamar Briggs. Miss Eden—she'd been married a couple of times, but she'd always remained "Miss Eden." Those birdlike brown eyes of hers and that thin little beaky nose had been poked relentlessly into the business of everybody from starlets to dictators, mobsters to athletes, for the past forty years, and they always seemed to see or smell crime or scandal. In her sixties, she was still at it. The network news had recently had pictures of her scrambling across rooftops in Bosnia, following up information on a phony charity that was bilking relief-minded contributors in the States.

She was wearing her trademark jodhpurs, riding boots, and safari shirt, and she looked at me like a teacher with a promising but so far disappointing student.

"Mr. Cobb!" she said. "I've researched you. You're good. Why do you waste your talents helping *management,* for heaven's sake?"

"Management has the money," I said blandly.

"Nonsense!" she sniffed. "I've made more money than you ever will. If you must work for that network, get on the air! Expose some corruption! Make waves!"

I told her I'd keep it in mind, and turned and shook

hands with Lamar Briggs. He was tall, much taller than my six-two, with a tall man's slouch and an air of slow competence about him. He was dressed in rumpled tweeds, and he looked a lot more like a college professor than a lawman.

"Don't you mind Ms. Eden," he said in a deep drawl. "Seein' me just brings back bad memories for her."

"How's that?"

Briggs showed me a sly grin. "Back in nineteen hundred sixty-three, she come down to my county lookin' to find out who killed this fellow from up North who was gettin' Nigras out to vote. She come lookin' because she didn't think I would be, you see. She was what you call prejudiced."

Ethel Eden took in a sharp breath. "I don't appreciate that, Lamar."

"Sorry, ma'am. Anyway, the day she breezes in, askin' me what I intend to do, I brought her in the back room and showed her I'd already done it."

"Done what?" I asked.

"Found the killer. It was a peckerwood named Sam Pettison. I guess you'd call him a white supremacist, which is kind of pathetic, considerin' Sam probably wasn't superior to a single livin' thing on earth. Anyway, I caught him, we prosecuted him, the good people of the county convicted him, and he's in the penitentiary yet. I bet you never heard about this."

I admitted I hadn't.

Ethel Eden sniffed again. "I wrote about it. I wrote all about it. I told the truth."

"Yes, ma'am. I think it appeared on page forty-seven of *The New York Times*."

"A reporter has nothing to say about where her story appears," the journalist protested.

"No, ma'am," Briggs said. "But, Ethel, darlin', as

I've told you before, I remain convinced she learns real fast what kind of story makes the front page and what kind doesn't."

"You're impossible," Ethel Eden said, but there was affection behind the asperity in her voice. "Almost as bad as Doug Empsey."

"Yes," Sharon Empsey said. "I wonder where Dad is?"

"I'm here, I'm here," said a hoarse voice, familiar from dozens of TV interviews. The well-known form of Doug Empsey followed. He wasn't tall, but he was impressive, even into his seventies, square and stocky and powerful-looking. There was a little softness around the middle, but he still looked tough enough. He wasn't wearing his trademark dark suit and fedora. He was wearing a blue plaid sport jacket over an open-necked sport shirt, and his unruly mop of hair had gone gray. The face was still the same, though, nose mashed slightly to the left over a good-natured crooked grin.

Then we shook hands, and I knew the difference. Sharon had mentioned her father's arthritis, but I hadn't figured it would be as bad as this. He sort of reached over my hand and pinched it with his fingertips. I didn't squeeze back—his fingers felt as fragile as a handful of bread sticks.

It was kind of sad. The fists that had laid waste to the Brooklyn mob, the hands that had held the famous .45 that ended the career of the kidnappers of three-year-old Nancy Salliman, now probably needed a tool to open a can of beer.

It didn't seem to bother him. Of course, he'd had a while to get used to it, over twenty years since he'd retired, I realized. He told me he was glad to see me, patted Briggs on the back and said, "Lamar," then put an arm around Ethel Eden's waist and gave her a large and enthusiastic kiss.

It was a bit of a shock—I mean, *I* wouldn't have dreamed of kissing her, but then again, I didn't know her when she was young and cute. Ethel Eden, it is fair to say, was not revolted. She, in fact, kissed back in a way that said she'd been down this particular road before, and hadn't minded the trip in the least.

When they broke she said, "Hello, Douglas. I see you haven't changed."

"You either, doll. I hope the kid got that on film. It'll help his movie."

That was disingenuous, since Gary Oshen had been popping in and out of everybody's line of sight, sticking a camera in our nostrils at the slightest provocation, and telling us to ignore him anytime one of us looked in his direction.

"No one," Ethel Eden intoned, "wants to see two old relics kissing."

"Except the old relics themselves," Empsey said.

Sharon looked at her watch and said dinner was ready. As she chivied us into the dining room, her father called over his shoulder to Oshen, "Don't worry, kid, we'll find something to liven up your film."

I woke up. I couldn't see. I tried to rub my eyes, but I couldn't move.

I tried to call for help, but I made no sound. There was something in my mouth, but I couldn't spit it out.

I didn't think I was dead. Dead people didn't get this mad—or this scared. I had visions of myself in total, insensate paralysis, trapped inside my own head, getting crazier and crazier from isolation, with no one knowing it until I died.

I started thrashing around. I could move that much, even if my arms seemed to be tied down. I shook and twisted all I could until someone came and stuck a needle in me, and I was gone again.

I don't know how long I was out this time. I still couldn't see or move my arms. I think I began to cry, but I made no sobs.

The only sounds I heard were metallic rasps.

I could feel the panic welling up in me again, but I fought it. It hadn't done me any good the last time.

A woman's voice said, "Mr. Cobb? Mr. Cobb?"

I could turn my head a little. I turned it in the direction of the voice.

"Mr. Cobb, I'm Dr. Clara Connor, you're in the University Hospital, and I've been treating you. Nod your head if you understand."

I nodded.

"Very good. Now, I suppose you want to know what's wrong with you." She didn't wait for an answer. "You have been severely poisoned—by poison ivy, to be precise."

Poison ivy? I thought. Impossible. Of course, I'd seen some on the way up to the cabin with Ethel Eden, but I'd been careful to avoid it. In the fall, when the shiny leaves are bright red, poison ivy is even easier to avoid than it is the rest of the time. And if you're wondering how a city boy like me knows about poison ivy, I'll take you to Central Park and show you at least six lovely patches of it.

"Someone had burned a large quantity of poison ivy in the fireplace of the cabin you entered, and droplets of the irritant oil were disseminated by the smoke. You were lucky you got out of there when you did."

I'll bet I was. The doctor's words also informed me that Ethel had been right—Doug Empsey had to be dead. I thought of the blisters all over him, on his eyes and lips, and shuddered. What the hell did *I* look like?

Dr. Connor was psychic. "You have a serious skin

rash on your face, head, neck, and part of your chest, and a slightly lesser irritation on the palm of your left hand."

Every place she mentioned began to itch. I wished she'd shut up.

She didn't. "In addition, your eyes and throat were severely affected. Don't worry though, there should be no problem in getting completely well. Your eyes are bandaged, and your hands have been tied to the bed frame to keep you from rubbing your eyes in your sleep. There is an oxygen tube in your mouth. For the first thirty-six hours, we had an airway to your lungs, but we were able to remove that."

The *first* thirty-six hours? What the hell day was it? How long had I been here?

Either the doctor's psychic powers failed her, or she didn't want me to know. Instead she said, "You have been receiving intravenous medication—lidocaine, Demerol, and an antihistamine to fight swelling. You have responded well to the medication. Now, I'm going to run down a list of symptoms. You nod for me if any of them applies to you."

She did. The only one that made a difference was sore throat, of which I had a beaut. The doctor explained in the talking-to-kids voice she used that that was the result of pouring almost pure oxygen on a throat already irritated by poison ivy. Still it was important that I get as much oxygen as possible because my throat was still swollen, and if I liked, she could increase the dose of painkiller.

I thought about it, but realized it was probably the painkiller that had made me act so crazy the first time I woke up. I was figuring out a few things in spite of the fog that surrounded me. For instance, poison ivy doesn't grow wild in fireplaces. If it had been there, somebody had put it there, and Doug Empsey had been deliberately murdered. Furthermore, the fact that I wasn't dead as well seemed to be only the rarest good luck. Therefore, I owed somebody a major stomping, and I wanted my wits about me to make sure it got delivered to the right address.

I shook my head no.

"Sure now? All right then. Now, I want to remove the bandage from your eyes."

I nodded enthusiastically. I could hear my breath start to rasp in the respirator.

"All right, calm down, now. Lean back and let the nurse and I—that's it."

I heard scissor blades grate softly near my ears, then I felt gauze being unwrapped until I felt a cool breeze on the bridge of my nose and around my temples.

I still couldn't see. I tried to grab for my eyes.

"Relax, relax," the doctor said. "You still have gauze pads on your eyes. Please keep both eyes closed until I tell you to open them."

I didn't obey her, but I didn't jump the gun by enough to make her mad. At least I waited until both pads were gone.

I blinked against the light, though I didn't want to, because the light was glorious. Colors and fuzzy shapes, at first, then after a few more painful blinks, colors and sharper shapes.

Dr. Clara Connor was pleasant enough looking, in a fatigued sort of way, but in that moment she was beautiful. If I had my arms, I would have hugged her. If I'd had my voice, I would have proposed.

She saw the look on my face, and decided not to replace the bandage. "But," she warned me and the nurse, "this room must stay dim." She turned to me exclusively. "You get some more rest. We'll take out that air thing and see how your throat is this evening. The police will want to talk to you."

That was fine with me. For a New York blabber-mouth such as myself to have his mouth taped shut was sheer torture, especially when I had a murder to catch up on. The cops? Hell, I'd be happy to talk to the Nuremberg Tribunal or the Ronkonkoma, L.I., PTA as soon as I could get my pipes working again.

The nurse immediately dimmed the lights, and I could see even better. I just enjoyed looking at things for a few minutes—the competence with which the nurse adjusted the drips on my IVs, the red rubber bellows whose falling and rising matched the rasping noise of the respirator, the neat white boxing glove of gauze on my left hand, the soft but strong pieces of cloth that bound my wrists. Eventually, if I knew myself, I'd come to hate it all, hate the hospital, hate myself for being sick.

Right now, though, I was just happy to be more or less alive. I put my head back on the pillow and let the respirator lull me to sleep.

There's a saying in the TV biz that controversy makes a good show. There's no doubt Gary Oshen believed it—he was practically licking his chops behind the camera when the subject of the Skeggens case came up.

It was Lamar Briggs who raised the topic, which was a surprise, considering how intimately both Doug Empsey and Ethel Eden had been involved in the thing. On further consideration, though, it occurred to me that they both might just have been avoiding it.

". . . A lawman, you see," Briggs said with a sly smile, "has to go by the *rules*. He can't go *houndin'* someone to death the way you did that Skeggens boy out in Ohio."

Doug Empsey ran his tongue around his cheek, but said nothing.

It was the early seventies, the height of anti-Vietnam protesting. A high school kid named Chucky Scott blew himself to bits in the closed offices of the Mycroft, Ohio, draft board, apparently attempting to plant a bomb. There was suspicion that Chucky had been provided with the bomb by a friend, a college sophomore named Lester Skeggens, who was a science whiz (which Chucky definitely was not) and who had fallen in with some very radical pals on campus.

Suspicion, but no proof. The cops had had to leave it there, but Chucky's father hadn't. He'd hired Doug Empsey to find out what had happened. Empsey had proceeded to investigate. He questioned everybody. He questioned Lester Skeggens four or five times. The media picked it up, including Ethel Eden, who heretofore had been a close friend of Empsey's (a lover, if Sharon could be believed). Her position was that she had "sources" who told her that Chucky had been sacrificed by a group of right-wing plotters who wanted to discredit legitimate war protests.

Doug Empsey had had one comment for the record—"Bullshit." He'd gone on with his investigation. He questioned Skeggens one more time.

Later that night, Lester Skeggens took poison. The case sort of petered out after that. Empsey took expenses but no fee from Chucky's father. A short while after that, he retired.

"That's not fair," Ethel Eden said. "Doug might have been hopelessly wrong in that case, but he did what an investigator has to do. Gracious, if I worried about how my subject's feelings would be affected by my investigation of something, I'd still be writing up tea parties for the society page.

"Of course, my forthcoming autobiography, *What's She Doing Here?* will have what I consider to be the final word on the topic." She smiled demurely. "You'll all have to buy it to find out."

The conversation went on to other things. I noticed Doug Empsey didn't say much. He just kept looking at Ethel with an expression it was impossible to read.

Eventually, we broke it up for the night. I was eager to talk with my fellow guests off the record, but by the time I found a phone, called Roxanne, and wished her good night, they'd all dispersed. Only Sharon Empsey was left in the lounge.

"Where'd everybody go?" I asked.

"Lamar Briggs claimed age and walked off to his cabin. He asked for one of the cabins, you know. Dad and Ethel went for a walk."

"Oho."

Sharon grinned at me. "Oho yourself. They haven't seen each other for a long time, and they've got making up and catching up to do. Did you see my father looking at her?"

"I did. I don't know what he was thinking, but he was thinking it hard."

"Must be wonderful to be fascinating to men," she said.

"You just have to get to a place where you can meet more men. If I'd met you a couple of years ago, who knows what might have happened?"

"Is that supposed to cheer me up?"

I smiled and shrugged and decided I might as well get to bed, too.

Dr. Connor came in next morning and took the respirator out. I had a drink of water. It was fabulous. I got to take about five natural breaths when Stephen King walked in. Well, it wasn't really Stephen King. It was investigator Harry Terzo of the state police. But he was tall, with an angular face, deepset blue eyes, black hair, and a weedy Maine-tinged voice, so the mistake was natural.

"Do you know you look like—" I stopped. My voice sounded weird—weak, rough, and far away. I realized it was the first time I'd heard it in days.

"Yeah, yeah. Are you up to a few questions, Mr. Cobb?"

"Sure," I said. "I've got a million questions."

"I meant are you up to answering a few? Then maybe I can answer some for you."

"Okay. What do you want to know?"

"Just tell me what happened that night in your own words." He frowned. "What's the matter?"

I grimaced. "They must have cut my medicine down. I'm starting to itch. Especially my left hand." I looked at it, but of course all I could see was the gauze mitten. I flexed it a few times, just to bring the flesh in contact with the fabric of the bandage and get some scratch action that way. It helped a little, not much. I did much better concentrating on my story.

There must have been something in the air up there. I slept like a rock until four a.m. Then there was a knock on my door. Something in my brain always knows what time it is within ten minutes or so, but I checked my watch anyway. "Who is it?"

A woman's voice said, "Cobb, open up. It's important."

I came wider awake now. "Ethel?" I was puzzled. I hadn't been expecting a woman to come calling in the middle of the night, but if it was going to be one, I'd have expected it to be Sharon Empsey.

"Yes, it's me. Open up."

"I'm not dressed."

"I've seen a naked man before. This is important."

"Wait a second." I pulled on my pants and got the door. "Come in," I said.

Ethel Eden was fully dressed in her trademark jodhpur outfit. She'd added a leather jacket and a battered safari hat to the mix. She looked like Indiana Jones's mother.

She pointed at my pants. "That's a good start," she said. "Keep getting dressed. And do it right. We're going through the woods."

She was so sure of herself that I kept getting dressed, even though I didn't have the slightest idea what she was talking about. That much, I thought, I could fix. "Will you kindly tell me what the hell is going on?"

"I got a phone call."

"A phone call? There's a phone in your room?"

"There's a phone wherever I go. Cellular. Communications technology, young man. I thought that was your field."

"Only peripherally. What was this phone call?"

"From Doug. He's in trouble. He's hurt. Or something. He didn't say much before he stopped talking."

I sat on the bed and started pulling on my shoes. "Shouldn't you tell his daughter?"

She made a noise. "Her. She hates my guts. She'd waste too much time talking. Not that it looks as though I've done much better with you."

"Ha, ha."

"I'd get Briggs, but he's way out there in the row of cabins somewhere."

"All right," I said. I pulled on my nylon windbreaker, stuffed a pair of gloves into my pocket. Let's go."

It was a steep path up the hill to Doug Empsey's private cabin. In the false dawn, it was just possible to pick your steps. Empsey, according to his daughter, ran this path like a mountain goat—no wonder he was in such good shape. The path was crossed constantly with roots and vines, and I could hear creatures out there in the underbrush.

At one point, Ethel missed her footing, and if I hadn't spun around and grabbed the right sleeve of her jacket, we would have gone rolling backward to the bottom of the hill.

Doug Empsey's place was in a clearing on a ridge. Light leaked from around wooden shutters. There was nobody around, no screams, no outward signs of trouble.

As I got close to the door, I smelled something nasty. I backed away and pulled on my gloves. Ethel wet a scarf in a puddle, and gave it to me to put over my face.

"I'm going to have to get this door open," I said. "I'll probably have to bust it in."

"Try the knob," Ethel Eden said. "He keeps it open. With his arthritis, it's hard to work a key."

"You stand back a little," I told her. "If I run into trouble, you get more help, I don't care who hates your guts."

She patted the phone in her pocket. "I called the police before I woke you up," she told me.

"Yeah," I said. I twisted the knob, hit the door with my shoulder, and walked into the poison-ivy fumes.

"If I can add a personal comment," I told Terzo, "this is about the nastiest goddamn murder I ever heard of."

Terzo's mouth was a tight line. "You got that right. The poor bastard in there with his useless hands. All the killer had to do was climb the roof, drop a bunch of poison ivy down the chimney—no big trick to climb that roof by the way."

"I know. I saw it. Go right up the side of the chimney. A fat lady could climb it in heels."

"Right. Then slide down and hold the door closed until you were sure he was unconscious. What could he do about it with those hands?"

Terzo scratched his jaw. Then he pulled a visitor's seat close to the bed and said, "Cobb, I'm going to let you in on this. You don't actually have an alibi, but nobody would have gone in there like you did if he knew what would happen. You nearly got killed yourself."

"Tell me about it. But you never know. Remember that schmuck in Boston who killed his wife, then shot himself in the stomach."

"Not the same thing. He was aiming at his leg. Also, you don't have the ghost of a motive."

"Okay. You convinced me. You should let me in. In on what?"

"It would have been even easier. Empsey used to take painkillers at night, according to his daughter. Strong stuff. Knocked him right out, slept like a log."

"So if the killer knew, he could just waltz in with an armload of poison ivy and dump it on the fire. Even light a fire if he needed to."

"Exactly."

"Who knew?"

"Too many people. The daughter and the whole staff of the place. How many outsiders could they have told? Infinity."

"How's Sharon taking it?"

"Hard. I get the impression her whole life has been wrapped up in her old man. But she'll be okay. She's tough. I like her."

"What about the rest?"

He shrugged. "Your fellow guests? Professionals. Deadpan. Of course, they don't have motives, either.

I suppose Eden could be nursing a broken heart from way back, or something, but I doubt it. And I saw the videotape. Briggs was busting Empsey's ass on the Skeggens thing, but if that was anything more than some innocent ball busting, I'd have to have it shown to me."

"What about the young producer?"

"Oshen? He's eating this up with a *spoon*. Keeps following *me* around with a goddamn camera. I'm about an inch away from punching him in the mouth. I'm almost ready to believe he did it to liven up his goddamn TV show."

I told him that was true to form both for Oshen and for a cop. "Find anything else?"

"Like what?"

"I don't know. Footprints on the roof? Threads snagged in bushes around Empsey's cabin? Anybody come down with poison ivy and can't explain it?"

"Just you, and you've got an explanation."

"Tell me about it," I said again.

"All we found was some stuff in the fireplace. Hardwood ash, from the regular fire, you know, poison-ivy ash, remains of some papers somebody burned in there, and some burned-up leather. Probably the killer's gloves."

"Smart," I said.

"Yeah. Use them to protect your hands, then burn them, so you don't get poison-ivy juice on things and give yourself away. You can't really wash that stuff off leather very well."

I closed my eyes. I couldn't believe how tired I was.

After a few seconds, Terzo said, "Well?"

I opened my eyes. They still took a few seconds to focus. Not all better yet.

"Well what?"

"You had your eyes closed. I thought you master detective types did that to concentrate."

"Don't listen to Gary Oshen, all right? I closed my eyes because I was tired."

"Oh. Maybe you want to sleep."

"I suppose. It's hard to read with your hands tied up."

"Well, you've got another visitor out here. Been making a nuisance of herself for days. Threatened bodily harm to the doctor."

I could feel my irritated face stretching in a big smile. "Roxanne is here? Send her in for God's sake!"

"Sure. I was just going. You think about this, okay?"

"Yeah," I said grimly. "I'll think about it. Terzo, this joker almost killed me, too, remember?"

"I didn't think you'd need to be reminded of that. See you."

He opened the door. Roxanne almost bowled him over running into the room.

"Hi, honey," I said.

She came to the bed and stood over me. Her face got more and more frantic.

"What's the matter?" I demanded.

"Shit!" she said. "There's nowhere to kiss!"

"We'll make up for it later."

"Darn right we will. Oh, Matt, I'm so glad to hear you talk. They let me in here during the first couple of days. You were a *mess*."

"I don't want to hear about it," I told her. "Let me think."

"All right. You can even go to sleep if you want to. I'll just sit here and watch you." Then she reached out and gave my hand a little squeeze. My left hand.

"Ow!" I said.

Rox was apologetic, but I wasn't listening to her. I

was looking at my left hand, my poison-ivy-infested left hand. And, as promised, thinking. Really thinking about how Doug Empsey died.

It took about a half hour. "Rox?" I said.

"Yes, Matt. I'm sorry about your hand."

"Don't worry about it. You solved the case."

She looked at me. "I did, huh?"

"You sure did."

"Gee, I must be brilliant."

"A genius. But I still need more help. I assume everybody is still around."

"Sure. Terzo won't let them go."

"Good. Here's what I want you to do . . ."

The killer came carefully into my room.

"You're looking better. Sorry I haven't been by. Things have been hectic."

"That's okay," I said. "Lying here helpless is a full-time job. Nice jacket," I said. It was white canvas, still stiff.

"Yes, I decided the old image had to go."

"Right," I said, "and you can pop that one right into the washing machine, can't you, Ethel?"

"Yes, you can. Not that there are always washing machines where I travel."

"There isn't always poison ivy, either. What did you do with the leather one?"

"I got rid of it. Really, you're not making any sense."

"No? Then I'll be more specific. I've got poison-ivy rash all over my head and neck and face, and inside my throat from being exposed to the irritating oil in the smoke from Doug Empsey's fireplace. Fine. I've also got poison ivy on my left hand. Only my *left* hand. How did that happen? Not from the smoke. I put my gloves on when I went inside. I didn't get it on the path, when we were headed up to the cabin. The only thing I touched on the way up was the sleeve of your jacket when you lost your balance heading up the hill. I caught your right arm with my left hand. How did I get poison ivy from your jacket? Because of the sap left on it by your carrying armloads of the stuff to put in Doug's fireplace.

"He never had a chance. When you went for your walk, did you go up to his cabin? Were you going to sleep together for old times' sake? Or did you leave and go back, after he'd taken his painkiller and you knew he'd be sound asleep? It didn't really matter, did it?"

"You're a sick man, Matt. It's the drugs they've given you. They've affected your brain."

"I don't think so. Nobody considered you for the crime; you had no motive. We'll get to that in a second. The crime itself was easy. Nobody would have an alibi; you'd have my swollen body—dead or alive— to prove you tried to help. All you had to do was to wait outside and listen. When the agony of breathing poison woke him up, as we know it did, all you had to do was hold the door closed while Doug scrabbled around with his crippled hands trying to get free. Did you enjoy it? Did you imagine the pain he was going through? I have to tell you, there's nothing quite like it."

"I find this very offensive."

"Too bad. You also made a big mistake. When, in the course of choking to death, and thrashing around trying to get out, did he have time to phone you?"

She ignored it. "You admit yourself, I have no motive."

"That's what everybody thought. But a possible motive occurred to me when I thought about what you'd said that night. About how your book was going to reveal the truth about the Skeggens case, how—"

Just then the phone rang. I chuckled and looked at my hands. "Would you mind getting that? Usually the nurse picks up and sticks it by my ear, but we don't want to be interrupted, do we? Just take a brief message, if you would."

Ethel Eden was still looking disgusted, but she'd decided the pose of humoring me was the best way to handle things, so she picked up the phone.

She listened for a second, then put the phone against the front of her shoulder. "It's someone named Roxanne. She says she and Sharon found it."

"That's great!" I said. "She probably heard that. Tell her I said not to open it."

Ethel put the phone back to her ear. "She heard that, too." She said good-bye and hung up the phone.

I was grinning. "Motive. There's your motive."

"I think you've been seeing the wrong kind of doctor."

"Well, the envelope will tell. I assume it's an envelope. Could be a box, I suppose. Duplicates of the papers Doug showed you the other night. The ones you burned with the poison ivy. What were they? Proof that Skeggens was guilty?"

Ethel was silent.

"I knew it had to be that. Doug had proof all along that Skeggens gave Chucky Scott that bomb, but he sat on it all these years. Quit the business. The poor bastard must have really loved you. Fat lot of good it did him.

"He'd taken the heat for years, let your reputation grow with your big conspiracy theory. Sacrificed his own reputation for you. But when you started touting a book that's going to 'tell the whole truth' once and

for all, when he knows all you're going to do is en-
shrine a lie—that was too much to take.

"So he showed you the proof. Or reminded you he
had it. And you killed him. In the nastiest possible
way. You're really something, woman."

"He was a pig," she said. "How *dare* he cover up
the truth for the sake of my reputation! I didn't need
his *protection*. Said he did it because he *loved* me. He
pretended to respect me and my career, but he treated
me like a little mindless girl-creature. God, I wanted
to kill him *then*.

"I deliberately talked about my book to get him to
show me the paper—it was Skeggens's suicide note,
by the way. Doug went there after Skeggens killed
himself, found the body and note, and stole the note.
Skeggens admitted his guilt. I wanted to lay my hands
on it. Then I could destroy it, and Doug Empsey, and
the hold he thought he had over me."

She sniffed and drew her head up. "I am not sorry.
I would have gotten away with it, if he hadn't lied to
me to the end, and said there was only one copy."

"Oh, that," I said. "No, he didn't lie. You burned
the one and only copy. The call from Roxanne was a
bluff. She's in the waiting room downstairs. I told her
to watch you come in, wait five minutes, then call."

"Then you have no evidence. No evidence at all."

"There's my hand."

"That won't convince a jury of anything."

I gestured with my chin. "There's also this little
black thing on the bed. It looks a lot like the button
you use to call the nurse, but it's not. It's a miniature
TV camera, the kind they put inside football players'
helmets. Communications technology." I smiled. "My
field. If you lift my sheet, you'll see a microphone
there at the foot of the bed. And if you'll look out
the window, you'll see Gary Oshen out on the fire

escape, getting it all on tape. And drooling. Right, Gary?"

"Right!" The reply was a little muffled through the window, but came through clearly enough.

"You can't use this. It won't be admitted as evidence."

"Think again. We all signed blanket releases allowing Gary Oshen to videotape and air all our activities 'in the community of Orinoo, Maine.' This tape may not make it to court, but it's for damn sure making it to the network. You're through, Ethel."

"I've faced down dictators. You don't scare me."

"I don't care if I scare you. On behalf of my lungs, I just want to punish you. Which I have done."

She turned and walked out, but when she opened the door, the space was filled with Harry Terzo. Roxanne must have called him for the payoff, afraid that Ethel would slit my throat or something.

"Please come with me, Ms. Eden."

She turned and looked pure hatred at me.

"I suppose you think you've proved something."

I couldn't resist a parting shot. "Sure," I said. "I proved I can outsmart a very nasty killer . . . even with both hands tied behind me."

NICOLE
A Matthew Gereghty Story
BY TED FITZGERALD

It was midweek in mid-September, a clear day with little humidity and a temperature in the low eighties, and the ferry from Falmouth to Martha's Vineyard was crowded with retirees on day trips and late-season vacationers out to beat the crush. Rolling off the ferry at Oak Bluffs, I turned past the bike rental stands and headed for the Joseph Sylvia Public Beach, a streak of white sand located halfway between Oak Bluffs and Edgartown. The entire setup—the genteel, rushed phone request the afternoon before, the trip to the Vineyard, the inconvenient meeting place—was designed for privacy but it also spelled out a power move. And my prospective client was no stranger to power. She practiced it weeknights at six and eleven.

I spotted the light gray Saab she'd described, parked my dulled silver Escort behind it, then crossed over a long tuft of grass to make my way across the sand. She was twenty yards ahead, stretched out in a portable aluminum recliner, clad in a one-piece jet-black bathing suit that accentuated a well-toned body whose only concession to its wearer's nearing fifty was small potbelly. Her skin was taut and lightly bronzed, set off by a gold necklace and matching ankle bracelet, both catching the noon sun and storing it for a winter memory. Her hair, black as the suit and normally a lengthy pageboy on the tube, was tied back with a red ribbon. Ebony-lensed sunglasses masked her eyes and completed the dark motif. Hearing my approach, she turned her head and slid her body around. She feinted a rise and extended her hand, not fully standing until I gripped it.

"Matthew, I'm so glad you came," she said in a voice that had deepened over the years into a sultry whiskey tenor.

The effect was State Street, not the Plymouth County bedroom community in which she'd once lived. Coolness and influence and polished restraint; an aura of total confidence. The last time we shook hands there had been a band of white skin on the ring finger of her left hand and her hair had been flatter and streaked through with gray. That was ten years ago. I'd just graduated college and was down on the island with the great love of my undergraduate life who'd waited until then to tell me about her boyfriend. Nicole's husband had dumped her for a younger, more vibrant, he'd said, woman and she'd come here to get away, period. We ended up talking and after a day decided to play out the obvious romantic fantasy placed in front of us. It was fun and wistful and not quite real and we implicitly agreed not to let it continue beyond the week. She left with a strong handshake and a soft-spoken vow that things would improve.

And they had. Some details I'd gleaned from the papers and others from Nicole when we'd met at a political fund-raiser a year or so back. She'd gotten into PR, increased her wattage, developed a strong personal style, and built up a reputation as a high-powered events organizer. She eventually began penning an outrageous gossip column for a trendy business weekly and two years ago the perennial third-place TV station in Boston hired her for the evening news. While the ratings budge hadn't been massive, it was still enough that Nicole Bannister became a visible celebrity in her own right. And now she wanted to hire me, Matthew Gereghty, whose investigation business was so shitty at the moment that I was almost ready to go back into politics.

"I'm a sucker for a good mystery," I said in response to her greeting.

Nicole laughed and took my arm, guiding me down the beach and toward the surf. "Matthew, tell me: How *are* you?"

"Fine. Making a living."

"Just living or are you taking the time to enjoy it?"

"I have my moments. This may even be one of them. I still don't know if this is business or pleasure."

She paused and looked up at me. "Which would you prefer?"

"Like my old boss, the congressman, I'm greedy. I'll take both."

Nicole stepped back and shook her head. "Uh-uh. Choose one."

"Work, dammit."

"I saw your old boss. At a party in Palm Beach."

"With all the campaign funds he walked off with after the defeat, where else would the old pirate be?"

"He spoke highly of you, Matthew. So did some other people I know. The word I hear about you is 'discreet.' "

"That's politicospeak for 'Keeps his damn mouth shut.' In need of discretion, Nicole?"

"Still perceptive, Matthew." She gave me a warm smile. "Does that help in locating missing persons?"

"It doesn't hurt. Who's missing?"

"I have a special friend. His name is Giancarlo." Nicole was carrying a small black leather bag. She fished through it and came up with two photographs. She handed me one. It was of a slim, dark youth who looked like a model in an artsy jeans ad: curly black hair, narrow, delicate eyes, and thin, pale lips, clad in white chinos and displaying a hairless chest and a smile that could just as easily have been a smirk.

"And he is . . . ?"

"Mine," she replied with too much speed and vigor to support the laugh that followed.

"Boyfriend?"

"Lover would be the accurate term. Friend would do in easily shocked company. Easily shocked, Matthew?"

"Tell me about him. What does he do?"

"For a living? He's a waiter." Nicole shed her glasses and eyes I remembered as hazel were now onyx, glittering with the sharp bright points of the reflected noondday sun. "And don't worry, Matt. He's legal." She cocked an eyebrow ever so slightly. "Not that it would matter. If he were sixteen and filled me with passion the way he did this summer, I'd have him. You must understand." Her tone suggested that all civilized people did.

"How long has he been gone?"

"About three weeks. He would sometimes go off for a few days. With friends, I suppose. We didn't keep tabs on one another. He spent a lot of time at my place but he didn't actually live there."

"Why did he leave?"

"We had a spat."

"Concerning?"

"His wandering eye or mine, I forget which. We were very creative with petty jealousy. And the summer was coming to an end and I was wondering if this arrangement would continue and . . . well, I thought he'd cool off and come back."

"After three weeks? I doubt it, Nicole."

"Yes, And if he's not coming back, neither is this."

She passed over the second snap, this one displaying a gold bracelet with green stones draped on a blue velour base. "For insurance purposes," she explained. "It's only worth about two thousand but it has, as they say, great sentimental value. I think he took it only to spite me."

"And you want it back."

"I want it back *from him*. I want to see him, talk to him. I won't be deserted! You know I went through that once and I vowed it would never happen to me again. If he wants to end things, fine, but he has to justify it to me!"

"If you want me to rough him up when I find him, I'll have to charge you extra to watch."

Nicole's eyes narrowed until there was no light to be seen in them and her mouth opened slightly, to either speak or spit at me.

"Nicole, it's been a decade but I don't want you to set yourself up for a big hurt."

"That's not your concern, Matthew. I am not the same woman I was ten years ago."

"I know. You were a mess. Your own words. You told me you were going to take complete charge of your life and you obviously have. But it doesn't mean you should hit yourself over the head . . ."

"I can get plenty of people to do this job, Matt," she said coldly. "I picked you because I placed myself in your trust once and you didn't betray me then and I know you wouldn't now. I'm in a delicate professional position. I air people's bad judgments but I certainly don't want to read about myself on page six of the *Herald*. And my friends also tell me you're not exactly setting the world on fire financially."

I thought about the computer system I'd ordered and didn't yet have the money to pay for and the property developer I quit working for when I found what he really wanted was a glorified thug.

"Will you take my money or do I give it to someone who won't pass judgment on me?"

"You've got me." Letting a faint memory of feeling and an ongoing need for solvency wash away any random ethics, I quoted a hefty fee, twice my daily rate. Back at the recliner, Nicole wrote out a week's retainer in a light spiral hand and passed the check over to me. I asked some background questions on the elusive Giancarlo and learned that they'd met last summer, been casually involved, and that the relationship caught fire in the late spring of this year. She knew of two places he'd worked but little else: no friends, no relatives, and, surprisingly, no last name for lover boy.

"You two have been together since May and you don't know his last name?"

"I never thought to ask," she replied casually. "There was no need."

I peppered her with a few more questions, the when and the where but not the why—they never tell you that even if they know—then trudged off to the bank, an erstwhile local institution that now wore the name of a Providence-based chain thanks to a Friday afternoon visit from the federal regulators. Nicole gave me the name of another "dear" friend, Bud McCray, a ruddy-faced vice president with a hearty manner and an old jock's body, who gladly cashed the check, transferred most of it to my own bank via EFT, and left me the rest in walking-around money. We made polite chitchat while waiting for the transfer to go through and when he asked me my profession I gave in to a congenital disrespect of bankers and vaguely alluded to "personal services," leaving him to guess exactly what sort of contract that might constitute between Ms. Bannister and myself.

I found a bed-and-breakfast, wrote my notes, and planned my strategy. With little to go on but a first name and a photo, I knew that a lot of legwork would be required. That night, I ate dinner, then made the rounds of the Edgartown hot spots. It was a small world, the Vineyard, and Giancarlo had worked in two places that Nicole had known of: a cream-colored upscale seafood emporium dubbed The Oyster and a basement rock-'n-roast called the Down 'n Under. She'd met him at the former, no surprise. I spent the evening at both places, sipping Sam Adams's, shooting the breeze with the bartenders and observing the wait staff, overhearing names and listening to kitchen conspiracies, getting a feel for who was the staff gossip and knew the most about everybody else's business and therefore be able to tell me something.

The summer crowd—the students, anyway, who might have worked with Giancarlo—was mostly gone. Still, the mild New England autumns of recent years had extended the "season" well into October and there were enough recent college grads, members of two-income families working a second job, and folks otherwise battered by the recession to staff the restaurants and clubs. One of them might know something.

Or not. I hit three restaurants, four clubs, and— thanks to not finishing all my beers—no walls. Nor any jackpots. My display of Giancarlo's photo resulted in much shaking of heads and remarks of the "Yeah, I seen him" and "No, don't know where. Around, you know?" school. No strong reaction, no hostility nor any apparent evasion. My sole glimmer of light was at last call at the Down 'n Under. An outgoing young woman about twenty-two named Cory, who looked like a heavy metal groupie but possessed the clear, enthusiastic nature of a camp counselor, struck up a conversation while waiting for her friend to come off duty. Cory was visiting but had worked on the Vineyard this summer and last, and she laughed and smiled when I held up Giancarlo's photo.

"Alfredo!"

"That was his name?"

"No, it was something Italian. Puccini, Petrocelli, Mussolini. No last name. Like an artist or something. He mumbled a lot anyway, so I started calling him Fettucini Alfredo to bust his balls."

"Did you know him well?"

"Well enough to know he wasn't Italian. And that we weren't his type."

"Define type."

"We'd work these parties, you know, catering gigs for the people with money. And he'd be there sucking up to them. If he was working he'd strut around and snap his fingers, acting like a goddamned dictator and if he was there as somebody's guest, he'd treat us like shit and the next day at the restaurant he'd be all 'Carly this' and 'Dan Ackroyd that.' I'll put up with that for a paycheck and a tip but I won't for free."

"Did he have any friends, anyone he hung around with?"

"No, just the rich people he sucked up to. Although I'll tell you, he had something going with that woman on Channel Seven, the Elvira with all the face-lifts?"

I hadn't thought of Nicole in terms of nip-and-tuck or horror movie hostess, but this was after all the younger generation. Even for me. "What makes you think he wasn't Italian?"

"Hey, I grew up in East Boston. I know how the guys speak who got it from their grandparents and I know how the old country people speak. He was faking it. Probably to impress his rich friends. Maybe he wanted to be a model or an actor or something and he figured it'd help, I don't know."

"Know where he lived?"

"Everyone rented out rooms in houses. One of them, I guess." Curiosity finally caught up with her natural enthusiasm and she popped the question. "Why you looking for him anyway?"

"May have taken something that didn't belong to him."

"What a surprise," said Cory and she broke into a raucous laugh.

The next morning I made the rounds of shops and restaurants, the car and bike rental places, flashing Giancarlo's mugshot and giving out a phony name and a lame pretext about a family reunion. It brought vacant stares and vague recognition and enough discouragement to drive me to the bars once they opened. It was a strictly professional decision: I'd always found the day bartenders in resorts to be older, often year-rounders or veterans of enough previous seasons that they possessed the institutional memory the kids lacked. Combine that with a probable dislike for the young and the pretentious and one of them might hold some useful information. Also, by hitting The Oyster and the Down 'n Under during the day, I might pick up some employment information: last name, Social Security number, address.

The manager at The Oyster was a supercilious Austrian who considered it an affront to answer any question put to him by an uppity native. The day man at the Down 'n Under was friendlier: skinny, in his forties, with thinning red hair and beard, wearing jeans and a polo shirt with the club's name imprinted on the breast pocket. He seemed grateful for the early

company and it wasn't until we were well into a conversation about the Red Sox and nothing much that I
saw he might be lonely as well. He was visibly startled
when I produced the photo, switching his eyes from
it to me and back again, his face taking on the appearance of a suddenly slapped child.

"What do you want him for, Captain?" he asked
tentatively.

I more or less gave him an outline of the truth.
"Woman who cares for him very much wants to see
him. She misses him."

Red took his time with his answer. "If she cares
that much, she should stop looking for him."

"Why's that?"

"Any woman interested in him, no. No good."

"You saying he holds dual citizenship?"

He caught the meaning and chuckled. "Yeah. That's
pretty good, yeah." Then serious again: "You know,
he's very young. And cruel."

How would you know that, I thought. "A player?
A user?"

"Could say that, Captain." He focused on a beer
tap, squeezing it with his fingers. "He hasn't been hurt
enough to worry about pain. Giving it or getting it."

"You're a poet, my friend."

"No!" he snapped. "Just a bleeder."

"Don't sell yourself short."

"That buys you a beer on the house." He gazed at
me with the eternally nervous and hopeful smile of
someone who's never received enough affection in life.
He poured out a draft and passed it over to me. In
return, I placed a fifty of Nicole's retainer on the bar.

"I'd appreciate the beer and I'd appreciate your
help even more, but all I can offer you is something
I'm not sure you'd take." I slid the fifty across the

bar. Red stared at it, then caught it between his fingers and held it there.

"I'm too old to be a saint," he said. "You want to beat up on him, Captain?"

"Not what I'm after."

"Don't know what I can tell you. Didn't know him well. Or long."

"Start with his full name. I doubt he was christened Giancarlo or that he came from Naples."

"He's got an accent but it's not Italian. And not from around here unless you grew up around here. Know what I mean?"

"Local boy?"

"This part of the state. Portuguese, not Italian."

It made sense. Resorts like the Vineyard often attracted people wearing faces they weren't born with.

"We're all posers," Red said, reading my mind. "Some of us do it close to home."

"How far in miles from here would you say is home?"

He shook his head. "All I'm saying is, he talked a lot about Italy. I was there when I was in the navy. What he knew came out of a book."

"Where was home for him on the Vineyard?"

"Whoever'd be stupid enough to take him in, I guess."

I tried to get past that but he was sullen now, ignoring my questions and staring at the money as if it were a traffic ticket. Finally, he tossed it back at me.

"I don't want your fuckin' money, Captain," he muttered.

"Give it to a friend," I said, pushing it back. "You worry about people, you'll find somebody who needs it."

"Fuckin' drugs is what I need!" He crumpled the bill between his fingers, turned, and hook-shot it into a tip glass located beside the cash register and beneath a makeshift sign reading "No good deed goes unpunished." He kept his back to me as he spoke. "You want to find him and hurt him and, Jesus Christ, I want you to, too. Get out of my bar, Captain."

I tried to argue but he wasn't buying and I didn't really want to see his face when he turned around. Walking out, I felt his eyes boring into my back as I wondered if the tip jar sign contained the words he lived by.

It was time to check out Giancarlo's possible lodgings and the fifth house I visited turned out to be my lucky pick. A gnomelike man, bald except for thick tufts of hair peeking out from behind each ear, was bent over the toilet in the downstairs bathroom, working a plunger with more relish than the task usually demanded. He jumped slightly when I knocked on the door frame, scowled at me through thick-lensed glasses, and told me he had no rooms and was closing up the house for the winter.

"I'm not looking for a room," I replied. "Looking for someone."

"Well, congratulations. At least you're on the right island."

"Hope so." I flipped up the photo. Like Red, my owlish friend drew back.

"Oh, him. The Duke of Tuscany. He's been gone for weeks. Found other living arrangements."

"Know where he went?"

"Where do they all go? Probably home to mommy and daddy."

"Any idea where that is?"

"Not Italy, that's for sure."

"That seems to be common knowledge. Not much else, though. Know anything about him?"

"Just that he was an angry little boy pretending to be special so he could play with the grown-ups. Paid his rent and thought that entitled him to be treated like royalty."

"How's that?"

"Oh, he preened and . . . look, most of these kids are pigs. Here on a holiday, they don't pick up after themselves, they break windows, shove things down toilets. It's a full-time job keeping up with them but at least most of them don't complain if I move their junk around to clean up the place. He did. Pissed and moaned whenever he wasn't name-dropping."

"I hear he liked the lifestyles of the rich and famous."

"He was a terrible hanger-on. Always trying to get close to someone who could help him."

"What sort of help?"

"Give him money or toys. It was all a game with him. I've seen his type. Their whole goal is to get close to someone and have them react to them. Get something out of them."

"Any particular Samaritans?"

"Well, if you must know . . . That TV woman? On the Boston station? The gossip?"

"Nicole Bannister?"

"That's the one. He had his hooks in her all summer. And I mean she went through them fast and furious until he came along! I bet she'd know where he went."

"True love, the two of them?"

"Be serious! True grit would be more like it."

"He stayed here, didn't he need to fill out an application? Leave a security deposit?"

"I just take care of the properties. You want that information, you talk to the owner. He runs the bank. Mr. McCray."

*   *   *

To save time, I called Nicole rather than try to find
her place. Her voice was places-to-go-and-things-to-do
crisp and there was a pause after I explained what I
wanted her to persuade her dear friend Bud to do.

"Aren't you clever, Matt? I never knew Bud owned
Giancarlo's lodgings. Of course, I'll ask him to help
you in any way. I'm leaving for Boston now. I have a
taping tonight. Call me in town when you have
something."

It was almost closing time and Bud McCray did not
appear pleased to see me but he showed me into his
office where he said he kept his records. He thumbed
through a card file, grunted in a show of puzzlement,
retrieved a large folder from a file drawer, and began
pawing through that.

"That's very strange," he said. "I checked for this
house and my other rental properties and I can't seem
to find your boy."

"Doesn't everyone fill out an application and post
a security deposit?"

"Yes, but . . ."

"Could he have used another name?"

"No, I recognize most of these. I'm sorry, Mr. Gereghty. Age or too many Manhattans, I'm not sure
which." He peered over bifocals at the now famous
snapshot. "I recognize him. He's someone I saw
around, waiting on me at The Oyster or with Nicole.
He's not someone I'd normally be interested in knowing. Perhaps you should speak with Roger, my
caretaker."

"He's the one who sent me to you, Bud." I tapped
my fingers on the edge of the chair and waited.
McCray was too much the banker to give away anything, including an honest reaction. He was bull-
shitting me and I wasn't sure why. Either Giancarlo

hadn't filled out an application or Bud had deep-sixed it. The only certainty was that it was coming up on cocktail hour and Bud probably wanted to toast the sunset with a glass, not a rental form, in his thick fingers.

"How do people find out about your rooms? Do you advertise?"

"Word of mouth mostly."

"Know who recommended our friend?"

"No, I don't recall. Look, Mr. Gereghty, leave me your card. I'll double-check at home. If I find anything, I'll give you a call. I have an appointment."

Standing up, I picked up a card from a desktop holder. "Better yet, Bud, I'll take one of yours. If you learn anything, I'll give you a call. We'll be talking."

As he struggled with what that meant, I knew I had Bud McCray's number. And, in some as yet undefined way, so did my quarry.

It was too late to catch the ferry without rushing, so I rested, eating supper, drinking spring water, walking the beach, and mulling over what I had: a model-thin, almost pretty young man, say, twenty-one or -two, allegedly Italian but more likely an American with a bad accent and a southeastern Massachusetts twang in his voice. No name and no SS number, nothing solid to work with for a trace. Just amorphous recollections of an ambiguous, unlikable, pretentious young boy toy who apparently wanted in the worst way to be in with the glitterati. I didn't know him and already I didn't like him. Less for who he seemed to be than for what he represented in terms of my client. I had been going along on autopilot, collecting the facts, not dwelling on the proprietary nature of the Nicole/Giancarlo relationship, hoping personal feelings wouldn't intrude. Standing on the sand, listening to a steady, lulling surf roll in, I tried to reconcile the supremely confident, unapologetic diva who'd paid for my services with the vulnerable woman who'd wept in my arms a decade ago. I couldn't do it. So I shifted back to the hunt and well into my surfside walk I came up with a solid idea on how to get some purchase on the phantom Giancarlo.

Back on the mainland I started hitting the libraries, beginning with Falmouth and working my way east from the lower Cape to Bristol County—Wareham, Fairhaven, New Bedford—checking high school yearbooks for the preceding five years, looking for a photo that resembled the one I had.

In Fall River I hit paydirt. Monsignor Connolly High, three years back. The hair was longer and the face fuller but the eyes that focused on some distant point were the same. His name was Brian Azevedo. Pep squad. Drama society. Latin club. Helped design the sets for a production of *The Glass Menagerie.* Played a small role in *Becket.* Plenty of candids, most with a frail-looking Brian surrounded by young women, laughing with them. Delicate-looking, artistic, flamboyant, and undoubtedly possessing a different world view than many of his classmates. In my high school days, someone fitting that description was automatically in for a lot of grief. No, make that a lot of shit. There was nearly twenty years between us, but in a Catholic school in a mill town many things remained constant over the years. There would always be more than enough ostracism to make an outsider want to pretend to be other than who he was the first chance he got.

His entry contained a street address in Fall River. Cross-checking with city directory gave me the rest of the family: father, Hector, a meat cutter; mother,

Christina, a seamstress; and an older brother, Raymond, a warehouseman. I copied it all down along with the phone number, then called Glenn Briody, a coworker from the congressional days who was now a Bristol County prosecutor, and offered to buy him lunch. He said make it dinner, then asked me what I really wanted. I gave him what I had on Brian Azevedo and asked if the name was familiar. He said he'd check and to call him later. That done, I headed out to locate the Azevedo residence and do a little presurveillance cruise of the neighborhood.

The Azevedos lived in north Fall River, in a two-story house with pale green aluminum siding that was perched three-quarters of the way up the slope of one of the steepest streets in the city of hills, mills, and porkpies. It was a thickly settled residential neighborhood with narrow, potholed side streets filled with parked cars. I knew at once that surveillance was going to be a problem. Fall River is a city of closely packed neighborhoods, chiefly Portuguese, Irish, and French, where children inherited their parents' homes and very few new faces popped up. Parking unobtrusively anywhere nearby was out of the question.

One of the city's ubiquitous factory outlets occupied much of the block below the Azevedos' and its parking lot offered an unobstructed view of the house, but the beefy security guard who hugged the entrance and occasionally strolled the lot precluded that possibility. A few hundred feet to the left was an untended cluster of trees, still overgrown with leaves, which I could burrow into with a set of binoculars and still be within sprinting distance of my car. It would have to do.

Supper turned out to be beer, sausages, and a Red Sox game on the tube at a sportsmen's club a few blocks from the courthouse. Between innings Glenn filled me in on what he'd learned.

"I didn't recognize the name but one of the other ADAs did. It was a case she'd had a couple of years ago, a hate crimes sort of thing. Some guys on a softball team beating up on this Azevedo because he looked light in his loafers. Janice was disappointed it never came to trial."

"Why didn't it?"

"Officially, he declined to press charges. The family wanted to protect its privacy. The real reason: the DA talked 'em out of it. He didn't want his office perceived as advocating for homosexuals. Not in this town. Not in an election year, anyway."

"Was Azevedo gay?"

"The clowns with the bats thought so. And perception's what the case was all about."

"No argument there, my friend."

Since Fall River is a city where many of the people go to work early, I was parked and squirreled under the trees before dawn the next morning, working on a large donut shop coffee and gazing up at the Azevedo house. A man in his mid-fifties, the father I assumed, headed off at 6:20 A.M. and a younger man, brother Raymond no doubt, left fifteen minutes later. Cars started up and left yards, kids piled out of houses and were scooped up by school buses. At 8:35, a short, thickset woman with gray hair stepped out on the side porch to shake out a dust mop, then crossed the street to another house. She returned an hour later and there was no further movement until half past twelve, when she came out to start up a well-kept Chrysler Le Baron that was several years old. She opened the car's side door, went back to the porch, and helped a very thin, very pale Brian Azevedo carefully negotiate the porch steps. He slipped into the passenger seat and she closed the door for him.

I bolted to my Escort and nudged it up to the corner in time to see them head up the hill and take a right. We drove south, then east, for about ten minutes until they turned into a hospital parking lot. I pulled into a space in another aisle and watched as they entered the building, Mrs. Azevedo struggling to keep from grasping Brian's elbow.

When she returned a few minutes later, I made my choice to stay. I entered the same way and found a waiting room to my left but no Brian. I strode through different corridors, adopting the quizzical squint of someone looking for a particular room. I spotted him through a narrow glass window embedded in a door marked Conference Room. He was one of several men and women sitting in a circle, some chatting, Brian flipping through a copy of *Premiere,* a comfortable smile/smirk on his face. It might have been a twelve-step group, except some of the people looked haggard as hell, including Brian, who was much thinner than the photo but unmistakably my Giancarlo.

"Can I help you, man?"

A large black hand was poised above my forearm, ready to swallow it whole in its grasp. I turned to face an orderly with a determined cast to his face, the look of a man who expected trouble as a response and was well equipped to handle it.

"Are you here for the clinic?" he asked, not raising his voice.

"I'm looking for a friend."

"Here?" He pointed a thumb at the door.

"I'm not sure. He wracked up his foot on his bike. Called, asked me to give him a lift home."

"Emergency's that way." He pointed the way I'd

come. "Go down there and keep on walking. Know what I mean?"

I did and I was gone, pausing only to grab a copy of the hospital newsletter on my way out. Figuring the orderly would alert security, I drove out and circled surrounding blocks until I found a nearby donut shop with a view of the parking lot. I bought a coffee and sipped it at a window seat while skimming the newsletter. In it I found an article about one of the hospital's programs and figured out why the orderly had been so suspicious of outsiders and so protective of the people behind that door.

The job had been unsettling from the beginning, due in no small part to my own conflicted feelings about a woman I'd known briefly but felt I'd known well and the changes a decade and inner drive had brought about. On an objective level, the question of motivation moved to the forefront. The stolen bracelet seemed spurious now, Nicole's sole motivation being an anger ignited and fueled by much more than desertion. If she'd been a complete stranger I might have walked, but now I needed to see it through, to know if what I'd learned meant what I thought it did. And if so, decide what I could and would do about it.

Dan Rather's voice was declaiming through open windows when I parked in front of the Azevedo house. I chose the side door, approaching as the friendly family insurance agent rather than the Jehovah's Witness on the march. Mrs. Azevedo answered and stared at me with large, suspicious eyes.

"Who're you?" The words tumbled out as one.

"My name's Matthew Gereghty, Mrs. Azevedo." I held up the photostat of my license in one hand and the photo of Brian in the other. "I'm a private investigator. I'm looking for your son, Brian."

"Not here!" There was panic in the two words. "Go away!"

"Do you know where he might be, ma'am?"

"No! No! No! Go away!" As she started to close the door, I wedged in my foot. At the same moment, there was movement behind me, then someone's breath on the back of my neck and two hands on my forearms, vising them into immobility. From behind Mrs. Azevedo, the father appeared, his thick face flushed red with anger. He motioned with his head and I was pushed through the door into the kitchen.

"Who're you and what you want with my boy?" His voice lacked his wife's hysteria but not her energy and concern.

"That's between me and your son, Mr. Azevedo."

"Smart-ass! You leave my family alone. My son done nothing."

"I'd like him to tell me that."

"Dad, let's just knock him around and get him out of here!" said the voice behind me.

Mr. Azevedo was considering this when an airy, singsong voice emerged from adjacent hallway.

"Ask him who hired him."

The hallway was dark but light from an upstairs source illuminated bare feet and a pair of blue-jeaned legs on the stairway. I looked at the Azevedos but spoke to the hallway.

"Tell Brian I'm working for Nicole Bannister."

"Let him go, Raymond," said the voice. "If he's working for her and he hasn't killed me yet, he won't hurt me now."

Raymond whispered a "Jesus!" and released my arms. Mr. Azevedo turned away and looked down at the floor. Mrs. Azevedo gazed with worry into the hallway. No one moved for a few moments, then I took a tentative step, to see if anyone would stop me. When they didn't, I walked out and started up the stairs. Brian was poised on the top step and staring down at me, his face obscured in shadow under the glare of an overhead light.

"Come on up into my parlor."

I followed Brian Azevedo into a large room with a bed in one corner, a small sofa against one wall, a television and stereo and two chairs, one of which faced a set of windows that provided a view down the hill to the Taunton River, gray and deep red in the setting sun, and the town of Somerset on the other side.

"I saw you out there this morning," he said casually, taking the chair. "Sprawling around in those trees like a kid playing soldier. I wondered if you had a rifle and I was going to be struck down by a sniper's bullet."

I took the other chair. "Why would you think that, Brian?"

"You don't think she would let me live, do you? I've been waiting for someone to come after me since the day I left. That's why I asked Walter to keep an eye out for strangers."

"Walter the orderly?"

"Yes. I don't know what he thinks of us deep down but he does know what it's like to be an outsider. He's very protective of us."

"I suppose the sessions might draw some cranks."

"Believe it! Not everyone is understanding." He pointed a finger at the floor, indicating the kitchen below us. "There's still a lot of fear and loathing."

"How long have you known you were HIV positive?"

"About a month."

"So you waited a few days before taking off?"

"It was very confusing at first. I was numb but then

I usually was. I carried on the best I could until Nicole called me in a rage one day and told me to come right over. I knew what it had to be. Probably a regular checkup with her doctor and 'surprise!' It was ugly. She made threats and came after me with a kitchen knife. See?" Brian lifted up his T-shirt and revealed a jagged slash of red along his abdomen. "I took the knife away from her and calmed her down, but I was scared. All of a sudden I actually felt something. Maybe I'm only a coward but I wasn't ready to check out."

"She tried to kill you?"

"This was just a snap reaction. But she's had time to dwell on it and you can believe that nothing short of nailing my balls to her front door will satisfy her now. She knows people, you know."

"What sort of people?"

"Dealers, club owners, people with connections. Nicole did a lot of entertaining and you don't entertain without a lot of controlled substances. She could pay someone to waste me."

"How do you know I'm not that someone?"

"Because my father and brother are standing outside that door with a baseball bat and a hammer and they'll be on you in a flash if you so much as make a move toward me."

"That's not why I'm here, Brian. Tell me about the bracelet."

He erupted in a full-throated laugh, one so deep and wide that it seemed better fitted on a man his father's size.

"That's wonderful! There is no bracelet, Mr. . . . is your name a secret?"

"Gereghty."

"Of course, you must be for real! She sold you that story. Why else would you look for me? Whenever she was pissed at me, she'd hold that above my head, threaten to tell the police I stole her jewelry, get me arrested and thrown in the tank with a bunch of predators."

"She said she wanted to confront you. That she felt abandoned and deserved an answer as to why you left her."

"You have a talent for getting people to open up if Nicole told you that."

"Let's just say I'm a careful listener."

He caught an irony in that I hadn't intended.

"You know her, don't you?"

"Once."

"From before she became 'Nicole'?"

I nodded.

"Tell me, what do you think of her now?"

Not much, I thought. But what I said was: "Everyone changes. She put together a new life after the old one turned to shit. Not the only person to do that. Some people change themselves after they get beaten up for no good reason and no one does anything about it."

Brian stared at me openmouthed. "Nicole did get her money's worth from you. I never even told her my real name or anything about Fall River. How did you do that?"

"With a great deal of difficulty. You didn't leave footprints. Bud McCray couldn't even find your rental application. Some reason?"

"That was Nicole. He was an old beau. Resented me, by God, but a puppy dog that jumped every time she told him to. Waived the paperwork and the rent because she asked him."

"That doesn't make sense. He would have helped locate you, to please Nicole if not out of jealousy."

"Maybe he had his own motive." Brian stared out

the window, the pale rose sunset light bathing his face. It was a conscious pose, but the tone of his voice was sober now. "You probably think I infected Nicole but maybe it was the other way around. We think of ourselves as the recipients not the initiators."

"Are you saying she infected Bud?"

"Like the ad on TV: 'You tell two friends and they tell two friends . . .' Neither of us were aggressively monogamous, Mr. Gereghty. There were nights she pointedly told me not to come around because she was entertaining someone from a network or a national magazine and the entertainment wasn't reading her columns aloud. And I'd use those nights to get fucked up and . . . explore. I'd say old Bud got the bad news from his doctor and he wanted to confront Nicole or me."

The thought of an angry Bud McCray bird-dogging my tail. Dammit, I hadn't considered the possibility. Or any motive other than Nicole's seeking emotional satisfaction.

"I was hired to find you, not put you at risk, Brian. You might want to activate the Azevedo family underground railway for a few days. I can tell Nicole I found you but withhold the location until I'm sure McCray isn't after you."

He came up with a weak smile. "You've been so busy chasing me, I bet you haven't had the time to read the newspaper, have you?"

I shook my head and pondered the punch line that must be coming.

"Here." He reached beside the chair and lobbed over a copy of that afternoon's Fall River *Herald News*. "Down at the bottom of page three."

It was an AP brief, datelined the Vineyard. Local banker Walter "Bud" McCray found shot to death in his home, an apparent suicide.

"Suicide, my ass," said Brian Azevedo.

"Could be."

"No!" He was completely serious. "I know her. He confronted her and she did what she always does with a problem, she removed it. If she finds out where I am, Mr. Gereghty, she will kill me."

"She doesn't have any feeling for you?"

"We both had our compassion stripped off too many times. We don't give, we use." He waved his hand around the room. "Don't think I haven't been using my family's guilt to be well treated. When we absolutely cannot get our way, we hurt. Nicole will want my life for taking hers. That's how she'll see it."

The door opened and Mr. Azevedo stood there. With a hammer in his hand. "My son make up a lotta things," he said. "But this woman, she hurt him I'm sure."

"Convince me about the bracelet," I told Brian. "Then I'll do some checking. Then we'll see what's what."

Nicole drew back with the speed and snap of a cobra, a look of disbelief on her contorted face as the knife slipped from her fingers and fell silently onto the rug. She struggled against the arms of the tall man who held her, then froze as she heard the sound of her own voice caught on tape. The threat, the venom, the sheer viciousness of her tone echoed through the bedroom, sounding odd in its distance and disembodied quality.

"*. . . years putting myself together. Taking care of me! I was never going to be at anyone's beck and call ever again! Now you've taken that all away from me, you silly little boy. You were an amusement, to fill my needs, not fill me with poison!*"

Brian Azevedo's voice emerged in response: "*That*

doesn't stop you from finding another me, sweetie. The Vineyard's full of us. So's Boston. And you're not going to tell anyone you tested positive, are you? Even the owner of that little TV station of yours. He'll find out the way Bud did, won't he?"

"You little prick!"

"Must've gotten the word from his doctor, 'Bud, I have some bad news for you . . .' "

"Cocksucker!" On the videotape the knife was a silver blur in Nicole's hand, raised and ready to plunge when the off-duty Fall River police detective stepped through the door into Brian's bedroom and ordered Nicole to drop it.

Now, Nicole teetered on her heels, shifting in the cop's arms, wanting to lunge at someone or something, but confused as to who in the room was now her worst enemy. I helped answer that question by stepping inside. Right behind me was Rickey Moreia, a New Bedford criminal attorney with a reputation as a major hardball player in and out of the courts. He didn't give Nicole time to react.

"Once you've calmed down, Ms. Bannister, we're either going to broker a deal here or you're going to jail. Right now, you're facing a charge of assault with intent to commit murder. We're ready to push it to the limit. But you have an option. The Azevedo family would like to maintain its privacy, allow Brian to wait out his illness in peace. That means not worrying that you or someone you hire will come around again and try to kill him. I understand how shattering the experience of testing positive must be, but there's no proof my client infected you. And your sheets are hardly unsullied, ma'am."

"What do you want?" Nicole's voice was a cold sliver.

"The deal is this: You leave my client alone. You

sign a statement to that effect which I will hold. You leave this area: the Vineyard, Boston, New England. Yours is a gypsy profession. Seek other employment opportunities."

"You're a smug son of a bitch."

"Bet your ass, lady. If we go public, I will get dirty. And you do have kids. They may be grown-up and living with their father—your revenge on him, I take it—but if you feel anything at all for them . . ."

"I get your point." She turned to the detective. "I have cigarettes and a lighter in my bag, May I?" He looked at Moreia, who nodded. The cop released Nicole and extracted a slim gold lighter and a pack of Vantage from the bag. Nicole lit up with a snap, made a display of exhaling smoke, then fixed Moreia with an all-business stare. "We have a ways to go. Let's negotiate, tough guy."

The negotiations took two hours and seemed more and more absurd as the night went on. By the time it was done, the signed statement was history but Nicole allowed the tape to remain in existence, to be locked in a safe deposit box, one key for her and one for Brian. In return, the family agreed to press no charges and say nothing about the events of the evening. It was all probably illegal but it was also the epitome of small-city justice. The fix was in but it had saved a life.

Moreia did tell Nicole that she was on her own in the matter of Bud McCray. She said she wasn't overly concerned about the efficiency of the Vineyard cops. I didn't mention the state police.

On her way out Nicole stopped in front of me, acknowledging me for the first time since I'd stepped in the room. "Your idea?" she asked.

"Once I knew, I had to know if you'd try to kill him. Even for friends, I don't set people up."

"But you take your client's money."

"Check's in the mail."

"I'll send it back. I pay my bills. I pay my way. In fact, I pay for everything, don't I?" Deep crimson lips pulled back from her teeth to form a grin and the small laugh that emerged with her next words was bitter. "Enjoy your life, you judgmental bastard!"

State police or no, Nicole dodged the bullet on Bud McCray. She resigned abruptly from the TV job, citing a desire to "expand her horizons," though Molly Benedict, in her column in the Boston *Globe,* alluded to rumors of some sort of impropriety hastening Nicole's departure. Several months later I received a rambling telephone call from Brian Azevedo, wondering if I'd seen Molly's squib about "once-sultry Nicole Bannister, with more eyeliner and lacquered hair than the EPA will allow in the Bay State, is now delivering grit-'n-gossip to the good farmers of Mobile, Alabama." I steered the conversation back to Brian, who admitted he'd tired of playing the invalid and had started courses in stage design at the local university. He seemed sincere but there was enough of a wiseass tone in his voice to make me wonder if he'd matured at all. His next sentences convinced me he hadn't.

"Guess she's too far away to hurt me."

"Not likely, Brian."

"You're a detective, right? You find things?"

"What is it, Brian?"

"Why don't you find me Geraldo Rivera's phone number? I've got a great idea for a show for him."

"He vacations on the Vineyard, kid. Go ask him yourself."

He laughed long and loud on that one and said good-bye. I sat and pondered how people can be made to feel so bad about who they are that they become someone else and hurt so often that victims become predators. Then I thought of Nicole and where she was and the anger and the secret she carried with her and I shuddered for a few of the good citizens of Mobile.

But I still didn't call directory assistance.

SIDEWAYS
BY REX MILLER

Annie Stranucella is dead. I miss her. I hadn't seen her for a couple of years, but when she surprised everybody by marrying Ritchie Brown three years ago they sent me an invitation to the wedding. We were always tight, in our fashion, Annie and me. I knew all three of her husbands and her father. Went to school with her. Worked for her dad once. Never knew either of her sons but—hell—nobody knew her sons. Dead at forty-five. Ain't it a shame, as they say. My tears fell like rain when I heard about it from one of the guys at Meirhoffer's.

She was, in her day, the girl who had it all—or so everybody thought. She was gorgeous. To the day she died she had the best-looking legs of any woman in St. Joe. Beautiful face. A smile that killed. The whole schmear. Lovely looker from head to toe. Smart. Funny. But she was one of *those* kind. The kind who—for whatever reason—like to hurt themselves. That's all over now. Finally.

We had a lot in common, Annie and I. We both smoked, drank, kissed, and liked to do the hootchie-koo. In all the years I knew her I never made a pass at her. I knew better. We kissed and hugged and cuddled all over hell and gone. But she trusted me and we were pals. As much as a horny guy can be pals with a beautiful honey like Ann. She had some terrific qualities.

She was hilariously funny when she wanted to be. That was her best feature—next to her mouth, that killer mouth, those shapely Hollywood legs, that great behind, nice hard little—well, for god's sake the lady was hot stuff. But she was funny and nice and tough and a stand-up chick and you could depend on her and she would be there for a friend at three a.m. and she didn't bad-mouth people and she paid her debts and I guess the truth is . . . I loved her. In our fashion we always loved each other. I know she loved me as a friend, and I loved her because how could you not? What was not to love about old Stranootch? How the *hell* can she be dead at forty-five? Oh, boy.

She had her faults. I'll be the first to tell you that. Who doesn't? She went through one of her worst times, I guess, in the early sixties. That was when her dad hired me to follow her. Very sad, weird business it turned out to be.

I was twenty-three and had just quit the county gig, where I'd put in an unpleasant year in Prisoner Transport, mostly taking scared black kids to Booneville, and I hung out my first P.I. ticket. That was over across the line in Cowtown. Eventually I moved back home, where private investigators aren't licensed by the state—they operate under the St. Joseph Municipal Code—but that was later.

You can't even find the *block* my first office was in, much less the old Gateway Arcade Building. It was at Eleventh and Commerce, and the front door was inside *another* front door—you couldn't find it even then! Sheldon Zimmler, the bail bond guy, had his offices next to the antique shop that he also ran, on one side of the arcade lobby, and Gateway Finance was on the other side. In the middle of the lobby was the second door that led downstairs. I can still see that big painting of an ugly hand with a cocked thumb and first finger like a *gun* pointing down toward hell. Breaks me up every time I think about it. And there was a sign that told what offices were down the stairs.

Somewhere at home in a box of junk or a scrapbook I know I still have an old photo of that sign. I was proud of it, if you can imagine, with my name TERRY KOCHENGE, PRIVATE INVESTIGATOR. So fucking corny I have to laugh remembering what a punk I was. But I was a kid. Twenty-three. World by the tail. Not a bad kid as St. Joe punks go. I was an okay guy, I guess. My philosophy was try to never hurt anybody. Sounds simple, I know. But it's the way I tried to live my life for a long time. I didn't want to leave anybody worse than I found them. That's probably why I hated Prisoner Transport so much.

Private-eye stuff isn't much like you'd imagine it. If your experience is books, movies, TV, you'll have an image that's fun but it has nothing to do with the work. It's basically just routine investigative work, paperwork, surveillance, that kind of thing. Nowadays it's completely different, of course, with investigative agencies specializing in such things as parental kidnappings—but when I started it wasn't the colorful business you might have imagined.

A kitchen table agency could pretty much sculpt their business to run any way they wanted it to, and if one was honest and worked hard, a rep could be established without too much trouble. We only had a couple of local people in it back then, when I started in Cowtown. There was a guy who specialized in industrial work, a security guy, a sleazeball who just did domestic stuff—and the kid here. I came in with an advantage. Everybody in my family had been in law enforcement.

My dad had been a state trooper for eight or nine years, my uncle John was with the feds all his life—

so I was "with the program." I already had ties to the locals, I was leaving County with my bridges intact, I was in Kappa Alpha Pi (Zeta Chapter), with the sons of the big attorneys, I'd gone with the daughters of the guys who owned a couple of the biggest insurance agencies in St. Joe—and—you can see where I'd started with the advantages of familiar contacts. St. Joe back then was like a big family. A big *unhappy* family, but still . . .

You read about the beautiful, sexy blondes who come into the private eye's office looking to find black statues with jewels hidden in them, or you see the movie or TV show with the wisecracking tough guy. Sorry. I never had a blond woman get *near* my office. A couple of blond (bleached) wrestlers once, but no females. I was my own secretary. I dealt with trust officers at the bank, lawyers, and insurance agents. None of these guys encourage a whole lot of ha-ha on the job, although I've known some folks in all three professions who were pretty damn flaky.

It's not like law enforcement work either. It's largely civil stuff and you're trying to help build cases, essentially, or provide background information, and you want a *cherry* rep. That's why I decided from the first I wouldn't do any domestics, I wouldn't pad anybody's bill, I wouldn't do any of the schlock stuff the ma-n'-pa shops do—I would go the high road. I think that's why I lasted so long. I kept a low profile and played it as straight as I could.

It wasn't that easy, when I was getting started. Old man Zimmler upstairs called me a few times—wanting to get me to do some things. I stayed away from it— even though I was doing a lot with the insurance people. Basically he got guys to work as bounty hunters: you'd go after bail jumpers on straight commish, for a quarter or third of recovery, typically. You look for patterns and trails, and a good hunter can score better than half the time. But I would have hated that kind of stuff—to me they were worse than repo men. It just wasn't my gig.

My reason for going into all this is so you can understand what sort of an office I was running. I didn't do hardly any walk-in business. You'd have been pretty disappointed if you'd have followed the big finger down the linoleum-covered stairs into the basement or "sublevel," as they called it, of the Gateway Arcade. Harmony Records' entrance was to the left, the Black Dragon Tae Kwon Do outfit was in the center, and I was on the right. If you tried the doors you'd generally find them all locked!

The couple who had owned Harmony had gone belly up before I opened for business, and the "5th Degree Black Belt Instructors" who'd tried to make a go of the martial arts thing had also fared poorly. I was such a social nerd—when it came to *business* as opposed to partying—that I kept my door locked most of the time. This used to piss my dad off so bad I cannot tell you.

"How do you expect to build a business when you've got your office door locked?" he'd ask me.

"Mr. Zimmler keeps his door locked and he makes more'n you do," I'd wise off to him. It was true, of course, but that was the door to the antique shop. I didn't make a habit out of wiseing off to my old man, by the way. He was six-two, 230, big and rough like all the male relatives on his side of the family, and if you screwed with him on a bad day he'd knock your sorry butt to *China.* Trust me on that one.

All of which brings me back to Annie.

It was Dad got me the thing shadowing her, which was hard-earned dough in the end.

Dad and D.D. Stranucella were old bar-hopping

buddies. Before my old man joined the rods, when he was fresh out of the Corps, he and D.D. used to go to these badass roadhouse joints and clean them out. This was their idea of fun, or so my uncles told me. Personally, being devoutly chicken is a serious religion, and I brook no threats of violence. I can't imagine a situation where getting into a bar fight would be *fun.* Clearly I was the recipient of all the wussy genes in the Kochenge line.

I truly fear all forms of violence and have never been in a fight in my life. Not a fistfight. A couple of *gun*fights but . . . No, I'm kidding. Trying to put on a happy face. No—I would be petrified if someone pulled a weapon of any kind on me. I do not own or carry a weapon, and have never been in the kind of situation where one needed a club or whatever for self-defense. Lawyers, insurance guys, bank people—they can *kill* you—but they very seldom *hit* you.

Violence, the kind I've seen, is always experienced ex post facto. I look at a lot of the aftereffects of violence, but that's different. I don't even handle cases involving violence. Domestic violence stuff I generally refer to one of the big K.C. houses like Wells or Pinks—one of those shops. Back then, as I said, we had a guy who'd take child and spouse abuse cases and the like. I stayed clear of them. Prissy little punk that I was.

Imagine my surprise when the Chief of Police of the St. Joseph Missouri Police Department asked me to tail Ann, his daughter.

I was in my Chevy tooling through Krug Park, as I recall, and suddenly I looked up and saw a red ball in my rearview mirror. *WHEEEP,* one time with the siren. I saw the driver, a tough Mexican who Dad said was on the wrong side of the bars, and D.D.

D.D. was physically a juggernaut of contradictions.

Massive, quick, fireplug stout, diffident in manner, fearless, shy—the sort of dude you'd never completely know. I guess Dad knew him as well as anybody. He had some bizarre first name; one of those odd daffy double ding-dongs like Donald Duck or Dick Daring that he was ashamed of, probably Denise Darcel or something—so he was D.D. or Stranooch, which was how I got to call Annie that, hearing Dad talk about how "ole Stranooch jumped over the bar at Red's with a sawed-off cue." But I never called him anything but chief.

"Hey, boy," he said, blotting out the sun as he came up by the window.

"Howdy, Chief."

"You in a big hurry?"

"No, sir—" I said, misunderstanding him. "Was I going too fast?" He just smiled.

"Probably. I wanna talk to ya. Come on out of the car a minute."

I wondered how I had stepped in it. I got out. Standing next to him was an awe-inspiring experience, and I was used to being around large, tough, powerful men. Athletes. Guys who liked to roughhouse for fun. He was more like a pro football player—you *felt* the raw power. There we were, with me completely vulnerable: the tough Mexican cop in the car, staring straight ahead through his shades; D.D., like a small tree; both these guys armed to the teeth. Krug Park Drive—not a chipmunk in sight. If he told you to shit you'd be straining in the dirt, it was that simple a deal.

"You went to school with Ann."

"Right. Great girl." I smiled brightly. Fatuously. Three bags full.

"Yeah. Me n' your father 'tipped a few back' together—did you know that?" He moved away as I began to answer him. "Come on—let's walk."

We walked, down the grassy slope of the shoulder where my Chevy was parked. The tough guy *followed* us—it was weird—right off the road down the bank. No road there but hell, never mind, I guess he followed the boss. It was fortunate Stranucella didn't go wading or he would have probably driven into the duck pond.

"I want her tailed. I want it confidential. I want her watched around the clock and I want to know who her dope connection is."

"Sorry?"

"Her dope connection. Her *drug dealer*."

"Oh." What do you say . . . ? If you'd ever *seen* Annie you'd know how totally Looney Tunes that was. Annie doing drugs? Naah.

"Surprised?" A shy look for just that one second.

"Yes, sir—I sure am."

"She's a hype. She's got tracks all over her. Arms. Legs. Needle marks in her *feet for Christ's good sake!*"

"You know how long . . ." I stopped the question instantly.

He closed his big, droopy eyes and shook his head.

"No. I know she's a mess. Acts goofy as all get out—but she's always been like that." He looked at me as if I were the cause of her acting that way. "She's getting worse. I made her show me her arms the other day and she's scarred from Atchison to Topeka—man she is definitely on the needle. I want you to get as many people as it takes and find out who. It shouldn't take more than a few days. She may even be doing bad things to get the money. I want to know everything—understand? Where she gets it. Who the dealer is. What she's into. How she comes up with the cash—everything. I'll handle it from that point. And this can't be fucked up—read me?"

"Yes, sir." I guess there was no question of whether

I'd accept it or not. He could close *Cowtown* down, and me with it. He'd squash me like a flea. "I'll do my best."

"Outstanding. You come to me personally—at the station or at home—when you know something."

"Sure. I'll get right on it." No question of cost. I'd always heard Mrs. Stranucella was the one with the money—that the chief had married into big loot. When they don't ask how much they're either loaded or they're not going to pay. One of the two.

I wanted this gig like I wanted surgery. There was no coke back then—a few doctors and rich folks—but not in Cowtown or St. Joe. There was hash, reefer, mescaline, LSD was coming along—and of course heroin. Annie on smack was so absurd on the face of it I wondered what the hell was involved, and what she was into. I'd heard her marriage to Hog Haner had already gone on the rocks.

Parenthetically, Hog Haner (despite his nickname) was a handsome jock star from Benton whose father had fixed him up with an executive job over at Hoof & Horn Cattle Auctions in Elwood. I'd heard Ann had moved out of the house on Libel in Elwood, Kansas, when she'd become pregnant with their first child— Carl.

I hated the case from the very start. I'd never had anyone legit talk to me in that manner, in that tone to begin with; but to supply no information, no background; not even wait around for my questions! (Did I put enough negatives in that sentence? If not, here's another—it didn't feel right. Not for a heartbeat.)

I went to Dad. He said exactly what I figured he would say—he told me I was in business, this was business, no problem—take it. Take the case and do your best. To Dad it was an easy world. Everything was black. White. No gray areas. You went in a bar, minded your business, someone screwed with you, you picked up a pool cue and knocked their dick in the dirt. Why make life difficult? Do your work and be happy in your work. Simple.

I hired four operatives. Three hours on. Nine hours off. TFN. Everybody got the same; and depending on the outcome we'd split the pie five ways. Pay your own expenses. I brought two in from Kansas City, one from Savannah, and a girl all the way from Des Moines. (She could play street tag for *days* and you'd never make her. Very slick, and *so* pro!)

Ben somebody, a guy from K.C., was on her when we got onto the thing. Fourth day of the case. She and some street skuzz went into the old Player's in Cowtown. He came out to the house and told me about it when it went down. The guy was watching the pair of them from across the width of the darkened lounge. Saw them feeling each other up, messing with one another beneath the table. Goofing off, acting very high, giggling all the while. He assumed that between the time he'd laid back—waiting in the parking lot—and then gone on in as if he were a customer walking in for a drink, that they'd had time to fix or drop or snort whatever it was. There's quite a bit of noise in the place anyway, but after a bit the waitress came over. Said something. There was very loud talking. Laughter. Yelling. The bar owner or bouncer came out and made them leave.

Ben got up to follow them and walked by the booth where they'd been sitting. The waitress was trying to get the mess cleaned up. Ben said to her, "What happened? Somebody get hurt?"

"Two *massies*," she said. Hell, neither Ben nor I had ever heard the expression. "Massies. They're high or whatever and they get their rocks off with razors.

They were over here cutting each other's legs. Crazy idiots!"

I told the man. Got him out of bed, wondering whether he would be relieved she wasn't hooked on heroin or sad to learn she was this screwed up. Obviously she needed a good doctor's care and I said so. He agreed but old cops are not easy to rattle. He thanked me for my work. Told me to send him our bill. That was pretty much it.

I supposed that her first marriage had gone sour. I could scarcely believe my gorgeous Annie had taken a turn down such a dark road, but—what did I know? Personally, I didn't know a massie from Raymond Massey. It was out of my league.

My bill consisted of expenses for the ops and a nominal fee—a hundred and change for the four days—and he paid it promptly. I did pretty much as I'd been instructed and put the case out of my mind. I don't know what I thought about it all. Who am I to judge someone? If persons want to stick needles in their feet or slash one another with razor blades for *laughs*—I frankly find it so far outside my understanding as to be completely beyond me. I never could fathom the real freaky stuff.

Years later—her folks were dead, my folks were both gone—I was pleased to hear she'd remarried and was apparently happy. She had a couple of nice-looking boys, one with Haner, who had also remarried, and one who lived with her. Over the many years we'd see each other around town, and hug on the street the way you do—St. Joe is a big hick town. Then we lost touch for a while.

Three years back, when I learned the news about Ritchie, who comes from big-time Roubidoux-era money, and Ann getting married, I was happy for both of them. When people drift in and out of marriages

over the years you always wish the best for them but—
let's be honest: you never expect too much. Ritchie
and Annie seemed like an odd couple but sometimes
those turn out to be the best marriages. I knew her
own sons were long gone from the nest. One had
dropped into the drug culture apparently. The other
was in Florida and doing well, so the gossip had it. I
never knew either boy.

The moment I heard from the funeral home I had
an inkling—just a nudge—that it was a case without
a bottom. Supposedly it was a cut and dried suicide,
and perhaps since I knew about her past I assumed
the worst, that she'd been up to her old tricks and
someone got carried away. Went too far dealing out
the pain. But no. She'd taken gas, they told me.

I had to walk in my old buddy's footprints a little.
I went out to where they'd come across her. In back
of a small frame home out on Messanie.

She was found dead in an old gal's collapsing garage. Nobody knew why she'd picked that place. It
was full of magazines. Moth-eaten, ratty old chewed
National Geographics and back issues of *Life* moldering away; *Look*; the old *Saturday Evening Post*—big
slick mags going back thirty or forty years—*Collier's*.
All these old magazines around the garage. Ruined by
age and dampness. Annie in her new car, dead.

Even after the gas was cleared out it stunk of death
in there. Smelled as only stacks of old paper or a
"sideways" can smell: it is a rankness of moist, slimy
things, spiders, snakes, rats, mice, tiny furry creatures,
and mildew; rotting pulp stained by the high tides of
a thousand rainstorm leaks, in a garage full of carbon
monoxide traces and dashed dreams. She'd come to
buy old magazines—"all you can carry away" for five
bucks, the landlady had advertised. I have not a clue

as to why she wanted them. It's not relevant. The whole deal stunk.

I was going outside for some fresh air and one of the guys whom I've known for years commiserated with me about her. We'd both been schoolmates with her and he knew that she and I had been close friends through her three marriages and assorted problems.

"Hell of a damn waste. So pretty and all," he said.

"Yep. Sure is."

"She had a rough life, you know. I guess you know better than I do."

"Mm—" I didn't know what to say.

"You know there were always rumors of incest and things . . . in her family." He said it softly, assuming I already knew.

"I never heard that," I told him, truthfully.

"Just rumors—years ago. Christ! I don't even know the details." I could tell he was sorry he'd said anything.

"You mean—her father?"

"Yeah . . . Her father and her. And then—you know, she and the boys. I don't *know* any of that you understand. It could just be typical St. Joe bullshit. You know this fuckin' town."

"Yeah." I smiled. "Too well." I waved. "So long."

"Take care."

The boys, Carl and Michael (and the stepson, I saw the names in the *News-Press* obit), they couldn't be located I'm told. Not that they would come to the funeral anyway. Ritchie Brown didn't show up either.

I've seen a lot of suicides and I didn't totally like the look of it but, hell—I'm not that involved one way or the other. It's remotely possible she sat there reading old magazines and sucking gas. It could also be a homicide—you know how it is, in my business you learn to think the worst of people. Maybe she messed with Ritchie Brown's boy and he put her to sleep. Suicide, homicide, or—we have a word for it in the P.I. game—a "sideways." A sui-sideways. Could go either way, right? One thing sure, it's all over for Annie.

I'm not going to do anything about it. Fuck it, It's history. But, old habits being what they are, I dragged down the case law on Missouri 565.032, and I'm sitting here reading about OFFENSES AGAINST THE PERSON and missing Annie Stranucella and feeling weird.

CAN SHOOT
BY MICHAEL COLLINS

The misery, greed, and hate that breed most violent crime, and the vanity and arrogance that account for the rest, exist in Santa Barbara as well as New York. But Santa Barbara isn't New York, and out here walk-in trade is rare in my line of work.

"It's my brother, Mr. Fortune. He was murdered down here and the police won't do anything about it. They won't even listen to me. They just—"

"Slow down, Mr.—?"

My office is in our house, the address is unlisted, and in southern California nobody actually walks, so walk-in means a phone call from someone I don't know. A stranger with a problem who found me in the phone book under "Investigators—Private."

"Morgan Jones. My brother was David Jones. Mr. Bowan had no reason to shoot him. No—"

"Humphrey Bowan?"

Humphrey Bowan was one of Montecito's richest residents. He'd bought an old Dodge estate up on East Valley Road where the rich liked to build in the last century: away from the foggy ocean and not in the hot and dry mountains. Bowan lived there half the year, spent the rest of his time up in San Mateo County at his corporate headquarters—Bowan Industries, Inc., with interests in lumbering, mining, insurance, etc.

"He killed Dave right there on his big estate."

"Come out to my office."

When he came in the office door he looked exactly like his voice. A heavy man in his fifties, with a full head of thick dark hair going gray and a shy manner. He saw my left arm was missing, looked stricken for me, and tried hard to not look again.

"It's okay," I said. "I lost it forty years ago, give or take. And you can sit down."

Morgan Jones sat down. He took off his John Deere cap, held it in his lap. We sat there looking at each other.

"You can talk, too. You said your brother was killed 'down here.' Where are you from, Mr. Jones?"

"Placerville. Dave lived in King City. I came down to Santa Barbara to talk to the police, but they won't listen."

"What do you do, Morgan?"

"I run a farm. It's small. Dave worked with all kinds of big animals. He always liked the horses. That's why he went to college up at Davis, got to be a doctor."

"Doctor? You mean a veterinarian?"

"He was the smart one. That's why I know Mr. Bowan didn't have any cause to shoot him. I don't know what he was doing there, but I know for sure it wasn't to steal anything."

"Who says he was there to steal something?"

"Mr. Bowan and the cops. They say he had a gun, broke into the house, and stole some money and other stuff."

"Did he have a gun? Had he stolen anything?"

Morgan Jones was stubborn. "David never even owned a gun. And he didn't need any money. Vets do real good up in farming country. He had three kids in college, and he didn't owe a dime to anyone. He even left me money in his will."

"We don't always know everything about someone else, even our brother. How close were you?"

Jones looked at his hat in his lap. "We didn't see each other so much. I mean, him in King City, and me all the way up around Placerville. But I knew Dave, and he wasn't on that estate to steal or hurt anyone."

"Why was he on the estate?"

He looked longer at the hat. "I don't know."

"Did he know Bowan? Anyone else on the estate?"

"I don't know."

What he really wanted was to know there had been a reason for his brother to die like that. He had to know, one way or the other. He wanted someone besides the police to tell him his brother had died because he'd been a thief.

"Okay, Morgan, I'll look into it. How did you find me, by the way? Yellow pages?"

"I told the cops I was going to get my own detective. That Sergeant Koons said I should call you."

Sheriff's detectives don't usually send me business.

Sheriff's headquarters is in Goleta out near the city dump and across from the county jail. In his office, major crimes detective Sergeant Josh Koons pulled the file out of his desk.

"The lieutenant says if the brother was like him, no wonder he got shot. The undersheriff says it's a closed case."

"What do you say?"

Koons opened the file. "We got this call about midnight, three weeks ago Thursday. Homicide in Montecito. When we got there, we found David Jones dead inside the twelve-foot wall around Bowan's estate. He'd been shot once in the head with a high-powered rifle, died instantly. Bowan, his chauffeur, and his head groundskeeper were waiting with the body.''

He closed the file, recited from memory, "Bowan's up in his bedroom reading when he hears someone out on the grounds near the house. He looks out, sees a man in dark clothes outside French doors into his office-den. He keeps cash and valuables in a safe in the den, so he runs down. The den's empty, the French doors are open, one pane is broken. He grabs one of his rifles from the wall, shoves in a clip, runs out. The chauffeur, William Berra, hears the man, too, comes out of the garage with the gun he carries because they drive around with large sums of cash. The head groundskeeper, Anselmo Cortez, also hears someone and goes out to look. They all meet, hear the guy running through the trees and brush toward the wall. They chase him, and Bowan spots him. He fires a couple of warning shots in the air, and when the guy doesn't stop, shoots to wing him. The guy zags when he was supposed to zig, gets hit in the head. When we arrive we find a gun on him, cash and jewels from the safe in a bag. The guy's dressed all in black with a ski mask. We check Bowan's rifle, three shots are gone. Bowan is upset as hell, but the coroner's inquest takes ten minutes to bring in justifiable homicide.''

Koons finished, put the file back into his desk.

I looked at the drawer where he'd put it. "That's it?"

"Tragic, but the guy was committing a felony.''

I said, "If it had been me, and I'd shot a guy in clear self-defense, I'd still go to a grand jury."

Koons shrugged. Humphrey Bowan wasn't me.

"You trace his gun?''

"An old Colt .45 automatic that disappeared way back in World War Two. Hadn't shown up anywhere since.''

"Jones was in the service? Maybe his father?"

"Both of them were conscientious objectors."

"Jones has a long burglary sheet?"

"No real sheet at all."

"What does 'no real sheet' mean? Does he have a record or not?"

"He'd been arrested three or four times."

"For what?"

"Damaging federal property. Resisting arrest." Koons looked out his window. "He was an antinuclear nut, a peacenik, an environmental activist back in the seventies."

"He was in bad financial trouble. Needed money."

"Yearly income over a hundred thousand, half a mil in bonds. Three kids in college. A widower who owned his own house and had a steady girlfriend his own age who said he was solid as a rock. Didn't gamble, drink, or chase other women."

I said, "Let me see if I've got this straight. You can't trace the gun to him. He's got no record of ever using a gun; in fact, he's antiwar and weapons. He has no criminal record at all, when ninety-nine-point-nine percent of burglars are pros with sheets longer than Bowan's family tree. He doesn't need money, is an educated professional man and a solid pillar of the community. Have I got it right?"

Koons looked out his window. "He was dressed all in black with a ski mask. He had the gun, he had the loot. Even if the gun and loot were planted, I found no connection at all between him and Bowan or any-one else on the estate. And how could they have had a complete black outfit in his exact size, and a black ski mask, on hand to dress him in?"

"It's possible."

"The labels in the clothes were all from King City stores. I went up there to check the stores. Three different places remembered selling 'the Doc' the pants, the turtleneck, and the ski mask. I was up there a week, and I found no connection between Jones and Bowan or anyone on the estate. All I found was he'd bought the clothes a couple of days before he came down here. That's when the lieutenant said it was my last trip on the case, and the undersheriff wrote closed."

We both sat there looking out his one window. There's a lot of noise in a police headquarters. All kinds of voices, laughs, whines, violent shouts, radios.

"It doesn't bother you a little?"

"It bothers me a lot. But look at it from the other angle. Bowan fired warning shots, then shot an armed burglar and accidentally killed him. He has two witnesses who back him up. The dead man had a gun, the loot, and was dressed for burglary. He had a leather bag with him for the loot. An investigation found no connection between Jones and Bowan, and no reason to doubt the story told by Bowan and the other two. The sheriff said anything more would be harassing a man because he was prominent. Bowan puts money and time into the county and into the sheriff's campaigns."

"You traced the bag to Jones?"

"No. With the gun, it's the two things we can't trace."

I listened to the headquarters noises some more. "Bowan grabbed the rifle from his wall. Does he have a lot of rifles on that wall? Maybe pistols?"

"Rifles, shotguns, pistols. Trophy heads of all the world's large predators. He's a gun nut and a hunter."

"How far was he from David Jones when he aimed to wing him and hit him dead center of the skull?"

"Coroner says about fifty feet."

"Feet?"

"Feet," Koons said. "It was dark, the trees and brush are thick out there."

"How did Jones open the safe?"

"It's an easy safe. Bowan says he might have left it open."

"Jones's fingerprints on it?"

"He wore gloves. Black."

I listened to the sounds outside the office some more. "The two witnesses both work for Bowan."

"Why was Jones there that night? Dressed like a burglar?"

"They won't let you do any more on it."

"Not a prayer."

"Well then, it looks like I need to find a reason for David Jones to have been on the estate dressed like a burglar."

"I never said that. But it's funny, somehow I feel I missed something."

There are two ways to drive north from Santa Barbara. Both are beautiful drives, each takes the same time, give or take a few minutes depending on traffic. The longer freeway is faster and safer, the mountain pass is shorter, slower, and more varied. I told Kay, the lady who lets me live with her, I'd be back in a few days or less, and took the pass and backcountry route. It's more peaceful and relaxing.

The pass road rejoined the freeway beyond Los Olivos, and from Buellton north the drive alternated between the warm, dusty, and brown inland valleys, and the cool, foggy, and green coast. With mountains always somewhere to the right or left or both. A pleasant land, southern California, with gentle days and easy rhythms, where the only extremes are earthquakes, fires, floods, and man. North of the Cuesta grade the day ended in a long twilight at Paso Robles, and by King City night had settled in.

King City is the dusty and brown interior. One of those small inland cities of California that seem to have no particular reason to exist except to provide fast-food stops and gasoline stations for the stream of travelers on the freeway. The real reason is in the two main features of the city: the restored and rebuilt Mission San Antonio de Padua, twenty miles southwest, founded by Fr. Junípero Serra on July 14, 1771; and the Monterey County Agricultural and Rural Life Museum right in town.

David Jones's house was two miles out of town on county highway G14 toward Jolon, the military reserve of Fort Hunter Liggett and the wooded mountains of the Los Padres National Forest. A large, three-story white frame Victorian, it had probably once been the mansion of a local ranch baron who married into the old Spanish land grant hidalgos, ended up with the girl and the land. His veterinarian's shingle hung out front, and his office, like mine, was in the rear. I rang at the front door.

The young woman who answered appeared to be in shock. Her eyes were glazed. She stood in the doorway without speaking.

"Ms. Jones? Can I talk to you about your father?"

"My father's dead."

She would have closed the door except she didn't seem capable of moving. Two youths appeared behind her. For a while no one spoke. The oldest took a deep breath, knew he had to say something.

"Someone shot our father. We don't know why."

"He wasn't a crook!" That was the younger boy.

"Can we go inside and talk about it?"

The older one recovered partially from his paralysis and led the way into a large living room. It had molding, hardwood floors, fireplace with a marble mantel, old-fashioned wallpaper and furniture, and green velvet drapes, but it wasn't a museum piece. Lovingly restored and cared for, it was also comfortable and even relaxed. The people who had put the room and the house together were determined, meticulous, and gentle.

"Do any of you know what your father was doing on Humphrey Bowan's estate down in Santa Barbara?"

The three of them looked at each other, looked back at me, and shook their heads one at a time. They were normal young people, wrapped up in their own lives, needs, and dreams. Without a mother, away at college most of the year, and not concerned about what their father happened to be doing except sending them money. They also didn't know what the future was going to be for them and they were scared. Abandoned and frightened.

"Do you know of anything he was involved in that might connect him to Humphrey Bowan or anyone who works for Bowan?"

I knew it was useless. David Jones had been their father, the source of money and support, and at their age very damn little else. Unless what I needed was totally obvious I wouldn't get it from them, and if it had been that obvious Koons would have found it.

"Does he have an office in the house?"

Even that was a hard question for them. The oldest one realized he knew the answer. "No."

"Could I maybe see his real office then?"

They looked at each other, apparently decided that with their dad dead and buried they had nothing to protect him from. The older one nodded. "I guess so. You have to go outside. You need a key."

He told the younger boy to give me a key. He

would get used to being the man of the family only too soon. Then the other two, especially the girl, would begin to rebel and tell him he wasn't their father.

The office was another large, comfortable room with armchairs and side tables, a battered desk and daunting rows of file cabinets. There were three doors in addition to the outside door. David Jones had been primarily a large animals vet, few if any of his patients would have come to the office, but one door opened into an examination room with sterilizers and a surgical table for smaller animals. Another door was into a storage room and pharmacy. The last was a fully equipped darkroom made out of a closet.

Two walls of the main room were for the filing cabinets and bookcases. The other two walls were for the windows, and displays of diplomas and hundreds of framed photos of animals, protest marches, nuclear picketing, and fine landscapes. Jones had been an amateur photographer, which was interesting but he had certainly had the money to support a lot more expensive hobby than that.

I looked through the desk first, and after about an hour found nothing that looked in any way relevant. Then I tackled the files. Four hours later I gave up. Every file folder was for a veterinarian client, all local. None of them had any remote connection to Bowan, his estate, or Santa Barbara I could see. I had come directly to the house after checking into a motel, hadn't eaten, and after five hours was getting hungry. I drove to the motel, asked where I could get some dinner at the late hour, and was sent a block to a Denny's. King City.

In bed, the freeway still noisy outside even at midnight, and neon flashing in the windows of the room,

I lay awake and went over it. Koons had done everything I had done so far, had talked to everyone in town who had known David Jones, and had come up empty. The people, none of whom believed David Jones had been a burglar, clothes or no clothes, were not going to tell me anything they hadn't already told Koons. If there was a reason for Jones to have gone to Santa Barbara and Humphrey Bowan, other than burglary, it had to be somewhere in his office.

This time I had breakfast before I went out to the big old Victorian on G14. I still had the key, let myself in, and went around the office once more from the top. The desk, the files, every drawer and shelf in every room. By the time my stomach was rumbling for lunch, I still had nothing.

I was about to take care of my stomach before starting on the third go-around when the door opened and a woman came in.

"Who are you?"

I told her who I was.

"Morgan always did think far too much of Dave to accept that man's pack of lies as the police have."

"You must be Dave's lady?"

"I suppose I must. Do I gather you haven't accepted Bowan's blatant drivel either, Mr. Fortune?"

"Why would Bowan lie, Ms.—"

"Drusilla Barnes. Dave called me Drusie. I even liked it." There was more grief inside her than inside the dead man's kids, but she had it under iron control. "He lied because he killed Dave and needed an excuse to justify murder."

"Why did he kill him?"

"He had a reason."

"But you don't know it."

She sat down in one of the armchairs. A small, compact woman on the edge of being stout. In her mid-forties, brown hair cut short, wearing dark blue pants, a white blouse, and soft black medium-heeled boots. Not a wild swinger, but individual.

"You have no idea what he could have been doing on Bowan's estate? Dressed like a burglar?"

"No."

"Had he been involved in some environmental cause recently?" Bowan had interests in lumber, mining, and other fields the EPA and the environmentalists were hot on.

"Not for years. With the end of the Cold War he hadn't done any peace marches or protests either."

"He never mentioned Humphrey Bowan or his estate to you?"

"No."

"Santa Barbara?"

"No."

Every "no" sounded like a shovelful of dirt falling on David Jones's coffin. I didn't really believe a third try would do anything to help. Drusilla Barnes looked around with something close to tears in her eyes. She fixed on the walls of photographs.

"He loved his photography so much. An art and a record, you know? He carried his camera everywhere."

I stared at the walls of photos. Then I stood up. "Look for it. Look everywhere you can think of."

"Look? For what?"

"His camera. Any camera. I've searched this office twice, and I don't remember a camera. You go inside and do the house. Every room. Get those kids to help, if they're still around."

I did my third search. There was no camera.

Drusilla Barnes came back. "It's nowhere in the house. He used an expensive minicamera, a Minolta.

I remember it very well, he nearly always had it with him. If he didn't take it with him, he left it here in the office."

"Let's say he *did* take it with him. That he went down to Santa Barbara to take pictures of something. Something he knew Bowan wouldn't want photographed. That would account for the dark clothes and the ski mask, for him sneaking onto the estate."

"But what, Mr. Fortune?"

"Did he mention anything about taking special photos?"

"No."

"Anything at all unusual? Anything he was upset about? Anything—"

"Well, he was disturbed one evening recently by an emergency call he'd made, but he was often upset after a call, he hated to see animals suffer."

"Why did you happen to recall this one time specially?"

She frowned. "I'm not sure. Perhaps . . . yes, because he seemed more angry than upset. We had dinner that night, and I asked him why he was angry. He said he didn't want to talk about it until he was sure."

"Do you remember who the client was?"

She shook her head. "No, I—"

"Think, Drusie!"

But she couldn't.

I took Drusilla Barnes to lunch, coaxed and coached her the whole time, but no bells rang.

I tried the other vets in town. There were only three, and only one large animal. "Hell, Dave and I talked every day, but damned if I remember him being angry about any call he'd made."

I tried the feed stores and the Monterey County Agricultural and Rural Life Museum. They all knew

Dave, none had a clue about anything disturbing him recently.

I tried the police. The sheriff's deputy at the local office knew Dave, but not all that well. "Like I told Sergeant Koons when he come up here, Dave Jones was a real nice, quiet guy never had trouble with anyone I know. Never saw him get mad about anything."

After another not exactly sensational dinner at Denny's, I headed back to Jones's house to take one more look through his case files. This time I knew I was looking for something that had made Dave Jones angry, something out of the ordinary, something unusual, different, and I found it at once.

It was a single file folder. Not suspicious in itself, only . . . different. First, it was out of order. Second, it was at the front of the file drawer—as if it had been haphazardly dropped back in because Jones's mind was on something more important that the orderliness of his records. Third, it was empty except for an engraved business card, torn and dirty, with a name, Walter J. Bachman, and an address and telephone number in Bakersfield.

The label on the file read: Monterey Club Ranch.

I used the telephone. There was no answer in Bakersfield. I used the phone again.

On the other end, Drusilla Barnes said, "There's a Monterey Ranch out near Jolon. A big spread, and old. It's been in the same family since the last century. The Walkers. I heard they'd had some hard times, but I never heard of any club."

The Monterey Ranch was past Jolon on the county highway toward the wooded mountains of the Santa Lucia Range that touched the ocean on the far side. A night so dark I almost missed the sign over the entrance to a narrow blacktop road: Monterey Ranch.

A half a mile up the side road I was almost on top of it before the small white house emerged from the dark as well cared for as a museum exhibit. I drove on past, and saw a single light at the rear of the house and a forest service pickup truck.

The blacktop road went on in the night past the house. Few rural ranches in California had blacktop roads leading to them, and fewer still had the blacktop go on to something else beyond. Another mile and a half in, the road curved around the shoulder of a steep slope in the night under the edge of the mountains, and I saw a large number of buildings ahead.

I parked, got out, and looked at the shadowy buildings. They didn't look much like those of any working ranch I'd ever seen. A central frame building in the center of a dusty dirt yard was ringed by smaller cottages under old oaks and other native trees I couldn't name. To the right were a series of low buildings with doors every ten feet or so. There were no cars. The central building and the cottages looked deserted, but I heard movement in the low buildings to the right, and some dogs were barking in that direction.

I walked through the night to the low buildings. The barking of the dogs grew louder and more agitated as I walked along the buildings. All the doors were locked with padlocks. I went around to the rear and found the dogs. The buildings were cages. Most of the cages were empty, but the dogs barked and leaped in some. In two others there was a fat old leopard who watched me with eyes that could have belonged to one of the hound dogs who wanted to be petted, and a feeble-looking Bengal tiger far back and frightened in the corner of its cage. As I walked closer, the tiger tried to get up but failed, and the leopard tried to lick me.

I didn't hear the footsteps until they were behind me.

"Put your hands behind your head. Now!"

I put my lone hand on the back of my neck. Someone made a sound, but patted me from shoulder to toe anyway, inside my legs and out.

"Turn around."

They were two sheriff's deputies with their guns drawn, and a man in a uniform I didn't recognize but could guess.

"What are you doing here?"

I told them.

The three men in the office were a Monterey County sheriff's lieutenant, an assistant district attorney, and a regional director for the U.S. Fish and Wildlife Service. The office was in the King City Division of the Monterey County Municipal Court; the subject was the Monterey Club Ranch. The main talker was Assistant D.A. Marcus Delaney.

"The Monterey Ranch, Mr. Fortune, is a cattle ranch. It's run by Mr. Jackson Walker. Mr. Walker is well known here, the ranch has been in the Walker family for five generations, they tell me. It's a large spread in fairly remote country, with the forest and military reserve next to it. Some years ago Walker decided to increase his income by using the ranch for a sideline: hunting wild boar and deer."

Sheriff's Lieutenant Tom Fierro wanted me, or maybe the U.S. Fish and Wildlife Service, to understand. "A lot of folks around here work as hunting guides. Deer, quail, doves, varmints like coyotes and such. Maybe fifty, seventy-five years ago, a rich guy over toward Big Sur imported these European wild pigs so him and his friends from back East could hunt 'em on his estate. They got loose, been running wild

n Los Padres ever since. Tough damn pigs, and good
huntin'. Jack Walker got a lotta land, plenty of wild
pigs on it, so he got this idea to make some extra
money. Ranching ain't been so good around here,
axes keep going up on people's land."

"Monterey Club Ranch," the U.S. Fish and Wildlife
Service man, Bill Mikoyan, said. "Walker started advertising it down in L.A. and up in San Francisco.
Even back East. A thrill for city people. Custom killing. Bring your gun, we supply the dogs and the
targets."

He held a business card out for me to take. It had
the name of the club, the embossed heads of a wild
boar and a deer. It listed the hunting of the wild pigs,
deer, dove, and quail.

"The problem," assistant D.A. Delaney continued,
"is that Mr. Walker didn't stop there. Two years ago,
he—"

Lieutenant Fierro leaned forward in his chair in the
quiet office, the moonlight bright outside now over the
brown fields and distant mountains. "Five, six years of
drought. People are hurtin' around here. The damned
drought made Jack Walker sell off half his cattle, drove
the pigs 'n deer deeper inside Los Padres when food
and water dried up on his ranch. He didn't have
enough grazing for his beef, lost his barley farming
operation when he had a really bad crop, couldn't
afford to buy even enough feed for the cattle he had
left. He had to do something if he was going to survive
and maybe not lose the whole ranch."

He looked around at all of them, pleading a case I
hadn't heard yet, but could put together without a lot
of trouble from what I'd seen and heard so far.

"Exotic animal hunting," I said. "Lions, tigers, leop-
ards, jaguars. Old and toothless. Couldn't outrun a fat
poodle or harm anyone over six. A 'can hunt.' "

"An African or South American safari can cost over twenty thousand dollars," the wildlife man, Mikoyan said. "These kinds of sick operations are growing all the time. We must have ten other investigations going on right now across the country."

Delaney said, "Walker conducted five of these 'can hunts' in three months this year. Most of the animals come from zoos that no longer want them because they're too old and feeble. Some were pets people became afraid of or that grew too old to be fun. Some are raised specially in Mexico and Texas. Walker never kept them more than two or three days. It cost too much to feed them, I imagine. He only imported them when he had a 'hunt' lined up. These 'hunters' shot most of them a few feet from the cages, not that it mattered. Most of the animals didn't have enough teeth left to chew a chicken or the strength to run a mile. Some wouldn't even come out, were shot right in the cages."

I said, "For trophies. Have you charged anyone beside Walker? Any of the clients?"

"We do if we can catch them with identifiable dead animals, the pelts, or the heads."

"What's the charge and sentence?"

Mikoyan, the Fish and Game director, shook his head. "Mostly violating endangered species laws and permit procedures. We don't respect animals in this country. This world, for that matter."

Delaney said, "Misdemeanors. One year in jail and a small fine on each charge. Enough to do damage to Walker's business, but not a lot more."

Mikoyan said, "Federal charges of interstate transportation and killing of endangered species could be filed. Those are both felonies."

"With a decent lawyer they'd get off with a slap anyway. Free enterprise carries a lot more weight than an old tiger," I said. "You have the names of the clients?"

"Walker didn't keep records. Under the table all the way."

"Then how'd you find any clients to charge?"

Delaney looked down at his file. He didn't have to, but he didn't like what he had to say. "Photos of the trophies. Those who supplied Walker had records of the animals. Sometimes the original owners had records."

"Photos? From where?"

"Anonymous," Mikoyan said. "They just came into my office in the mail with the names of the clients."

"The clients didn't know the photos had been taken?"

"No."

I thought about it for a time. "How did you learn about the can hunts at all?"

Mikoyan said, "Same way. Anonymous tip. We followed up, then brought in the sheriff."

David Jones had gone to Monterey Club Ranch to treat some lion or tiger, and seen something about the animals that made him angry and suspicious. He'd tipped the federal wildlife people, but that hadn't been enough. He wanted the hunters.

Mikoyan said, "There's something sick about shooting an old, feeble animal at short range and then claiming a trophy. The shooters even took photographs and videotapes."

"Sure, can shootin' is bad," Lieutenant Fierro said, "but I don't see nothing wrong with hunting the exotics if the chase is fair. What's the difference between that and lettin' folks go out and hunt deer and boar?"

Everyone looked at him.

"The difference," Mikoyan said, "is that the exotics

aren't wild. They're tame animals, Fierro. Old and sick. They're goddamn pets!"

I said, "I don't really see all that difference myself, Lieutenant. Except that deer aren't even as dangerous as pets, and damned few of us need to put meat on the table anymore."

They all looked at me.

I sat in my Tempo outside the address in Bakersfield. It was a storefront on a back street with houses all around and simple black-bordered gold lettering on the door: Walter J. Bachman, Taxidermist.

I guessed that David Jones, on an emergency call to Monterey Ranch to treat one of the exotic animals, probably told that they were "caring for" the poor beasts in their last days, had been made suspicious by something and had found the card, too. He had called the number hoping to find a witness to confirm or deny his suspicions, and found instead Walter J. Bachman's trade. Why would somewhere that "cared for" old exotic animals need a taxidermist? (It was obviously something Jack Walker and Walter Bachman had thought of, too, hence nothing but name and address on the card.)

A sign in the window listed Bachman's hours as 8:00 to 12:00 and 1:30 to 5:30. It was like my business, not a lot of walk-in trade. I staked it out until the taxidermist locked up and went home for lunch. Then I broke in. David Jones had to have found the names and addresses of the can shooters somewhere. Walter J. Bachman, taxidermist, had to have records. He did.

Not in his regular account books, but in a special book in a locked drawer and coded. The drawer was simple to open, and the code was just as simple. Next to the names and addresses of the clients, the fees, and the delivery dates were a series of letters: T, L,

J. Maybe the taxidermist was proud of his skill, wanted to recall every exotic job he did. Whatever, he'd given David Jones his leads to find the clients and get his damning photographs, and next to Humphrey Bowan's name were three letters: T, J, and P.

I knew why David Jones had been on Humphrey Bowan's estate dressed all in black like a burglar. Now all I had to do was prove it.

I got back to my Summerland hacienda before dark. Kay was waiting for me, and so was Morgan Jones.

"He's been here every day," Kay said, not pleased.

I shooed Jones away after telling him I might have an answer for him soon, be patient. I didn't shoo Kay away. What I had in mind to do on David Jones couldn't be done well at night. What I had in mind for Kay could. She agreed.

She slept in, I made my own breakfast and considered the possibilities. David Jones had come down here to photograph Humphrey Bowan's illegal trophies, but no camera had been found on or near the body, or in his car parked on the side road. Either it had been found by Bowan and his people and probably destroyed, or it was still out there. Fifty-fifty odds.

I drove out to East Valley Road, parked on the same side street Jones had. It had been dark when he scaled the wall. I was going to have to do it in daylight. He had had two arms, I had one. Nobody ever said detective work was easy. With the aid of a friendly low-hanging sycamore branch, I made it over the wall and located the exact spot where, Koons had found Jones dead. It wasn't hard to spot even after three weeks. The thick brush had been trampled and flattened for ten yards around, there was even still a trace of blood. What there wasn't was a camera.

I worked outward in a circle, one eye alert for anyone who might spot me. The trees and brush were so thick the massive fifty-room imitation English manor house was invisible, but I still felt as exposed as a zebra in a pride of lions. As I moved closer to the house I heard voices through the trees, saw the chauffeur working on a limousine in front of the garages that had once been a coach house. But I didn't find a camera, and went back to the wall to think about it.

Assuming David Jones had gotten into the mansion and taken his pictures, as the broken French door panes indicated, and Bowan or the other two had spotted the camera, they'd have grabbed it. If I was going to find it, they had to have missed it. What would I have done with the camera if I were being pursued? Jones couldn't have imagined anyone would shoot him, so his main concern would have been to preserve the photos, his evidence against Humphrey Bowan, even if they caught him and turned him over to the police for trespassing.

He had been shot near the wall. If I had felt no one could see me, and I was at the wall, over the camera would have gone.

I used the same sycamore, went over again, worked my way through the brush between the wall and East Valley Road, and there it was.

A mini-Minolta that had landed in a thicket of manzanita, intact and undamaged.

I took the film to one of those places where they claim to develop and print your roll in one hour, but always take half a day at best. It was late afternoon when I spread the prints out on my office desk. Fifteen close-ups, from every angle, of three mounted heads on a wall between other heads and racks of guns. A grizzled tiger with a scarred eye, a jaguar with one ear bald and the other half-gone, and a puma older than my grandfather after he was dead.

The chauffeur, William Berra, came out of the gates of Bowan's mansion at exactly six p.m. He never slowed down until he got to the Miramar Hotel bar. A muscular, dark-haired man with a thick neck and a battered, stubborn face, he wore narrow gray slacks that showed his slim waist, a sky blue sport shirt loose and wide over his muscles, and running shoes. Thirty-five or so, thick-haired and handsome.

He settled onto a stool at the piano bar, flirted with the waitress, and eyed three women at the bar. Older women. Berra's smile said he expected them to appreciate his open attention. A confident man without a care in the world. He had two more margaritas over the next two hours, looked at his watch, patted the waitress, and left. I followed him back to Bowan's estate.

He didn't come out again for the next two nights, and when he did it was the same controlled ritual.

Anselmo Cortez did nothing the first day. The second day he came out in midafternoon, went alone to a bar in the barrio of the lower east side, and drank for hours without a word. Brooding. He did the same on the third day, got drunk, and his wife found him and drove him home. When he came out later that same night, his dark face both angry and pale, I had my man.

He went to the same barrio saloon. I took a seat three stools up and waited. I was the only Anglo in the place, but with one arm I didn't look like a cop. I didn't look like an easy mark for the macho young punks either, wasn't nervous, so they left me alone. When you're a minority, you tend to be wary of a member of the majority who doesn't fit the normal pattern.

On his third tequila, I moved next to Cortez.

"Women don't understand when a man's got trouble, amigo."

Cortez nodded gloomily. He was a tall, slim man with a worn and craggy face like saddle leather. Someone who had spent his life outdoors, and not always on a plush estate.

"The cops'll find out, you know that."

He nodded again, sorry for himself, and then the import of my words that echoed his own fears reached him and he froze.

"An honorable man like you shouldn't cover for someone like that. He's a coward, Anselmo, you know that."

Now he looked at me in abject terror.

"It's a good job, right? Your family? I understand that. But even the best job . . ."

"Who . . . who are you?"

"You didn't know he had a brother, did you? The man your boss killed. The murder you're covering up for him."

"I don' know what you say."

"He sent me, the brother. I'm a detective and I know what happened. It won't help your family if you go to prison."

He drained his tequila, didn't wave for another.

"Then I'll tell you. You heard someone outside, went out to look. You ran into your boss with his hunting rifle. Berra, too, with his gun. You all chased the intruder. You all . . ."

"Boss say we got big hunt. Boss—" He stopped. "You go. I don' talk to you no—"

"Hunt?"

A hunt! For a fleeing burglar! Bowan hadn't fired

any warning shots. His first two shots had simply missed. Had they all missed until Bowan's fatal shot, or was the hunt only for Bowan? A hunt for the biggest game. A burglar, a criminal. Who would ask any questions? Especially when they put a gun with the body and a bag of loot.

"David Jones wasn't a criminal, Anselmo. He wasn't there to steal anything. I know why he was there that night, and when I tell the police it's all going to come out. You—"

The other patrons in the bar were all looking at us. Even the bartender. Not a friendly look. It was one thing to let a questionable Anglo alone; it was another to let him attack one of your own. I had to finish fast.

"I guess it comes down to this, Anselmo. You want to go down with your boss, lose your cushy job *and* your freedom, or lose just your job and feel . . . ?"

He pushed his empty glass away, walked to the door and out into the night. I sat and finished my beer. If I'd tried to go after him, I wouldn't have reached the door.

It was going to be a matter of timing.

Hair-trigger timing. But I didn't have much choice. Unless someone talked, all I had was conjecture. Nothing proved David Jones didn't take a gun as well as his camera, or decide to lift some loot on the side.

I borrowed the house from some friends of Kay's. It sat deep on a wooded acre off El Bosque Road two miles from Bowan's mansion. I waited until dark and made the first call.

"Humphrey Bowan?"

"Yes. Who is this?"

"My name doesn't matter. What I know does. I know what David Jones was really doing on your estate that night, and you don't. When I tell the police, they'll know he wasn't any burglar. I know and they'll know what really happened. Now I'm a reasonable man. Dave's dead, what does he need, right? I'm alive, and I need a whole lot of things. So let's talk about what you got a lot of, right? I mean, it ought to be worth maybe six figures, right?"

"I don't know what—"

"One word, Mr. Bowan. *Hunt.* How's that? A hunt."

The silence dripped with more venom than the voice when it finally came again. "Where are you."

"That's better. I'm at 184 El Bosque. It's pretty isolated, and I can see real good, so come alone."

"Half an hour."

He hung up. I sat and watched the grandfather clock in the borrowed house. He would need to gather the troops, make a plan, and drive the two miles. Say, fifteen minutes if he moved fast. I waited five and then called Sergeant Koons.

"Koons? Dan Fortune. You want Humphrey Bowan, get out to 184 El Bosque, and fast."

"Fortune—"

This time I hung up. Twenty minutes for Koons, at most.

I left the lights on inside the house, drew the curtains, and went outside into the shadows of a grove of old oaks fifty feet from the house. They stood, thick and shadowy, at a corner of the large yard where I could watch both the side of the property that bordered East Valley Road and the front on El Bosque. It was a dark night, but the moon was coming up. So was what I hoped was the end of the game. I had my Sig-Sauer, and fifteen minutes later I had them.

Anselmo Cortez parked his pickup at the front on El Bosque. He got out and walked up the driveway toward the house. He had no gun, walked slowly and warily as if cautious. What he was doing was decoying the man they expected to be watching greedily from the house to see his money walking toward him. After all, the blackmailer on the telephone was only a dumb crook, right?

The chauffeur, Berra, and Humphrey Bowan came through the brush from East Valley. They moved as silently as big cats, I'll give them that. After all, Bowan was a big-game hunter. He was a tall, lean shadow that passed in the night toward the house and carried a hunting rifle ready to go to the shoulder or the hip.

I let them make their approach right up to the house. They signaled Cortez to climb the steps to the front door and knock. I heard the first distant siren, faint and still some miles away. When Cortez was on the porch, I stepped to the edge of the grove of oaks, half in and half out of the moonlight, my Sig-Sauer out and steady.

"Well now. Look who's trespassing, and with guns, too."

Cortez recognized my voice. "That man is the—"

Berra came around with his pistol, got off two fast shots.

Too fast. He didn't come close. I shot twice, got his hand. The gun disappeared somewhere in the night, and he went down cursing and holding a broken and bleeding hand. Humphrey Bowan moved the rifle maybe an inch, and we faced off for maybe half a minute. Then he lowered the rifle.

"Yeah," I said. "You like it better when the target can't bite or shoot back."

"Mister, you better have a good explanation for this, or the police—"

I heard the car glide to a silent stop out on the road. I smiled to myself. I'd had a hunch Koons would come first and silent. Bowan was too busy intimidating me and planning a quick escape to notice the car. Berra was too busy with his pain to hear anything. I couldn't tell if Cortez heard or not.

"Oh, I've got a good explanation. David Jones didn't steal anything from you, and he didn't have a gun that night. He was unarmed, and you shot him down in cold blood. Because you were sure you could get away with it. No other reason. A hunt, some sport. Another 'can shoot' just like up in Jolon. Only this time the quarry wasn't some scared and toothless old pet, but an unarmed human being who'd only come to your estate to help stop the killing of helpless animals."

And then I talked to Anselmo Cortez on the porch. "You're going to have to make up your mind, Anselmo. Are you going down with him, or are you going to tell us how he made you do what you're ashamed of?"

As if on cue, the sirens were suddenly close in the night, coming along East Valley Road. Cortez heard them.

"He tell us don' catch the man, on'y chase him. Make sure he don' get away. Make the man stay on the land so he, Mr. Bowan, can hunt the man like animal."

"The brave hunter," I said.

"He's a liar!" Bowan snarled. "You can't prove a damn thing. The sheriff won't listen—"

"I think he will. With Cortez talking, Berra will talk, too. And with what I've put together, it should convince a jury."

That was when Sergeant Koons stepped out of the trees. "It's convinced me."

There were five of us in the lieutenant's office. I said, "Morgan Jones didn't believe his brother could be a thief. Neither did Koons, and neither did I. So there had to be a reason for him to be on that estate dressed the way he was. That's what I found in King City. He was there to take photos of the trophy heads from the 'can shoot' up in Jolon. At first, I thought Bowan must have spotted him and the camera, known what he was doing, even though proving Bowan shot those helpless animals didn't sound like enough motive for murder. Not with the small penalties involved, but you never know. Some men, especially rich and arrogant men, would kill to keep from being humiliated, made to look small. If that had been what happened, the camera would be long gone. I would know what had happened, and so would you, but we could never have proved it. So when I found the camera I knew he had to have been shot for some other reason. Cortez told me the reason—a hunt."

Koons said, "They heard Jones, but they never saw him in the house, and they never spotted the camera. Bowan saw a chance to have a big thrill he'd never had. He'd never shot a man. He told Cortez and Berra to block Jones, shoo him back to where Bowan could get a clear shot. It took him three shots, the last at fifty feet. They planted the gun and the loot on the body and called us."

The lieutenant said, "That Berra better talk, too. Otherwise it's the Latino's word, and Fortune's story, against Bowan and his lawyers."

"Christ," the assistant D.A. said. "There's going to be hell to pay. Bowan funds half the goddamn charities in the county."

The undersheriff said, "The boss is going to shit purple."

"With Bowan's money he can appeal forever," the assistant D.A. groaned. "Jones *was* trespassing. He *was* wearing clothes that made him look like a god-damn burglar."

"Yeah," I said. "A real dangerous criminal."

The undersheriff glared at me. "Why the hell didn't that fucking Jones mind his own goddamn business."

"I think you'll all come out okay," I said. "Second degree, or at least voluntary manslaughter. I mean, you can get the poor old animals in. Everybody cares about cruelty to animals if not to people."

Nobody seemed to think that was funny.

EASY AS PIE
BY ARTHUR WINFIELD KNIGHT

I had the pistol in my pocket. It was an unregistered .38 Smith & Wesson. I wasn't sure I should have brought it but Karl had said, "I've never asked you for anything before. Please, don't say no."

It was raining when I got to Tomales Bay. I pulled off Highway One onto the dirt road leading to Karl's cabin. I could see a light inside.

I parked underneath a eucalyptus tree. When I got out of the car, the wind from the bay blew the rain into my face so I kept my head down, making my way toward the cabin in the darkness.

Somewhere in the trees nearby, I could hear the strange croaking sounds egrets make. You could see the birds wading a few yards out from the beach at dawn, their long necks bent over as they looked for fish, but at night they nested in the tops of the trees.

Karl opened the door, the yellow light spilling out like molten wax, and the hot smell of the cabin mixed with the sweet scent of the eucalyptus when I reached the porch.

I hadn't seen Karl in a couple of years. He was three years older than me, fifty-six, but he looked a lot older. Maybe because he was a smoker, and I wasn't. Or maybe I just liked to think he looked older than I did. Maybe I didn't really see myself when I looked into the mirror; a lot of people go through life fooling themselves.

I'd seen Karl's picture on the front page of the San Francisco papers, but it didn't prepare me for his appearance. His face was so gray it looked as if someone had embalmed him, and he must not have shaved for days. His beard was as gray as his face.

"Come in. Quick," he said, but he didn't need to.

I was glad to get out of the rain.

I hung my coat with the pistol in it on a peg next to the bathroom. The pistol thumped against the unpainted plyboard wall, but I didn't think Karl heard it.

We sat at the long table next to the sliding-glass doors that led to the deck. The rain burst against the glass, and the marijuana plant in a large wooden tub on the deck bent over in the wind. Karl had hung red paper balls from the plant so the cops who scanned the shore from a helicopter, looking for marijuana, would think he was growing tomatoes. I thought he was fooling himself, but he hadn't been arrested. Not yet.

Karl lit an unfiltered Pall Mall and said, "I didn't mean to do it." His hands were shaking.

"I know."

Karl was one of the most placid people I'd ever met. When he and I were college roommates, I'd rage against the inequities of the world while Karl drank Grace Brothers beer and ate huge bowls of popcorn. He'd listen to my rants, shrugging, and say, "What're you gonna do?" He was so calm it was maddening. Now he was accused of murder.

"Do you want to tell me about it?" I asked.

Karl walked to the sliding doors, leaning on them, his palms against the glass. The backs of his hands were orange in the light. It looked like the raindrops were exploding against his fingertips.

"Did you bring the pistol?" he asked.

I didn't want to answer him. I said, "You wouldn't be in trouble if you hadn't had a gun three days ago."

"I'd probably be dead."

He'd begun carrying a pistol when he'd gone to graduate school at the University of Texas at Austin. Everyone "packed" one in Texas, he'd told me. Housewives took them to the supermarket. His girlfriend carried one in her purse when they went to the movies, and he knew high school kids who wouldn't go to McDonald's without carrying a "piece."

The San Francisco papers said Karl had shot a black kid who was unarmed.

Karl put his cigarette out against the glass, letting the butt drop onto the floor. Then he sat in the torn leather chair next to the TV.

I said, "I know you didn't murder anyone."

"I'm not sure what I did," Karl said. "It just happened. All of a sudden. I was driving up Ashbury Street, not far from where we used to live." He paused, staring at the logs burning in the fireplace. I was sweating under my arms, but Karl didn't seem to notice the heat.

"Someone in an old Escort started to back up toward me when I pulled up behind him at a stop sign," Karl said. "I blew the horn and the car stopped just before it hit mine. This black kid leaned out the window and began yelling, swearing. 'Fuck you, fuck you.' He was shouting, giving me the finger, and I didn't even know why he was mad. He would have hit me if I hadn't honked. But I guess he didn't think about that. He just knew some white guy had honked at him and he was furious. Maybe it wouldn't have been so bad if it hadn't been for the Rodney King business, if the cops in L.A. hadn't been acquitted for beating him. I don't know. Maybe he was on drugs."

Karl slumped into the chair. He'd always had lousy

posture, and his clothes always looked worn, even when they were new. He reminded me of a disheveled Walter Matthau.

"I was on my way to the U.C. Medical Center for chemotherapy and I didn't really want to go because it isn't doing any good and maybe I shouldn't have laughed when the black kid was swearing, maybe that's what made him go crazy, but it was ludicrous. Here he was, young, healthy as hell, but mad at the world, and here I am . . ." He shrugged and for a moment I thought he was going to say, What're you gonna do? but he didn't.

"I didn't know you were . . . sick," I said. I'd almost said dying but caught myself.

"Yeah. The doctors gave me six months, but that was eight months ago." He smiled. "They told me I ought to quit smoking, it's lung cancer, but it's a little late now. I've lived with the habit all these years. I might as well die with it." As if he were proving the point, Karl lit another cigarette.

"I'm sorry," I said and felt stupid, but I didn't know what else to say. I wondered if he was sorry he'd smoked all those years, but I didn't ask. He had enough grief.

I said, "I'm not an arms dealer. I don't buy and sell weapons. So why did you phone me?"

I must have sounded angry because Karl said, "I knew you could find a gun if you wanted to."

Karl was right about that. I'd called a friend who was a Zen poet and a small-time arms dealer along the Russian River. He sold switchblade knives, submachine guns, rocket launchers, and he probably did some low-level drug dealing. I didn't want to know. The guy lived with his mother.

I knew all sorts of people, but you wouldn't want to meet most of them. That's why I'd gotten out of the business. I'd worked as a detective for Hargrave Secret Service in San Francisco until I'd taken an early retirement and returned to Petaluma, thirty-eight miles north of the city.

Occasionally, I still took part-time jobs to supplement my income, but I didn't believe in the work anymore. I'd become a detective because I didn't know what else to do with a degree in creative writing and because I thought I might be able to move the world a quarter of an inch, positively—it was something a poet I'd met claimed he wanted to do—but I'd spent most of my time spying on people. I hoped the poet had better luck than I did.

"Tell me what happened with the black guy," I said.

"He pulled his car into a driveway across the street, then he came running toward me. He was still cursing, waving his fists, but I'd locked the doors and rolled up the windows so I couldn't hear him.

"Before I could get up the hill, he began banging on the hood with his fists, then he came over to the window on my side, beating on the glass. I thought it was going to break.

"All I could see was his black face. He had a scar under his left eye and his nose was running. Sometimes, he'd wipe his nose on his knuckles, then he'd beat on the glass some more, smearing it with his snot.

"There were drops of spittle on his lips and chin. It was almost like he was foaming. I groped for the .357 Magnum in the glove compartment, aiming it in his direction without even thinking. It was slippery in my hand. All of a sudden, he froze for a second; I guess he saw the pistol. The last word he ever said was 'Fuck,' but I finished the sentence for him. 'You,' I said as I pulled the trigger and he disappeared; the bullet smashed through the window where his mouth used to be, and I was covered with blood and glass."

Karl stopped to catch his breath, and he put his cigarette out in a dirty ashtray.

"I'd just killed a guy and I felt relieved—elated. I've never believed in violence, you know that; I don't think it's a solution to anything, but I was smiling when I gunned the car up the hill. I was alive. That's all I could think. Dying but alive."

Karl got out of the chair slowly, and I realized how tired he was. How sick.

He said, "I tossed the gun over the side of the Golden Gate Bridge when I drove north so no one could trace it to me, but they traced my license plate number, so I threw the gun away for nothing. The whole thing was for nothing." Karl had that what're you gonna do look again. "That kid will never see another sunrise, never make love with his girl, and I'm alive." He almost seemed ashamed of it.

The kid had been in trouble with the authorities from the time he was in grammar school, and he'd robbed a couple of convenience stores, threatening the proprietor with a tire iron, according to the papers. He wouldn't be doing that again, either, but I didn't tell Karl that. He was almost enjoying his misery. Maybe it made him feel more alive.

"Why didn't you go to the police?" I asked.

"I was tired. Tired of chemo. Tired of trying to make sense of things that were senseless." Karl had a Ph.D. in sociology. "There'd be a trial."

"They'd acquit you."

"I don't think I'd live long enough to get through it, and I don't want to die in jail."

"There's bail."

"What would I use for money? This place is mortgaged and I haven't taught full-time in five years. No one would put up a bond for me."

I didn't know what to say. Maybe he was right. The world could be a pretty crummy place at times.

I went over to the glass doors and looked out at the bay. I could see the moon's reflection in the water, but it looked pockmarked when the rain hit it.

Karl lived with a woman who was a social worker in Concord, but it was only a matter of days, maybe hours, until the cops traced him here. "What'll you do then?" I asked. I couldn't imagine him shooting it out with them. That wasn't why he wanted a pistol. He'd always believed you have to work at changing a sick society, and now he was part of the sickness.

Karl said, "I'll be gone."

"Where?"

"Just . . . gone. You know."

He couldn't buy a pistol because there was a waiting period, and besides, he'd be recognized since his picture had made the front pages. And he didn't want me to bring him a registered gun because he didn't want it to be traced back to me when the cops finally caught up with him.

I knew what he was going to do.

Jesus.

I went to the small refrigerator, opening it, and found a bottle of Watney's Ale. I opened it, pouring it into two glasses that looked like they hadn't been washed in months, and I handed one to Karl. We drank the beer, not saying anything. We'd drunk a lot of beer together in thirty years.

I put the glass on the counter separating the kitchen from the living area, then I took the pistol from the pocket of my jacket and set it next to the glass.

The pistol looked obscene.

Karl said, "I spent the summer with my grandparents in Excelsior Springs, Missouri, when I was nine. Grandma was always working: milking cows, churning butter, baking. She hardly had time to listen to the radio at night. I'd never seen anyone work like that and I asked her, 'How do you do it?' She just laughed and said, 'It's easy as pie,' and I wasn't sure what she meant." Karl put his glass next to mine and touched the pistol with the tips of his fingers. "The world has changed, hasn't it?"

"Yeah."

"Nothing is as easy as pie now."

I remembered the first time I'd come to the cabin. It was a Saturday afternoon and Karl was out on the bay in a small sailboat with his dog, Boswell, and I read part of a book titled *The True Believer* by Eric Hoffer and drank a beer while I sat in the shade on the deck under an indigo sky and waited for Karl. We were going to live forever.

When I'd retired, Karl had let me use the cabin for a week while I looked for a place in Petaluma, and I'd found a dog food coupon that had expired in November '63 in one of the kitchen drawers. When I told Karl about it he said, "My dog died," as if that explained why the coupon was still there.

Life turned out differently than any of us imagined.

Karl had been married and divorced. He had a daughter who was in her late teens who lived in Germany for some reason—his ex-wife taught college in Missoula, Montana—and I knew he never heard from the girl.

I'd been married and divorced twice and, the second time, Karl had been my best man. I never had kids.

"Yeah. Nothing is as easy as pie now," I repeated.

Neither of us mentioned the pistol.

I said, "It's never hopeless." I was lying. "You can still turn yourself in and you can go back to chemo. I had a friend who was given eight months to live and he fooled the doctors. He even went to Yucatán and

Egypt, then he moved to Chapel Hill. He lives near his daughter now." My friend had gone to Yucatán and Egypt, but he was dead now.

"Thanks," Karl said, "for everything," and I knew he wanted to be alone. There wasn't anything left to say—to do.

My coat felt light without the gun in the pocket.

Karl and I shook hands and I still wanted to say something, but I didn't.

I heard the door to the cabin shut before I got to my car. When I reached it, I held my breath and listened.

I didn't know if I was crying or if it was just the rain running down my face in the darkness. I stood there, waiting.

FAMILY VALUES
BY MATTHEW CLEMENS

He was a huge man. At least half a foot taller and a hundred pounds heavier than me. He filled the doorway. Greasy hair hung to his shoulders and his dull brown eyes studied me with the curiosity of a child's.

"You wan sumpin'?" he asked, revealing jagged teeth that had been thrown in his mouth at random.

"I'm looking for Earl Strong. Is he here?"

My question seemed to baffle him. He tilted his head slightly and stared through me. I tried to see around him, wondering if there was someone inside I could talk to, maybe someone with a brain.

The place was a run-down, one-story farmhouse with a dilapidated porch, nestled tightly into a grove of pines. It needed paint. No, it needed to be condemned. The corpses of two cannibalized Chevys lay to one side. The '74 Monte Carlo that was probably the Strongs' family car sat on the lawn pointed toward the lane.

I tried again. "Do you know Earl Strong? He's supposed to live here . . ." My voice trailed off as confusion crossed the monster's face again.

"He's sleepin'."

"Could you wake him?"

He shook his head slowly.

"When will he be up? I can wait."

This was not what the moron wanted to hear. "You leave, now!"

"But . . ."

That was as far as I got. I didn't duck fast enough and he grabbed me by my neck.

"I said," he grumbled, "you leave."

With one hand, he shook me. My world turned upside down, treetops spun and colors swirled. His fingers pressed on my carotid artery, my blood roared like jet engines in my ears. I smelled his foul sweat and my fear. The colors faded into a shapeless blackness.

I heard a faraway voice. A woman's voice. "Archie, whatcha doin' with that guy?"

Archie swung me behind his back so the woman wouldn't see his new toy.

"Archie . . ." The voice rose, a question, a threat.

I wanted to pry his fingers from my neck, but my limbs were no longer obeying my brain. The woman's voice and the jets in my ears began to fade away. It occurred to me that my first case was less than one day old and I was about to die.

He threw me down. The jet engines roared louder than ever. My lungs burned as I fought to breathe. I took a quick inventory as I lay there in the dirt, unable to move. I seemed to be alive. I was surprised.

The woman's voice forced its way into my brain. "Who are ya, mister?"

My tongue and brain still weren't speaking. Whatever I tried to say came out a raspy jumble.

"Who are ya?" she repeated, stepping closer.

Archie tried to help. "He was askin' questions 'bout Pa."

I seemed to be on autopilot nodding my agreement.

The women bent down close to me, her face a grayblue blur. "Whatcha want with Earl? You a cop?"

I shook my head as I struggled to my hands and

knees. A shaft of flame burned the length of my spine every time I moved.

"If you ain't a cop, who are ya?"

I pushed myself up to my knees so I could face her. "Twain," I said, trying to focus on her face. "I'm a private detective. Ezra Strong hired me."

The woman began to come into focus. She was fifty or so, rail-thin with a pinched face and pointed nose. Her hair was a chocolate-colored beehive, her eyes brown marbles. One of those too-long, skinny cigarettes was pasted to her lipstick. Her pink flowered blouse was knotted at her waist and the fuchsia slacks she wore were a size too small.

"Ezra's a no-good, lyin', two-faced . . ." Her voice still held a trace of Arkansas. She took a breath and tried to think up more insults.

I jumped in. "You Dottie?"

She nodded, tilted her head like Archie had earlier, and her glare turned icy. Ezra Strong had warned me about his sister-in-law when he'd called me the night before.

I'd picked up on the fourth ring. "Twain."

There was a pause, then the thready voice of an old man. "Is this the Triple-A Detective Agency?"

"Yes. I'm Twain. What can I do for you?"

Ezra Strong was calling from Stockton, California. He told me about Earl loaning him fifty thousand dollars, thirty years ago, to start a business. When the business failed, he couldn't repay the debt.

Ezra knew Earl lived in Morehouse, Illinois. A town of about a thousand just across the Mississippi from Northport, Iowa, where I live. He had tried to talk to Earl, now that he could repay the loan, but he couldn't get past Dottie.

"Did you tell her you wanted to pay back the loan?"

"Dottie keeps telling me he's out or doesn't want to speak to me. She never liked me, Mr. Twain. She's never forgiven me . . . or Earl." He sounded tired.

"You think she's trying to keep you apart?"

"Yes, sir. I want you to be my emissary, Mr. Twain. Find Earl, tell him I just want to talk to him, then I'll pay him back and send along five thousand to you for your trouble."

My ears perked up at the mention of money. I grabbed a pencil.

"I've got two questions, Mr. Strong. What's Earl's address?"

He told me, I wrote it down. "Why me?"

"Triple-A was the first detective agency listed in the Northport yellow pages. Will you help me, Mr. Twain?"

"Yes, sir. I will."

"There's one more thing, Mr. Twain."

That was when he warned me about Dottie. He gave me his phone number and hung up. I had sat at the table that night grinning at how well my advertising had worked. When I got my license, I had called myself AAA for the very reason Ezra Strong had chosen me. I went to bed that night knowing I was about to make an easy five grand. That was how it began.

Five grand had seemed like easy pickin's before I met Dottie and Archie Strong. Now, lying at their feet in a heap, I knew I'd been wrong. Real wrong.

"If that bastard wants to pay us back, you tell 'im to mail us the check. Till then, me and Earl got nothin' to say to 'im."

My head began to clear. "Look, lady, I could give a shit about . . ."

Archie cuffed me, sending me sprawling and replaying the colored light show. I came up to my knees and looked at him.

"Don' cuss in fron' a Ma. She's a lady."

Glancing at Dottie, I saw a wisp of a smile nibbling at the corners of her mouth. I waited for the multicolored fireflies to disappear. "Why don't you have Earl call Ezra? He just wants to talk . . ."

"Earl," she interrupted, "don't wanna talk to him. He stole from us, his family. He stole from us."

"But . . ."

"But nothin'. Ezra turned on his own. Me and Earl don't want no part of 'im."

"If I could just talk to Earl. Maybe I could convince him to talk to Ezra . . ."

"I said 'No.' Earl don't like strangers any better'n he likes Ezra. He took a shot at one a month or so ago. Now haul your ass off our place 'fore I call the sheriff."

"But, Mrs. Strong . . ."

"Money talks, mister. He mails the check, maybe we talk to 'im." She turned and walked into the house.

I tried to follow.

Through the screen she said, "Archie."

Archie stepped into my path. I reconsidered, went to my car, and drove away. Something was wrong at that house. I didn't know what, but I would.

My Pinto glided into Morehouse. The main drag had a small convenience store with gas pumps, a church, two bars, and a post office. It wasn't much.

Knowing nothing of Earl, I decided to start at the post office. It was a one-room building split by a counter. On the right side were numbered metal boxes. The left side was a barred window. Peering out was a small, moon-faced woman of forty or so, who'd had her share of acne. Her name turned out to be Shirley Wayne.

Shirley told me how Dottie Strong showed up on the first of every month to pick up Earl's disability check, and about the Strong children. Besides Archie, there were four more. The youngest, Floyd, was a spoiled mama's boy of eleven. His sister, Rose, was a year older. Jamie and Janie were seventeen-year-old twins. I thanked Shirley and was about to leave when she stopped me.

"And, Mr. Twain . . ."

I turned to face her. She scanned the room to make sure no one was listening, even though we were alone.

"Watch out for Dottie. She can be a mean old bitch and she uses Archie like an attack dog. The boy ain't bright, but he is obedient and he dotes on his mama."

"Thanks. I'll remember that," I said, closing the door behind me, wishing I'd met Shirley a couple of hours earlier.

Across the street was a two-story brick building with a large sign that invited me to Bert's Bar, cold beer and mixed drinks. Stopping just inside the door, I let my eyes adjust to the darkness.

Bert's was one of those places where the locals congregate, simply because there's nowhere else to go. The jukebox was quietly belching out some Garth Brooks song. Behind the bar was a middle-aged, chubby, balding man that I presumed to be Bert.

In a back corner sat two older men wearing seed company caps, probably regulars, who stopped talking when I entered. When I sat on a stool at the bar, they went back to their conversation.

Chubby came over to me. "What'll you have?"

"Got any coffee?"

The man didn't say anything, just waddled to the other end and poured coffee into a heavy ceramic mug.

"Cream or sugar?" he called.

I shook my head, he trundled back and set the cup in front of me. It was steaming and smelled bitter like it had been on the hot plate since yesterday. He hovered around until I pitched a buck on the bar. He stuffed the bill in the register and didn't bring me any change.

"My name's Twain."

He didn't even look up.

I went on. "Maybe you could help me . . ." I let my voice trail off, leaving him an opening.

"Bert," he offered. "This is my place."

"It's nice," I said, not looking around.

"Thanks. What'd you say your name was?"

"Twain."

"Well, Twain, we don't get a lot of strangers in here. What can I do for you?"

"I'm looking for someone. Earl Strong. You know him?"

Bert glanced at the two guys in the corner, then back at me. "You a cop?"

"No. His brother Ezra hired me to find him. It's a family thing."

Bert nodded like he understood family things. He stroked his chin. "Family can be a tough thing. But I don't think I can help much. Hell, I can't even remember the last time I saw Earl . . . Had to have been two, three years at least." He turned to the boys in the corner. "You guys seen Earl Strong lately?"

I watched them think, look at each other, then think some more. The boys shook their heads in unison.

"Kind of funny nobody has seen him for so long in such a small town, isn't it?" I asked.

Bert shook his head as he looked at me. "Earl always was sort of a homebody, if you know what I mean?"

I nodded.

"He and Dottie," he went on, "used to come in

here on Friday nights for a while. Then they just sorta stopped comin' around."

I nodded again. I was getting nowhere.

"Wait a minute," Bert said. "Dottie was in here a month or so ago. Had some guy with her. Lyle, I think she said his name was. Yeah, that's it, Lyle Bensen. Said he was her cousin. But they weren't actin' like cousins, if you know what I mean?" Bert winked at me as he said that last part.

I knew what he meant. "They been back?"

He shook his head. I thanked Bert, drank my cold coffee, and slipped a ten under the cup when I set it on the bar. As I walked out, I heard Bert over my shoulder. "Thanks, Twain. You come back now."

Outside, the autumn sun was fading into the west. It still seemed bright after the darkness of Bert's Bar. I struck out at the other bar, a sleazier dive than Bert's.

The girl on duty at the convenience store, who said her name was Peggy, knew the Strongs. She told me that Earl used to come in for coffee and doughnuts in the morning, but she hadn't seen him for a while. Dottie still came in regularly, sometimes with the kids. Peggy liked the twins, who were about her age, but was scared shitless of Archie. And like Shirley at the post office, she thought Dottie was a bitch. When I asked about Lyle Bensen, I got a blank look.

I started back to Northport with nothing good to report to Ezra, a stiff neck, assorted bruises and bumps, and the possibility of the easy five grand setting with the sun. It had not been a good day.

I needed a fistful of aspirin, a good night's sleep, and a chance to sort it all out. Instead, I decided to drive to the sheriff's office.

The jail was a long one-story concrete bunker squatting on the edge of Stone Island, the county seat, about nine miles from Morehouse. The lobby was empty. Behind the counter was a woman wearing a drab brown uniform of a deputy. Her name tag read, CPL. S. MARSH. She was about five-six and built like she belonged on the vice squad.

"May I help you?" she asked.

"Just cuff me, frisk me, and I'll confess."

She chuckled.

"Is Gerking here?"

Duane Gerking was a good cop with a dumb name. He was in his fourth term as sheriff and I'd known him for most of that time. With that name, he'd heard a lot of stupid pickle jokes. He was a big man with a blustery voice to match.

We'd met through my other business, Peaches and Chuck Security. PAC handles security for rock bands on the road. It has made my partner Jesus "Peaches" Gomez and me a lot of money in the last ten years. Enough that Peaches opened an antique shop and I began Triple-A.

PAC had donated security at some local events in Stone County over the years, so we got to know Gerking pretty well. We'd become friends. From his office, I heard him bellow, "Twain, is that you? Get your ass back here. I haven't seen you since . . . hell, I can't even remember."

The deputy smiled, nodding for me to go on back. I shrugged, tried to match her grin, then wandered back following the echo of Gerking's voice. He pumped my hand too hard and long, as some politicians will, then waved me to a chair.

He went behind his desk, sat down, and leaning back precariously in his overstuffed leather chair, he put his feet on his desk. He lit his pipe, glanced at me, and shook out the match. This was Duane's way of letting me know he was ready. He started fishing. "Social call, Twain?"

I shook my head, lit a Camel, and plunged in. "You know a guy named Earl Strong over in Morehouse?"

Gerking nodded, his feet came off the desk, and he sat up straighter. "Why?"

I told him about Ezra, Archie, and Dottie. He nodded and puffed as I went.

"Yeah, that Dottie. Man, she's a piece of work, ain't she?"

It was my turn to nod and drag on my smoke.

Duane went on. "Haven't seen Earl in a long time. Sent a couple of my boys out there to check. Dottie wouldn't even let 'em in the house, claimed Earl was outta town but wouldn't say where. Said if we wanted in the house to come back with a warrant."

"Yeah?" My neck hurt. I tried to turn my head and couldn't.

He nodded. "Tried to get one, too. Judge Stevens said we didn't have probable cause, wouldn't give it to us."

"Hear anything about Earl taking a shot at some guy?"

Duane shook his head, looked surprised. "When?"

"Month ago. At least, that's what Dottie told me."

"Nobody reported anything." He shrugged, giving me one of those what-are-you-going-to-do looks.

"You think Archie's smart enough to lie?"

Gerking rubbed his forehead grinning. "Doubt it."

I nodded my agreement. Dottie would probably lie to God, but not Archie. He was just too simple. "So, Duane, your hands are tied?"

"Yeah. Unless Dottie commits a crime, or Earl turns up, there ain't a damn thing I can do. Sure would like to see Earl though, find out where he's been."

"What about this Lyle Bensen?"

Gerking shrugged again. "Sometimes he's there for as long as six months, then he's gone for a long time. Go figure."

There was one way to find out what the story was in that house and Gerking wouldn't want to know about it, so I didn't burden him with my idea. I said thanks and we shook hands. On my way out, I chatted with Corporal Marsh long enough to get her first name, Sara, and her home number.

In my apartment, I curled on the couch with a Camel, a cup of coffee, and my cats, Leopold and Loeb. We talked about my idea until I had the kinks worked out and the cats had fallen asleep. The next morning I cleaned up and drove downtown.

Riverbank Antiques, Peaches's place, sits on a corner overlooking the river. A small bell attached to the door announced me.

Peaches was rising from his desk in the back when he saw it was me. He sat back down. "Twain," he said, grinning. "What's up, Babe?"

Gomez would call Satan "Babe." Slightly taller than me and chiseled, his body was all muscles and ripples. Thick, peroxided hair flowed to his shoulder blades. That day, as usual, it was in a blond ponytail contrasting against his cinnamon skin. A black belt, master of weapons, and student of all things Eastern, Peaches was the only Mexican warrior-monk I knew and that was precisely what I needed.

"We need to talk," I said, settling into the chair next to his desk.

He sat back, hands clasped behind his head. "So, Babe?"

I explained the situation and my idea. Peaches frowned.

"Why do you always hate my ideas?"

Peaches failed his "sugarcoating" class. "Because they are inevitably dumb."

"Got a better plan?"

He didn't and we both knew it. Finally, he agreed to serve as my backup. The next morning, the first of November, would be the day.

It was still dark when we drove toward Morehouse. We parked the car in the woods about half a mile from the Strong farm. Peaches circled around into the woods. He would be behind me.

With the dead cornstalks crackling like gunfire, I crawled through the field until I was in a position to see the front of the house and the Monte Carlo in the yard, and waited.

It was a simple plan. When Dottie and Archie drove into town to pick up Earl's check, I would break in and search the house for some sign of Earl. The four youngest kids would be in school. The only glitch would be if Lyle Bensen was there.

Lying on my stomach in the field, the frost beneath me soaked into my black jeans and not heavy enough jacket. My legs and ears got numb, my fingers stiff from the cold. I didn't think I could be seen from the house. I glanced back toward the woods. No sign of Gomez, but I knew he was there.

I watched the Strong kids board the school bus. The dead stalks chafed against my hands and face. An hour later, Dottie and Archie climbed into the Monte and sped down the lane. I waited another five minutes before I made my move.

The hulks of the Chevys were my first target. Sprinting across the field, the only sounds were the snapping of cornstalks and my heavy breathing. I huddled between the cars, heart pounding. Peering over a fender at the house, I saw no signs of activity. I hightailed it around to the back of the house to the safety of the shadows and the pines.

Sweat slithered down my back and my adrenal gland was pumping at triple time. Except for a dog in the distance and the throbbing of my heart, it was quiet. I wedged up next to the door and tried the knob. It was locked. Fear constricted my throat, breathing came hard. I checked the woods, no sign of Peaches but that was to be expected. He wouldn't show himself unless I needed him.

The top half of the door was glass. Wrapping my jacket around my left hand, I punched it. On the second blow, there was a crash, then a chorus of shards shattering on the kitchen floor. Tiny needles poked every inch of my fist, then began climbing my arm. I tried to shake them free, but my hand felt broken. Sticking my right hand through the hole, I undid the latch and let myself in.

It was a small, dingy room. To one side sat a Formica table and four folding chairs. The dishes in the sink and on the counter looked like a penicillin factory. The windows were covered with grease and gunk and barely any light filtered in. I hurried into the next room.

The living room was just as dark. I tried to get my bearings, but it was hard. The windows were covered with both curtains and some kind of blinds. These people lived in a cave. I tripped over something and sprawled to the floor in the darkness.

Pain shot through my hand again. Sweat trickled down my brow searching for my eyes. With my nose buried in it, the cheap carpeting smelled of mildew.

My hand throbbed and fear nibbled at my heels as I crawled down the hall licking my lighter at each doorway.

The first room was a grimy, windowless bathroom.

Beyond that, a bedroom, probably Archie, Jamie, and Floyd's. Bunk beds mirrored each other from opposite walls and the sheets smelled as if they hadn't been changed ever. The room was cluttered with junk whose only common quality was that it was all broken.

The dirt was less pronounced across the hall in Janie and Rose's room, but it was hard to tell with clothing piled everywhere.

The last room was dominated by a king-size bed that nearly filled it. Against the wall, at the foot of the bed, was a cot. There was a mound under the blankets. If it was Earl or Lyle they could sleep through anything considering how much noise I'd made getting there.

My legs quivered as I rose. I took two tentative steps and touched the blanket. A couple of deep breaths and I was ready to pull it back.

There was a grunt that wasn't my voice and I found myself on my stomach on the big bed. The weight on top of me was crushing as I screamed into the sheets. My mind found a foothold in reality. It was Archie. I didn't know how, but it was Archie. His rancid breath enveloped me as I tried to fight back. It was useless. With dead weight alone, he had me pinned to the bed. He jerked my head up by the hair. It felt like he was trying to pull my crotch through the top of my head, but I forgot that pain when he punched me in the chest. My lungs collapsed. As I hung there limply, I wondered if a heart attack hurt worse.

My world became a black cloud filled with blurry faces. My mom and dad, Leopold and Loeb, Peaches. Where the fuck was Peaches? I couldn't focus. A vague light appeared, a tunnel. I tried to move toward it.

Archie slapped me back into the reality of the room

and held me so Dottie could glare into what was left of my eyes.

"I told you not to come back," she snarled. "I could call the cops. But that'd be more trouble than we need."

She took a step to the cot and raised the blanket. "We might have to explain this then." She nodded toward the cot. My gaze followed hers and I finally met Earl Strong.

Earl, or what was left of him, had been mummified and laid to rest on the cot at the foot of Dottie's bed. The bed where she slept, where, presumably, she fucked Lyle Bensen. A skeletal frame and a few clumps of wispy hair were about all the rats had left. I figured Earl had probably looked better, but judging from his offspring, not much.

Dottie let out a sick cackle as my stomach somersaulted and I tried to climb over Archie to get out of that room, that house.

"Je . . . Jesus Christ," I stammered.

"What'd you 'spect?" Dottie said coolly. "He's been dead for a couple of years now. But me and the kids needed his checks. We couldn'ta made it without 'em. So we couldn't tell nobody."

My skin was crawling, snakes filled my guts. "But . . ."

Dottie didn't need me, she was on a roll. "Really it was Lyle's idea. He's smarter than Earl ever was. Anyway, I woke up one morning and there was Earl lyin' next to me, dead. Musta had a heart attack in his sleep or somethin'. So I called Lyle right away and he says, 'Why tell anybody?' " She shrugged. "So we didn't."

I gagged. "What about the kids?" I managed.

"Oh, they love their dad. I 'splained to 'em that if we ever told anybody, that they'd take Daddy away. And well, you know kids, mister. They didn't want to lose their daddy so they went 'long with it. Hell, they still have dinner with Earl, talk to 'im 'bout their troubles and stuff."

Ezra Strong didn't have enough money, not for this. I felt tears sliding down my cheeks.

"You know, mister, now that you know our little secret," she paused, "you can't leave here."

I tried to break away. Archie slapped me again, a glancing blow this time, which sent me flying on top of Earl. We fell together on the floor, wedged tightly between the cot and bed, Earl on top of me.

I heard Dottie's cry of "Earl!" over my own screams. I tried to push Earl off me, my hand shoving through where his stomach should have been to his spine. I kicked and punched to no avail. Earl didn't care, he just lay there trapping me.

Dottie was hysterical, screaming for Archie to save Earl and to "Kill that son of a bitch!"

Earl's arm crackled like the cornstalks as it splintered off on the edge of the bed, allowing me to crawl free before Archie jumped onto the pile.

What was left of Earl went up in a cloud of dust as Archie lit on top of him. I got to my feet and kicked Archie in the face as hard as I could. He groaned and sagged. I jumped across the bed and caught Dottie with a picture-perfect right cross. The scream died in her throat as she fell into the closet.

I could hear Archie lumbering after me, bellowing like a wounded animal as I ran down the hall. He got a piece of my shirt as I crashed through the back door. We tumbled to the ground in a heap, Archie on top, crushing the wind out of me.

He had me by the head again, about to snap my neck, when Peaches stepped from the shadows. I don't think Archie ever saw the flat-hand blow that drove his nose bone into his undersized brain.

"Where the fuck have you been?" I wheezed.

Peaches was cool, as always. "Waiting until you needed me, Babe."

"I . . ." I let it go. I was too tired to fight.

Peaches stood guard over Dottie while I called Gerking. Fifteen minutes later, Duane, Marsh, and half a dozen deputies showed up.

It took two months for the whole story to come out. Lyle was arrested in Vegas and flown back. He and Dottie were tried for concealing a death, fraud, child abuse, and a bunch of other shit. They should be out of jail for Rose's high school graduation. The kids became wards of the court and the local mental hospital. Maybe with the money their Uncle Ezra sent them, they can get some decent therapy.

With Dottie and Lyle in jail, and the kids put away, nobody showed up at Archie's funeral except Ezra, Peaches, and me. I had no anger toward Archie—it wasn't his fault. All he'd wanted to do was make his mother happy. He probably could've been all right except for the accident of his birth, but you can't pick your parents.

I used part of the five grand Ezra gave me to pay for Earl's headstone. EARL STRONG, 1932–1990, A GOOD FATHER. Gerking rode the publicity of the case to a fifth term as sheriff.

Deputy Marsh, who drove me home that day, and stayed for the two days it took for the shock to wear off, became a good friend. On those nights when the nightmares come and I see Earl on top of me with black holes for eyes or Archie's teeth coming for my neck, Sara still picks up the phone on the first ring. It's good to have friends . . . and a family.

THE GIRL, THE BODY,
AND THE KITCHEN SINK
BY MARTIN MEYERS

I walked into the barbershop just as the shooter placed the gun to the toweled head of the man in the chair. I wanted to turn and run but I couldn't.

"No, don't," I shouted.

The shooter pulled the trigger and the man in the chair was dead. I still couldn't move. All I could do was stare at the bloody pulp that used to be a head.

"Tough luck, Fatso."

He meant me. I turned away from the mess in the chair in time to look into the eyes of the shooter as he put one in my stomach.

"Oh, my God." I fell to the floor clutching my gut. "Oh, God, please don't let me die." I screamed it over and over. "Oh, God, please don't let me die."

The phone rang as he fired again and again. I couldn't move. I let the machine handle it.

The shooting had happened over twenty years ago, yet it continued to haunt my dreams.

My tough luck for sure. The proverbial innocent bystander. I had wandered into a mob execution. They dug three bullets out of me that night, all from my big gut. The extra layers of fat probably saved my life. A fourth slug had caught me in the left knee. While all this was happening I was in dreamland. I came out of it two weeks later, a trimmed-down svelte 235 pounds. And with a knee that did tricks.

You want to hear the worst of it? My draft board,

which had been rejecting me because of my weight, now considered me 1A, fit for duty. Forget about the trick knee. I was drafted.

I checked the clock radio. Just before eleven. I pressed PLAYBACK on the answering machine. "Pat? Sol Schiff. Couple of days' work. But only if you get right back to me."

I tapped out Sol Schiff's number. Zola, the receptionist, put me through.

"Pat? All my people are out covering *Manhattan Mirage,* the drug movie that's shooting. Sabotage threats. I need you to come in and man the phones for a few days."

"Be still my heart."

"Don't be a wiseass. You coming in?"

"When?"

"Ten minutes ago."

"I'll be there. If my heart can take the strain."

"Wiseass."

Everything in New York is show business. But I'm not an actor. I'm a private investigator. My name is Patrick Hardy. I used to work strictly for myself, but what with the way the economy's been, I free-lance to other agencies. Mostly for Sol and the Victory Investigation Bureau.

The army put me in a special unit of misfits. Experimental. The Pavlov Platoon. They brainwashed all of us so that frightened or not we would act aggressively when danger threatened. I was still a chicken heart, but a fighting chicken heart.

Each and every man in the unit was a grade A foul-up. After a wholesale AWOL we were hauled in. Uncle had given up on us and was sending us back home. We were on a truck heading for the plane that would take us to Tokyo, then home. The truck hit a mine. Blap. Everybody got dead. Except me. Not a scratch.

I served out the rest of my time in Germany. MPs. I warmed a chair and pushed papers around.

Paris. It wasn't everything the movies told me it was but it was okay. I took my separation there. And found out that women liked the thin me. Yeah. At twenty-eight I discovered sex. I liked it. But I also still liked food. So, if I wanted women and food I had to work out.

When I got back to the States I found I wasn't qualified to do anything. Lucky for me the old man left a little bit. But not enough to sit on my ass. Since I needed to work but couldn't act or sing and certainly not dance, I became a private investigator.

For the last twenty years or so I've been playing the P.I. game, making a buck, but never big bucks. Eventually I even nailed the bastard who shot me. An asshole by the name of Ben Pelligrin. He changed my life. And I never even had a chance to thank him before he died.

I used to smoke too many Marlboros, drink too much scotch, pop too many Libriums, and screw . . . Well, you can never screw too many women.

I guess I'm what you'd call one of those bimbo-chasing detectives. Put it this way: I'm one of the reasons for the feminist movement and for political correctness.

My frame can handle 235 but often, when I ate too much and exercised too little, I added as much as thirty pounds to that. My bum knee always gave me problems and my blood pressure was always too high. Now that I've finally stabilized my weight and blood pressure, my cholesterol is too high. And the knee is worse than ever. Can't win for losing.

What it boils down to is my life had been dedicated to sex and food and exercise. With a little work on the side. Maybe that's overstating it. I love to read and watch old movies on TV. And I have to admit that for the last few years I've been getting more food than sex. I'm forty-eight. And I'm tired.

I was tired that day.

My eyes popped open. Sol was going to have kittens. I dressed and drank a container of Tropicana while a cab took me from my apartment on Riverside Drive down to the Chanin Building on East Forty-second Street and Lex. It was the middle of September, but more like spring than fall.

I stepped out of the cab and right into some dog's bad manners. I slid a few feet and in keeping myself from falling into the crap, I wrenched my bad knee. Wonderful.

I plunged into the Chanin, which is an art deco delight of chandeliers and white marble all about and underfoot, the kind of place you'd expect to find a private investigator's office.

On the ninth floor I pushed open the frosted glass door of the Victory Investigation Bureau.

"About time," said Sol, shouldering past me. Sol's an ex-cop. You'd never know it to look at him. Average. About forty, medium build, brown eyes, brown hair, you wouldn't notice him in a crowd. Good look for private investigator. "Field the calls, interview the people. Don't make trouble."

"Nice to see you, too, Sol."

Zola's a sweet young serious thing and I learned long ago she wasn't interested in anything I was selling. We had the office all to ourselves. I grabbed some ice and a Coke from the small fridge in the cubbyhole kitchen near her desk and parked myself in Sol's cherry-wood office.

While she worked at her computer and answered the phone, I iced my knee and finished my Steven Saylor paperback, *Roman Blood*. Because I hadn't thought to bring more than one book, I spent the rest of the day alternately thumbing through Sol's stack of old *New York Times* and staring at the wall and trying not to think of booze, cigarettes, and women. Every so often Zola would let me deal with one of the calls.

For lunch I had four calzones. A calzone is an Italian turnover made with pizza dough and filled with ricotta or mozzarella and herbs and spices and garlic and good things like that. I had two with prosciutto and ricotta and two with mozzarella and sausage.

About four fifty-five Zola interrupted me at my push-ups to tell me that a Ms. Arden Nash was on the line.

"Patrick Hardy. How may I help you, Ms. Nash?"

"I want you to follow my husband for me." Her voice was honey, warmed in the sun that only shone the other side of Mason Dixon. I envisioned white blond hair and breasts young as springtime and as round and firm as oranges.

"Is this for a divorce proceeding, ma'am?" I pulled a work sheet to me, and wrote her name.

"That's what I want you to find out."

"When would you like surveillance to begin?"

"Now."

Like Sol, like the world, everyone nowadays wanted everything right now.

"Are you there, Mr. Hardy?"

"Yes, ma'am."

"I'm calling from just outside Trump Tower. You know where that is?"

I sneered. "Yes."

"My husband, Kipling Nash, has offices there." I recognized the name. Like I said, everything in New York is show business. Except me. And sometimes I'm not so sure about me. Kipling Nash was the new wunderkind. Wasp America's white bread answer to Spike Lee and Martin Scorsese. "I will meet you in the lobby in ten minutes with a cashier's check for twenty-five hundred dollars."

"There's my other line."

"I don't have time . . ."

I put her on hold. "Zola, do you have a number to reach Sol?"

"No. I'm getting ready to close up."

"Okay." I retrieved Ms. Southland. "I'll meet you in the Trump lobby in ten minutes." I was lying. Only if I ran could I get there in ten minutes. And I wasn't about to run.

"How will I know you?"

I thought of the shtick and props Sol kept in the painted white closet in the corner of his office. I'm not much for beards and such but over the years, when my knee went bad, I learned that people took a man with a cane for granted. I like that. It gives you an edge. I didn't really need it today. Or did I? No matter, I'm partial to props, and that cane is a good weapon. It has six ounces of lead in its foot. "I'll be carrying a walnut cane. See you soon."

The walnut stick was waiting for me. I grabbed it and the gray aluminum attaché case, which was the surveillance kit, and hustled out to the front. "If you talk to Sol tell him I'm doing a surveillance gig for a Ms. Arden Nash. On hubby, Kipling Nash."

"Ooh," said Zola. That was not awe. That was sarcasm.

"Yeah. Ain't this a fascinating, exciting business?"

"Yawn, yawn."

"Paperwork's on Sol's desk. Start-up money is twenty-five hundred. I'll call the message box and the machine."

'Right," she answered, putting a cozy over her computer.

From the Chanin at Forty-second and Lex to the Trump on Fifth at Fifty-sixth Street is only fourteen short street blocks and three long avenue blocks. I made it in fifteen minutes. My knee was almost fine. The cane was all ornament that I had twirled much to my own delight. I took another minute to stop my heavy breathing and made a vow to get more bike work in.

We spotted each other at the same time. I suppose you could say she had auburn hair, but that would be an understatement. Spun copper gossamer was more like it. Down to her shoulders. And the face of an angel. She was petite, juicy, with a voluptuous figure, only a few pounds shy of plump. The black leather coat accentuated rather than hid her curves. "Mr. Hardy, I presume."

"Call me Pat." I was immediately on the make. Juvenile, I know, but old habits are hard to break.

"Mr. Hardy," she repeated, her bright blue eyes sharpening into bits of steel. Many Southern women have that confectionery facade and underneath they are icy bitch. Arden Nash didn't bother with the facade. She was pure ice maiden. Short and mean.

"When my husband comes down I want you to follow him."

"Simple enough. But I could use a little more background."

"There he is now. The elegant man in the camel's hair coat." She was looking at a tall, thin man with sleek dark blond, almost honey-colored hair, who

looked as if he'd time-traveled from a 1920s Arrow
Shirt ad.

I had seen his picture the week before in *People*.
Not with Arden. "I know what he looks like," I said,
getting the small Canon camera out of the kit.

"Doesn't everyone?" Her look was pure venom.
For me or him? Who knew? Either way her expression was icy enough to put frost on my pumpkin. "Had
you gotten here earlier," she said in best bitch fashion,
"I would have been able to oblige you with some per-
tinent details." She thrust a pale green number ten
envelope at me. "The check and my card. Let me
know where he goes and who he sees. Don't worry, I
have call forwarding."

I was a little late with the camera. I should have
checked the time and date gizmo sooner. I did now.
"Don't the two of you live here?" With the camera
waist high I grabbed a shot. I owed the tape recorder
a commentary.

"He does, I don't." She'd almost snarled it.

"You want him covered around the clock?"

"And so close you can hear him fart." Not only
bitchy, crude, too. But—as she brushed past me on
her way out, I thought I caught the curve of a smile.
Had she been jerking my chain? But there was no
time for such idle thoughts. Kipling Nash had faked
me out by slipping onto an elevator. Going back up?
Or the basement? I shoved the camera in the pocket
of my blue blazer and followed.

Elevators are not conducive to tailing. Unless
there's a mob, you're readily noticed. Like now. We
were alone in the car. He had pressed eight. I stood
there trying to be as anonymous as possible. Gray
surveillance case in one hand, cane in the other. The
damned cane didn't help. Dumb, the cane.

When he got out on eight, so did I. We marched

off in opposite directions. After a bit I went into my I-don't-know-where-I'm-going act and turned. Just in time to see an extremely pretty woman open the door to a jeweler's shop and let Nash in. She was almost Nash's height and perhaps just out of her thirties, with delicate bones and straight jet hair.

A jeweler's shop window in Trump Towers is very tasteful. A great deal of crushed blue velvet and minimum ostentation. Perhaps the simplicity is the ostentation? There was a glass display window but all I could see was the tasteful display of only a few gem-studded bracelets and necklaces on the blue velvet. Nothing of the shop itself.

A quick shot of the exterior and I found a space where I could take out the small tape recorder from the surveillance case. I told the recorder the date and time and that Kipling Nash was my subject and that he had just entered Ormont Jewelers on the eighth floor of Trump Tower.

I backed off and watched the door, all the time debating which was worth more? A picture of the girl or a check-in call on the portable phone. I decided not to chance the call. In less than ten minutes Nash was out. I clicked a hip shot at a glimpse of the woman, hoping the camera saw her better than I did. As expected, Nash headed for the elevators. Once more there were no other people about. Go figure. In New York. In the Trump Tower.

He was a director, trained to observe. Would he retreat within himself as most people did on an elevator? Or would he be twenty-four-hour Herr Director who would eyeball me with intensity and etch me into his brain. I had to think the latter. One more elevator ride with the two of us together and we'd be engaged.

After that, as far as following Kipling Nash was concerned, I'd be useless as tits on a bull.

Of course, one car could come right behind the other, and I could dash for it and chase him down, offering my elevator a tip not to let the subject get away. And those bulls could grow wings while they were at it.

Or? I did or. I bet that he was going directly to the lobby and coming out on Fifth Avenue. So with the camera in my right pocket and the tape recorder in the left and the portable handset and small flashlight clanking around the surveillance kit with other paraphernalia, I ran down eight flights of stairs. Let me tell you, the detective game ain't what it used to be. And it sure is hell on my jackets.

While I waited on the street, favoring my sore knee, I used the portable phone to call Victory's message box. Nothing for me. I called the other number and got the machine. "Hardy," I told it. "Five-forty. This is going to go on for a while. I'm going to need a relief shift in about eight hours. Might even need a partner now. I'll check back with the box next chance I get. For God's sake, don't ring me." It's happened. Hot on a subject's ass and the portable rings, clueing the subject and blowing an entire operation.

After five more minutes of waiting, I grew very concerned that I had screwed up big-time. I patted my jacket for a cigarette. Pitiful. I'd quit my two-box-a-day Marlboro habit five years earlier but I still craved the damned things. I was saved from the next stage of checking out butts in the gutter by Kipling Nash finally coming out of Trump Tower.

He took a cab. I took a cab. The way it works in New York, there are two kinds of cabs. Metered and not-metered, gypsy. Most gypsies had a sign in the front window: CAR SERVICE. Take your pick. His was metered. Mine was not. Metered cabs are easy. You pay the meter. With the others there's a negotiation.

"Where you going?" asked the driver. From his speech I figured Indian or Pakistani. No turban. That means something but I forgot what.

"Just follow that cab." I nodded at the vehicle just ahead, waiting for the light.

He turned and smiled at me through the plastic partition, eyebrows arched. "Such service will take some sensitive shmoozing."

Shmoozing? "What would you charge me for the next eight hours?"

He grinned, then turned to gun the gas and follow Nash's taxi. "How does one thousand dollars sound?"

"Terrible, but I admire your spunk."

"I would assume you have good spunk, too. Five hundred."

At Second Avenue we turned downtown, which is good because that's the way Second Avenue goes.

"What's your name?"

"Shelly Ansari."

"Well, Sheldon, how does two hundred sound to you?"

"Terrible, tawdry, and trashy. And my name is Shelly, not Sheldon."

"Like the poet. Two-fifty."

"No, like my father. Three."

At Forty-seventh the taxi ahead went west. Did Nash know he was being followed?

"Lay back, Shelly. And let me think." I used the interim to bring the tape recorder up-to-date. Then I took a few shots of Nash's cab. Fills the client file.

Just east of Broadway Nash's cab suddenly parked. Nash was getting out. Shelly was preparing to pull in behind.

"Drive past. Drive past."

With a quick wrench of the wheel he did. Taking Second Avenue to get to the West Forties was sure a long slide for an out. If Nash didn't know he was being followed, he was at least making sure he wouldn't be. But he hadn't looked around to check the terrain.

I watched him going into the Hayes Hotel. The Hayes is strictly for rent by the hour. Correction. By the quarter hour. Ten stories high, I don't know how many rooms on a floor. Hookers have been using it for years to turn their tricks. Bottom line. Lots of gash, lots of cash.

"Stop." We did with a very noisy squeal of brakes. "You're too erratic for my kind of work, Shelly. How much for the ride?"

"Thirty."

He was overcharging but I paid and hustled my ass to a spot just across the street from the hotel. Question was did Nash go out a back door or was he staying for a while? In my young days I would have barged right in and found out. And maybe gotten a few lumps for my trouble. Don't get me wrong, I wasn't tough. Just stupid. Sol wasn't paying me enough for lumps. I watched and waited.

"Taxi, sir?"

It was Shelly.

"Go away."

"Apparently you are here for the duration. I'm through for the day. Get in. Be my guest. Gratis."

I got in. I took several shots of the Hayes and told the tape recorder about it. After that I attempted to use the handset but it wouldn't work inside the cab. So, half inside and half out I called the mailbox. Nothing for me. I called Sol's answering machine and brought it up-to-date. That was not a long talk. But then again, it was to a machine.

Three girls, two with short skirts, the third with

long, were now congregating in front of the Hayes. Their hair agreed with their skirts. The long-skirted one had her hair wrapped neatly in an old-fashioned bun. They all wore dark blue pin-striped suits, no blouses. And black mesh hose. All, good long legs. Besides their makeup the only splash of color was their red pumps.

They most definitely were hookers. Two blocks away from the Hayes they could pass for dancers. This was the middle of the whore district and the theater district. A close call. It was odd to see them so uniform. Like a team. Or a troop. Or a gang.

I took pictures of them and observed as after a bit one by one they peeled away with johns and went into the hotel. When they were gone Shelly and I talked. About the girls and about morality. I took a pass on sexual morality. Killing people, starving people, that's an easy call. Sex? I think it's a wonderful thing. If only so many people didn't get hurt because of it. But you could say that about money and power, too.

We compared Eastern philosophy and Western philosophy. Not my best subject but I can bullshit about most anything, and apparently so could Shelly. At nine I got antsy, slipped Shelly another thirty, got receipts for our two transactions, and went across to the Hayes Hotel.

I had a few options. I could just ask for Nash. I could register and look around. I could be straightforward and ask about Nash. Or say I was supposed to meet him. I could show money. I could show muscle.

"How much for a room?"

"Say what?" He was a skinny white kid with a geeky fade haircut. His damn head looked like a white radish with moldering top greens.

"I need a place to crash for a couple of hours. How much?"

"I got you." He winked. What the hell he thought he was being conspiratorial about I have no idea. At that moment it occurred to my slow brain that if I wandered these halls, I'd be fighting pimps and johns all night. I switched to plan B. "Nash get here yet?"

"Who?"

"Tall, thin guy, shiny sort of blond hair. Wears a camel's hair coat."

"What's that?"

"Never mind. Did he get here?"

"Yeah. Three-oh-five. You're in three-oh-seven." The kid smirked. "Maybe you two could have a drink together. And if you get lonely I could come up and join you."

I smirked back. "I'll consider your kind offer." Sleaze factor aside, it was easier than I could hope for. Why a man like Nash would want to screw around in a sewer like the Hayes was beyond me. Perhaps he thought he was so well known this was the only place he could avoid detection. A rented apartment would be better. Then again, some people think sex is only good when it's degraded. Perhaps Nash and Miss Pretty liked screwing in a toilet. Maybe it did something for their libidos that clean sheets in a nice place couldn't do. The whole situation confounded me. But if I could take a couple of pictures of him in the sack with whomever, I could call it a night, go home, pig out on salami and potato salad, and watch a movie.

I entered my closet of a room. God's gift to the weary traveler. The rug had more dust in it than Oklahoma. The bed promised to be just as gritty. A promise I did not want it to keep.

As I started to shut my door, I heard 305's creak open. Being lucky is better than being born rich or good-looking. I crept my door in till it was not quite closed and watched through the crack. A female form wearing a tan raincoat went past. I thought I saw an ice bucket. I opened my door a quarter inch more. It creaked, too. I stood stock-still and waited.

Pretty soon back she came, jiggling the bucket, making happy noises that matched the expectant grin. It was the woman from the jeweler's shop.

There was no listening device in the kit. A stethoscope would have done the job. I figured I'd do all right with the bathroom glass. The glass was plastic. Wrapped in cellophane, too, which did wonders for my sanitary concerns but did nothing to help me hear what was going on in 305.

I was forced out to the hall. The door was thinner than the wall. Nothing that route either. And no keyhole to peep through. I was bored, hungry, and just plain pissed off. I knew I had to get inside that room. Waiting wasn't going to cut it. I had to get a shot of them with the smoking gun. There's an image for you.

Back to my room. The surveillance kit also contained a power lock-pick. The instrument looks like the crossbreed issue of a toy electric drill and cake mixer. All you do is insert the tines and give her the gun. Zip-zap. The lock unlocks. I pulled the trigger. Nothing. I checked the batteries in the handle. They were dead.

I hadn't been in the Boy Scouts for nothing. Always prepared. The tools in the worn leather case in my inside pocket had done the job for the past fifteen years. With the camera strap hooked around my neck I opened my door. Traffic. I retreated and waited. Did the traffic go into 305? I couldn't be sure. I hadn't heard a door and I still couldn't hear anything through the wall.

I waited five minutes, then tried the hall again. Clear. Quickly I drew out the special knife and small tension wrench from my leather case. The wrench is hooked on each end, like a long "s." The knife is narrow, its blade has a hump toward the front end. This is a rake blade.

I pushed the wrench in at the top of the keyhole into the cylinder. In a few seconds I felt the first pin in the tumbler. I eased the rake blade in and moved it clockwise, exerting just a little pressure with the wrench. Every time a pin opened I pushed the wrench deeper through the opening, stopped, held my breath, looked up and down the hall, and listened for sounds from inside. Nothing on all fronts. When I passed the final barrier, the lock clicked. I kicked open the door and brought the camera up. Through the viewfinder I saw Kipling Nash's beautiful camel's hair coat soaked with blood. Like the battery, Kipling Nash was dead.

The woman was framed in the window, backlit by the neon lights of the club across the street.

The dead man with the bloody wounds was distracting, but she was more distracting. Her black hair that now flowed loose around her wide shoulders had downy traces of gray in it that I hadn't noticed earlier. Her eyes were light green. So light I thought extraterrestrial. She was a vigorous young woman with a healthy body. Covering some of it was a pale green blouse and lacy black panties. The blouse was hanging open but covering her brass.

I couldn't avoid seeing the gory remains of what had once been a human being in the bed and I knew that someone had stabbed him to death and that someone could have been this woman, but I was fascinated by her exposed skin. What can I tell you? I'm an aging detective, almost inured to violence and death and stuck in my depraved horny sexist ways. And I dig legs. And stomachs. And I am very aware of AIDS but that didn't stop me from wanting her.

Investigator instinct clicked in for a microsecond.

Just enough. On the floor was a black satchel. She saw my eyes flick to it and her hands came up and away. She undulated, the blouse undulated, exposing breasts that merely swayed. I stared.

I never think about my age until I'm face-to-face lusting after an attractive woman. Then I remember the years and wonder how jowly my neck appears. I was a good-looking young man. Never mind the corpse. All I could think was, does she think I'm attractive. After this was over should I hit on her? Will she think I'm a silly old fart or will she be interested?

Somebody kissed me. With a sap. Right at the base of my dumb skull. As my cop friend, Gerald Friday, used to say, in my world, life was just one paperback cliché after another. I guess I am stupid.

Dreaming again. This time of Ruby. She was young. I was young. Hell, the whole world was young. Ruby was wearing a net bra and a G-string and her red hair was flowing wildly. She was calling to me. "Come on, stud. Let's go."

I remembered. I would never stop remembering.

In the days when I was a testosterone grenade with the pin pulled, I knew a girl by the name of Ruby Red Rose.

Ruby Red. In a purple light. The first time I saw her she was wearing the traditional prima ballerina costume from *Swan Lake* and stripping to Tchaikovsky's music. The first thing she bared was her hair, her beautiful red hair. When the purple light changed to red, she bared her large, firm, round breasts.

We were lovers. When each of us was in the same place. That went on for a while. Except. After one of her trips out of town, she never came back. And I never checked to see why.

*   *   *

When I woke up all seemed well. I was in bed. And the dark-haired woman was right next to me. Trouble was it was the same bed Nash was in. He was on the other side of her. And he was still dead. More trouble was the woman. Her healthy body was no longer healthy. And her otherworld light green eyes were now doing the staring. She was dead, too. Like Nash she had been knifed to death. Yeah, I'm stupid.

I had barely placed my feet on the floor when the door burst open. A tall man, thin as bare bones. When he saw me the hunting knife suddenly appeared in his right hand. He must have had a rig in the sleeve of his denim jacket.

I've always been physically cautious. That's code for chicken. But I was trained to react. To fight. And even at forty-eight if I'm threatened my reflexes want to react. Except my reflexes are forty-eight, too.

So, I'm a little bit slower on the get go. And when I hit someone it can hurt my hand as much as the person I hit. Good enough reason for me not using my hands. My bones are too brittle for that sort of nonsense. Lack of calcium, I guess. That's why I like the cane. Too bad it was in the other room.

The speedy bastard was on me in a heartbeat. I couldn't go back and he was in front. Sidestepping his left, I feinted with my right. The blade came low. And fast. God, was he fast. Barely, I grabbed his right arm and heaved. He smashed into the wall. I must have scrambled his brain. He kept stabbing away, hacking the wall until finally he had punched so deep and tight he couldn't get the blade out. The wall could have been me.

He seemed so out of it my reflexes relaxed. Scared to my gut, I threw up.

While I was busy he ran. I was grateful. The knife

was no longer in the wall. He could have finished me. Much against my nature I ran after him. Why? Who the hell knows? I'm supposed to be a smart coward. Sometimes the wrong buttons get pressed and I do these things. I went into the stairwell and listened. The pound of his feet above me was unmistakable. I followed him up to the roof.

Lots of buckets and scaffolding littered the area. Apparently work was in progress. Shit, instead of one bad guy there were now two. This other was shorter and heftier. No matter shorter, I don't relish taking on two anyones. I tried to get away. Short whacked me with a bucket. Both sons of bitches grabbed me. Punching and kicking everywhere. My reflexes were functioning, I was slipping and counterpunching. But not well enough. Tall got me in a full nelson and held me while Short battered away. Then Short had a brilliant idea. "Let's throw him off the roof," he said, in a perfect announcer's baritone. Another out-of-work actor. The city was full of them.

They hoisted me over the four-foot security rail. There was about a one-foot walk space between the fence and the edge of the roof. The tall one leaned over the fence. I started a punch but he was still faster than I was. He grabbed my arm and shoved his knife almost up my nose. I could count the flecks of blood from the victims and the grains of plaster from the wall on it. "Your choice. The knife or the jump." His voice was pitched for perfect villainy, all growl.

There was a rope tied to scaffolding on the side of the building. I leaped for it, climbed, and slid down as fast as I could. The two above started shaking the rope and yelling about cutting it, but by that time I was past the eighth floor and almost to the seventh and literally at the end of my rope. Jesus, my heart stopped and I was ready to wet my pants. I was hang-

ing onto the swinging, twisting line for dear life with
my feet trying to grab the inches-wide ledge over the
seventh-floor window.

It was quiet up above but I didn't know if they were
sawing away, or if they had gone, or were waiting for
me to climb back. I kicked at the window. The shades
flew up, revealing a naked woman. She opened the
window, looked at me, and started screaming.

"Don't scream, lady," I shouted, "I'm one of the
good guys."

Behind her I saw a naked man running out the
door. She grabbed her clothes and followed him.

My hands were slipping. I was running out of rope.
I had only one option. I took it. I swung toward the
window and let go of the rope. Thank you, God, for
old and rotting windows.

With a crash and a shatter I was on the floor among
the broken glass and wood, waiting for my body to
stop shaking and for my pulse to settle somewhere
near to normal.

I needed a drink. I needed a smoke. A woman
would have helped. Or a ham sandwich. I picked myself up, brushed myself off, and went out into the hall
on seven. No one. But I could feel eyes. Not willing
to deal with the stairs, I took a chance on the elevator
to get back to three.

The two bodies were still in 305. Amazingly, so were
my camera and pick case. Something was missing but
I was in too much of a hurry to think what. I immor-
talized the two dead people on film.

When I went into my room to wash my face, I saw
in the mirror that there were tiny little cuts all over
my hands and face. As long as there were no big ones
I was not complaining. My blue blazer was red-
specked and shredded, but again, I was not complain-

ing. And my knee didn't feel too bad. So you see, I was not complaining.

I collected my gear and this time used the stairs to get the hell out of the Hayes Hotel.

I wanted a drink. But I knew if I had one I might have another and I had stuff to do. The familiar gypsy cab was still across the street. Shelly was sitting there reading a paper. Suspicion niggled but I was too grateful for sanctuary. I crossed the street. "Shelly?"

He looked up from his *News*. "Sir?"

I got in. Now that he was serving his purpose, I ignored Shelly and shared what I knew with the tape machine. Clients love that stuff. I concluded that Mrs. Nash would be an exception. The cops would be thrilled.

The phone still wouldn't work inside. Again I did my half-in–half-out act and checked in with Victory. First the mailbox. Not a word. I called Sol's machine and told it the bad news. I called 911. Then I called Arden Nash.

"There's been some complications."

"Such as?" She didn't sound too bitchy. I remembered what was missing from 305. The black satchel. On a whim I shoved a suction cup onto the receiver and started the tape machine.

"I'm afraid I have some bad news. Your husband has been hurt."

"What?" The bitch was back. A disappointed bitch it sounded to me. I followed my whim. "But I've got the black bag."

"What?" This wasn't a bitch, this was a wounded lioness. Her dialogue was monotonous.

"The satchel." I grasped at straws. "The diamonds."

"What?" Broken record.

"The diamonds your husband and the girl were stealing."

"How did you get them?" The straws had become brass rings.

"The cops have the two bozos you sent to hijack the jewels and kill your husband and the girl."

"I never told them to kill anyone and you can't prove I did."

The familiar New York sound of sirens split the air. "I don't have to. Not my job. That's the cops' job. But you and I have just helped by supplying them with a lovely tape of your confession."

"It won't stand up. I know my rights. I haven't been Mirandized."

"That, too, is not my job. Anyway, this will point them in the right direction. What was the plan? To lay it all on me? Mox nix. The game's over. You lose. Sol will send you a bill and a complete copy of my report." I broke the connection and envisioned lighting a Marlboro.

Shelly's hand was at the money drawer in the plastic partition. "I'll take that tape, please."

"Oh, shit, Sheldon. Are you one of the bad guys?"

"No," he said, flashing his gold detective shield at me. "I'm one of the good guys. How did you know we caught the two perps?"

I shook my head. "I didn't. Just more bullshit."

It was his turn to shake his head. His voice was an echo from the past of my cop friend Gerald Friday. "I can't believe this. I work long hours, using up brain and muscle tracking this thing, and you wrap it up like a cliché paperback detective, on bluster, bluff, and bullshit."

That night after a double scotch I ate a large corn-beef sandwich from the Carnegie Deli. On seeded rye, slathered with plenty of their spicy Düsseldorf mus-

tard, washed down with a Dr. Brown's cream soda.
Hog heaven. I didn't have a Marlboro. Or a woman.
But I watched Ty Power on the tube triumphing as
Zorro, and slept like a baby.

LESSONS
BY JEREMIAH HEALY

1

There was a real bite to the November air outside my office, so I had only one of my two windows open, and that just an inch. Over the noise from the crowd milling around at the corner of the Boston Common across the street, I could barely hear the grind and yaw of trains pulling into the Park Street subway station. In front of me on the desk were the makings of a report to a couple in Iowa who had asked me to find their daughter. She'd overstayed her vacation in Cambridge visiting her boyfriend from Cedar Rapids. What had taken me a day would have taken less than an hour if the boyfriend had owned a telephone, because when I finally found him he gave up the name of another guy his "former" girlfriend had met in one of the few coffeehouses still extant on the planet. The girlfriend had moved in with the other guy, and she called her parents in my presence. It seemed important to her to prove that she hadn't been trying to hide on them.

I was doing the multiplication for the hourly rate when a pair of knuckles rapped on the pebbled glass that had JOHN FRANCIS CUDDY, CONFIDENTIAL INVESTIGATIONS stenciled on it. "It's open."

The man who swung the door wide looked like swinging it took most of his remaining energy. He was pencil-thin and elderly, that stage where you might be seeing a wasted seventy or a spry eighty. His gray hair was thin and slicked back like the movie idols of his youth, the facial bones sharp above and around hollow cheeks. His eyes were a shade lighter than the hair, the lips just a couple of lateral lines under a hook nose. I saw a tie whose width was almost fashionable, but the shirt collar and shabby cloth topcoat seemed two sizes too large for him. He held a homburg in the hand that wasn't on my doorknob. The hat shook, and the doorknob rattled.

"You're John Cuddy?"

"I am, Mr. . . . ?"

"Vogel, Joseph Vogel."

I rose. "Come on in. Can I take your coat?"

He closed the door. "Rather keep it on. Kind of chilly one today."

I extended my hand to shake, but Vogel didn't seem to see it as he looked at both my client chairs on his side of the desk.

"Please, have a seat."

I gestured to either of the chairs. He took the one closest to him, using a hand on each armrest to lower himself into it.

Sitting back down, I brought a fresh pad to center stage on the blotter. "What can I do for you, Mr. Vogel?"

"You can find my son Keith."

My week for missing offspring. While I appreciated Vogel's directness, my guess was Vogel, Jr., wasn't running in the same circles as the girl from Iowa.

"How old is your son?"

"Thirty-six, next birthday."

"When's the last time you saw him?"

"Year ago last month."

Direct answers every one, but not much information volunteered around the edges. "Mr. Vogel, maybe it'd be best if you told me the problem in your own words."

A short breath, then an abrupt nod, then a deeper breath. "I got married before I went into the service, but my first wife died while I was overseas. You have any idea what that was like?"

"Some."

Vogel paused. "You lost your wife, too?"

"Yes, but not while I was overseas."

"Vietnam?"

"That's right."

Vogel said, "I was in the Sixty-ninth Infantry Division of the First Army. Twenty years young when I hit Omaha Beach in June, '44."

I thought, He's not even seventy yet.

"We reached the Rhine at Remagen by March, then the Weser and finally the Elbe in April, where we met up with the Russkies. Ukrainians, wearing fur hats instead of helmets. Like deer hunters they were, swapping their Tokarev pistols for some of our surplus .45s."

I started wondering what this had to do with his son as he reached it.

"When I got back from Europe, I started teaching school. Didn't feel much like marrying again, waited five years, then married a girl almost ten years younger than I was. Emily bore me three children. Roger was the oldest and went into the marines. We lost him when they shelled Khe Sanh. You there?"

"No. I was army, mostly Saigon."

"Well, Roger getting killed, that nearly killed Emily herself right there. Diane was the baby, kind of . . . unplanned. But we loved her, and when we lost her a year and a month ago, that did kill Emily. Like a stake through her heart, outliving two of her children.

Keith's the middle one but my last left. I learned some lessons from my losses, and I want to see him again."

I thought about the dates. "The last time you saw Keith was at your daughter's funeral?"

"That's right."

"But not at your wife's."

Vogel seemed to have trouble swallowing, then coughed like a squeezebox with a hole in it. "He'd moved, no forwarding. With everything else, I . . . didn't take the time to find him."

"What makes you think he's still in the area?"

"I don't know that he is, for sure. But he used to hang out at a bar down Commonwealth. You might start there."

"Which bar?"

"Place called Shooters."

I'd been by it but not in it. A hole-in-the-wall dugout on Commonwealth Avenue just past Boston University's athletic complex. "Why don't you save yourself some money, go there yourself?"

"I did. Three weeks ago. Got nowhere."

"Mr. Vogel, I don't want to waste your money. I—"

"Got plenty of money to waste, as far as you're concerned. What I don't have is time." He swallowed and coughed again, controlling it more quickly this time. "Doc over at the VA in West Rox gives me two months. Maybe."

I closed my eyes. "I'm sorry."

"No need to be. You didn't make me sick, and you can't make me well. What you can do is find my son. Or at least give it a decent try for whatever you get a day now."

I quoted him half my usual rate and asked for two days in advance. He dipped into a breast pocket of the old coat and came out with an older wallet, a blue rubber band around it. He removed the band and produced a wad of twenties that looked fresh from the bank and counted out the right number of them onto my desktop.

As Vogel counted, I said, "You know, even if I find Keith, I can't make him see you."

"I realize that. Just call me before you approach him, and I'll come there."

"You have a picture of Keith?"

The hand that replaced the rubber band and the wallet went to another inside pocket and produced a small, framed photo. He passed it to me, holding it by the frame so the glass wouldn't be smudged.

"High school yearbook picture."

I nodded. The photo showed a boy with greedy eyes and a cold smile. He wore muttonchop sideburns and long hair combed down over the eyes and to the sides. The face was distinctive, though, especially with Vogel Senior's hook nose and flat lips.

"Any changes from when you saw him a year ago?"

"About the same height and weight, which is to say six feet and maybe one-sixty. Hair's a lot shorter, no sideburns. He was trying to grow a mustache, didn't even shave it for his sister's funeral. Don't have any photos from that. Didn't seem a time for taking pictures."

I mentally revised the yearbook shot. "Can I take this out of the frame?"

Vogel moved his tongue around inside his mouth. "Will I get it back?"

"Frame now, photo after I've had some copies made."

"Then keep both together, till you can give me the photo back in the frame. Don't want to take any chances with it, case you don't find him."

"I'll get on it this afternoon. How can I reach you?"

"Had to sell the house after Emily's medical bills.

I'm staying at a place takes boarders over by the Wang Center. Here's the number of the pay phone down the hall."

I took the slip of paper from him, torn from the corner of a *Boston Herald* newspaper.

Vogel said, "You call me, just let it ring awhile. I'll get to it before one of the Asians does."

"Asians."

"Lots of them in the place, three, four to a room, but that's okay. They're quiet, and I never had to fight any of them."

"Fight them?"

Vogel gave me a slow-student look. "In the war. I was European theater, remember?"

2

Shooters turned out to be all you'd expect and less. Seven steps down from sidewalk level, it had a DOLLAR DRAFTS hand-lettered sign in its one window next to a flickering neon logo of a beer brand. The floor was dark, marbled linoleum and tacky from sloshed or spilled drinks, a little tug from the tiles every time you took a step. The bar itself once had a brass rail, but now just the supports for it, sticking up like coat hooks. A bartender was actually trying to swab it down for two college girls who looked as though they were having second thoughts about staying long enough to order. At the far end of the bar, a little guy with a scraggly beard looked up from a Coors long-neck just long enough to make sure I wasn't a buddy who might stand treat for the next round.

I took a stool midway between the girls and Scraggly, leaving me a margin of three stools either way. If the jukebox worked, it wasn't being fed, and the mirrors above the barkeep's head were cracked and taped over with the black stuff electricians use.

The college girls decided to pass and left. The keep gave them the finger to their backs, which made Scraggly giggle and say, "They ain't impressed, Dukey." Then the bartender who might be named Dukey came down to me but didn't bother with the wipe cloth.

"Get you something?"

"A draft would be fine, Dukey is it?"

The keep nodded and went off to draw my beer. About five-ten and pushing forty, he had short, sandy hair that couldn't quite hold a part on the right side. There was a lot of scar tissue around his eyes, a broad nose that had been broken a few times, and a weak chin, which might explain the scar tissue and nose. As Dukey finished off the draft, I noticed there wasn't much head. Flat from last night's last keg.

He set it down in front of me, no coaster.

I said, "Thanks. What do I owe you?"

"Buck."

I put a five on the bar with one of the copies of Keith Vogel's photo I'd had duplicated at a passport shop around the corner from my office. "You know him, you can keep the change."

Something passed behind Dukey's eyes. "Sorry."

I said, "How about double or nothing?"

He took the five, left the photo, and went to the old-fashioned cash register. He rang in a dollar, came back to me with one dry single and three soggy ones.

Dukey put the bills on the bar. "Still wouldn't be able to help you."

This was getting interesting. "Make it twenty then."

"No. You deaf or what?"

"Maybe or what."

Dukey didn't like something he saw in my face. He went through a little door behind the bar and out of sight, though he left the door open, and I didn't hear another door or a phone.

Scraggly slid off his stool and came toward mine, saving me a trip to him. He didn't look so much like a derelict as somebody who just didn't care about clothes. His shirt was half in and half out of old blue jeans with a slit at one knee and a patch at the other. Old hiking boots for shoes and a pencil behind his ear under a 1986 Red Sox League Champion hat that looked like he'd washed the car with it.

Scraggly said, "Can I see the picture?"

I showed it to him. He grinned, a couple of missing teeth on his right side. "That's Keith, ain't it?"

"Keith Vogel."

"Sure, I recognize them eyes. Nasty boy."

"You seen him lately?"

"For how much?"

He knew he was a live one, and he knew I knew it, too.

I said, "Last bid was twenty, and it won't go any higher."

"Sure it will."

I expected I smiled. "Twenty-five."

"Fifty."

"Not in this economy."

He giggled. "Okay, account of I like your style. Keith, he had this girlfriend named Dana, college broad gone wrong, mainly thanks to him. You need a pencil, write down her address?"

"I'll remember it."

He recited number and street, including a description of the house about a mile from where we were sitting.

I said, "You have a last name on Dana?"

"No. But she lives on the first floor there."

"Thanks. What's your name?"

"Don't want you to know it, case Dukey decides he wants to try something."

"Where'd Dukey go?"

"Bathroom."

"Bathroom?"

"Yeah. He always likes to take a pee before he whales the hell out of somebody."

I laid twenty-five on the bar and decided that at half rate, discretion was the better part of valor. By the time I hit the door, Scraggly was slurping my beer.

3

I parked my old-model Prelude about three houses down from the address I'd been given. The building was a wooden three-decker, pretty typical for the neighborhood. Missing shingles, peeling paint, patchy lawn with two decent, chest-high bushes. Climbing the steps, I counted four spindles missing from the balustrade around the shallow porch.

There were three buttons next to the front door. The bottom one had no plastic cover and said, "D. Gins . . ." The remainder of the last name obliterated by the weather. I tried it. Six times.

A day and a half later, the door swung open, the woman behind it looking other than pleased. She had a terry-cloth exercise band around dishwater blond hair that stood up and out like palm fronds, but if she'd been working out she'd been doing it in a knit long-sleeved sweater and black, clingy stirrup pants.

"What?"

"My name's Cuddy." I had my ID holder out and open for her to read if she cared to. She didn't.

"Whatever it is, I don't know anything about it."

"Keith Vogel says otherwise."

She grinned. "What you want, it can get Keith into trouble?"

"Maybe."

"Then come on in."

"Thanks, Ms. . . . ?"

"Dana's all you need."

It wasn't until I followed her into the open door of the first-floor apartment that I realized how wired she was. Dana Gins-something was bouncing on the balls of her feet like a Tennessee Walker, her right shoulder caroming off the inside of the doorjamb as though that were the way everybody entered a room.

She gestured toward a gut-sprung chair near a thirteen-inch TV on top of a cardboard liquor box. A floor lamp stood next to the chair, and some college anthologies on philosophy, English literature, and American poetry were scattered at the base of the lamp.

As I took the chair, Dana flopped into a daybed with a holey chintz cover and triangular pillows as backrest. "So, how can I hurt Keith?"

"Maybe by telling me how you got to know him."

"Sure." Dana lapsed into a debutante voice. "My sophomore year. Diane introduced us."

"Diane?"

"Keith's sister. We were classmates, and one day big brother stopped by the dorm. Keith and I took one look at each other, and I knew we were lost."

Not quite *Of Human Bondage*, but I got the idea. "How long did you see him?"

"Hot and heavy for like a year, then on again, off again for a few months after that. Diane's dying kind of took the edge off things for me."

"When's the last time you saw him, then?"

"Her funeral, whenever that was."

"Any idea where he is now?"

"I don't know. Ask . . ."

"Ask who?"

The glint of suspicion came into her eyes. "You said

before you talked to Keith. How come you don't know where he is?"

"Because he's changed addresses since then."

"Yeah, well, if he changed since then, he's changed at least one more time than I know about. Just which cops are you from?"

"I'm not."

"But you said—"

"That I wanted to talk with you. I'm a private investigator."

"But I saw a badge."

"No. You saw an ID holder, and you didn't bother to read it. But I'm curious. Why have it in for Keith?"

Dana debated something, probably whether she was more mad at letting herself be tricked by me or more interested in hurting Keith if she could. When she smiled, I figured she'd decided on a compromise.

"I tell you what, Mr. . . . Curry?"

"Cuddy."

"Cuddy. You should learn to articulate better, so people would remember your name."

"Sound advice."

"I'll tell you what, Mr. *Cud*-dy. When you find out why I have it in for Keith, I'll bet you kick yourself. Real hard in a soft spot."

4

Walking down Dana's steps, I already was kicking myself for botching the interview with her. That might explain why I didn't hear him, but it certainly doesn't excuse it.

As I passed one of the chest-high bushes, the familiar voice behind me said, "This Intratec Tec-9 fires thirty-two nine-mil rounds without reloading."

I stopped cold, hands at my sides. "I'm persuaded."

"You carrying?"

"Probably."

A giggle. "Good. Give me a reason to shoot, I don't like what you do."

"What would you like me to do?"

"Walk over to your car, chauffeur me to a man wants to see you."

"What about?"

"He'll tell you when we get there."

I moved to my car, his footsteps, behind me on the sidewalk.

"Unlock the passenger's side first."

I did.

"Now climb in and over the stick and parking brake."

"I've done that before. It's not easy."

"Try it. For me."

I managed, a little tearing noise coming from the inseam of my pants.

"Now put the keys in the ignition, but don't turn it on."

"Okay. Now what?"

The scraggly guy from Shooters hopped nimbly into the passenger's seat and closed the door behind him. "Now we go see the man." The ugly, perforated nose of the Tec-9 nestled against my right rib cage. "And if your right hand don't stay on the gear knob the whole way, I give you about half of these."

Starting the engine, I said, "I knew I should have stayed at twenty bucks."

Scraggly giggled again and joshed me with the muzzle, showing his appreciation of "my style."

The office had no windows, not that the view outside would have been worth the cost of framing and glass. The furnishings, though, were carefully chosen. Original tin etchings and artist proof prints on the walls. Some kind of Afghan carpet over a polished hardwood floor. Admiral's chairs for visitors, padded with what looked and felt like real leather, oiled and buffed. The desk was sleek, black, and lacquered. You might have said the same for the man behind it.

He had no hair on top, a diplomat's trimmed beard riding downward from his fringed ears like a delicate lobster bib. He wore horn-rimmed glasses and as many sapphire and ruby rings as he had fingers less the thumbs. He tented his hands and rings on his tummy as he looked me over, the hands like a steeple with opaque stained-glass windows.

"Trevor tells me you expressed an interest in Keith Vogel."

"Trevor?"

From behind my chair, Scraggly said, "That's me."

My host said, "Trevor isn't much to look at, which makes him perfect in my business. Too many competitors believe they need be slaves to fashion."

That last from the voice box over a Louis's suit, silk tie, and brocaded shirt. I said, "What's your name?"

"No."

I shook my head. "Sorry, but that's how I started with Trevor at the bar, and look where it got me."

A tease of a smile, requiring him to push up the bridge of his glasses with an index finger that then returned to the steeple. "Let's just call me Frosty."

"As in the Snowman."

"Correct."

"Which gives me a rough idea of the business you compete in."

"Also correct. A business which finds itself missing one Keith Vogel for reasons I cannot fathom."

"Vogel an employee?"

"If he were a competitor why would I care where he was, except to construct an appropriate alibi?"

"So Vogel's absent without leave."

"For nearly a month."

"And?"

"And Trevor has been kind enough to stake out Shooters, Dana Ginsberg, even Keith's last place of abode—rather humble—without noticeable success."

"Vogel skip with some buy money or the proceeds thereof?"

One left to right movement of the bald head. "Neither. All accounts were squared, which is not an easy thing, dealing with the college crowd as Keith does."

I thought about it, but the wrong way. "So you're short one pusher for none of the usual reasons."

"For neither of the typical reasons. It may be that a competitor decided elimination was the sincerest form of flattery, not to mention increasing market share, but I doubt it."

"Why?"

"In the college game, there is truly plenty of room for everyone. It's only in the—God, I detest the term—*ghetto* that *turf* is an important aspect of the business."

"Well, I've already been to all the places Trevor here has tried except Vogel's old digs, so you're way ahead of me."

"Perhaps. Perhaps, also, however, you could divulge the name of your client so that we might expand our circle of inquiry."

"No."

An inclination of the head. "Trevor?"

A bolt or safety got thrown on the Intratec.

I said, "Still no."

"All I have to do is say a certain name again, and you will be like unto dust."

"I doubt that, given your care in decorating. But I'm still not going to tell you."

The skin around the glasses crinkled. "Why not?"

"Because I'm not nuts about your methods, and I'm not about to expose a client to them."

"A point of honor?"

"It's not that complicated, Frosty. I just don't like you."

The almost-smile reappeared. "Honor and courage. How refreshing."

I felt a trickle of sweat going down my spine. "I'm glad you think so."

"And grateful, too, I trust. Rugs can be replaced." He opened the steeple, then fluttered the pads of his fingers together again. "If you do find Keith, would you be willing to tell me?"

"Not a chance."

A full smile, the two front teeth with little gold star inlays. "I would have been disappointed if you'd agreed."

Trevor walked me back to my car, giggling at a private thought. Once I pulled away from the curb without him, I drove at a sedate speed for about three miles to the corner of Berkeley and Stuart Streets, parking illegally across from police headquarters and hoping the old Prelude would be mistaken for one of the oncoming shift's personal cars.

Upstairs, I found the man I was looking for. Slim, black, and streetwise. Dressed in a teal polo pullover and distressed jeans, a pair of cordovan brogue boots strapped to his feet. He lolled in a desk chair, legs stretched out in front of him, and didn't rise to greet me.

"Haven't seen you for a time, Cuddy."

"Good memory."

Ned Dawkins made a sour face. "Where you con-

:erned, babe, ain't no good memories. What do you want?"

"You still in Narcotics?"

He looked down at himself. "You ever seen Murphy over in Homicide dressed up like this here?"

"I wonder, if I gave you a name, could you run it for known associates?"

"Like the wind. But why would I want to do that?"

"One of our wholesalers has lost a retailer and doesn't know where to find him."

"You working for the forces of darkness now?"

"No. But a case I'm on crossed over a little, and I'd like to know what I'm getting into."

Dawkins regarded me, a little tic working under one eye that I didn't remember from the last time I'd seen him. "You got a name for the wholesaler?"

"No, just the retailer. Keith Vogel, been active in the college market."

"That supposed to motivate me?"

"That's supposed to help you decide if you want to help."

The sour look again. "Let's give it the old college try, then."

Ten minutes later he came back from another room and said, "Your Keith Vogel been running with Manson Olivette."

"Olivette a balding guy with an Oxford complex?"

"You mean does Manson think he's cultured, yeah. But cultured don't mean civilized."

"His enforcer a guy named Trevor?"

"Trevor McBride. Murphy's probably got two or three case files with his name in them but not enough for the grand jury."

"Anybody else in Vogel's jacket?"

"Just from his olden days."

"What olden days?"

"Back when he was doing B&Es, before he learned where the money tree grows."

"Name?"

"Dwayne Ulrich."

"Dwayne? Who'd call a kid Dwayne?"

"Not even Dwayne himself."

"What do you mean?"

"Goes by the name he used in the ring. 'Dukey.' Don't sound too tough, does it?"

I took a breath. "You never know."

5

I waited outside Shooters on a side street, my windshield diagonally across Commonwealth from the dugout's entrance. That way, I could follow Dwayne "Dukey" Ulrich regardless of whether he took automobile or subway east or west. That first night he came out the door at 8:05, reading a magazine as he walked casually to the Green Line trolley westbound. I trailed the trolley on Commonwealth. Dukey just sat in the car with ten or so other people, his head in the magazine until his stop came up about a mile farther on.

Ulrich left the trolley and walked down an intersecting street half a block before putting the magazine under his arm and climbing a set of outside stairs to the second floor of a brick two-family. Once inside, he was in for the night. Or at least until three a.m., when I called it a day.

The next night, same routine with magazine and trolley, only starting at 8:10. The third night, however, Dukey had lost the reading material and was alert coming out of the bar, as if the bell were about to ring for the last round. He took the trolley westbound again, but this time stood and watched around him. Ulrich got off two stops before his place, went into a small grocery, and came out a bag that looked fairly full. He was still walking on eggshells, getting on the trolley and standing again, even with the bundle. This time he went three stops past his place and started down a side street.

Dukey walked around the block once and might have made me if I hadn't been lagging in the car, looking for a pay phone. Seeming satisfied he hadn't been followed, Ulrich then went around the back of a yellow three-decker with no lights on the top floor. The lights came on just after I figured he would have reached the third-floor landing.

I walked back to the pay phone I'd spotted on the corner.

The man looked so awkward negotiating the bottom step of the trolley that I wished I'd told him to let me pick him up and drive him out. He saw the Prelude where I'd said it would be and came toward me slowly, bent over and into a wind that I hadn't noticed until he began struggling against it.

I got out the driver's side as he coughed, a spasm that sounded a lot worse than either had three days before in my office.

"Mr. Vogel, you all right?"

"No. I'm dying, remember?"

I gave him a moment. "You sure you want to go through with it?"

"This other person, the bartender, he still up there?"

"As far as I can tell."

"Well, that's not too private, but let's take the chance."

"There's something else you should know, something I didn't want to tell you over the phone."

"What?"

"Your son's been involved with the drug trade."

Vogel's flat lips parted. "I didn't say Keith was a saint. He's been in trouble before, but I still want to see him."

"Okay."

I moved with Vogel without helping him until we got to the stairs. I told my client to climb staying on the outside of the risers. He gave me the slow-student look as a reward. We went up in unison, me on the right side, him on the left, a slow step at a time.

At the door, I gave Vogel a questioning look. He stepped back and pantomimed a knocking gesture, so I did.

I heard two sets of feet cross the room inside, but only one came all the way to the door. As it cracked open, I put my shoulder into it hard enough to go through it, bulling over Dwayne Ulrich who on his best day was probably only a welterweight. As he got up, a shot rang out from behind me, and Ulrich's knee popped into a small fountain of blood.

I was half-turned when something metallic and solid tapped my skull behind the right ear, sending me down in a sprawling gesture. My chin kissed the floor of the kitchen, loosening a tooth. I wasn't quite out, vividly aware of Ulrich's screaming, less so of the man from the yearbook picture, his hands in front of his chest, the time-lapse illusion of aging on a face drawn taut with terror.

Keith Vogel said, "Pop, no, please!"

My client's voice from behind and above me was steady, rehearsed even with the emotion lacing it. "Two years I fought the Germans so kids like you could be free, Keith. Roger died in a bad war, Diane from bad drugs you gave her. This other piece of scum I shot told you I was looking for you, and you hid like a rabbit. You were right to hide from me, Keith."

"No, Pop! come on, here."

I managed to roll over onto my side, but the motor coordination to draw my weapon or get to my feet was at least ten minutes away. Joseph Vogel held a black, bulging automatic in his hand, none too steadily. Given the distance involved, none too steady would be more than good enough to take his son.

When my client didn't reply, Keith glanced at Ulrich still writhing on the floor. "Pop, please God, what are you saying here?"

"I'm saying, Keith, that you dishonored your brother and killed your sister, and that killed your mother. For all I know, the heartache over those losses brought on my cancer. I do know I learned a lesson from the soldiers who traded me this Tokarev pistol, a lesson they learned from fighting the Germans."

I said, "Mr. Vogel—"

His voice, now raspy with effort, rode over me. "It was a simple lesson, Keith, one I should have taught you at an age when it would have done some good. Something goes wrong, you deal with it yourself, make it right."

"Pop, no. For the love of—"

"God? Your sister? Maybe your mother. Take your pick, Keith. I haven't got much longer left, but I'd like to spend that time talking, to the papers, to the TV, whoever. You're going to be a lesson, too, Keith, a lesson on what should happen when something you've created goes haywire, on what a parent's duty is to society for a child gone wrong."

"Jesus God, Pop, let me—"

Vogel Senior had run out of speech, or run out of patience, but he hadn't run out of bullets. Spaced a heartbeat apart, the first punched his son against the sink, and the second spun him around the pantry door.

The next two pinned him to a wall before he started sliding down, leaving vertical smears of crimson behind him roughly on a line with where his lungs used to work.

My client dropped the Tokarev onto the table and pulled out one of the old vinyl chairs. He slumped into it, coughed once, and looked down at me as he rummaged a hand in the glove pocket of his overcoat. "Probably don't have a phone here, so you'll have to go back to that pay station on the corner."

"Mr. Vogel—"

He came out with a dime and tossed it at me. "Go ahead. You put this thing into it and dial, remember?"

A FAVOR FOR SAM
A Nick Delvecchio Story
BY ROBERT J. RANDISI

1

"Sam! You're a day early. You weren't due back from Chicago until tomorrow."

She was sitting on the floor with her back against my door as I came down the hall. She was wearing jeans, a T-shirt, and she was barefoot.

"Oh, Nick!" She started to cry.

I stared at her, unsure what to say, so I slid down and sat next to her. She looked at me and then wiped at an errant tear as it worked its way down her face.

"Lisa's my friend . . . a writer who I see at these conventions. When she didn't arrive I called her and . . . and she told me on the phone that she tested positive for . . . for the HIV virus."

She was talking very fast, the way people who are upset do. I'd never seen her this upset. She just about collapsed in my arms and started sobbing. You have to understand about my neighbor, Samantha Karson. She's smart, gorgeous, sensitive, and confident. I'd never seen her cry before.

"And . . . and that's not the worst part. She really loved this guy, Nick, the guy who . . . who gave it to her. At first she didn't want to believe that she got it from him, but there was no one else."

"Did she confront him?"

"On the phone. She called him and told him that

315

she had AIDS, and do you know what the son of a bitch said to her?"

"What?"

"He told her it was her fault, that she should have been more careful."

"What? He gave her AIDS, and *she* should have been careful?"

"That's what he said."

"What a shit."

"He also said it wasn't his responsibility to tell her."

"Then whose was it?"

"He told her that she should just treat everybody like they have AIDS."

"That's good advice—funny, too, coming from him. What kind of shape is she in?"

"She said she's on some kind of medication and she's responding well to it, but you know that will only put the inevitable off for a while. She's going to die, Nick."

"I'm sorry, Sam."

"There's something else."

"There's more?"

Sam nodded.

"She found out from another girl that the same guy gave her AIDS."

"Before or after your friend?"

"Before. She was his girlfriend before Lisa."

"Too bad Lisa didn't meet her earlier."

"I feel terrible."

"Why?"

"I wish there was something I could do."

"Like what?"

Sam shrugged. "I don't know. Something."

"Well, I wish there was something I could do to help you, Sam."

Sam looked at me sharply and said, "There is."

I looked back at her and asked, "Did I just walk into that with my eyes wide open?"

"Nick, Lisa wants to confront the guy—face-to-face."

"So?"

"She doesn't know where he is. She can't find him."

"I repeat. So?"

"You could find him. You're good at that."

"Sam—"

She stopped me by putting her hand on my arm.

"Please, Nick. There's so little that can be done for her. If she could confront him . . ."

"Aw, Sam . . ."

She kept staring at me, her eyes pleading. How could I turn her down? And what would it cost me to try? It would probably make *her* feel like she was doing something, which would make her feel better.

"Okay, Sam, I'll see what I can do. Where does your friend live?"

"St. Louis."

"Saint— Okay, well, where does the guy—what's his name—live?"

"His name is Ted and he lives in St. Louis, too."

She had a wary look on her face, like she was waiting for me to explode.

"St. Louis? Sam, that's in Missouri. That's all I know about St. Louis—"

"What do you have to know? If you're looking for a missing person, don't you do the same things, no matter where he lives? Check his home, his work, and . . . and whatever else you check?"

"Well, sure, but I don't know my way around St. Louis—"

"Lisa said she can tell you how to get anyplace you want to go."

"Lisa said—you already told her I would come?"

"Well . . . you don't think I expected you to pay your own airfare, do you?"

2

Sam said her friend Lisa didn't have much money but she did have enough to pay for airfare from New York to St. Louis. Of course, I had to lay out the two hundred and forty-eight dollars and she'd reimburse me later. Oh, and Sam said there was a catch—she was coming, too. She said she wanted to spend some time with Lisa. Since I considered that I was doing the whole thing as a favor to Sam, I didn't argue as long as she did what she was going to do while I did what I was going to do. She agreed.

Lisa Carlson lived in a suburb of St. Louis called Shrewsbury. Well, they didn't call them suburbs, they called them cities. That meant that within the city of St. Louis were all these other little cities such as Shrewsbury, Webster Groves, Clayton, and others. Being from New York, it was confusing to me, so I preferred to think of them as suburbs, or even boroughs.

We rented a car at the St. Louis Airport, which was the biggest airport I'd ever been in. One entire section of it was the TWA hub and we seemed to walk miles before we left the gate area and got into the area with the ticket counters, shops, and transportation.

When we got in the car I got behind the wheel and asked Sam where we were going. That's when she explained about all the little cities and told me the one Lisa lived in.

"How do we get there?"

"She gave me directions."

She started telling me about I-270, and something called the inner belt that was also known as I-170, and

then there was Highway 44—I let her get that far and
stopped her.

"I'll drive," I said, "and you just point."

"Okay."

With her pointing we only went the wrong way
twice but we finally ended up in Shrewsbury, getting
off the highway at a street called Laclede Station Boulevard. Lisa lived in an apartment complex on Big
Bend Road, and when she opened the door to greet
us she and Sam embraced warmly. Lisa seemed genu-
inely touched by Sam's presence, and at that point I
was glad I was helping both of them.

Sam made the introductions and then we sat down
at Lisa's table with coffee and cookies and I took a
good look at her. Outwardly there were no indications
of the disease. She was slender and attractive, with
brown eyes and long dark hair.

"You can't see it," she said to me.

"Oh, I'm sorry." I thought I'd been staring and she
caught me.

"It's all right. Actually, I don't have AIDS, I simply
tested positive for the HIV virus."

"But that will become AIDS, won't it?" Sam asked.

"Maybe," Lisa said, biting her bottom lip, then,
"probably. It depends on how well I continue to respond to the medication."

We were silent for a while and when it became awkward, Lisa broke it herself.

"I'm glad you came here to help me, Nick. What
do you need?"

"Well, Sam says the guy's name is Ted. I need his
full name, his home address, where he works, who his
friends are—if you know them—and some other
women he might have seen."

"His name's Ted Drew. I can write down his address for you. I know the last place he worked, but I

don't think he works there anymore. Um, I know one or two of his friends, but I don't know their addresses."

"Maybe you could give me some idea where they hang out."

"Sure, I can do that. As for other women, there's his former girlfriend—"

"Sam mentioned her. I definitely want to talk to her."

"I have her address and phone number. We're kind of, uh, well, members of the same club."

"What condition is she in, Lisa?"

"She's showing some signs, Nick. She's lost a lot of weight."

"What about medication?"

Lisa looked down.

"She was on the same medication I am. It worked for a while, but now she's getting worse."

"And how about Ted? What kind of shape is he in?"

"The last time I saw him you couldn't tell he had anything wrong with him."

I frowned at that. What kind of justice was there when he could go around infecting innocent, trusting women and not be suffering himself. AIDS is not something I know a lot about. Okay, I'm ignorant, like a lot of other people. I know that safe sex is advised, and I've had those kinds of conversations with women, but I didn't know that someone could have it, pass it on, and not show any sign themselves.

That sucked.

"Why don't you write all that information down for me, and anything else you think might be helpful?"

"All right."

Sam and I waited, drinking coffee and munching

without appetite on cookies, while Lisa got a lined
pad and wrote for almost ten minutes.

"There." She stopped writing and pushed the pad
across to me. I tore off the sheet, scanned it, folded
it, and put it away.

"I want to ask you something, Lisa."

"All right."

"Do you think Ted is deliberately infecting women
with this AIDS virus?"

"Well, he knew he had it when he slept with Kitty—
that was his girlfriend before me—and then when
he and I were together. I guess that means it's de-
liberate."

"If that's the case," Sam said, "he could be brought
up on charges."

"No, what I mean is, is he the kind of man who is
looking to infect as many women as he can on
purpose?"

She frowned.

"That would make him . . . evil."

"I guess it would."

She thought for a moment, then shook her head
slowly.

"I really don't know, Nick."

"That's okay." I stood up. "I'd better get started.
Do you have any pictures of Ted?"

"I thought you might ask."

I'd noticed when we arrived that she was limping
slightly. Now she limped over to the counter and took
a picture from where she'd left it. Coming back she
saw me looking at her.

"I stepped on a nail a couple of days back. Here."

It was a wallet-sized head shot. Drew was a good-
looking man in his late thirties, brown hair falling
down over his forehead. I could see where a woman
might want to brush the hair back, maybe run her

fingers through it. He was smiling, looking for all the world like Beaver Cleaver all grown-up. The All-American boy, passing AIDS along like a bad joke.

Before I left, I came up with one more question.

"How long has it been since you saw him?"

"The day I told him I tested positive was the last time I saw him. That was about a month ago."

I walked to the door with Sam, followed by Lisa. I opened the front door and walked out, then turned and saw that Sam was still inside.

"Come on," I said, "we have to get a hotel room."

"Oh, we do?"

"Well, sure . . ."

"One room?"

"Well . . . it would be cheaper that way, wouldn't it?" I have to admit, the prospect of sharing a room with Sam was . . . interesting.

"I suppose it would, but I have a better idea."

"What?"

She smiled and said, "Get my bag out of the car. I'm staying here with Lisa."

"You had this planned all along, didn't you?"

She just smiled, so I got her bag from the car, gave it to her, and told her I'd call when I got to a hotel.

3

I found a Best Western nearby, off of Highway 44, and checked in. In my room I took out Lisa's sheet of paper and read it. I had gotten a map of St. Louis from the car rental, so I spent the next fifteen minutes finding addresses and marking routes in pen. Before I left the room I called Sam and told her where I was staying.

"Why don't you come back here for dinner?" she suggested.

I agreed, and we planned for me to arrive at six.

The first person I wanted to see was Kitty Marks, Ted Drew's former girlfriend. I had her phone number and called her. She had spoken with Lisa, and said I could come right over. She lived in Brentwood and since I had her on the phone I asked the best and most direct route to her. Armed with that, I got to her apartment in twenty minutes.

Her illness was obvious because she was at least five feet ten and seriously underweight. There were also dark hollows beneath her eyes. Her hair was dirty blond, almost brown, and listless. She kept her arms folded, with her elbows in the palms of her hands. I noticed that her right hand was bandaged.

"I can't tell you much," she said, "except that the son of a bitch gave me AIDS."

"I hope you'll excuse me if I ask you how you know it was him."

"I was with only him for six months, Mr. Delvecchio."

"Nick, please." Even as I spoke it sounded inane to me. I'd probably never see this girl again in my life—or hers.

"Nick . . . and before that I hadn't been with anyone for over eight months."

"Did you or he have an AIDS test before you started seeing each other?"

"I mentioned it, but he refused. He said how could I claim to love him and think he wasn't clean?" She looked ashamed. "I bought it."

"After you found you he had AIDS did you tell him?"

"You bet I did. You know what the bastard did?"

"What?"

"He moved out the same day. Quit his job and moved out."

"Did he express . . . remorse? Say he was sorry—"

"He said I should have been more careful."

Same thing he said to Lisa.

"You know what pisses me off? He's probably out there right now giving it to some other poor unsuspecting girl. I'd like to cut off his dick!"

I couldn't blame her for that.

"Can you give me some idea of where to find him? Who he hung out with?"

"I can tell you who he hung out with when we were together, but I don't know where he goes now."

"That'll be good enough."

I left Kitty Marks's place with a couple of more hangouts I could try in my search for Ted Drew.

I went from her house to the home address I had for Ted. It was an apartment complex on Manchester Road. I knocked on the door, but no one answered. I went to the office to find out if he still lived there. The woman there told me he didn't, because he was two months behind in the rent. Even if he returned, she said, he wouldn't get back in. I asked if he had left anything behind and she said no. She added that the apartment was furnished, so the furniture wasn't his. I thanked her and left.

My next stop was the place where he was working while he was seeing Lisa. It was a print shop, and when I asked for him the owner angrily told me that Ted had simply stopped coming in, with no notice at all.

I left there and stopped at a Hardee's to eat. There are no Hardee's in New York, but there are Roy Rogers, and since Hardee's owns Roy's, I tried the fried chicken and found it the same. I think Roy's has better chicken than KFC.

Over my lunch I thought about Ted Drew. Why would a man who has a disease make the conscious decision to spread it? Did he figure he'd gotten it from a woman, so he was trying to pay all women back? As I understood AIDS it was statistically more likely that a woman would get it from a man than the other way around. Also, the people most susceptible to contracting AIDS were gays and drug users. I'd have to call Lisa and ask her if Ted used drugs.

The fact that Drew had abandoned both his home and his job fit the man's pattern. When he found out that Kitty tested positive, he moved out and quit his job. Lisa hadn't been living with him, but he left his apartment anyway and stopped going to his job, in effect quitting.

How far back did this pattern go? I wondered. Did he sleep with women until they tested positive, then move, quit his job, and start over? Was he doing this all over St. Louis? If he did it long enough, wasn't he bound to run into an old girlfriend or boss?

Since he'd infected two women I knew of, I wondered if Ted Drew hadn't already left town, moved to another city where he could start fresh with new victims.

Jesus, I thought, if women started dying because he was infecting them, did that make him a serial killer?

4

I hit a couple of bars where Drew hung out when he was with Kitty Marks. I didn't see any way around asking for him. I didn't have the time to start staking places out, waiting for him to show up.

I tried to be casual about it, but bartenders these days are a suspicious bunch. As soon as you say, "Hey, Ted Drew been around lately?" they want to know who you are and where you're from. If you happen to tell them that you owe him money and want to find it, that's the end of it. They shut up. You're better off saying that he owes you money.

In the third place I tried I caught a bartender's interest.

"Owes you money, huh?"

"Yep."

"A lot?"

I played with my Busch bottle and said, "Enough to make me want to find him."

"Gambling, huh?"

I looked him in the eye and said, "He picks the wrong teams."

"Don't I know it. You're shit out of luck, pal. He already owes a couple of regulars money and he don't come here no more."

"Any idea where he does hang out?"

He didn't mince words. "What's it worth to you?"

"You sell the information to your regulars, too?"

"Fuck them. He owes them forty, fifty bucks from a one-night bet. They ain't making book."

He assumed I had booked bets for Drew, and consequently figured that Drew was into me for a lot.

"I'll go ten."

"Make it twenty."

"Fifteen."

"Twenty, and I think I can tell you where to find him."

We matched stares for a while, and then I gave in.

"Okay, twenty."

"Let's see it."

See? What'd I tell you. A suspicious lot. I handed him the twenty.

"Check the Landing. I heard from a guy that he saw Drew down there."

"What landing?"

"Laclede's Landing, by the river."

"What river?"

"Where you from, pal? The Mississippi."

Yep, that was a river, all right.

I got back to Lisa's place at six. She and Sam had prepared dinner and while we ate I told them what I'd been doing. When we were done Lisa gave me directions to Laclede's Landing.

"A lot of people hang out down there," she added. "There are lots of clubs and restaurants and you can walk along the river."

"The Mississippi," I said to Sam.

She gave me a funny look and said, "I know."

Sam wanted to come to the Landing with me, but I vetoed the idea. I figured when I found Ted Drew he wasn't going to be real happy, and I might just find him in his own turf, with his friends around him. I explained that to her. She walked me to the door.

"If you find him like that," she said, touching my arm, "be careful. Don't approach him."

"I'll just tail him and find out where he lives. That's all."

"That's all she wants."

"I'll remember."

I left the house and got into the rental car. Lisa just wanted to confront him. I'd started this thing as a favor for Sam, but the more I thought about Drew deliberately infecting women with a deadly virus, the more I just wanted to smash his face in. How the hell could somebody justify doing that? I just couldn't understand it, and I doubted he could ever explain it to me.

5

There were plenty of bars and restaurants down on the Landing, as Lisa had said, but I'd already been to three places where Ted Drew used to hang out, and they were all of a type. They all served food, but none of them could have been called restaurants. With that in mind I walked along and stopped at bar and grill type places, had one beer and looked around. A couple of them catered to a younger crowd, so after a single beer I rejected them. Both Lisa and Kitty were in their thirties, so I figured that was the kind of girl Drew would go for.

I didn't ask questions this time, either. If he was currently hanging out in any of these places I didn't want to scare him off. If he was the barhopping type— which he seemed to be—then if I didn't spot him this night, I would the next, or the one after that. He wouldn't be able to stay away.

I worked the Landing for three days and nights until the bars closed, staying away from Lisa and Sam until dinner. I had made up a list of the places I thought Ted Drew might show and I had a beer in one, then moved to the next one, and so on. On Friday, I caught a break, which is usually the way my job finally gets done.

I was in a place called The Big Muddy, sitting at the bar nursing a beer. When the beer was done I was going to move on to the next place on my list. A woman in her early thirties with long brown hair came up to the bar and stood about five stools from me. She was wearing a light blue shirt and dark blue jeans. She stood there and waited for the bartender to notice her.

"Has Ted been around?" she asked, and my ears perked up.

"Not yet," the bartender said.

"Come on, Maury, he's not home he must be—"

"He ain't been in, Lynn, I swear."

"Is he coming in?"

The bartender, a beefy man in his forties, just shrugged.

"He's hiding from me—"

"He's not hiding, Lynn. Why don't you just give up?"

"I don't want to, Maury. Do you think he's at the Rock?"

"I don't know. You could try."

The Rock was another bar that was on my list. When she left I decided to follow her.

Walking along behind her I couldn't help wondering if she'd slept with Drew yet, if she'd been infected. From her conversation with the bartender, it sounded like she wanted to find Drew, but he didn't want any part of her. Maybe there was something I could do before anything happened.

She went into the Rock and I stepped in behind her, remaining just inside the door. She went up to the bartender and talked to him, and I saw him shake his head and shrug. She slammed her hand down on the bar once and he spread his hands in a helpless gesture. As she turned to leave, a patron sitting at the bar said something to her and she spoke sharply, cutting him down, and started past him. He reached out and grabbed her arm and I saw her wince.

The man was in his late thirties and big, but he was carrying some extra weight around his middle that would slow him down. This looked like my chance to meet Lynn.

I moved toward the bar and stopped just on the other side of the man.

". . . think you're too good. You ain't even that good-looking."

"Then let go of my arm." Lynn's voice sounded calm, like she'd dealt with this kind of thing before. Up-close I could see that the man was wrong, though.

She was kind of cute, and I'd walked along behind her from the Muddy and knew she filled her jeans out okay. He was just smarting from being brushed off.

The bartender came over to me and I said, "Busch, in a bottle."

Lynn was trying to soothe the man's wounded ego now, telling him she was sorry but she just didn't have time.

"It didn't sound to me like your man was gonna be around, so why not have a drink with me?"

"Look, I'm trying to be nice—"

"No, you ain't," the man said, cutting her off. "That's the problem."

The bartender brought my beer, cast a look at Lynn and the man, and walked to the other end of the bar.

I picked up my beer in my left hand and with my right I tapped the guy on the shoulder.

"Huh?" He turned his head to look over his shoulder at me. With my rigid index finger I poked him in the eye.

"Ow, Jesus!" He released Lynn and put both hands up to his face. I pushed my beer in front of him and looked at Lynn.

"Come on," I said.

She looked unsure, but I took her hand and led her outside.

"T-thanks."

"That's okay. With that kind of guy you just have to give them something else to think about."

She examined my face, then smiled and said, "That makes sense."

"I heard you asking for Ted. Would that be Ted Drew?"

"Do you know Ted?"

"No, but I'm looking for him, too."

Now she looked suspicious.

"Oh, yeah? Why?"

"Are you his girl?"

She bit her lips a moment, then said, "I thought I was."

"And you'd still like to be?"

She stared at me a moment, then nodded.

"Let's go someplace and talk."

"I don't know—"

"There something very important you should know about Ted."

"I thought you said you didn't know him?"

"I don't," I said, "but I know something about him."

"What?"

"Let's get a drink, Lynn."

I figured she was going to need one.

6

There was a McDonald's on the Landing so we went there to talk instead of a bar. We both got coffee and found a table.

"What do you want to tell me about Ted?" she asked.

"First, can you tell me where he lives now?"

"What for?"

"I want to find him, Lynn."

"Are you a cop?"

"Is Ted afraid of the cops?"

"No, why should he be?"

"Why are you asking me if I'm a cop?"

"You look like a cop."

I looked at her and smiled. "How many cops do you know?"

"None."

"Lynn, how . . . close are you and Ted Drew?"

"We're . . . tight."

"That explains why you can't find him."

"We had a fight. It's nothing serious."

"But he's avoiding you."

"So what? He . . . he loves me. I know he does."

"Lynn . . ." I leaned forward. "Have you slept with him?"

"Sure I have."

She said it too fast. I sat back in my chair.

"Lynn, I'm a private detective. I know two girls who have been infected with AIDS by Ted Drew."

Her eyes went wide. "That can't be true."

I took the picture Lisa gave me from my pocket. "Is this Ted?"

She looked at the picture and nodded.

"Then it's true. He's given two women AIDS that I know of. There could be many more. I'll ask you again. Have you had sex with him?"

She looked drugged.

"No." Her tone was listless. "I wanted to, but he didn't want no part of me."

"You're a lucky girl, then."

She rubbed both hands over her face, then looked at me.

"Is it true?"

"Yes, it's true."

"Jesus. I never thought I'd feel so glad a guy dumped me. But . . . he doesn't look sick .. except he wasn't feeling too good the last time I saw him. He said he had a . . . a bug, or something."

He had a bug, all right.

"I've got to find him, Lynn. Will you help me?"

"I can give you his address. He wasn't home when I banged on his door."

"When was that?"

"All week."

"Give me the address and I'll check it out."

I took a small pad out of my pocket and she wrote his address on it, then told me how to get there.

"Count yourself lucky, Lynn. Be more careful in the future who you pick."

She laughed ironically and said, "You know the first day I went to his place I thought he was cheating on me. I mean, I felt like he was."

"Why?"

"I saw two women coming from his apartment."

"Coming out of his apartment?"

"No, just from that direction. I banged on his door and when there was no answer I figured I was wrong. Besides, there looked like something was wrong with one of them."

"Like what?"

"She was holding her arm stiff, and the other woman was supporting her."

"What'd they look like?"

"Well . . . they looked like me, sort of. Long dark hair, slender, about my age. I thought maybe Ted liked that type, you know? He wasn't home, though, so they weren't coming from his place. I guess I ought to thank you, mister. You probably saved my life."

"Maybe. From now on, though, make sure you save your own, all right?"

She nodded and I left, feeling like a commercial for safe sex.

I followed her instructions to an apartment complex on Gravois and Grand. When I got to Drew's apartment there was no bell, just a knocker. I used it a couple of times, then peered in the window next to the door. I saw furniture, but if he rented furnished apartments that explained that. There was other stuff around, though. Magazines, newspaper, some fast-food wrappers on a coffee table. It looked to me like someone still lived there.

The apartment was one of six in this building, and it was on the first floor. I walked around to the back and saw that there were patios, and sliding-glass doors. The gate was on a latch and easy to open. When I got to the sliding-glass door I found it locked. I couldn't see any way to get in short of breaking the glass, and that wasn't my place to do. I peered into the room. It was a kitchen, with a cheap aluminum table and two metal folding chairs. I was about to give up when I spotted something else. I moved all the way to my right to give myself a better angle and saw what it was. Sticking out from behind the kitchen counter was a shoe—with a foot attached.

7

Ted Drew was dead. He'd been stabbed in his kitchen. The place was a mess behind the counter, which I was unable to see from outside the door. There were pots and pans and glass all over the floor, and a lot of blood.

I told the police the whole story. There was no reason not to. I also told them I was doing a favor for a friend, not working for a fee. After all, I wasn't licensed in the state of Missouri. They took my statement, my name, address, and phone number. After that they let me go. I drove directly back to Lisa's house.

"How was he killed?" Lisa asked.

"He was stabbed. Well, actually it looked as if he was stabbed during a fight."

"So then he didn't . . ."

"No, he didn't die of the disease."

"That's too bad. I'll call Kitty and tell her."

She was cold, real cold, but who could blame her. She just wanted him to die of the same disease she knew she was going to die of.

"I guess there's not much more to say, Nick. Thanks for trying to help."

She made it sound like I had failed. Hell, she wanted me to find him and I did. It wasn't my fault he and Kitty had killed him.

"Sam, it's time to leave."

"But—"

"I really think it's time to leave. We can change our tickets at the airport." We'd been scheduled to leave in two more days, but I didn't want to stay any longer.

It took Sam fifteen minutes to pack. She and Lisa embraced, but over Sam's shoulder Lisa's eyes met mine, and I think she saw that I knew.

"Stay in touch, please," Sam said.

Lisa promised she would, but it was a promise she never kept. Ultimately, she locked herself away from her family and friends and just waited to die—or go to jail.

On the way to the airport I explained it to Sam.

"I don't believe it," she said. "How could you think that Lisa and Kitty killed him?"

"They're members of the same club, remember?"

"Nick—"

"It all fits, Sam. Lynn saw two women walking away from Drew's building last Monday. According to the M.E., Drew would have been dead about then. That's why he didn't answer the door when Lynn knocked."

"So how does—"

"Let me finish. She said one of the women was supporting the other, and one was holding her arm. I don't know who was supporting who, but Kitty has a bandage on her hand. I think she got cut during the fight."

"And Lisa?"

"She's limping. There was broken glass on the floor. I think that's what she got in her foot, not a nail."

"But why would she kill him, and then ask me to help?"

"Did she ask you for help? For my help?"

"Well . . . no, now that I think of it. I offered to have you help her, but that was only when she said she wished she could find him."

"She knew he was dead when she said that, Sam. She just thought that was what she was supposed to say. When you offered to have me find him, she must have thought it would sound suspicious if she refused. Besides, it'll make a good argument when they arrest her. She'll ask the cops why she would have me searching for him if she killed him."

Sam folded her arms across her breasts.

"I don't believe it."

"Well, I do."

We drove in silence for a while and then she asked, "What are you going to do?"

"Nothing."

"Nothing? You think they committed murder and you're not going to say anything to the police?"

"No."

"Why not?"

"Because if I figured it out the cops will, too, eventually. Let Lisa and Kitty think they got away with it a little longer."

"Why would you do that?"

"Because they don't have anything else. Besides, I don't think they went there to kill him. I think they went there to confront him, and things got out of hand. Maybe he ridiculed them and there was a fight, and the two of them were able to kill him. He was only stabbed once, so it could have been an accident.

If they'd gone there to kill him I think they would have both stabbed him several times before stopping."

We drove a little more in silence before Sam spoke again.

"I still can't believe it."

At least she didn't say she "didn't" believe it.

"Forget it, Sam. Let's just get back to Brooklyn."

KADDISH FOR THE KID
A Nathan Heller Story
BY MAX ALLAN COLLINS

The first operative I ever took on, in the A-1 Detective Agency, was Stanley Gross. I hadn't been in business for even a year—it was the summer of '33—and was in no shape to be adding help. But the thing was—Stanley had a car.

Stanley had a '28 Ford coupe, to be exact, and a yen to be a detective. I had a paying assignment, requiring wheels, and a yen to make a living.

So it was that at three o'clock in the morning, on that unseasonably cool summer evening, I was sitting in the front seat of Stanley's Ford, in front of Goldblatt's department store on West Chicago Avenue, sipping coffee out of a paper cup, waiting to see if anybody came along with a brick or a gun.

I'd been hired two weeks before by the manager of the downtown Goldblatt's on State, just two blocks from my office at Van Buren and Plymouth. Goldblatt's was a sort of working-class Marshall Field's, with six department stores scattered around the Chicago area in various white ethnic neighborhoods.

The stores were good-size—two floors taking up as much as half a block—and the display windows were impressive enough; but once you got inside, it was like the pushcarts of Maxwell Street had been emptied and organized.

I bought my socks and underwear at the downtown Goldblatt's, but that wasn't how Nathan Heller—me—

got hired. I knew Katie Mulhaney, the manager's secretary; I'd bumped into her, on one of my socks and
underwear buying expeditions, and it blossomed into
a friendship. A warm friendship.

Anyway, the manager—Herman Cohen—had sum-
moned me to his office where he filled me in. His desk
was cluttered, but he was neat—moon-faced, mus-
tached, bow- (and fit-to-be) tied.

"Maybe you've seen the stories in the papers," he
said, in a machine-gun burst of words, "about this
reign of terror we've been suffering."

"Sure," I said.

Goldblatt's wasn't alone; every leading department
store was getting hit—stench bombs set off, acid
sprayed over merchandise, bricks tossed from cars to
shatter plate-glass windows.

He thumbed his mustache; frowned. "Have you
heard of 'Boss' Rooney? John Rooney?"

"No."

"Well, he's secretary of the Circular Distributors
Union. Over the last two years, Mr. Goldblatt has
provided Rooney's union with over three thousand
dollars of business—primarily to discourage trouble at
our stores."

"This union—these are guys that hand out ad
fliers?"

"Yes. Yes, and now Rooney has demanded that Mr.
Goldblatt order three hundred of our own sales and
ad people to join his union—at a rate of twenty-five
cents a day."

My late father had been a die-hard union guy, so I
knew a little bit about this sort of thing. "Mr. Cohen,
none of the unions in town collect daily dues."

"This one does. They've even been outlawed by the
AFL, Mr. Heller. Mr. Goldblatt feels Rooney is nothing short of a racketeer."

"It's an extortion scam, all right. What do you want me to do?"

"Our own security staff is stretched to the limit. We're getting *some* support from State's Attorney Courtney and his people. But they can only do so much. So we've taken on a small army of night watchmen, and are fleshing out the team with private detectives. Miss Mulhaney recommended you."

Kate knew a good dick when she saw one.

"Swell. When do I start?"

"Immediately. Of course, you do have a car?"

Of course, I lied and said I did. I also said I'd like to put one of my "top" operatives on the assignment with me, and that was fine with Cohen, who was in a more-the-merrier mood, where beefing up security was concerned.

Stanley Gross was from Douglas Park, my old neighborhood. His parents were bakers two doors down my from father's bookstore on South Homan. Stanley was a good eight years younger than me, so I remembered him mostly as a pestering kid.

But he'd grown into a tall, good-looking young man—a brown-haired, brown-eyed six-footer who'd been a star football and basketball player in high school. Like me, he went to Crane Junior College; unlike me, he finished.

I guess I'd always been sort of a hero to him. About six months before, he'd started dropping by my office to chew the fat. Business was so lousy, a little company—even from a fresh-faced college boy—was welcome.

We'd sit in the deli restaurant below my office and sip coffee and gnaw on bagels and he'd tell me this embarrassing shit about my being somebody he'd always looked up to.

"Gosh, Nate, when you made the police force, I thought that was just about the keenest thing."

He really did talk that way—gosh, keen. I told you I was desperate for company.

He brushed a thick comma of brown hair away and grinned in a goofy boyish way; it was endearing, and nauseating. "When I was a kid, coming into your pop's bookstore, you pointed me toward those Nick Carters, and Sherlock Holmes books. Gave me the bug. I *had* to be a detective!"

But the kid was too young to get on the force, and his family didn't have the kind of money or connections it took to get a slot on the PD.

"When you quit," he said, "I admired you so. Standing up to corruption—and in *this* town! Imagine."

Imagine. My leaving the force had little to do with any "standing up to corruption"—after all, graft was high on my list of reasons for joining in the first place—but I said nothing, not wanting to shatter the child's dreams.

"If you ever need an op, I'm your man!"

He said this thousands of times in those six months or so. And he actually did get some security work, through a couple of other, larger agencies. But his dream was to be my partner.

Owning that Ford made his dream come temporarily true.

For two weeks, we'd been living the exciting life of the private eye: sitting in the coupe in front of the Goldblatt's store at Ashland and Chicago, waiting for window smashers to show. Or not.

The massive gray-stone department store was like the courthouse of commerce on this endless street of storefronts; the other businesses were smaller—resale shops, hardware stores, pawnshops, your occasional

Polish deli. During the day things were popping here. Now, there was just us—me draped across the front seat, Stanley draped across the back—and the glow of neons and a few pools of light on the sidewalks from streetlamps.

"You know," Stanley said, "this isn't as exciting as I pictured."

"Just a week ago you were all excited about 'packing a rod.' "

"You're making fun of me."

"That's right." I finished my coffee, crumpled the cup, tossed it on the floor.

"I guess a gun is nothing to feel good about."

"Right again."

I was stretched out with my shoulders against the rider's door; in back, he was stretched out just the opposite. This enabled us to maintain eye contact. Not that I wanted to, particularly.

"Nate . . . if you hear me snoring, wake me up."

"You tired, kid?"

"Yeah. Ate too much. Today . . . well, today was my birthday."

"No kidding! Well, happy birthday, kid."

"My pa made the keenest cake. Say, I . . . I'm sorry I didn't invite you or anything."

"That's okay."

"It was a surprise party. Just my family—a few friends I went to high school and college with."

"It's okay."

"But there's cake left. You want to stop by Pa's store tomorrow and have a slice with me?"

"We'll see, kid."

"You remember my pa's pastries. Can't beat 'em."

I grinned. "Best on the West Side. You talked me into it. Go ahead and catch a few winks. Nothing's happening."

And nothing was. The street was an empty ribbon of concrete. But about five minutes later, a car came barreling down that concrete ribbon, right down the middle; I sat up.

"What is it, Nate?"

"A drunk, I think. He's weaving a little . . ."

It was a maroon Plymouth coupe; and it was headed right our way.

"Christ!" I said, and dug under my arm for the nine-millimeter.

The driver was leaning out the window of the coupe, but whether man or woman I couldn't tell—the headlights of the car, still a good thirty feet away, were blinding.

The night exploded and so did our windshield.

Glass rained on me as I hit the floor; I could hear the roar of the Plymouth's engine, and came back up, gun in hand, saw the maroon coupe bearing down on us, saw a silver swan on the radiator cap, and cream-colored wheels, but people in the car going by were a blur, and as I tried to get a better look, orange fire burst from a gun and I ducked down, hitting the glass-littered floor, and another four shots riddled the car and the night, the side windows cracking, and behind us the plate glass of display windows was fragmenting, falling to the pavement like sheets of ice.

Then the Plymouth was gone.

So was Stanley.

The first bullet must have got him. He must have sat up to get a look at the oncoming car and took the slug head on; it threw him back, and now he still seemed to be lounging there, against the now-spiderwebbed window, precious "rod" tucked under his arm; his brown eyes were open, his mouth, too, and his expression was almost—not quite—surprised.

I don't think he had time to be truly surprised, before he died.

There'd been only time enough for him to take the bullet in the head, the dime-size entry wound parting the comma of brown hair, streaking the birthday boy's boyish face with blood.

Within an hour I was being questioned by Sergeant Charles Pribyl, who was attached to the State's Attorney's office. Pribyl was a decent enough guy, even if he did work under Captain Daniel "Tubbo" Gilbert, who was probably the crookedest cop in town. Which in this town was saying something.

Pribyl had a good reputation, however; and I'd encountered him, from time to time, back when I was working the pickpocket detail. He had soft, gentle features and dark alert eyes.

Normally, he was an almost dapper dresser, but his tie seemed hastily knotted, his suit and hat looked as if he'd thrown them on—which he probably had; he was responding to a call at four in the morning, after all.

He was looking in at Stanley, who hadn't been moved; we were waiting for a coroner's physician to show. Several other plainclothes officers and half a dozen uniformed cops were milling around, footsteps crunching on the glass-strewn sidewalk.

"Just a kid," Pribyl said, stepping away from the Ford. "Just a damn kid." He shook his head. He nodded to me and I followed him over by a shattered display window.

He cocked his head. "How'd you happen to have such a young operative working with you?"

I explained about the car being Stanley's.

He had an expression you only see on cops: sad and yet detached. His eyes tightened.

"How—and why—did stink bombs and window smashing escalate into bloody murder?"

"You expect me to answer that, Sergeant?"

"No. I expect you to tell me what happened. And, Heller—I don't go into this with any preconceived notions about you. Some people on the force—even some good ones, like John Stege—hold it against you, the Lang and Miller business."

They were two crooked cops I'd recently testified against.

"Not me," he said firmly. "Apples don't come rottener than those two bastards. I just want you to know what kind of footing we're on."

"I appreciate that."

I filled him in, including a description of the murder vehicle, but couldn't describe the people within at all. I wasn't even sure how many of them there were.

"You get the license number?"

"No, damnit."

"Why not? You saw the car well enough."

"Them shooting at me interfered."

He nodded. "Fair enough. Shit. Too bad you didn't get a look at 'em."

"Too bad. But you know who to go calling on."

"How's that?"

I thrust a finger toward the car. "That's Boss Rooney's work—maybe not personally, but he had it done. You know about the Circular Union and the hassles they been giving Goldblatt's, right?"

Pribyl nodded, somewhat reluctantly; he liked me well enough, but I was a private detective. He didn't like having me in the middle of police business.

"Heller, we've been keeping the union headquarters under surveillance for six weeks now. I saw Rooney there today, myself, from the apartment across the way we rented."

"So did anyone leave the union hall tonight? Before the shooting, say around three?"

He shook his head glumly. "We've only been maintaining our watch during department-store business hours. The problem of night attacks is where hired hands like you come in."

"Okay." I sighed. "I won't blame you if you don't blame me."

"Deal."

"So what's next?"

"You can go on home." He glanced toward the Ford. "We'll take care of this."

"You want me to tell the family?"

"Were you close to them?"

"Not really. They're from my old neighborhood, is all."

"I'll handle it."

"You sure?"

"I'm sure." He patted my shoulder. "Go home."

I started to go, then turned back. "When are you going to pick up Rooney?"

"I'll have to talk to the State's Attorney, first. But my guess? Tomorrow. We'll raid the union hall tomorrow."

"Mind if I come along?"

"Wouldn't be appropriate, Heller."

"The kid worked for me. He got killed working for me."

"No. We'll handle it. Go home! Get some sleep."

"I'll go home," I said.

A chill breeze was whispering.

"But the sleep part," I said, "that I can't promise you."

The next afternoon I was having a beer in a booth in the bar next to the deli below my office. Formerly a blind pig—a speakeasy that looked shuttered from the street (even now, you entered through the deli)—it was a business investment of fighter Barney Ross, as was reflected by the framed boxing photos decorating the dark, smoky little joint.

I grew up with Barney on the West Side. Since my family hadn't practiced Judaism in several generations, I was *Shabbes goy* for Barney's very Orthodox folks, a kid doing chores and errands for them from Friday sundown through Saturday.

But we didn't become really good friends, Barney and me, till we worked Maxwell Street as pullers—teenage street barkers who literally pulled customers into stores for bargains they had no interest in.

Barney, a roughneck made good, was a real Chicago success story. He owned this entire building, and my office—which, with its Murphy bed, was also my residence—was space he traded me for keeping an eye on the place. I was his night watchman, unless a paying job like Goldblatt's came along to take precedence.

The lightweight champion of the world was having a beer, too, in that back booth; he wore a cheerful blue and white sport shirt and a dour expression.

"I'm sorry about your young pal," Barney said.

"He wasn't a 'pal,' really. Just an acquaintance."

"I don't know that Douglas Park crowd myself. But to think of a kid, on his twenty-first birthday . . ." His mildly battered bulldog countenance looked woeful. "He have a girl?"

"Yeah."

"What's her name?"

"I don't remember."

"Poor little bastard. When's the funeral?"

"I don't know."

"You're going, aren't you?"

"No. I don't really know the family that well. I'm sending flowers."

He looked at me with as long a face as a round-faced guy could muster. "You oughta go. He was working for you when he got it."

"I'd be intruding. I'd be out of place."

"You should do kaddish for the kid, Nate."

A mourner's prayer.

"Jesus Christ, Barney, I'm no Jew. I haven't been in a synagogue more than half a dozen times in my life, and then it was social occasions."

"Maybe you don't consider yourself a Jew, with that Irish mug of yours your ma bequeathed you . . . but you're gonna have a rude awakening one of these days, boyo."

"What do you mean?"

"There's plenty of people you're just another 'kike' to, believe you me."

I sipped the beer. "Nudge me when you get to the point."

"You owe this kid kaddish, Nate."

"Hell, doesn't that go on for months? I don't know the lingo. And if you think I'm putting on some fuckin' beanie and . . ."

There was a tap on my shoulder. Buddy Gold, the bartender, an ex-pug, leaned in to say, "You got a call."

I went behind the bar to use the phone. It was Sergeant Lou Sapperstein at Central HQ in the Loop; Lou had been my boss on the pickpocket detail. I'd called him this morning with a request.

"Tubbo's coppers made their raid this morning, around nine," Lou said. Sapperstein was a hard-nosed, balding cop of about forty-five and one of the few friends I had left on the PD.

"And?"

"And the union hall was empty, 'cept for a bartender. Pribyl and his partner Bert Gray took a whole squad up there, but Rooney and his boys had flown the coop."

"Fuck. Somebody tipped them."

"Are you surprised?"

"Yeah. Surprised I expected the cops to play it straight for a change. You wouldn't have the address of that union, by any chance?"

"No, but I can get it. Hold a second."

A sweet union scam like the Circular Distributors had Outfit written all over it—and Captain Tubbo Gilbert, head of the State Prosecutor's police, was known as the richest cop in Chicago. Tubbo was a bagman and police fixer so deep in Frank Nitti's pocket he had Nitti's lint up his nose.

Lou was back: "It's at 7 North Racine. That's Madison and Racine."

"Well, hell—that's spitting distance from Skid Row."

"Yeah. So?"

"So that explains the scam—that 'union' takes hoboes and makes day laborers out of them. No wonder they charge daily dues. It's just bums handing out ad circulars. . . ."

"I'd say that's a good guess, Nate."

I thanked Lou and went back to the booth where Barney was brooding about what a louse his friend Heller was.

"I got something to do," I told him.

"What?"

"My kind of kaddish."

Less than two miles from the prominent department stores of the Loop they'd been fleecing, the Circular Distributors Union had their headquarters on the

doorstep of Skid Row and various Hoovervilles. This
Madison Street area, just north of Greek Town, was
a seedy mix of flophouses, marginal apartment buildings, and storefront businesses, mostly bars. Union
HQ was on the second floor of a two-story brick building whose bottom floor was a plumbing supply outlet.

I went up the squeaking stairs and into the union
hall, a big high-ceilinged open room with a few
glassed-in offices toward the front, to the left and
right. Ceiling fans whirred lazily, stirring stale smoky
air; folding chairs and card tables were scattered everywhere on the scuffed wooden floor, and seated at
some were unshaven, tattered "members" of the
union. Across the far end stretched a bar, behind
which a burly blond guy in rolled-up white shirtsleeves
was polishing a glass. More hoboes leaned against the
bar, having beers.

I ordered a mug from the bartender, who had a
massive skull and tiny dark eyes and a sullen kiss of
a mouth.

I salted the brew as I tossed him a nickel. "Hear
you had a raid here this morning."

He ignored the question. "This hall's for union
members only"

"Jeez, it looks like a saloon."

"Well, it's a union hall. Drink up and move along."

'There's a fin in it for you, if you answer a few
questions."

He thought that over; leaned in. "Are you a cop?"

"No. Private."

"Who hired you?"

"Goldblatt's."

He thought some more. The tiny eyes narrowed.
"Let's hear the questions."

"What do you know about the Gross kid's
murder?"

"Not a damn thing."

"Was Rooney here last night?"

"Far as I know, he was home in bed asleep."

"Know where he lives?"

"No."

"You don't know where your boss lives."

"No. All I know is he's a swell guy. He don't have nothin' to do with these department store shakedowns the cops are tryin' to pin on him. It's union busting, is what it is."

"Union busting." I had a look around at the bleary-eyed clientele in their patched clothes. "You have to be a union, first, 'fore you can get busted up."

"What's *that* supposed to mean?"

"It means this is a scam. Rooney pulls in winos, gets 'em day-labor jobs for three dollars twenty-five a day, then they come up here to pay their daily dues of a quarter, and blow the rest on beer or booze. In other words, first the bums pass out ad fliers, then they come here and just plain pass out."

"I think you better scram. Otherwise I'm gonna have to throw you down the stairs."

I finished the beer. "I'm leaving. But you know what? I'm not gonna give you that fin. I'm afraid you'd just drink it up."

I could feel his eyes on my back as I left, but I'd have heard him if he came out from around the bar. I was starting down the stairs when the door below opened and Sergeant Pribyl, looking irritated, came up to meet me on the landing, halfway. He looked more his usual dapper self, but his eyes were black-bagged.

"What's the idea, Heller?"

"I just wanted to come bask in the reflected glory of your triumphant raid this morning."

"What's that supposed to mean?"

"It means when Tubbo's boys are on the case, the Outfit gets advance notice."

He winced. "That's not the way it was. I don't know why Rooney and Berry and the others blew. But nobody in our office warned 'em off."

"Are you sure?"

He clearly wasn't. "Look, I can't have you messing in this. We're on the damn case, okay? We're maintaining surveillance from across the way . . . that's how we spotted you."

"Peachy. Twenty-four surveillance, now?"

"No." He seemed embarrassed. "Just day shift."

"You want some help?"

"What do you mean?"

"Loan me the key to your stakeout crib. I'll keep night watch. Got a phone in there?"

"Yeah"

"I'll call you if Rooney shows. You got pictures of him and the others you can give me?"

"Well . . ."

"What's the harm? Or would Tubbo lower the boom on you, if you really did your job?"

He sighed. Scratched his head and came to a decision. "This is unofficial, okay? But there's a possibility the door to that apartment's gonna be left unlocked tonight."

"Do tell."

"Third floor—three-oh-one." He raised a cautionary finger. "We'll try this for one night . . . no showboating, okay? Call me if one of 'em shows."

"Sure. You tried their homes?"

He nodded. "Nothing. Rooney lives on North Ridgeland in Oak Park. Four kids. Wife's a pleasant, matronly type."

"Fat, you mean."

"She hasn't seen Rooney for several weeks. She says he's away from home a lot."

"Keeping a guard posted there?"

"Yeah. And that *is* twenty-four hours." He sighed, shook his head. "Heller, there's a lot about this case that doesn't make sense."

"Such as?"

"That maroon Plymouth. We never saw a car like that in the entire six weeks we had the union hall under surveillance. Rooney drives a blue LaSalle coupe."

"Any maroon Plymouths reported stolen?"

He shook his head, no. "And it hasn't turned up abandoned either. They must still have the car."

"Is Rooney *that* stupid?"

"We can always hope," Pribyl said.

I sat in an easy chair with sprung springs by the window in room 301 of the residential hotel across the way. It wasn't a flophouse cage, but it wasn't a suite at the Drake, either. Anyway, in the dark it looked fine. I had a flask of rum to keep me company, and the breeze fluttering the sheer, frayed curtains remained unseasonably cool.

Thanks to some photos Pribyl left me, I now knew what Rooney looked like: a good-looking, oval-faced smoothie, in his mid-forties, just starting to lose his dark, slicked-back hair; his eyes were hooded, his mouth soft, sensual, sullen. There were also photos of bespectacled, balding Berry and pockmarked, cold-eyed Herbert Arnold, V.P. of the union.

But none of them stopped by the union hall—only a steady stream of winos and bums went in and out.

Then, around seven, I spotted somebody who didn't fit the profile.

It was a guy I knew—a fellow private op, Eddie

McGowan, a Pinkerton man, in uniform, meaning he was on night watchman duty. A number of the merchants along Madison must have pitched in for his services.

I left the stakeout and waited down on the street, in front of the plumbing supply store, for Eddie to come back out. It didn't take long—maybe ten minutes.

"Heller!" he said. He was a skinny, tow-haired guy in his late twenties with a bad complexion and a good outlook. "What no good are you up to?"

"The Goldblatt's shooting. That kid they killed was working with me."

"Oh! I didn't know! Heard about the shooting, of course, but didn't read the papers or anything. So you were involved in that? No kidding."

"No kidding. You on watchman duty?"

"Yeah. Up and down the street, here, all night."

"Including the union hall?"

"Sure." He grinned. "I usually stop up for a free drink, 'bout this time of night."

"Can you knock off for a couple of minutes? For another free drink?"

"Sure!"

Soon we were in a smoky booth in back of a bar and Eddie was having a boilermaker on me.

"See anything unusual last night," I asked, "around the union hall?"

"Well . . . I had a drink there, around two o'clock in the morning. That was a first."

"A drink? Don't they close earlier than that?"

"Yeah. Around eleven. That's all the longer it takes for their 'members' to lap up their daily dough."

"So what were you doing up there at two?"

He shrugged. "Well, I noticed the lights was on upstairs, so I unlocked the street-level door and went up.

Figured Alex . . . that's the bartender, Alex Davidson . . . might have forgot to turn out the lights, fore he left. The door up there was locked, but then Mr. Rooney opened it up and told me to come on in."

"Why would he do that?"

"He was feelin' pretty good. Looked like he was workin' on a bender. Anyway, he insists I have a drink with him. I says, sure. Turns out Davidson is still there."

"No kidding?"

"No kidding. So Alex serves me a beer. Henry Berry—he's the union's so-called business agent, mousy little guy with glasses—he was there, too. He was in his cups, also. So was Rooney's wife—she was there, and also feeling giddy."

I thought about Pribyl's description of Mrs. Rooney as a matronly woman with four kids. "His *wife* was there?"

"Yeah, the lucky stiff."

"Lucky?"

"You should see the dame! Good-lookin' tomato with big dark eyes and a nice shape on her."

"About how old?"

"Young. Twenties. It'd take the sting out of a ball and chain, I can tell you that."

"Eddie . . . here's a fin."

"Heller, the beer's enough!"

"The fin is for telling this same story to Sergeant Pribyl of the State's Attorney's coppers."

"Oh. Okay."

"But do it tomorrow."

He smirked. "Okay. I got rounds to make, anyway." So did I.

At around eleven-fifteen, bartender Alex Davidson was leaving the union hall; his back was turned, as he was locking the street-level door, and I put my nine-millimeter in it.

"Hi, Alex," I said. "Don't turn around, unless you prefer being gut-shot."

"If it's a stickup, all I got's a couple bucks. Take 'em and bug off!"

"No such luck. Leave that door unlocked. We're gonna step back inside."

He grunted and opened the door and we stepped inside.

"Now we're going up the stairs," I said, and we did, in the dark, the wooden steps whining under our weight. He was a big man; I'd have had my work cut out for me—if I hadn't had the gun.

We stopped at the landing where earlier I had spoken to Sergeant Pribyl. "Here's fine," I said.

I allowed him to face me in the near dark.

He sneered. "You're that private dick."

"I'm sure you mean that in the nicest way. Let me tell you a little more about me. See, we're going to get to know each other, Alex."

"Fuck you."

I slapped him with the nine-millimeter.

He wiped blood off his mouth and looked at me with hate, but also with fear. And he made no more smart-ass remarks.

"I'm the private dick whose twenty-one-year-old partner got shot in the head last night."

Now the fear was edging out the hate; he knew he might die in this dark stairwell.

"I know you were here with Rooney and Berry and the broad last night, serving up drinks as late as two in the morning," I said. "Now you're going to tell me the whole story—or you're the one who's getting tossed down the fucking stairs."

He was trembling, now; a big hulk of a man

rembling with fear. "I didn't have anything to do with he murder. Not a damn thing!"

"Then why cover for Rooney and the rest?"

"You saw what they're capable of!"

"Take it easy, Alex. Just tell the story."

Rooney had come into the office about noon the lay of the shooting; he had started drinking and never topped. Berry and several other union "officers" rrived and angry discussions about being under sur- veillance by the State's Attorney's cops were accom- panied by a lot more drinking.

"The other guys left around five, but Rooney and 3erry, they just hung around drinking all evening. Around midnight Rooney handed me a phone number ne jotted on a matchbook and gave it to me to call or him. It was a Berwyn number. A woman answered. I handed him the phone and he said to her, 'Bring one.' "

"One what?" I asked.

"I'm gettin' to that. She showed up around one o'clock—good-looking dame with black hair and eyes so dark they coulda been black, too."

"Who was she?"

"I don't know. Never saw her before. She took a gun out of her purse and gave it to Rooney."

"That was what he asked her to bring."

"I guess. It was a .38 revolver, a Colt I think. Any- way, Rooney and Berry were both pretty drunk; I don't know what *her* excuse was. So Rooney takes the gun and says, 'We got a job to pull at Goldblatt's. We're gonna throw some slugs at the windows and watchmen.' "

"How did the girl react?"

He swallowed. "She laughed. She said, 'I'll go along and watch the fun.' Then they all went out."

Jesus.

Finally I said, "What did you do?"

"They told me to wait for 'em. Keep the bar open. They came back in, laughing like hyenas. Rooney says to me, 'You want to see the way he keeled over?' And I says, 'Who?' And he says, 'The guard at Goldblatt's.' Berry laughs and says, 'We really let him have it.'"

"That kid was twenty-one, Alex. It was his goddamn birthday."

The bartender was looking down. "They laughed and joked about it till Berry passed out. About six in the morning Rooney has me pile Berry in a cab. Rooney and the twist slept in his office for maybe an hour. Then they came out, looking sober and kind of . . . scared. He warned me not to tell anybody what I seen, unless I wanted to trade my job for a morgue slab."

"Colorful. Tell me, Alex. You got that girl's phone number in Berwyn?"

"I think it's upstairs. You can put that gun away. I'll help you."

It was dark, but I could see his face well enough; the big man's eyes looked damp. The fear was gone. Something else was in its place. Shame? Something.

We went upstairs, he unlocked the union hall and, under the bar, found the matchbook with the number written inside: Berwyn 2981.

"You want a drink before you go?" he asked.

"You know," I said, "I think I'll pass."

I went back to my office to use the reverse-listing phone book that told me Berwyn 2981 was Rosalie Rizzo's number; and that Rosalie Rizzo lived at 6348 West Thirteenth Street in Berwyn.

First thing the next morning, I borrowed Barney's Hupmobile and drove out to Berwyn, the clean, tidy

Hunky suburb populated in part by the late Mayor Cermak's patronage people. But finding a Rosalie Rizzo in this largely Czech and Bohemian area came as no surprise: Capone's Cicero was a stone's throw away.

The woman's address was a three-story brick apartment building, but none of the mailboxes in the vestibule bore her name. I found the janitor and gave him Rosalie Rizzo's description. It sounded like Mrs. Riggs to him.

"She's a doll," the janitor said. He was heavyset and needed a shave; he licked his thick lips as he thought about her. "Ain't seen her since yesterday noon."

That was about nine hours after Stanley was killed.

He continued: "Her and her husband was going to the country, she said. Didn't expect to be back for a couple of weeks, she said."

Her husband.

"What'll a look around their apartment cost me?"

He licked his lips again. "Two bucks?"

Two bucks it was; the janitor used his passkey and left me to it. The well-appointed little apartment included a canary that sang in its gilded cage, a framed photo of slick Boss Rooney on an end table, and a closet containing two sawed-off shotguns and a repeating rifle.

I had barely started to poke around when I had company: a slender, gray-haired woman in a flowered print dress.

"Oh!" she said, coming in the door she'd unlocked.

"Can I help you?" I asked.

"Who are you?" Her voice had the lilt of an Italian accent.

Under the circumstances, the truth seemed prudent. "A private detective."

"My daughter is not here! She and her-a husband, they go to vacation. Up north some-a-where. I just-a come to feed the canary!"

"Please don't be frightened. Do you know where she's gone, exactly?"

"No. But . . . maybe my husband do. He is-a downstairs. . . ."

She went to a window, threw it open, and yelled something frantically down in Italian.

I eased her aside in time to see a heavyset man jump into a maroon Plymouth with a silver swan on the radiator cap and cream-colored wheels, and squeal away.

And when I turned, the slight gray-haired woman was just as gone. Only she hadn't squealed.

The difference, this time, was a license number for the maroon coupe; I'd seen it: 519-836. In a diner I made a call to Lou Sapperstein, who made a call to the motor vehicle bureau, and phoned back with the scoop: the Plymouth was licensed to Rosalie Rizzo, but the address was different—2848 South Cuyler Avenue, in Berwyn.

The bungalow was typical for Berwyn—a tidy little frame house on a small perfect lawn. My guess was this was her folks' place. In back was a small matching, but unattached garage, on the alley. Peeking in the garage windows, I saw the maroon coupe and smiled.

"Is Rosalie in trouble again?"

The voice was female, sweet, young.

I turned and saw a slender, almost beautiful teenage girl with dark eyes and bouncy, dark shoulder-length hair. She wore a navy-blue sailorish playsuit. Her pretty white legs were bare.

"Are you Rosalie's sister?"

"Yes. Is she in trouble?"

"What makes you say that?"

"I just know Rosalie, that's all. That man isn't really her husband, is he? That Mr. Riggs."

"No."

"Are you here about her accident?"

"No. Where is she?"

"Are you a police officer?"

"I'm a detective. Where did she go?"

"Papa's inside. He's afraid he's going to be in trouble."

"Why's that?"

"Rosalie put her car in our garage yesterday. She said she was in an accident and it was damaged and not to use it. She's going to have it repaired when she gets back from vacation."

"What does that have to do with your papa being scared?"

"Rosalie's going to be mad as h at him, that he used her car." She shrugged. "He said he looked at it and it didn't look damaged to him, and if Mama was going to have to look after Rosalie's g.d. canary, well he'd sure as h use *her* gas not his."

"I can see his point. Where did your sister go on vacation?"

"She didn't say. Up north someplace. Someplace she and Mr. Riggs like to go to, to . . . you know. To get away?"

I called Sergeant Pribyl from a gas station where I was getting Barney's Hupmobile tank refilled. I suggested he have another talk with bartender Alex Davidson, gave him the address of "Mr. and Mrs. Riggs," and told him where he could find the maroon Plymouth.

He was grateful but a little miffed about all I had done on my own.

"So much for not showboating," he said, almost huffily. "You've found everything but the damn suspects."

"They've gone up north somewhere," I said.

"Where up north?"

"They don't seem to've told anybody. Look, I have a piece of evidence you may need."

"What?"

"When you talk to Davidson, he'll tell you about a matchbook Rooney wrote the girl's number on. I got the matchbook."

It was still in my pocket. I took it out, idly, and shut the girl's number away, revealing the picture on the matchbook cover: a blue moon hovered surrealistically over a white lake on which two blue lovers paddled in a blue canoe—Eagle River Lodge, Wisconsin.

"I suppose we'll need that," Pribyl's voice over the phone said, "when the time comes."

"I suppose," I said, and hung up.

Eagle River was a town of 1,386 (so said the sign) just inside the Vilas County line at the junction of U.S. 45 and Wisconsin State Highway 70. The country was beyond beautiful—green pines towering higher than Chicago skyscrapers, glittering blue lakes nestling in woodland pockets.

The lodge I was looking for was on Silver Lake, a gas station attendant told me. A beautiful dusk was settling on the woods as I drove into the parking lot of the large resort sporting a red city-style neon saying DINING AND DANCE. Log-cabin cottages were flung here and there around the periphery like Paul Bunyan's Tinkertoys. Each one was just secluded enough—ideal for couples, married or un-.

Even if Rooney and his dark-haired honey weren't staying here, it was time to find a room: I'd been

driving all day. When Barney loaned me his Hupmobile, he'd had no idea the kind of miles I'd put on
it. Dead tired, I went to the desk and paid for a cabin.

The guy behind the counter had a plaid shirt on,
but he was small and squinty and Hitler-mustached,
smoking a stogie, and looked more like a bookie than
a lumberjack.

I told him some friends of mine were supposed to
be staying here.

"We don't have anybody named Riggs registered."

"How 'bout Mr. and Mrs. Rooney?"

"Them either. How many friends you got, anyway?"

"Why, did I already catch the limit?"

Before I headed to my cabin, I grabbed some supper in the rustic restaurant. I placed my order with a
friendly brunette girl of about nineteen with plenty of
personality and makeup. A road-company Paul Whiteman outfit was playing "Sophisticated Lady" in the adjacent dance hall, and I went over and peeked in, to look
for familiar faces. A number of couples were cutting
a rug, but not Rooney and Rosalie. Or Henry Berry
or Herbert Arnold, either. I went back and had my
green salad and fried trout and well-buttered baked
potato; I was full and sleepy when I stumbled toward
my guest cottage under the light of a moon that
bathed the woods ivory.

Walking along the path, I spotted something: snug-
gled next to one of the secluded cabins was a blue
LaSalle coupe with Cook County plates.

Suddenly I wasn't sleepy. I walked briskly back to
the lodge check-in desk and batted the bell to summon
the stogie-chewing clerk.

"Cabin seven," I said. "I think that blue LaSalle is
my friends' car."

His smirk turned his Hitler mustache Chaplinesque.
"You want I should break out the champagne?"

"I just want to make sure it's them. Dark-haired girl and an older guy, good-looking, kinda sleepy-eyed, just starting to go bald?"

"That's them." He checked his register. "That's the Ridges." He frowned. "Are they usin' a phony name?"

"Does a bear shit in the woods?"

He squinted. "You sure they're friends of yours?"

"Positive. Don't call their room and tell 'em I'm here, though—I want to surprise them. . . ."

I knocked with my left hand; my right was filled with the nine-millimeter. Nothing. I knocked again.

"Who is it?" a male voice said gruffly. "*What* is it?"

"Complimentary fruit basket from the management."

"Go away!"

I kicked the door open.

The lights were off in the little cabin, but enough moonlight came in with me through the doorway to reveal the pair in bed, naked. She was sitting up, her mouth and eyes open in a silent scream, gathering the sheets up protectively over white skin, her dark hair blending with the darkness of the room, making a cameo of her face. He was diving off the bed for the sawed-off shotgun, but I was there to kick it away, wishing I hadn't, wishing I'd let him grab it so I could have had an excuse to put one in his forehead, right where he'd put one in Stanley's.

Boss Rooney wasn't boss of anything, now: he was just a naked, balding, forty-year-old scam artist, sprawled on the floor. Kicking him would have been easy.

So I did; in the stomach.

He clutched himself and puked. Apparently he'd had the trout, too.

I went over and slammed the door shut, or as shut

as it could be, half-off its hinges. Pointing the gun at her retching naked boyfriend, I said to the girl, "Turn on the light and put on your clothes."

She nodded dutifully and did as she was told. In the glow of a nightstand lamp, I caught glimpses of her white, well-formed body as she stepped into her step-ins; but you know what? She didn't do a thing for me.

"Is Berry here?" I asked Rooney. "Or Arnold?"

"N-no," he managed.

"If you're lying," I said, "I'll kill you."

The girl said shrilly, "They aren't here!"

"You can put your clothes on, too," I told Rooney. "If you have another gun hidden somewhere, do me a favor. Make a play for it."

His hooded eyes flared. "Who the hell are you?"

"The private cop you *didn't* kill the other night."

He lowered his gaze. "Oh."

The girl was sitting on the bed, weeping; body heaving.

"Take it easy on her, will you?" he said, zipping his fly. "She's just a kid."

I was opening a window to ease the stench of his vomit.

"Sure," I said. "I'll say kaddish for her."

I handcuffed the lovebirds to the bed and called the local law; they in turn called the State Prosecutor's office in Chicago, and Sergeants Pribyl and Gray made the long drive up the next day to pick up the pair.

It seemed the two cops had already caught Henry Berry—a tipster gave them the West Chicago Avenue address of a second-floor room he was holed up in.

I admitted to Pribyl that I'd been wrong about Tubbo tipping off Rooney and the rest about the raid.

"I figure Rooney lammed out of sheer panic," I said, "the morning after the murder."

Pribyl saw it the same way.

The following March, Pribyl arrested Herbert Arnold running a northside handbill distributing agency.

Rooney, Berry, and Rosalie Rizzo were all convicted of murder; the two men got life, and the girl twenty years. Arnold hadn't been part of the kill-happy joyride that took Stanley Gross's young life, and got only one to five for conspiracy and extortion.

None of it brought Stanley Gross back, nor did my putting on a beanie and sitting with the Gross family, suffering through a couple of stints at a storefront synagogue on Roosevelt Road.

But it did get Barney off my ass.

AUTHOR'S NOTE

While Nathan Heller is a fictional character, this story is based on a real case—names have not been changed, and the events are fundamentally true; source material included an article by John J. McPhaul and information provided by my research associate, George Hagenauer, who I thank for his insights and suggestions.